DATE DUE

Maggie Shaw Fullilove

Who Was Responsible? Stories from *Half Century*

Mary Etta Spencer

The Resentment

AFRICAN-AMERICAN WOMEN WRITERS, 1910–1940

HENRY LOUIS GATES, JR. *GENERAL EDITOR*

Jennifer Burton *Associate Editor*

OTHER TITLES IN THIS SERIES

Charlotte Hawkins Brown	*"Mammy": An Appeal to the Heart of the South* *The Correct Thing To Do—To Say—To Wear*
Fanny Jackson Coppin	*Reminiscences of School Life, and Hints on Teaching*
Maud Cuney-Hare	*Norris Wright Cuney: A Tribune of the Black People*
Jessie Redmon Fauset	*The Chinaberry Tree: A Novel of American Life*
Jessie Redmon Fauset	*Comedy: American Style*
Sarah Lee Brown Fleming	*Hope's Highway* *Clouds and Sunshine*
Maggie Shaw Fullilove	*Who Was Responsible? Stories from* Half-Century *magazine*
Mary Etta Spencer	*The Resentment*
Gertrude Pitts	*Tragedies of Life*
Anne Scott	*George Sampson Brite* *Case 999—A Christmas Story*
Zara Wright	*Black and White Tangled Threads* *Kenneth*

MAGGIE SHAW FULLILOVE

WHO WAS RESPONSIBLE?
STORIES FROM *HALF CENTURY*

MARY ETTA SPENCER

THE RESENTMENT

Introduction by
P. GABRIELLE FOREMAN

G. K. HALL & CO.
An Imprint of Simon & Schuster Macmillan
New York

Prentice Hall International

Introduction copyright © 1996 by P. Gabrielle Foreman

All rights reserved. No part of this book may be reproduced or transmitted in any form or by any means, electronic or mechanical, including photocopying, recording, or by any information storage and retrieval system, without permission in writing from the Publisher.

G. K. Hall & Co.
An Imprint of Simon & Schuster Macmillan
1633 Broadway
New York, NY 10019

Library of Congress Catalog Card Number: 94-12994

Printed in the United States of America

Printing Number
1 2 3 4 5 6 7 8 9 10

Library of Congress Cataloging-in-Publication Data

Shaw Fullilove, Maggie, 1884–
   Who was responsible? and stories / Maggie Shaw Fullilove. The resentment / Mary Etta Spencer ; [general] introduction by P. Gabrielle Foreman.
     p. cm. — (African American women writers, 1910–1940)
   Includes bibliographical references (p.).
   ISBN 0-8161-1630-X (alk. paper)
   1. Afro-Americans—Fiction. I. Spencer, Mary Etta. Resentment. 1994. II. Title. III. Title: Who was responsible? and stories. IV. Title: Resentment. V. Series
PS3537.H455W48 1994
813'.54—dc20   94-12994
                                                                                               CIP

The paper used in this publication meets the requirements of ANSI/NISO Z39.48-1992 (Permanence of Paper).

808.83
SHAW FULL I LOVE

CONTENTS

General Editors' Preface vii

Publisher's Note xiii

Introduction by P. Gabrielle Foreman xv

WHO WAS RESPONSIBLE? 1

STORIES FROM *HALF CENTURY* 183

"Sermons in Stones" 183

"Navy Blue Velvet" 199

"The Precursors of the Dawn" 209

"Sweet Peas Between" 215

THE RESENTMENT 245

GENERAL EDITORS' PREFACE

The past decade of our literary history might be thought of as the era of African-American women writers. Culminating in the awarding of the Pulitzer Prize to Toni Morrison and Rita Dove and the Nobel Prize for Literature to Toni Morrison in 1993 and characterized by the presence of several writers—Toni Morrison, Alice Walker, Maya Angelou, and the Delany Sisters, among others—on the *New York Times* Best Seller List, the shape of the most recent period in our literary history has been determined in large part by the writings of black women.

This, of course, has not always been the case. African-American women authors have been publishing their thoughts and feelings at least since 1773, when Phillis Wheatley published her book of poems in London, thereby bringing poetry directly to bear upon the philosophical discourse over the African's "place in nature" and his or her place in the great chain of being. The scores of words published by black women in America in the nineteenth century—most of which were published in extremely limited editions and never reprinted—have been republished in new critical editions in the forty-volume *Schomburg Library of Nineteenth-Century Black Women Writers*. The critical response to that series has led to requests from scholars and students alike for a similar series, one geared to the work by black women published between 1910 and the beginning of World War Two.

African-American Women Writers, 1910–1940 is designed to bring back into print many writers who otherwise would be unknown to contemporary readers, and to increase the availability of lesser-known texts by established writers who originally published during this critical period in African-American letters. This series implicitly acts as a chronological sequel to the Schomburg series, which focused on the origins of the black female literary tradition in America.

General Editors' Preface

In less than a decade, the study of African-American women's writings has grown from its promising beginnings into a firmly established field in departments of English, American Studies, and African-American Studies. A comparison of the form and function of the original series and this sequel illustrates this dramatic shift. The *Schomburg Library* was published at the cusp of focused academic investigation into the interplay between race and gender. It covered the extensive period from the publication of Phillis Wheatley's *Poems on Various Subjects, Religious and Moral* in 1773 through the "Black Women's Era" of 1890–1910, and was designed to be an inclusive series of the major early texts by black women writers. The Schomburg Library provided a historical backdrop for black women's writings of the 1970s and 1980s, including the works of writers such as Toni Morrison, Alice Walker, Maya Angelou, and Rita Dove.

African-American Women Writers, 1910–1940 continues our effort to provide a new generation of readers access to texts—historical, sociological, and literary—that have been largely "unread" for most of this century. The series bypasses works that are important both to the period and the tradition, but that are readily available, such as Zora Neale Hurston's *Their Eyes Were Watching God*, Jessie Fauset's *Plum Bun* and *There is Confusion*, and Nella Larsen's *Quicksand* and *Passing*. Our goal is to provide access to a wide variety of rare texts. The series includes Fauset's two other novels, *The Chinaberry Tree: A Novel of American Life* and *Comedy: American Style*, and Hurston's short play *Color Struck*, since these are not yet widely available. It also features works by virtually unknown writers, such as *A Tiny Spark*, Christina Moody's slim volume of poetry self-published in 1910, and *Reminiscences of School Life, and Hints on Teaching*, written by Fanny Jackson Coppin in the last year of her life (1913), a multi-genre work combining an autobiographical sketch and reflections on trips to England and South Africa, complete with pedagogical advice.

Cultural studies' investment in diverse resources allows the historic scope of the *African-American Women Writers* series to be more focused than the *Schomburg Library* series, which covered works written over a 137-year period. With few exceptions,

General Editors' Preface

the authors included in the *African-American Women Writers* series wrote their major works between 1910 and 1940. The texts reprinted include all of the works by each particular author that are not otherwise readily obtainable. As a result, two volumes contain works originally published after 1940. The Charlotte Hawkins Brown volume includes her book of etiquette published in 1941, *The Correct Thing To Do—To Say—To Wear*. One of the poetry volumes contains Maggie Pogue Johnson's *Fallen Blossoms*, published in 1951, a compilation of all her previously published and unpublished poems.

Excavational work by scholars during the past decade has been crucial to the development of *African-American Women Writers, 1910–1940*. Germinal bibliographic sources such as Ann Allen Shockley's *Afro-American Women Writers 1746–1933* and Maryemma Graham's *Database of African-American Women Writers* made the initial identification of texts possible. Other works were brought to our attention by scholars who wrote letters sharing their research. Additional texts by selected authors were then added, so that many volumes contain the complete oeuvres of particular writers. Pieces by authors without enough published work to fill an entire volume were grouped with other pieces by genre.

The two types of collections, those organized by author and those organized by genre, bring out different characteristics of black women's writings of the period. The collected works of the literary writers illustrate that many of them were experimenting with a variety of forms. Mercedes Gilbert's volume, for example, contains her 1931 collection, *Selected Gems of Poetry, Comedy, and Drama, Etc.*, as well as her 1938 novel, *Aunt Sara's Wooden God*. Georgia Douglas Johnson's volume contains her plays and short stories in addition to her poetry. Sarah Lee Brown Fleming's volume combines her 1918 novel *Hope's Highway* with her 1920 collection of poetry, *Clouds and Sunshine*.

The generic volumes both bring out the formal and thematic similarities among many of the writings and highlight the striking individuality of particular writers. Most of the plays in the volume of one-acts are social dramas whose tragic endings can be clearly attributed to miscegenation and racism. Within the context of

General Editors' Preface

these other plays, Marita Bonner's surrealistic theatrical vision becomes all the more striking.

The volumes of *African-American Women Writers, 1910–1940* contain reproductions of more than one hundred previously published texts, including twenty-nine plays, seventeen poetry collections, twelve novels, six autobiographies, five collections of short biographical sketches, three biographies, three histories of organizations, three black histories, two anthologies, two sociological studies, a diary, and a book of etiquette. Each volume features an introduction written by a contemporary scholar that provides crucial biographical data on each author and the historical and critical context of her work. In some cases, little information on the authors was available outside of the fragments of biographical data contained in the original introduction or in the text itself. In these instances, editors have documented the libraries and research centers where they tried to find information, in the hope that subsequent scholars will continue the necessary search to find the "lost" clues to the women's stories in the rich stores of papers, letters, photographs, and other primary materials scattered throughout the country that have yet to be fully catalogued.

Many of the thrilling moments that occurred during the development of this series were the result of previously fragmented pieces of these women's histories suddenly coming together, such as Adele Alexander's uncovering of an old family photograph, picturing her own aunt with Addie Hunton, the author Alexander was researching. Claudia Tate's examination of Georgia Douglas Johnson's papers in the Moorland-Spingarn Research Center of Howard University resulted in the discovery of a wealth of previously unpublished work.

The slippery quality of race itself emerged during the construction of the series. One of the short novels originally intended for inclusion in the series had to be cut when the family of the author protested that the writer was not of African descent. Another case involved Louise Kennedy's sociological study *The Negro Peasant Turns Inward*. The fact that none of the available biographical material on Kennedy specifically mentioned race, combined with some coded criticism in a review in the *Crisis*, convinced editor Sheila Smith McKoy that Kennedy was probably white.

General Editors' Preface

These women, taken together, begin to chart the true vitality, and complexity, of the literary tradition that African-American women have generated, using a wide variety of forms. They testify to the fact that the monumental works of Hurston, Larsen, and Fauset, for example, emerged out of a larger cultural context; they were not exceptions or aberrations. Indeed, their contributions to American literature and culture, as this series makes clear, were fundamental not only to the shaping of the African-American tradition but to the American tradition as well.

Henry Louis Gates, Jr.
Jennifer Burton

PUBLISHER'S NOTE

In the *African-American Women Writers, 1910–1940* series, G. K. Hall not only is making available previously neglected works that, in many cases, have been long out of print, we are also, whenever possible, publishing these works in facsimiles reprinted from their original editions including, when available, reproductions of original title pages, copyright pages, and photographs.

When it was not possible for us to reproduce a complete facsimile edition of a particular work (for example, if the original exists only as a handwritten draft or is too fragile to be reproduced), we have attempted to preserve the essence of the original by resetting the work exactly as it originally appeared. Therefore, any typographical errors, strikeouts, or other anomalies reflect our efforts to give the reader a true sense of the original work.

We trust that these facsimile and reprint editions, together with the new introductory essays, will be both useful and historically enlightening to scholars and students alike.

INTRODUCTION*

BY P. GABRIELLE FOREMAN

By the morning of 28 October 1918, the Shaw siblings had sighed in relief. Their sister was going to pull through; the fever had broken. Maggie would soon be back singing in church and listening to her opera albums at home as if she herself belonged to the opera company; her short stories would continue to appear in national magazines; the neighborhood children would still find themselves gazing at the rows of titles in an expansive book collection at the Fullilove home instead of concentrating on their kindergarten or music lessons. Most important, Robert Fullilove wouldn't have to explain to Robert Jr., Daisy, and Beverly why Mommy wasn't there to sing "Happy Birthday" when Robert, the eldest, turned eight next July, or why he, their father, one of the two black physicians in town, couldn't save her.

By the twenty-ninth, Beverly, Preston, and Emma Shaw left their sister's in Yazoo City, Mississippi, for their own homes. They no doubt joined the small city's residents in fleeing what would later be known as the Spanish influenza epidemic of 1918. When thirty-four-year-old Maggie's fever broke, her siblings might have thought that her meeting and marrying a doctor, instead of a reverend and author like the prominent men in her family, was a blessing. Now her husband, Robert, elder sister, Henrietta, and younger brother, Joe, thought they would only have to watch over Maggie as she recovered. Instead, they would bury her. She died of a weakened heart on 30 October.[1]

Margaret Christine Shaw Fullilove was born to Mrs. Maria Petty Campbell Shaw and the Reverend Duncan P. Shaw on 27

Introduction

January 1884. That year Ida B. Wells successfully sued a segregated railroad company and won damages, only to have the Mississippi Supreme Court overturn the case the following year. It is in this historical moment that the Shaw family settled in Abbeville, Mississippi. Maggie was the middle child of five born to her parents, ex-slaves who were determined, in an era of increasing Jim Crow disenfranchisement and rising numbers of lynchings, to send all of their children on to college.[2] Following in both Ida B. Wells's and her own brothers' footsteps, Maggie attended Rust College, formerly named Shaw College, in Holly Spring, Mississippi. By the time his younger sister reached the campus, Preston was on his way to study for a LL.D. and then going on to receive his D.D. from Boston University. Beverly had already earned a master's degree, gone on to study Hebrew at the University of Chicago, and been a professor of classics at his alma mater for five years.[3] At Rust, Maggie studied opera performance and met Robert, the eldest boy of twelve children born to Taylor and Laura Fullilove. Maggie taught school while Robert traveled north to Memphis's Meharry Medical School. There he fulfilled his ex-slave grandmother's prophetic story about a young man who went away and came back a doctor: "And that doctor," she intoned again and again as she repeated the tale, "was you."

Maggie and Robert decided to settle down in Yazoo City, then a small town more than 150 miles south of Holly Springs. The Huddleston family's black insurance company, the Afro-American Sons and Daughters, was expanding to establish the state's first small black-owned hospital and training school for nurses, and the newly graduated Dr. Fullilove was eager to join the distinguished Floyd T. Miller as one of the two Afro-American sons on staff. While Yazoo City was too small for her to pursue her singing professionally, Maggie taught kindergarten and piano in their home. In 1917 she became a regular contributor to the nationally circulated African-American magazine the *Half-Century* and is said to have published in the white press as well.

A family story illuminates the complexities of the interplay of class, race, and status in this era. Maggie's love for opera inspired the couple to pile their three young children into their car and to head for New Orleans to sit, segregated but enraptured, while the

Introduction

New York Metropolitan Opera's traveling company performed *Faust*. Far from bored, their four-year-old son, Beverly, was ready to make his own deal with the devil, exclaiming, "If the bad man can really sing like that, I wouldn't mind going down there."[4] Shaw Fullilove's own elite economic context—out-of-town car trips to hear opera, a piano, and a large book and album collection—may make it easier to understand that the class dynamics of *Who Was Responsible?* (1918) do not call for its readers to assume that its racially indeterminate characters are necessarily white.[5] However, race is certainly not a central or even a tangential concern of this temperance novel, which, to borrow Hortense Spillers's characterization of another novel, "presses its polemical point by way of the story, which provides an occasion for the theme of social uplift."[6]

The opening third of the novel tells the story of John Drew, a reformed alcoholic, who has moved to Hollyville, a dry Southern county. Despite the loss of his wife in childbirth, Drew has prospered in this college town "on account of its high literary and moral standard,"[7] and has contributed to it both his own success as a merchant and his popular and much-courted son, Robert, who has just graduated from the college. Robert ventures to New Gate, the neighboring city of sin his father left years before, to begin his own career. Seduced by the glamour of high society generally and by the specifically dazzling form of Miss Grace King, he is induced to drink socially. Never having been warned away from alcohol, the young man soon progresses to stronger "medicinal" grog, breaks his father's heart, and fills a "drunkard's grave" (*Who*, 5).

Overcome by grief, John Drew tries to trace who is responsible for the destruction of this fine specimen of rising manhood. The saloon keeper who supplied Robert's final bottle sends Drew to the city liquor licenser, who directs him to a city councillor, who suggests the state legislator. Meanwhile, the formerly superficial and haughty Grace King realizes too late that she loves the deceased Robert and that she has been responsible for his fall. She vows to make amends by saving other young men from his fate, and goes for advice to her uncle, the influential New Gate councilman Mr. Anderson, who has also lost a son to drink. John Drew

INTRODUCTION

finds his way to Mr. Anderson almost simultaneously; the three of them decide to garner the necessary support and to lobby the state for prohibition.

At this juncture, with two-thirds of the novel yet to unfold, the narrative shifts its emphasis to Grace King's transformation into an effective political activist. While Robert Drew's death breaks his father, who gets progressively weaker and finally dies as the challenges of prohibition activism progress, Miss King thrives as a reformer. She joins the Women's Christian Temperance Union (WCTU), studies constantly, spearheads war conservation efforts, and becomes a savvy master of political analysis. When the state legislature announces that only national prohibition is expedient, she charges ahead to Washington. Her efforts inspire others—the press, medical and religious establishments, and individuals—to take personal responsibility for their part in allowing social evils to exist. Nor does she neglect personal interaction as she takes her campaign to the national level. Coming upon a charmingly neat but poor rural cabin that houses a refined woman and her intellectually precocious son, Jean, she learns that they have been cast out from both their class position and New Gate because the woman's husband, once a man of great promise and social standing, has turned into an abusive drunkard. When the man dies from alcohol abuse, she provides moral and educational support for Jean and his mother. The novel ends as Mr. Anderson successfully takes Jean in as an apprentice, while a happy Miss Grace King, still unmarried, enjoys a successful career as a speaker and writer for political reform.

It is no mystery why *Who Was Responsible?* has not been mentioned in critical discussions about African-American literature. The thematics of temperance and nonracial uplift, even more than the discourse on marriage, which Ann duCille brilliantly addresses in *The Coupling Convention* (1994), have been "all but dismissed as the author['s] dalliance with the petty preoccupations of white society that have nothing to do with the *real* material conditions of most black Americans."[8] Yet for these reformers, encroachments on the rights of humanity were connected sins; the mission of spiritual uplift "was as urgent in the late-nineteenth century as was organizing against lynching, rape, Jim Crow, and black disen-

INTRODUCTION

franchisement."⁹ Nor were Christian reformist and recognized black women's discourse disconnected. Indeed, the language of the National Association of Colored Women (NACW), with "Lifting As We Climb" as their slogan, was infused with religious imagery.

Despite the often unstated opposition between the thematics of radical protest and social uplift, temperance societies were part of black activist or self-help movements dating back to the 1830s. Black clergymen "combined temperance work with pastoring, abolition and mutual aid work," and the A.M.E., for example, formally disapproved of drinking.[10] Frederick Douglass and William Wells Brown, the two most prominent early black authors and activists in the United States, were temperance men. Douglass took the pledge in 1846 and delivered temperance speeches in Ireland; while in London later that year, he and William Lloyd Garrison attended the World Temperance Convention. The first women's temperance conventions in the United States were peopled with abolitionists who would eventually become women's rights activists.[11]

This sustained commitment to antidrink work bridged ante- and postbellum reform movements and involved a whole generation of early black women writers. In 1874, the year the WCTU was founded, William Wells Brown sponsored a writing contest to encourage the spurning of alcohol; the winning essay, "The Evils of Intemperance and Their Remedy," was penned by fifteen-year-old Pauline Hopkins, who would later become an important journalist and prolific novelist. Writer and educator Josephine Turpin Washington's first writing addressed the same theme. In the 1880s, T. Thomas Fortune, the outspoken editor of the highly influential *New York Age*, flirted with the Prohibition party. Black women in North Carolina founded their own temperance paper in the 1890s, while their sisters all over the South responded to the segregation of the WCTU by forming WCTU#2 chapters, many of which changed their names to Lucy Thurman WCTU in honor of one of three African-American women who participated in the national leadership. In the North, the NACW also had an office devoted to temperance work. Abroad, writer, speaker, and educator Hallie Quinn Brown lectured for the British Women's

Temperance Association and was a speaker at the World's Women Christian Temperance Union gathering in 1895.

Black temperance activity wasn't merely mimetic, local, or sporadic. Black women understood it in relation to both broader "transcendent" values of social uplift and to their own specific racially and gender-determined circumstances. Frances E. W. Harper, who served for more than a decade as the WCTU Superintendent for Colored Work, listed the three great evils of civilization as prostitution or "the social evil," lynching or "lawlessness," and intemperance.[12] We now know that Harper's second novel, *Sowing and Reaping: A Temperance Story*, was serialized in the A.M.E. church journal, the *Christian Recorder*, in 1876–77. *Who Is Responsible?* is no anomaly; forty years before Shaw Fullilove's text was published, Harper also used racially ambiguous characters to fight drinking as a social evil.[13] Organizing to fight these ills was not just an imperative Christian duty. A writer in the *Colored American Magazine* put it this way: "Our young women can do much to head off the drink habit among the young men . . . and it is for their own future well-being that they exercise their decisive influence to that end."[14] Lucy Thurman put it differently, announcing that temperance unions would be a "grand training school for the development of women."[15] While the first author implies that women's "influence" could protect the sanctity of the home and in turn protect standard spheres of influence and action, Thurman extends women's realm beyond the domestic sphere. Miss Grace King is an example of Thurman's model of women's active development and public force. Read in context, far from falling outside the pale of historical black activity, *Who Was Responsible?* is a logical literary extension of nineteenth-century black interest and activism.

That *Who Was Responsible?*'s temperance theme fits into a specific black historical context does not resolve the issue of the novel's racially indeterminate characters. While Shaw Fullilove's interest in temperance places her in the company of Frances E. W. Harper and Pauline Hopkins, her novel has less in common with their (radical) texts of race and romance than it does with the less well-known turn-of-the-century writings of A. E. Johnson and Emma D. Kelley-Hawkins. While Hopkins and Harper feature

Introduction

mulatta heroines who are phenotypically white, Johnson's *Clarence and Corrine; or God's Way* (1890) and *The Hazeley Family* (1894), Kelley-Hawkins's *Megda* (1891) and *Four Girls at Cottage City* (1898), and Shaw Fullilove's *Who Was Responsible?* include characters who are both textually and contextually racially indeterminate.[16] Additionally, *Megda* and *Clarence and Corrine* are both concerned explicitly with the fate of women and children plagued by men in league with the "demon whiskey." *Clarence and Corrine* and *Who Was Responsible?* could have been written, as Hortense Spillers categorizes the former, under the auspices of the WCTU (Spillers, xxii). Additionally, Miss Grace reminds readers of Kelley's character Megda and her friends, who transform from "callow, carefree schoolgirls to responsible, Christian women" (duCille, 57), just as Grace King and her cohorts are "the beautiful dazzling thoughtless creatures [who] were but shining lights to lure, charm, and bewilder the green youth—lure, and in the end destroy" (*Who*, 17).

The vast majority of critics either assume or argue that racially indeterminate characters are by default white, at least in U.S. economies of race. However, Ann duCille suggests that the effort to make these characters and the spiritual salvation and home protection that concern them transcendent, larger than race, may explain their racelessness, which shouldn't necessarily be interpreted as white.[17] One might add that in an era and region in which black men were the material and discursive targets of all sorts of violence, black authors were particularly sensitive not to create a script that could be appropriated as antiblack rhetoric. Temperance, with the surrounding debate on hereditary inclinations, could easily collapse into arguments about eugenics and black degeneration. Examples of white rhetoric about "weak" Native American populations' attraction to alcohol being an indication of their inferior stock abounded. Black men, too, were often the focus of intemperance abuse campaigns in the South. Emphasizing racially indeterminate and upper-class characters as the victims of the alcohol abuse, then, can be interpreted as an act designed to protect rather than erase black subjectivity.

It is also important to contextualize Shaw Fullilove's own literary-geographic circumstances. While Hopkins and Harper lived

INTRODUCTION

and published in the North at the beginning of Jim Crow, Shaw Fullilove's life almost exactly overlapped with the most repressive years of the South's most repressive state.[18] As historian Neil McMillan argues, "above all, black Mississippians [of that era] were expected to avoid controversy with the dominant race" (McMillan, 25). The Fullilove family's economic status itself made them a heightened target for white violence. When a black physician and his fiancée barely survived being forced off the road, beaten, and shot near Meridian in 1925, the NAACP determined that local whites were jealous of the doctor's new car and home. Local whites paid attention to the subtleties of black behavior. They would not tolerate black consideration of an exhaustive list of taboo topics that included, as Richard Wright later categorized it, "American white women; the Klu Klux Klan; . . . the entire Northern part of the U.S.; the Civil War; Abraham Lincoln; . . . slavery, social equality . . . or any topic calling for positive knowledge or . . . self-assertion on the part of the Negro."[19] Although extralegal codes gave form to Mississippians' interactions, a 1920 law illustrates the extent of juridical white overseeing of black-penned representations. Anyone found guilty of "printing, publishing or circulating printed, typewritten or written matter urging or presenting public acceptation [sic] or general information or suggestions in favor of social equality or intermarriage" could be fined up to $500 and/or imprisoned for up to six months (McMillan, 8–9). McMillan notes that, despite his dedication to the race, Lloyd Miller, Fullilove's senior surgeon, lived his public life in "scrupulous conformity to racial codes" (McMillan, 25). Black Mississippians like the Fulliloves were often forced to be social realists who carefully negotiated their personal and professional dedication to the race and their public representation of it. Creating a black Grace King, an activist clearly demonstrating the aforementioned "positive knowledge and self-assertion," might be suicidal for Maggie Shaw Fullilove or for the hospital of the Afro-American Sons and Daughters. While the facts of Jim Crow are all too familiar to us in the abstract, they inform what we might call the microintentionality—the specific and local oppressive circumstances that might call for an author's multivalenced textual codings—of a text like *Who Was Responsible?*

Introduction

Considering both the textual and contextual evidence, one can argue that Shaw Fullilove's novel is meant to be marked simultaneously by race and by its absence of metonymic stereotypes. Interestingly, Hopkins, Harper, and Kelley, among others, specifically portray their heroines as phenotypically white. In Hopkins's *Hagar's Daughter*, for example, "Jewel Bowen's beauty was of the Saxon type, dazzling fair, with creamy roseate skin. Her hair was fair, with streaks of copper in it; her eyes, gray, with thick short lashes, at times iridescent. Her nose superbly Grecian. Her lips beautifully firm . . ."[20] Shaw Fullilove, in contrast, offers conceptual rather than physical descriptions of her characters: Grace King is dazzling, Robert thinks, "all that a beautiful woman is said to be," while he is the very "impersonation of clean, healthy, wholesome young manhood" (*Who*, 19). Shaw Fullilove calls on readers to fill in the specific descriptive weft according to their own racially coded concepts of beauty and ideal man- or womanhood.

Few novels leave such imaginings to their readers. Both of A. E. Johnson's novels open with an illustration of her phenotypically white characters; the other pictures in her novels confirm that her characters do not, at least, look black. On the other hand, *Who Was Responsible?* is introduced with a photograph of a pretty and unmistakably brown-skinned woman with a decidedly non-Grecian nose who is announced in the caption below as Maggie Shaw Fullilove. J. Beverly Shaw's framing foreword reinforces the opening iconographics, and tells us that the author's parents were both ex-slaves without school advantage, who nonetheless sent all of their children to college. Shaw goes on to tell us that "Maggie Shaw was graduated from Rust University, Holly Springs, Mississippi."

The framing documents and Shaw Fullilove's Hollyville–Holly Springs conflation invite readers to use biographical data to inform the text's lack of racial commitment. The merchant John Drew's story of a man "with limited education acquirements" echoes the Shaws, for the narrative begins just as his son, like Maggie, has graduated from the much-vaunted college in Hollyville.[21] Moreover, although the characters in *Who Was Responsible?* may seem too wealthy and well connected to be

Introduction

African American, Beverly Shaw, obviously related to the author, has signed his framing introduction as the *president* of Central Alabama College. That Drew wants his son to be a professor at his alma mater, as parenthetically Beverly Shaw had also been, is not merely the stuff of fiction. The text opens by inviting its readers to read blackness into the borders of its racial indeterminacy.

It is not class, then, but status that eventually forecloses the multiple racial possibilities of *Who Was Responsible?* Mr. Anderson is Miss Grace's uncle and a New Gate councilman. His multiple "boyhood chums" are state senators; he and Miss Grace have almost unlimited access to national congressmen. Shaw Fullilove includes them in the inner political workings of the country at a time when Thomas Dixon, author of the best-selling book *The Clansman*, actualized his racist fictional narratives by convincing Edward White, chief justice of the U.S. Supreme Court, to arrange a viewing of *Birth of a Nation*, a film based on Dixon's book, for a group of Supreme Court justices, congressmen, and senators, and when Woodrow Wilson, showing the film in the White House, declared that it was "like writing history with lightening!"[22] This fictional-turned-filmic ideological apparatus directly informed increasing African-American disenfranchisement. Wilson segregated government employees and dismissed those African Americans who had managed to hold on to civil service appointments. Taking up issues of class and racial indeterminacy, Claudia Tate argues that sentimental texts of the previous generation work to inspire through their politically allegorical rather than realist conventions.[23] Ultimately, *Who Was Responsible?* suggests the allegorical as its logical interpretive option, for Shaw Fullilove's own personal social realism forecloses the possibility of her novel's grounding in racial realism as the narrative moves its political agenda forward.

The feminist workings of *Who Was Responsible?* open up at the very narrative juncture that its multiple racial possibilities begin to close down. In the first third of the story, Grace King is a careless girl at best, an agent of seduction and contamination in a story in which the temptations of women and wine seem to be explicitly connected. Yet, Shaw Fullilove's narrative strategies significantly undermine the feminization of "the curse" of alcoholics.

Introduction

The text seems to propose that Robert falls from all that is good, clean, and scrupulous as he partakes of Grace's "wine and her smiles" (*Who*, 24). Shaw Fullilove undermines this script, suggesting, in moments that foreshadow his fall, that Robert is not all "demigod." He "ruthlessly" kicks "discarded rubbish" that his beloved father considers "gold treasures of a very happy past" (*Who*, 14) before his lips touch a drop of wine or whiskey; in the "rage of passion" that accompanies his first drink, what Grace considers his chaste thoughts cover his "mad desire to kiss her—to devour her—to strangle her with love" (*Who*, 23); as his drinking problem progresses, Robert's sinister glances cause his beloved family caretaker's "heart to wither in her bosom" (*Who*, 45).

Just as Shaw Fullilove undermines Robert's inherent goodness, she destabilizes the script of Miss Grace's loss of perfect love and marital bliss at the hands of alcohol. In conventional ways the story of Jean's mother points to Grace's possible fate. The woman Miss Grace befriends, so different from Clarence and Corrine's enervated mother in A. E. Johnson's 1890 novel, remains nameless throughout the work to illustrate that any refined, gentle woman—even a woman like Grace—can marry a man like Jean's father, who once was "honest, intelligent, upright, a gentleman who came from one of the best families" (*Who*, 91). Again conventionally, Robert's death, even as it saves Grace from Jean's mother's fate, acts as a redemptive icon, the crowning love of her womanhood being given too late, and is "the means of transforming her into a woman of broadest sympathies" (*Who*, 139). Suffering and loss, as they are for Frances Harper's Iola and Pauline Hopkins's Sappho, become agents of angelic transformation.

Yet Shaw Fullilove displaces the primacy of suffering and the loss of potential marital bliss and instead emphasizes Grace's work. Moreover, it is not the higher spirituality of social uplift that fulfills Grace King, it is the personal pleasure she gains from the process and methods of work—her studying, lobbying, and her efficiency—that Shaw Fullilove stresses. Toward the close of the novel, Mr. Anderson notes that he

> was aware of the immense pleasure which his niece found in her work of usefulness. She was forever busy, working in the various

INTRODUCTION

well-organized clubs, in the church, in everything that pertained to the improvement of the city. All during those weeks in which she worked so assiduously, so efficiently, she was unconsciously drawing from the faithfulness of her work. . . . Her work constantly enabled her to gain in much valuable experience, in fine training, in increased efficiency, in splendid discipline, in self-expression, and in the strengthening of her beautiful character. (*Who*, 163)

Shaw Fullilove continually uses Mr. Anderson to articulate a conventional narrative she then displaces or augments. He emphasizes the "faithfulness of her work" and connects her pleasure to it. Yet, what lends her "beautiful character" fortitude is increasingly the characteristics of the public realm of commerce—efficiency, experience, training, discipline—not the qualities usually associated with an expanded sphere of sentimental femininity, such as faith, love, affection, and inspirational divinity.

Shaw Fullilove offers a model of effective political activism as true womanhood fulfilled. Robert's dying, the text suggests again and again, is the best thing that could have happened to Grace King. In addition, the author does not provide a suitable mate at the end of the novel to contain her heroine's radical happiness within the typical closure of the coupling convention, as Ann duCille characterizes the marriage plot in African-American women's fiction. The novel culminates with freedom, not with marriage, to paraphrase Harriet Jacobs, and with a passage that describes Miss King publishing diatribes in leading magazines, "ruthlessly . . . assaulting" America's drinking folly, and "demanding" that a God-fearing nation fight this enemy of "peace and order" (*Who*, 180) in language that hardly reflects the feminized discourse usually associated with "sentimental" Christian social uplift.

Who Was Responsible? is not a transparent text. The narration explicitly undermines Mr. Anderson's script, in which Grace is "a young girl whose soul is as white as an angel" who "gave her love to [Robert] and although he loved her and declared his love, he died before he could make her his wife" (*Who*, 74). Instead, as we have seen, Shaw Fullilove directs us to question Robert's ascendant greatness, and implicitly disrupts the text's sentimentalized

Introduction

discourse of romantic love. In many ways, this novel moves beyond the 1890s, and with its emphasis on process and efficiency is firmly rooted in its own era of mass production. Its heroine is preoccupied neither with marriage as a metaphor for civil liberty nor with sisterhood and women's community. Grace King is an individual public actor intricately involved with effective public policy and state intervention to protect the sanctity of the home through external and public rather than internal and affective regulation.

Although many of Maggie Shaw Fullilove's short stories foreground female desire, her magazine fiction and novel present different sets of issues. All of her extant stories were published in the *Half Century Magazine*, a national black publication founded in 1916 and based in Chicago, whose very first announcement was a notice of the National Association of Colored Women's biennial meeting. A typical issue contained notices for such associations as the National Negro Business League, the National Negro Press Association, and the National Medical Association of Colored Physicians, Surgeons, Dentists; news items reprinted from the *Chicago Defender* and the *Amsterdam News*; a domestic science division; and a special fashion segment, the first to feature "*our* people in the latest styles." The *Half Century* aimed to be "the greatest Colored short-story magazine in the world,"[24] and Maggie Shaw Fullilove was included as one of its first and most-featured authors.

The publication's aims (and so guidelines) in relation to its fiction are multiple and sometimes seem unaligned. In the issue in which the editors introduce "the well-known and popular writer Maggie Shaw Fullilove," they announce that the paper

> can't get too many short stories. So let them come fast and thick. . . . We aim to please the women and make [the magazine] popular. We do not want philosophy, science, sociology and eloquence—we editors have plenty of that ourselves. Our people—tired at the end of the day's work—have no time to consume reading solid literary stuff. They want diversion and recreation, and will read anything stimulating and refreshing. They will read light, airy fiction—full of snap, pep and go. And so we want: Stories that are easily digested.

Introduction

> Stories with plenty of action—full of romance, love and sentiment. Stories in which the superficial qualities are cultivated—"like fluency, and wit, and the glamour of money, and a few touches of pathos and purity and no difficulties for the understanding." . . . Don't go into the church-house for all your plots.[25]

The editors express a disdain for the "solid literary stuff" that they say their working readers will find too boring, brooding, or profound, and that in any case will take too much energy for their audience to unravel. Yet, the paper fills in the referents that provide meaning for words like "light," "stimulating," or "refreshing." What this race magazine wants from its fiction is not exactly superficial; it has, in fact, a decidedly sociological edge. Soliciting stories less than a year after its opening pronouncement, the editors announce that the magazine's contributions "as usual will have *only* Colored men and women, or boys and girls, as the case may be, as heroes and heroines, and will seek to inspire and elevate the race by having these to appear not always in comic or ignorant roles to indicate racial inferiority, racial subservience, or racial satisfaction with life as it is or has been; but, will aim to have their leading characters set forth in inspirational roles."[26] Despite the editors' casual request for stories stressing superficial qualities like the "glamour" of money, and the magazine's continual emphasis on its mission "to present facts in plain common sense language so that the masses may read and understand," the *Half Century* does not offer class escapism as a fictional panacea when it comes to the juncture of race and class. "As the Race Problem is ever with us," one editor comments, "we shall discuss and shall entertain discussions of the same from time to time. We appreciate that we are now living in a commercial era and that the factors of paramount importance in the solution of this problem are economy, industry—the making and saving of money—and business development. We also understand that in the upbuilding of the race, unity, cooperation and race patronage are essential."[27] One can't but notice that the ethos of the business era—the production and circulation of efficient social protest reflected in this statement—informs the way Shaw Fullilove frames Grace King's social, rather than racial, uplift work. Shaw Fullilove is explicit about quantifiable processes as

INTRODUCTION

well; drink is a drain on personal and commercial industry and enterprise. Alcohol, Grace King stresses again and again, hinders in the upbuilding not of the race, but of the nation.

Shaw Fullilove's *Half Century* publications differ from *Who Was Responsible?* because the social vision and feminist mechanisms of their expression are absent rather than augmented in her stories with black casts. We assume the protagonist in "The Precursor of the Dawn" is black because of the unmistakable illustrations of an African-American youth that accompany the story. Yet this makes no difference at all to the story; in his struggles against the "demon whiskey" he could be any youth, as his namelessness implies; he could be Robert Drew. Race is a given in all of Shaw Fullilove's *Half Century* stories, but it is not a factor. Unlike the novel, the stories do not take either social or racial protest as their subject. Personal desire and marital protest are her focus in these stories, which address, for the most part, the construction and conservation of domestic relations. And while some black women writers use the domestic realm in order to fashion important social critiques, in her short fiction Shaw Fullilove's formulations ultimately are either conservative or contained.

"Navy Blue Velvet," the first story to appear in the *Half Century*,[28] might be interpreted as an expression of female agency and self-assertion. Margaret Harding feels invisible because within her familial economy she continually represses her personal desires. On her way to the bank with her own fifty dollars, a sum her husband has earmarked for a springtime litter of pigs, she spies a navy blue suit in the latest New York style and, in an act of spontaneous protest, spends the entire amount on it. The suit leads her to the impractical purchase of a pair of glacé kid Cuban-heeled pumps, and a surreptitious trip to the theater—a frivolous waste of money according to Mr. Harding—alone, decked out, at night. Her husband catches her, of course, and many nasty things get said. She thinks of leaving him, then realizes she can't and doesn't want to. In the meantime, he takes back his words and reconsiders his motives, but can't find a way to tell her so. In the end he begins to buy her pretty things and finally allows her to have a flower garden where he formerly, for practicality's sake, would only allow her to plant vegetables.[29]

Introduction

What is interesting here is that this story, from its opening line, "Kensington's, the leading dry goods store of the little town, was beautiful that day," to its resolution, is much less about its putative topic of beauty and aesthetic appreciation than it is about consumption. Margaret Harding's freedom, her personal and feminine agency, is constrained by marital limitations on her status as a consumer. She becomes visible, that is, literally someone in view, only when she puts on this navy blue suit. Shaw Fullilove seems to conflate being the object of the gaze and the relation between commodification and visual consumption with self-expression. Mrs. Harding's protest is decidedly not about being a self-expressive agent. The conflict of the story is easily resolved, then, when her husband finds the thick New York catalogue out of which his wife chooses some children's clothes each year, and orders her a fur cape and muff. A product takes the place of communicative exchange; it speaks, we can infer, louder than words. When it arrives, she breaks down in tears of happiness, he admits he's been a fool, and all live happily ever after.

"Sermons in Stone"[30] starts with an even more forceful critique of woman's limited agency within marriage. After college, Evelyn follows her heart rather than her head and marries her classmate Lionel instead of another suitor who settles in the city. She finds herself disgusted with her cramped rural life. Hungry for something more, she decides to write the story she cannot live. Back from a hard day in the fields, her husband comes upon her with a lamp lit and

> spill[ing] a halo around Evelyn's dark head, piled high with masses of thick shining black hair. One of her quick-thinking moods was on her. He had seen her write like that when they were in school together. She could not get her words down on paper fast enough.
>
> She raised vague eyes to him, nodded abstractedly and kept on with her rapid writing. When they were in school together, he had loved her for this power of concentration. It showed her superiority above the others. She was a darling, a wonder who intrigued and delighted him by her willful cleverness. But now—O Lord! This time he groaned aloud. ("Sermons," May 1917, 18)

Introduction

He groans because he's concerned that her ardor for writing will impede her development into a fine homemaker, that "before long there might be a complete upheaval of all their domestic affairs" ("Sermons," May 1917, 18). Shaw Fullilove makes it clear that Lionel sees her writing and their marriage in oppositional terms. As much as he loves his wife and wants to make her happy, "there existed an under-current of foreboding and anxiety whenever he thought about her career. Somehow it seemed to come between them" ("Sermons," May 1917, 4).

In the opening segment—as the image of the halo suggests—the narrator is sympathetic toward Evelyn's assertion of domestic and artistic agency. Yet this agency is contained and undermined in the concluding section of the serial. Evelyn's work drives her away from her husband and home, the latter of which takes on a state of exaggerated filthiness. When, as the narrator tells us, Evelyn's story is rejected for publication because it simply isn't any good, she comes back to both her senses and her household. Yet, she doesn't give up writing; she simply finds an appropriate channel. By writing about housekeeping, she becomes a good housekeeper; and by becoming a good housekeeper, she becomes a good writer: "The shining stove, the clean shelves, the spotless cupboard, the glittering tins—all whispered in her ears. . . . Then followed paragraph after paragraph of good, wholesome, instructive ideas on how it is possible to make house-keeping a pleasure" ("Sermons," June 1917, 5). The story concludes with Evelyn's assertion that "It was pots and pans that gave me a true knowledge of life and taught my soul the gracious lesson of submission" ("Sermons," June 1917, 13).

At times it seems as if Shaw Fullilove were involved in a proleptic exchange with Nella Larsen. Shaw Fullilove seems to imply that Evelyn is not what Helga Crane will become in *Quicksand* (1928), because Evelyn quiets down her dissatisfaction, talent, and personal desire for the "great things in life" ("Sermons," June 1917, 13). Read at face value, far from fitting into a tradition of domestic fiction that encodes social and/or racial protest or uplift, Evelyn's move from creating imaginative love stories that disrupt the home to outlining domestic instruction that fortifies the home contains her own desires to express her own talent and

INTRODUCTION

agency. A more generous reading would infuse irony into Shaw Fullilove's seemingly exaggerated narrative of accelerated domestic destruction and the subsequent reconstruction, in which personified pots and pans become a girl's best friend. Shaw Fullilove's placement of the break in this serialized story might support such a feminist reading, for it gives Shaw Fullilove's readers a full month to absorb Evelyn's desires before the second segment suggests that they are selfish and disruptive. One might point to her next story, "Sweet Peas Between," for support[31]: while the hero is the popular writer, the heroine is the successful critic who applies her analysis to Tennyson, Shakespeare, Aeschylus, Dante, and the work of the novelist-hero, who will become her fiancée. Echoing Anna Julia Cooper, the heroine asserts that "we must admit that [the black writer in question] has framed some mighty men . . . but his women do not satisfy. They are weak, even foolish, entirely too sentimental. . ." ("Peas," May 1918, 13). Yet, while Shaw Fullilove undermines Robert Drew's "demigod" status throughout *Who Was Responsible?*, in "Sermon in Stones" she continually supports Lionel and justifies his expectations. Moreover, she undermines Evelyn's artistic motivations and implies that they are selfish; in contrast, Evelyn sends the instructive homemaking articles out not for their pecuniary value, but "with the hope that [they] might . . . perpetuate love and sunshine" ("Sermons," June 1917, 5). One might note that Shaw Fullilove's artistic development is the inverse of her character Evelyn's. By the time she pens *Who Was Responsible?*, she encodes subtle irony in what critics often dismiss as sentimentality, and gives voice to a feminist, although not racial, sensibility that extends the vision of African-American women writers of the previous generation.

Unfortunately, beyond her race, we know nothing about the life of Mary Etta Spencer, the author of *The Resentment* and the short story "Beyond the Years," published in the Urban League's journal, *Opportunity*. The "Who's Who" pages of that October 1929 issue hail Sterling Brown's and other contributors' achievements; about Spencer, however, not a word appears. What we know of her life

INTRODUCTION

we must glean from the dedication and "Author's Purpose" note that introduce *The Resentment*. She credits her mother for her literary talent and dedicates the volume to the "growing boys and girls" of "my race," whom she hopes to inspire "to be willing to endure struggle to become a man or woman of worth."[32] Ironically, although one of the chapters is entitled "I Will Not Always Be Called a Nigger," and although Spencer stresses race in her dedication, in the sparse commentary in which she is mentioned, critics assail Mary Etta Spencer for her willfully superficial treatment of prejudice and black disenfranchisement.

The Resentment chronicles the rise of Silas Miller, who is given "little consideration" on account of his "being only a Negro boy" (*Resentment*, 9) but who nonetheless struggles dutifully, goes to the North to work as hired help to raise money, and returns to the South to become a "Hog King" and the richest Negro in the state. Silas is a respectful boy who knows his place. And it is this understanding that facilitates his success, garners the support of his white neighbors, ensures his economic rise, and allows him to marry Margaret Kempt, the daughter of a wealthy Northern black family.[33]

Spencer also narrates the story of Silas's sister Nett, a prank-loving Frado-spirited girl who looks after Silas's first litter of pigs while he is up North earning money to buy more. After Silas returns, Nett also goes North to fulfill her goal of becoming a nurse. There she's transformed into a rather serious young woman who takes the blame and punishment for another student's wrongdoings without protest or bitterness, as Dr. Lionel, in the know, looks on with admiration. Nett the nurse-courted-by-doctor is familiar to readers of earlier African-American fiction; this subplot replicates Dr. Gresham's appreciation of Iola Leroy's angelic ministering abilities, except that by the 1920s, Nett is a sacrificing trained nurse in the now-urban slums rather than a volunteer during the Civil War. Eventually, as Iola's does, Nett's health fails from exhaustion; Dr. Lionel attends to her, telling her that he has "waited for her to taste both the joys and sorrows of the course that she had so nobly chosen" (*Resentment*, 198). Nett's conventional "reward," as the chapter in which Dr. Lionel proposes is titled, undermines the primacy of her work. Eventually, however, Nett helps Dr. Lionel with his practice, and with money Silas and Margaret give her, opens a modern health facility for African-American women. Nett directs the arrangements "to erect a building where [black] women could go to get free medical treatment from the best women doctors and nurses obtainable, and remain there until they became capable of caring for themselves" (*Resentment*, 202). Although Nett runs into absolutely no problems as she constructs and runs such a facility in the South, Spencer's attention to black women's health issues and her suggestion that women should continue to express themselves within marriage perhaps are the points she makes most successfully.

It is rare for a black feminist critic to find herself endorsing Robert Bone's generally dismissive assessments of an early African-American woman writer. Yet, he rightly observes that Mary Etta Spencer "stoutly maintains that there is no barrier to success which diligence and perseverance cannot hurdle. Rather than face the hard facts of caste, [she] prefers to indulge in crude success-fantasies. [Characters] 'play white' in [her] novel, much in the same sense as children 'play house.'"[34] *The Resentment* reads like a fictionalized illustration of Booker T. Washington's *Up from Slavery* philosophy, which calls upon Southern blacks to cast down their buckets and then fill them up with something whites need. Spencer accepts this philosophy as truth without recognizing Washington's complicated address and strategies.

Even more than Washington, Horatio Alger is Spencer's ideological and narrative model. The opening lines of his first and most famous novel, *Ragged Dick*, read: "'Wake up there, youngster,' said a rough voice. . . . 'Wake up, you young vagabond!' said the man a little impatiently; 'I suppose you'd lay there all day, if I hadn't called you.'"[35] Spencer's opening specifically recalls Alger's "'Come on, come on there, boy, you must think you are owner of half this county instead of being a good-for-nothing 'nigger.' Come, hurry up, we have got lots of work to do today, with the sun two hours high already" (*Resentment*, 7). Spencer places Silas into Ragged Dick's narrative; they literally begin at the same moment, around 7:00 A.M., and both young protagonists face a hostile disembodied voice that berates them for their laziness.

Introduction

Spencer seems to suggest that unlike Dick's situation, race rather than class will be the obstacle Silas will have to overcome. For a moment one might believe that Spencer will anticipate Richard Wright and *Native Son*'s opening "Brrrrriiiiiiiiiiiiiiiinng!," and that her depiction of racial obstacles foreshadows Wright's racial determinism. Within pages, however, it becomes clear that *Native Son* and *The Resentment* are on opposite poles. In Spencer's novel, race is superficial. Unlike Frederick Douglass in his 1845 narrative before him or Bigger after him, Silas is like Dick; he does not have to learn how to read in opposition to dominant codes and expectations. Instead, he receives his first encouragement as successful white men see his true inner nature. Again, Spencer's text mirrors Alger's; Silas's Mr. Walker recalls Dick's Mr. Whitney in that both give the young protagonists advice and encouragement. After seeing that the youngsters have imbibed their advice, they offer them monetary gifts as a token of their faith.

Spencer's Mr. Walker fulfills another purpose. Like Mr. Whitney, he had a "friendless youth" (*Resentment*, 57), but his rags-to-riches story also dispels the notion that race is the fulcrum of black misfortune. Walker, like African Americans, was a victim of a system as bad as slavery, despite his white skin. At the age of eight, Walker was bound out to cruel people for whom he worked ten years without pay. "In the summer I went barefooted and half naked," he confides to Silas; in the winter "one cheap suit, a pair of heavy boots and two suits of underwear to be worn the entire year" (*Resentment*, 18) were his provisions. In addition, he is subjected to so much physical abuse that he finally is compelled to leave. Spencer deracinates this familiar narrative of its roots in black slavery. By erasing race as a symbol of the past, she can ignore the racial obstacles of Silas's present and can narrate a story in which individual merit is rewarded. In these circumstances Walker and Whitney merge, as do, amazingly, Silas and Ragged Dick. Whitney's advice to Dick serves as the revoked frame to Spencer's narrative as well as its credo: "You know in this free country poverty in early life is no bar to a man's advancement" (*Ragged Dick*, 55).

Spencer even extends Alger's paradigm of individual meritorious success. Mr. Whitney's nephew Frank encourages Dick, telling him, "If you'll try to become somebody, and grow up into a respectable member of society, you will. You may not become rich—it isn't everybody that becomes rich, you know—but you can obtain a good position, and be respected" (*Ragged Dick*, 31). Ragged Dick makes his way from "rags to respectability"; Silas travels from rags to riches. In Spencer's revisionary mythology not only Mr. Walker, but all whites support Silas's success. After the opening line, Silas's only detractors are black. When he asks if he can buy pigs from Mr. Baxter, the Southern farmer whose epithets open the novel, and then before giving him the money asks, "Shall we go to the house and sign papers?" (*Resentment*, 28), Mr. Baxter thinks "what a bright little chap he was" instead of calling him impudent or knocking him senseless. Likewise, after his success has made him the "chief object of interest in Kent county," white farmers commented to each other "'that Miller is going ahead fast, give him a few years longer and he will be at the top of the ladder.' Still others referred to him as 'that smart black man,' but no one ever called him 'Nigger'—he had passed that stage" (*Resentment*, 104).

Spencer's fantasies of economic uplift—Southern whites' delight as a black man surpasses them—do violence to the material reality of racism. Of course, there were individual examples of successful blacks working with and being accepted by white Southern communities. Yet, after almost thirty years of Jim Crow, Spencer implies that racism is class based and that one can be past "that stage." Indeed, Silas appears to reach a stage where he seems to forget what it means to know his place. He refuses to haggle with white farmers, and instead gives them a "long talk," reminding them of the superior quality of his hogs; they listen attentively and acquiesce (*Resentment*, 88); in other instances he makes the point that he has "about twenty times" more stock than they do, and they laugh good-naturedly (*Resentment*, 121). Finally, he exhorts, "I have learned that when we help ourselves, others will help us. It has been a great misunderstanding among many persons of our race that the white man hates us: but I have found that the intelligent white man honors and respects the intelligent and prosperous black man" (*Resentment*, 211). Examples of this type abound in the novel, making it hard for all but the most assimilationist readers to direct "the resentment" toward the writer herself.

The anger and frustration that seep into critical assessments of novels that seem far removed from the lived experiences of the masses of black people are not new; they have been destructively wielded against early African-American women writers from Jacobs to Harper to Jessie Fauset. Yet, much of the misreading that has characterized such criticism stems from a fundamental misunderstanding of these authors' sophisticated negotiations of sentimental subversion. Spencer does not work within that genre. Hers is a tale of economic uplift told in the language of realism, a genre that "defines itself *against* the excesses of romanticism and romance [and] displaces metaphysical reality with social reality and substitutes historical, humanistic truth for ahistorical, transcendental truth."[36] The problem with this novel is not that it strays away from some set of acceptable African-American themes or that it doesn't address some authentic sense of blackness. Rather, the novel fails to either fulfill or subvert the terms of representation it employs. Nor does Spencer adopt other generic conventions that would admit more complex, nontransparent, formal mediations. Rather, *The Resentment* insists that it is a transparent paradigm for material black economic success and simultaneously fails to even approximate the historical realism it adopts, even when "history" and "realism" are expansive multiplicitous terms.

Black women's literature is also becoming increasingly expansive. As their first republication in this series illustrates, until recently interpretive models were lacking to address such novels as *Who Was Responsible?* and *The Resentment*, which fail to fit comfortably into established paradigms. The new questions about women and activism that historians now pose, along with theories that deaggregate race, gender, sexuality, status, and class, help to situate black textual workings with more understanding. As more and more early writing becomes available, readers can address the varied traditions these authors establish, expand, and subvert, the multiple strategies and conventions they adopt, and the multiple formal and political interventions they make.

Introduction

NOTES

*I would like to thank Jacquelyn McLendon for reading and talking through drafts of this introduction, DoVeanna Fulton for her extraordinary research assistance, Michael Roudette at the Schomburg Library for his smiles and for tracking down information on the Shaws, and Earl Lewis and Jacqueline Goldsby for providing me with helpful facts, figures, and references. A fellowship at the University of Michigan's Center for African and African-American Studies helped to facilitate this research. I thank them for their support.

[1] I am most grateful to Dr. Daisy Fullilove Balsley, Maggie Shaw Fullilove's daughter, and Dr. Robert E. Fullilove III, her grandson, for their help. I obtained the material that informs these opening paragraphs from them. Interview with Robert Fullilove III, New York, 18 October 1993. Interview with Daisy Fullilove Balsley, Chicago, 18 November 1993. Dr. Balsley also provided the photograph that appears in this volume.

[2] The five also had a half-sister from their father's previous marriage.

[3] For further information on J. Beverly Ford Shaw, a clergyman who went on to be a college president, see Joseph J. Borris, ed., *Who's Who in Colored America* (Yonkers on the Hudson, NY: C. E. Burckel & Associates, 1927). For more information on Bishop Nathan Alexander Shaw, see G. James Fleming and Christian Burckel, eds., *Who's Who in Colored America, 1950* (Yonkers on the Hudson, NY: Christian E. Burckel & Associates, 1950). Also see J. Beverly Ford Shaw, *The Life and Work of Bishop Alexander Preston Shaw* (N.p., n.d.).

[4] From author's interview with Dr. Daisy Fullilove Balsley, Chicago, 18 November 1993.

[5] The fact that the Fullilovs owned a piano, an extensive library, and a car indicates that they were very comfortably situated. See Ray Ginger, *The Age of Excess: The U.S. from 1871–1913* (New York: Macmillan, 1975), 229.

[6] Amelia E. Johnson, *Clarence and Corrine; or, God's Way*, ed. Hortense Spillers, in *The Schomburg Library of Nineteenth-Century Black Women Writers*, ed. Henry Louis Gates, Jr. (New York: Oxford University Press, 1988), xxvii; hereafter cited in text as Spillers.

[7] Maggie Shaw-Fullilove, *Who Was Responsible?* (Cincinnati: Abingdon Press, 1919), 7; hereafter cited in text as *Who*.

[8] Ann duCille, *The Coupling Convention: Sex, Text, and Tradition in Black Women's Fiction* (New York: Oxford University Press, 1994), 8; hereafter cited in text as duCille.

INTRODUCTION

[9] Emma D. Kelley-Hawkins, *Four Girls at Cottage City*, ed. Deborah McDowell, in *The Schomburg Library of Nineteenth-Century Black Women Writers*, ed. Henry Louis Gates, Jr. (New York: Oxford University Press, 1988), xxix.

[10] Darlene Clark Hine, ed., *Black Women in America*, vol. 2 (Brooklyn, NY: Carlson Publishers, 1993), 1154; hereafter cited in text as Hine.

[11] Elizabeth Cady Stanton was the chair of the first convention in 1851 and Susan B. Anthony the secretary. Abbey Kelley, the pioneering abolitionist, would later join the Massachusetts chapter of the WCTU. What I mean to suggest here is that recognized political activity like abolition was often linked to devalorized activities like temperance, not that these linkages were unproblematic, particularly when it came to racial politics. But black activists who believed in the temperance cause were often the first to critique the institutionalized racism of white reformers. Douglass blasted the American Temperance Society while in London. Almost fifty years later, also while in London, Ida B. Wells would forcefully condemn WCTU president Frances Willard's unpardonably racist courting of Southern support. Shaw Fullilove offers no such critique in *Who Was Responsible?*

[12] As quoted in Hine, 1154–56.

[13] Frances Smith Foster's rediscovery and republication of three Harper novels will rechart the field of nineteenth-century African-American letters. Their appearance corrects the previously held assumptions that between 1867 and 1886 no black novels were published. See Frances Smith Foster, ed., *"Minnie's Sacrifice," "Sowing and Reaping" and "Trial and Triumph": Three Rediscovered Novels by Frances Harper* (Boston: Beacon Press, 1994).

[14] As quoted in Hine, 1154.

[15] As quoted in Hine, 1155.

[16] The one exception to this indeterminacy is when the girls in *Four Girls at Cottage City* are forced to sit in "nigger heaven" when they go to the theater, despite all four's fair skin, and two girls' blue eyes.

[17] Discussing *Medga*, duCille notes that "taking as the most important question the color of the characters in any of these texts racializes precisely what the authors have endeavored to couch in religious rather than racial terms" (duCille, 54). She goes on to ask: "What does it suggest about our interpretive needs as critics and our interpellation as subjects of racial ideology if we assume that figures not clearly identified as black or white are necessarily the latter?" (duCille, 55). See duCille's excellent treatment of this era in *The Coupling Convention*, particularly chapters 2 and 3.

INTRODUCTION

[18]Neil R. McMillan in *Dark Journey: Black Mississippians in the Age of Jim Crow* (Urbana: University of Illinois Press) argues that the years between 1889 and 1919 constitute the height of Jim Crow in Mississippi. Shaw Fullilove's life spanned between 1884 and 1917. Her husband had *Who Was Responsible?* published after her death in Ohio, significantly, outside the boundaries of the South. McMillan hereafter cited in text.

[19]Richard Wright, *Black Boy* (New York: Perennial Press, 1966), 253.

[20]Although in *Hagar's Daughter* Hopkins plays with issues of type, revelation, and the prototypical description of the mulatta, Iola, Sappho, and the characters of A. E. Johnson's novels are described in painstaking and similar detail. See Pauline Hopkins, *Hagar's Daughter. A Story of Southern Caste Prejudice*, ed. Hazel Carby, in *The Schomburg Library of Nineteenth-Century Black Women Writers*, ed. Henry Louis Gates, Jr. (New York: Oxford University Press, 1988), 82.

[21]We do not find out until John Drew dies that he was "the descendent of one the best and oldest families in the State . . . [and] son of the well-known Colonel Hamilton Drew, of New Gate" (*Who*, 121). Of course, African-American fiction often ironically connects the ancestry of its black characters to the "best" families of the South, and Drew's all-important maternal lineage is not provided in his obituary.

[22]*Birth of a Nation* premiered in 1915. For further information, see Michael Rogin, "'The Sword Became a Flashing Vision': D. W. Griffith's *Birth of a Nation*, in *The New American Studies*, ed. Philip Fisher (Berkeley: University of California Press, 1991), 346–91.

[23]Claudia Tate, *Domestic Allegories of Political Desire: The Black Heroine Text at the Turn of the Century* (New York: Oxford University Press, 1992).

[24]*Half Century Magazine* (February 1917).

[25]*Half Century Magazine* (February 1917): 2.

[26]*Half Century Magazine* (July 1917): 3.

[27]*Half Century Magazine* 1, no.3 (August 1916): 3.

[28]Maggie Shaw Fullilove, "Navy Blue Velvet," in *Half Century Magazine* (February 1917): 5, 17; (March 1917): 4, 8, 17.

[29]One could note the autobiographical possibilities of this piece: the protagonist's name is Margaret; she loves opera, etc.

[30]Maggie Shaw Fullilove, "Sermons in Stones," in *Half Century Magazine* (May 1917): 4, 18; (June 1917): 5, 8, 13. Hereafter cited in text as "Sermons."

[31]Maggie Shaw Fullilove, "Sweet Peas Between," in *Half Century Magazine* (April 1918): 4, 13; (May 1918): 4, 9, 13; (June 1918): 6, 11. Hereafter cited in text as "Peas."

INTRODUCTION

[32] Mary Etta Spencer, *The Resentment* (Philadelphia: A.M.E. Book Concern, 1918); hereafter cited as *Resentment*.

[33] Spencer provides other examples that the road to success is paved by knowing one's place. A valued servant leaves his employers to "follow another vocation." He comes back from time each year to see if the family had any work they wanted done. "They always found something for him to do, as they liked him, and the children were wild about 'Tom'. . . To [the white family, Tom] did not show any knowledge above that of a mere working boy, but he possessed good manners, quiet, clean habits." Often, the white woman who narrates the story goes on, the white family commented on these good qualities "and gave the cause to the fact that he had worked for our race of people since a child. . . One day my friend was called to witness a very difficult operation. . . and was dumbfounded to learn that the doctor who was colored and when he looked more closely found it was Tom" (*Resentment*, 96). Humility and submission, Spencer implies, complement and facilitate black professional development.

[34] See Robert Bone, *The Negro Novel in America* (New Haven: Yale University Press, 1958), 49. He groups Spencer with the fiction of Oscar Micheaux and Henry Downing. I take the liberty of silently changing his language to the singular. Agreeing with Bone gives me pause. I hope a future critic will be able to elucidate this text with more success, and that we can then throw Bone's critique of Spencer, with his dismissal of Larsen and Fauset, on the critical trashheap of history.

[35] Horatio Alger, *Ragged Dick and Struggling Upward* (New York: Penguin Books, 1985), 3; hereafter cited as *Ragged Dick*.

[36] Bernard Bell, *The Afro-American Novel and Its Tradition* (Amherst: University of Massachusetts Press, 1987), 79.

Maggie Shaw-Fullilove

Who Was Responsible?

BY
MAGGIE SHAW-FULLILOVE.

CINCINNATI
PRINTED FOR THE AUTHOR BY
THE ABINGDON PRESS

Foreword

MAGGIE SHAW-FULLILOVE, the author of this story, was born in LaFayette County, Mississippi, January 27, 1884, and died in Yazoo City, Mississippi, October 30, 1918. She was the youngest daughter of Mrs. Maria Petty-Shaw and the Rev. D. P. Shaw, a preacher of the Methodist Episcopal Church. Her parents were ex-slaves, without school advantages, but with such a passion for education as found fruitage in the college education for all their children.

Maggie Shaw was graduated from Rust University, Holly Springs, Mississippi, with the degree of A. B. in the class of 1907. Soon thereafter she was married to Dr. Robert E. Fullilove, who afterwards located in Yazoo City, Mississippi. Three children were born to that union. A faithful and devoted wife and mother, she nevertheless found time to give to the writing of short stories for publication in newspapers and magazines. Various stories with moral and religious messages, such as "Sweet Peas Between," "Navy Blue Velvet," "Pass It On," "The Making of Leon Tony," and "Sermons in Stones" came rapidly from her pen. She never wrote for mere entertainment. She was a gifted singer as well as writer, and employed her talents in the local church choir. She

FOREWORD

lived a simple, unselfish, useful, and beautiful Christian life, and was an inspiration and a benediction to all who knew her.

This story is submitted to the reading public with the earnest hope that it may do its bit in crushing to the earth and keeping crushed the demon rum.

J. BEVERLY F. SHAW,
President Central Alabama College.
Birmingham, Alabama,
June 28, 1919.

Preface

I SUBMIT this book to the reading public with the earnest prayer and sincere hope that it may do its small share in arresting the tide of demoralization which some of the vices of society are spreading over the land.

THE AUTHOR.

Who Was Responsible?

CHAPTER I

A HANDSOME, middle-aged man stood looking out a window upon a street below. It was a fair street, extending north and south. The small but elegant mansions were placed each on its carpet of verdant grass, and a long flight of steps extended from every door to the pavement. Ornamental trees, the weeping mulberry, the tall maple, so lofty and bending, the graceful and gracious umbrella tree, the old-fashioned cedar, pearshaped and evergreen, grew thrivingly among brick and stone.

There were more streets running parallel to this one, but none equaled it in the grandeur of its aspect; for most of the aristocrats and the wealthiest people lived on this street. They called it College Street, so named because at the head of it, on a beautiful forty-acre campus, the college buildings stood—a strong, up-to-date institution, which appealed to the best class of young people, offering highest educational as well as social advantages. There was everything tending to the development of the ideal, capable young people. It was an ideal institution, and all things considered was as nearly perfect as the most considerate wisdom, benevolence, and humanity could make it. On account of its high literary and moral standard, it shed an atmosphere over the whole town, making it pure and clean.

It was a source of inexpressible pleasure to observe the almost imperceptible but none-the-less certain effect wrought by this institution upon the entire community of the small town of Hollyville; and to note the general humanizing tastes and desires it engendered, the affectionate friendships to which it gave rise, the amount of vanity and prejudice it dispelled.

Year after year it graduated young men and women of exceptional worthiness and capability, many of whom made their homes in the town of Hollyville.

All the citizens of the town took great pride in making it ideal in every respect. The town was beautiful and did not fail to impress all strangers very favorably. Its streets were kept clean of filth and dirt; and under the effect of local option, its business center was free from saloons and dives where young men are wont to linger in indolence and strife. There is no doubt that much of the intellectual refinement and superiority of the place was referable to the quiet influence of its institution of learning. The resident professors were gentlemen of learning and varied attainments, and were men who shed grace upon and did honor to the town.

Near the end of College Street the Drews lived—John Drew, the well-respected merchant of good character, and Robert Drew, the popular and much courted son. These two and a housekeeper comprised the inhabitants of the Drews' house. Though they failed to rank in wealth with the other dwellers of that street, they seemed to be the most favored. It was the recognized worth of private character which exhorted this homage. John Drew, although a man of limited educational acquirements, adorned his station in life, dignified the mercantile profession, vindicated the dignity of common life, and carried a large, high, and noble spirit into ordinary affairs; made men recognize something inviolable even in common humanity—this was the power and attraction of John Drew's life. Robert, the son, was a general favorite in the community. Every mother and father of them loved the young man: every mother's son of them sought his wholesome companionship, while every fair daughter of them cast shy glances upon his promising, vigorous young manhood.

It was John Drew, the father, who stood looking out the window, as was mentioned in the beginning of the story. As he looked, there advanced a single passenger on its farthest extent—a fine young man of twenty-one, who hastened forward with swift, swinging stride, slapping his left hand with his folded gloves, thus keeping time with his buoyant, ringing steps. As he came nearer he raised his eyes to throw a glance upward at the waiting gentleman.

"What a fine fellow he is," thought John Drew, as he fondly noted the broad shoulders, the towering height, the fine, strong, clean-cut features; eyes which flashed the ardor of youth, a mouth that was firm and strong. John Drew smiled in satisfaction as he realized what a future was in store for his son. He loved this son with all his soul. Indeed, the emotion seemed more than love and was closely akin to worship. He had loved the boy's mother as few men love their wives. When she died in giving birth to their son, at first he was crazed and wild with stubborn grief; but it was the boy who had brought back hope to his withered heart. It was the boy, a tiny mite of humanity, who grasped his big thumb in its firm baby fingers and led him back to life and love.

Since then he had lived, starved, striven, grappled with fate and conquered—all for the boy. Robert's deep love and devotion, his unbounded faith in the father, amply repaid all his parent's efforts, and made his paternal love and pride in his offspring an unbounded joy. In fact, the son electrified the father's world; the love of him was the lightning of his soul, illuminating his sky, clarifying the atmosphere of adversity, making every task delightful.

Robert paused before mounting the steps, looked up at his parent with remarkably bright and singularly sympathetic eyes; then, bounding up three steps at a time, he soon entered the room where John Drew awaited him.

"Well, Pater!"

"Well, Son!"

It was a simple greeting, yet each knew the full depth of the other's overcharged heart. There was little need of undue demonstration between these two. Each understood the other's eccentricity and respected it. Robert of twenty-one had outgrown those halcyon days of paper kites, toy boats, and knee-foot gallops to the market town. He had the same frank, boyish, open heart, was altogether adorable, yet withal he possessed a man's interests and capabilities.

"I've got a job, father." Robert paused in order to note the effect of his words, then continued: "I've

WHO WAS RESPONSIBLE? 11

been employed as clerk in Morgan & Sons—New Gate."

"New Gate!" The father gasped. Of all the Southern cities, New Gate was the very last in which he wanted his son to reside. It was a city in which society was corrupt. The free flow of alcoholics had washed away almost every vestige of clean, chaste manhood and even womanhood. Ignorance and vice stalked abroad in the streets. There was no law against drunkenness; and as there was no penalty, no man feared to get drunk.

John Drew was disappointed—not that he did not want his son to work; and he knew that this was a splendid opportunity for a man who had an inclination toward the mercantile profession—yet he had secretly hoped that his boy might choose some other profession. A position in Hollyville College would have met his approval sooner.

"Pshaw! I'm a whiney old woman," he told himself a few moments later as he sat down alone to think over the situation. "I need not hope to keep my boy tied to my apron strings; yet he might have chosen a more lofty position. Of course any occupation is lofty so long as it is honorable. But somehow I've always pictured the lad at the head of some institution of learning."

Robert had graduated from Hollyville College with honors, had been a favorite as a student, and no doubt could have secured a good position in his Alma Mater. John Drew strongly disliked the idea of Robert's working at New Gate. No one knew the city and its history any better than he did. It had been the home of his boyhood. He was acquainted with every dive, every hole and corner, every ill-reputed public house, every saloon—of the latter there were a great number. He could recall many unpleasant incidents connected with many of them. They had been his father's curse, had come near being his own curse, had it not been for the fact that Alice, Robert's mother, had led him away and taught him the value of love and home. He had shunned New Gate ever afterwards, as he would shun a black and fathomless pit which led to hell.

He sat there staring into the fire, his mind worked up into a sort of frenzy at the thought of Robert's going there to work—his boy, who had been brought up almost entirely without any knowledge of alcoholics. John Drew had been very careful about this thing. He had been careful not to even warn the youngster against it, for fear that he might try it out of mere curiosity. Curiosity had been one of the lad's weaknesses. He could recall many incidents of Robert's childhood which verified this. John Drew felt that it was better not to spend too much time warning him against the evil effects of alcohol, because he felt sure that Robert would try it just to see if it would in truth have the reputed effect. And John Drew feared that if he should taste it once, he'd taste it again and again; for was not his boy in danger according to the law of heredity? John Drew shuddered. His anxious mind began to picture the boy—his glorious Robert—mingling with the gay society of New Gate, joining in their sports, partaking of the so-called harmless dinners, in which wine and even whisky were served in abundance.

He felt that he would rather see Robert dead than to see him under the influence of alcohol once.

So intent was he in this line of unpleasant, bitter thinking that he did not hear the door open, nor see the ruddy face of Robert framed therein, until the young man's "Hello, Pater!" aroused him.

"You look as if you are about to be burned alive, Pater mine," said Robert, noticing his father's haggard and anxious countenance. "Come, cheer up! Does my going away affect you so? I verily believe you would keep me here in this little, stuffy town always. Why, father, I'm tired meeting the same people, doing the same things over and over. There's nothing to keep me here now that I've finished school. I want to make new acquaintances: I want to see the world."

John Drew looked at this full-fledged youngling and felt it to be utterly useless to protest. This young man before him must go away and work out his own destiny as thousands of other young men had done. Controlling himself with a mighty effort, John Drew spoke as bravely as he could: "You are right, my son. Go; nothing but good can come of it, surely. You are twenty-one now and should know how to keep to the right and shun the wrong. But you will find New Gate a different place from this. Its atmosphere is not so pure, its moral standard low, most of the inhabitants are of the baser sort."

"I'm going there to work, father; not to loll and idle among low-class individuals. I dare say I'll have little time to be led from the path of rectitude; then—I'm my father's son, you know!" He spoke proudly as he measured his height with that of his father and found himself even the taller of the two.

The father turned, placed a firm hand on each of the young man's shoulders, looked deeply and earnestly into the fearless eyes. There was something he was about to say—some grave warning; but a sudden fear clutched at his heart, and the warning did not come. If he had only known—but of course he did not know, could not know what the coming years might have in store for Robert.

After that John Drew forgot his fears in the close companionship of his son. In various ways the son revealed hidden traits of character which delighted his father's heart. He was indeed a son to be proud of. His society was delightful. He was brilliant in speech, possessing a keen sense of humor and wit, which rendered conversation with him charming. He possessed an indomitable courage; and his moral principle, his father believed, would steer him clear of evil-doing.

Their few remaining days together were memorable ones. Arm in arm the father and son strolled about the gay lawns. They found a sort of boyish pleasure in going over the old haunts and even renewing their old games. Each knew what this parting would cost the other. Robert knew that he was about to cast a cloud over his father's sky, which had hitherto been flooded with sunshine. Therefore he strove to bring back the happy years which they had known together. They even spent hours throwing pebbles into the little brook back of the wood-lot. Once they found the battered wheels of an old goat wagon. "Useless, outgrown relics of the past," thought Robert, ruthlessly kicking the rusted wheels from the heaps of discarded rubbish. But to the father they were gold treasures of a very happy past,

WHO WAS RESPONSIBLE? 15

and he secretly planned to return alone and store them away for safekeeping.

That day came all too soon for the parting. After Robert had actually gone, poor John Drew returned to his empty home—a forlorn gentleman, indeed. The old housekeeper's heart was touched when she saw him wandering about from room to room as if in search of someone.

A month later Robert, sitting at his desk in Morgan & Sons, penned a letter home, telling of his work and the pleasure he derived from it. He had written several letters home, but this one seemed to give his father more pleasure than all the others.

"I feel, dear Pater, that I am at last in the great game of life," he wrote, "and I find it exhilarating. I love the work. I have little time for anything else. I go to church on Sundays. Now and then I visit— in the very best homes, mind you. During my leisure hours—well, Pater, 'Libros, cum mihi est otium lego'; for when I do have a few leisure hours and would perhaps spend them in idleness, I find that 'Liber bonus me liberat periculo.'"

John Drew smiled at the Latin phrases. "The lad's as good as gold," he thought.

Another time he wrote: "Pater, I attended my first dinner party here. Little, stuffy Hollyville can't hold a candle to New Gate when it comes to affairs of this kind. They are simply dazzling! The very best people attend." Here followed a list of aristocratic names.

"The boy is indeed becoming a factor in the great game of life," thought John Drew as he read this letter. With a mighty effort he stifled the fear that would, in spite of him, find a place in his heart. He reasoned within himself that this was quite natural and proper. "A man cannot contribute anything worthy to society without putting himself into it, checking his fancies, and restraining his impulses. The constant appeal to the intellect, as he comes in contact with learned people, would serve to perfect his manners and bearing toward other people. It is absurd to suppose that the young man would absent himself from society. Since he had chosen this vocation, he would prove himself a failure if he did not enter into it as a part of the world's work, and not simply a means of getting a living. A man should regard his business as a part of the world's work, his share of the great activities that render society possible. There would be greater success in all the occupations of life if men did not too often pursue them simply for a livelihood, with no thought that they may contribute directly to true manhood and womanhood. That is an utterly low business which regards it as only a means of getting a living."

In this wise John Drew reasoned, and read the account of Robert's entering into society with a rising degree of pride. Another time Robert wrote a letter in which he gave a lengthy description of one of New Gate's fashionable dinner parties. "The young women here are wonderful," he wrote in all the fire and ardor of youth.

John Drew sat far into the late hours of that night, staring into the fire and conjuring up all sorts of morbid fancies. He too had once mingled with that class of young women. The beautiful, dazzling, thoughtless creatures were but shining lights to lure, charm, and bewilder the green youth—lure, and in the end destroy. Of course there were some among them who were ideal, good young women; but men rarely chose them—why, he did not know.

Once while he dozed he thought he saw a man walking along the street; his shoulders were stooped and sloven; his face red and swollen; his eyes restless and bloodshot. Over his head a row of burning letters spelled the words, "The Curse." The fellow stumbled and fell upon the pavement. John Drew thought he ran to lift the fallen creature, and behold, it was Robert!

John Drew awoke and spent nearly all the rest of the night pacing the floor in restless apprehension. But the new day dawned so lovely and bright that he scolded himself severely for his unreasonable and morbid fancies. "The boy is all right and I am the fool," he told himself.

CHAPTER II

ON the evening of the great event of the season, the King's banquet, Robert Drew found himself in a flutter of excitement which was quite an unusual thing for him. He had attended many a gay festival in his own little town, all of which were simple, innocent affairs in which those pure-minded young people took great delight. There was always soft music and dancing, cards and other simple games. But Robert had never witnessed such an affair as this social event promised to be. It was to be a ball, given in honor of Miss Grace King's return from abroad.

Robert was eager to meet this Grace King, whose praise was upon every tongue. Just after business hours he wrote his father concerning the great event, announcing himself as one of the honored guests.

That night, as he entered the banquet hall in company with one of his new acquaintances, he gave a little start of amazement and pleasure; and it was plainly evident that Raymond King, noted as he was for lavish expenditure, had outdone himself this time. The whole room was a bower of roses—great, climbing bushes, heavy with blooms. Cool, green ivy hid the walls from floor to ceiling, and were supported upon cunningly wrought trellises, through which hidden lights glowed softly like fireflies. Marble statuettes gleamed in certain nooks. They were so placed as to heighten the effect of space and to carry out the idea of a garden. In the center was a wide but shallow stone fountain, on the surface of which large-leaved pond lilies floated. Beautiful goldfish with filmy fins and tails like iridescent wedding trains propelled themselves indolently about. Two dimpled cupids held a marble cornucopia, out of which trickled a sparkling stream of water. Robert knew that the wonderful Miss King had wrought all this lovely arrangement herself.

There was a flutter of excitement and many words of inquiry as Robert and his companion entered. Many of the young ladies wanted to know who was the six-foot young demigod with the college air. Robert was indeed a very striking figure, rising head and shoulders above his companion—the very impersonation of clean, healthy, wholesome young manhood. He was not long a member of the gay throng before Miss King entered.

Her father, whom Robert had already met, led her through the throng leaning gracefully on his arm, and in a stately, old-fashioned way, introduced her to several of the young people. Robert was the last one to receive an introduction. He led the smiling young woman up to Robert, saying: "Grace, my daughter, this is Robert Drew, son of John Drew, a prominent merchant, and a friend of my boyhood."

Robert thought he had never seen so divine a creature before. To him she was a star, radiating brilliant rays of light which dazzled all who beheld her. In fact, he thought her all that a beautiful woman is said to be. She passed on to another group of young people, but not without an open admiring glance at Robert. Sometime after that she even sought him, evidently as much impressed as he.

Robert was at first somewhat shy and embarrassed, but this feeling soon wore off under the influence of her easy manner and charming grace. She was not timid or shy like the maidens of his home town: neither did he think her bold—just simply charming and very gracious. She was perfectly at her ease, and so prettily garrulous and confidential, telling little stories of her life abroad and describing scenery on some lake. After she had babbled sweetly about fashion, society, balls, receptions, operas, and theaters for several minutes, she turned upon him a marvelously penetrating glance of her dark eyes, a glance which startled him as much as an unexpected flash of light might have done. He returned her gaze wonderingly as she asked the perfectly simple little question, "And you, what do you do? How do you amuse yourself?"

"M—me?" he stammered, "I work."

"Ah, yes. You are in your father's business?"

"I clerk in Morgan & Sons."

"You must find it dull and tiresome to labor all day. You ought to rest sometimes. You must visit your friends and be gay. Don't you agree with me?"

"Assuredly," said Robert, becoming more at ease as he listened to her simple, childish chatter. "But perhaps I do not take my rest precisely like other people. I read a great deal—some day I hope to be able to write."

"What—books? How charming!"

Here their conversation was abruptly broken off, as Grace's mother, a dignified lady clad in richest silk, with huge diamonds gleaming here and there upon her handsome person, sailed up from a remote corner of the room, where she had no doubt been watching them with the speculative observation of a match-making matron.

The room was soon dinning with strains of the invisible orchestra, and the vocal chatter and exclamations of the guests. Presently the sound melted into the soft, alluring melody of a grand old waltz, and the dancing began. The couples floated over the floors like fairy folk in wonderland, so it seemed to Robert. He could dance well, but was reluctant to try his skill here in this assembly, where dancing was indeed an art. He said as much to Miss Grace, but that gracious young lady wouldn't allow him to refuse.

"Let me teach you," she said, sweetly, giving him another of those thrilling glances. He could feel her body tremble as he took her in his arms, and as they gently glided out on the floor, there was in her steps that indescribable quality born in natural dancers. Her supple body supplied all the deficiencies of his slightly awkward steps, and soon they were the center of attraction.

When the dance was over her eyes were twin stars, her cheeks were roses. Her rounded bosom heaved with intense excitement. When she took her place at the table and from sheer satisfied exuberance laughed her dear, trilly little laugh, Robert said under his breath: "By Jove! What a ripping girl!" Miss Grace did not fail to catch the fire of admiration in his eyes, and her own heart glowed in triumph. The diners soon arranged themselves and the dinner began. To Robert there was a complete absence of the stiffness at the formal banquets of his college home. The moments did not drag. A Bohemian spirit prevailed. The ardor of the men, encouraged by coquetry and smiles, rose quickly; wine flowed and a general intimacy began.

Without knowing why, Robert could not enter into the prevailing intimacy with Miss Grace. He thought her much more attractive than the girls of his acquaintance, and yet it was this very attractiveness and intimacy that alarmed his inbred social conservatism regarding women.

He began to become conscious of thinking rapidly and becoming excited. He wanted to appear well-bred in the eyes of this woman, yet drinking intoxicants of any sort was altogether alien to his custom. The exciting tendency increased as he set aside the glass which had been filled by the brilliant woman by his side. At this she looked up at him with large, soft, serious eyes. He hesitated no longer, but tipping his glass with hers, drank to her health. It was Madeira wine of such exquisite perfume and admirable flavor that Robert allowed his glass to be filled again and again. Being entirely unaccustomed to strong drinks of any kind, Robert soon felt a kind of dizziness about his head, and he longed to get out in the open air. Miss Grace continued her gay chatter and her dazzling smiles until Robert found himself mounted as if on golden wings. The dizziness gave place to hilarity as he partook of more wine. His boyish shyness and some of his scrupulous ideas concerning women slowly fell off like a cloak. In his

WHO WAS RESPONSIBLE?

wondering excitement and new joy, he leaned across the table, boldly took Miss Grace's hand in his, and talked freely with her—even a degree of flippancy tinged his speech.

After dinner the wonderful music began playing again. Other couples were dancing, so he seized the yielding body of Miss Grace in his arms and whirled her away. He wanted to dance in this way continually. He wanted to float away out into the soft, starlit night with this rare creature clasped in his arms. No one knew—not even Miss Grace herself was aware of the rage of passion that was racing through Robert. His incoherent thoughts were that he did not want to ever stop dancing with her. He had a mad desire to kiss her—to devour her—to strangle her with love.

When it was all over, and he had pressed her two small hands at parting, Robert knew that he loved Grace King—loved her as he would love no other woman. He was no longer master of his own destiny: Miss Grace was his fate.

The next morning when he took his place at the office, somehow his work did not seem quite so delightful as formerly. Amazement was so deep upon him that he moved about mechanically. Last evening's experience was so different from anything he had ever known. He was fascinated, bewildered, and yet—yet there was something about it all that he did not altogether like.

Whenever those conflicting emotions came over him, the face of Grace King floated before his vision —alluring, glorious, and compelling.

Robert became a frequent visitor at Miss Grace's home. He attended more such brilliant parties, partook of her wine and her smiles with increasing enjoyment, while she, fair siren, was more in love with her sense of triumph over this "country boy" than anything else. She gave him just enough encouragement to keep him at her feet, but never allowing him to rise and claim her as his own. There was as yet no love in her heart: in his absence she could even find it in her heart to laugh at him, whereas in all decency and conscience it would have become her to have wept for the mischief she had wrought.

CHAPTER III

ONE cold November evening Robert went to his room somewhat earlier than usual. He had been feeling sick all day. Having never been sick in his life, it was quite a new experience for him. Every joint in his body ached; he shivered from head to foot as he went out of the warm office into the open street. A cold rain had set in, and the dampness agonized his aching joints all the more.

Since his lodging was only a short distance from the office, he never thought of hiring a carriage or going on the car, but hurried on foot through the cold, drizzling rain to his apartments. His roommate, a young man who worked at one of the downtown saloons, had already arrived, built a fire, and set things to order. Robert soon removed his soaked, uncomfortable clothing, stretched himself before the fire, and was tolerably comfortable. "Let me mix you a little drink—something hot," suggested Jack. "Go to bed, old man; make yourself comfy. I'll warm you up all right—just you wait."

Then that amiable young man adroitly prepared one of those subtle drinks which is the beginning of the downfall of so many young men. He meant it as an act of kindness, of course, but all unconscious of it, he was rounding off the corners of the foundation which had been so subtly laid by those harmless beverages at the dinner-parties. He was all but putting the finishing touches to the thing which Robert's father lived in fear of and dreaded most.

Robert drank the steaming draught without question. Soon a sense of warmth and comfort stole over him and he fell asleep. The next day he was better and went back to his work. But Robert was far from well. Before noon he felt that he must even leave the office again. Mr. Leek, another employee in Morgan & Sons, noticed Robert's gray, pinched look and advised him to retire immediately.

"You'd better call in a physician, Drew," he said. "You look all in."

"I'll be all right when I'm tucked in. Jack, my roommate, is a capital nurse. He'll bring me around with one of his curious drinks, I dare say."

Sure enough, Jack tucked him in and administered another of those deceiving hot drinks which soothe for the time being, but leave an indelible trace of its poison lurking in the blood. Robert slept all night—a feverish, troubled sleep. The next day he was able to go to his work as usual. He tried hard to regain his old, buoyant spirit for work; but about ten o'clock a violent chill seized him and he hastened once more to his room. A strange sense of impending serious illness hung over him.

"Jack," he said to his roommate that evening, "I believe I'll write the Pater to come over here. I owe him a letter or two, and I'd love to see him about now." He attempted to rise and procure writing materials, but his aching body cried aloud in protest.

"Oh, hang it! I believe I'm going to be really ill!"

"Let me call a physician," suggested Jack.

"Well. No—but I'll tell you what I will do—I'll go home to-morrow! Yes, yes, I'll give the Pater

WHO WAS RESPONSIBLE? 27

a big surprise!" He was quite boyish in his eagerness. That night he made arrangement with his employer to be absent a few days—until he should recover—then he sat down to write a little missive to Miss Grace, his hand shaking so that he could hardly write the lines which that worshiped young woman would remember to her dying day. It read:

"My Beloved One: I am not well to-day—a foolish chill. Nothing of consequence, I hope. I leave to-morrow for home. I am delighted at the prospect of seeing the Pater. I'd so love to come to you once before I go, my beautiful queen, but I'm too ill. Farewell till I return again—all well.

"May the saints keep you ever, my dearest and best beloved.   Yours heart and soul,

ROBERT."

The next morning, while he was making preparation for his departure, Jack was moved with compassion when he beheld the ashen look of the sick man. "Why, old sport, you are really ill. You'd better defer that journey." At Robert's sign of negation, he urged, "Then you'd better see a physician before you go. We'll have ample time."

"Oh, bother a physician!" Robert said impatiently. "He will only advise me to go to bed; keep quiet; take nasty medicine. I'm all right—only I do seem so chilly."

"Well, suppose we go by Croggs's and get you a bottle of spirits. It'll brace you up as nothing else will. Come—what do you say? It will warm you up in a jiffy, old man; come. Try it."

Robert consented—anything to give warmth to his icy spine. He felt so wretched and ill at that moment that he was willing to submit to anything which would enable him to make the journey. He was struck with a mad desire to go home. He longed to feel his father's hand—strong, yet tender as a mother's—soothing his fevered brow. He wanted his father more than anything else on earth—more than he wanted Miss Grace even. When they entered the saloon his body shook with a chilliness which he was unable to conceal.

The keeper, Croggs, a shrewd little fellow with a narrow, keen eye to business, began to urge him to take a drink. "See how this one glassful will warm you up," he said, pouring out a small tumblerful. Robert made a faint sign of rejection, at which the keeper urged the more strongly. "Goodness knows, you need it this raw morning. Drink!"

Robert laughed a trifle nervously, and his hand trembled as he raised the glass to his lips. Slowly tilting the glass, he tasted the liquor. Why, it was delicious to his palate, exquisitely fine and delicate! In his pleasurable amazement, he drank half the tumblerful, readily growing conscious of an indescribably delightful sense of restorative. Warmth and comfort pervaded his whole system.

"Why, the stuff is excellent!" he cried, and without taking more thought as to what he was doing, he finished the whole draught. Robert had never given alcoholics a serious thought. Since his coming to New Gate he had made no special effort to steer clear of its evil influence; besides the thought of his own danger to drunkenness never entered his mind.

His father had never warned him against it—why should he give it serious thought?

The stuff was fine, bracing! Robert purchased a whole bottleful. When he was comfortably settled on the train, he drank more with increasing avidity. Previous to taking it he had been cold and shivering, but now he was thoroughly warm, agreeably languid, and a trifle sleepy. "The stuff has no equal when it comes to its medicinal properties," he said drowsily. The rumble and roar of the shrieking locomotive seemed afar off like sounds in a dream. He was in that hazy condition of mind common to certain phases of intoxication when the drunkard is apt to believe he is thinking, though really no comprehensible thought is possible to his stupefied brain.

It was pitch dark when he reached Hollyville. He got up slowly, walked—or reeled—out of the car. When he reached the street, he found himself exposed to a furious rain which poured down incessantly.

Robert had advanced down an obscure street only a little way—stumbling weakly—when he fell. Strange, incoherent sentences coursed off his lips with impetuous rapidity. His voice had a strange, piteous pathos in it. Robert was drunk!

The cold rain continued for some time. Finally the wind shifted and became a colder north wind, freezing the rain into sleet. It fell upon the pitiful figure of the young man lying there huddled in an insensible heap. He lay stunned for a few minutes, until brought back to consciousness by the cold sleet pelting his face. With a desperate effort he started upright and gazed wildly around. He could not make out his surroundings; neither did he realize the fact that he lay in a slough—a concoction of mud and liquid filth.

The darkness was intense. He looked upward and discerned no sky, not even an unfathomable void, but only a black and impenetrable nothingness, as though heaven and all its lights had been blotted from the system of the universe.

Mumbling and whining, he dropped his head upon his arm, half buried in the cold mud. A stony weight lay behind his temples, cold and hard and heavy. He tried to think and found it impossible. With an incoherent outburst, which he himself scarcely heard, he sank into unconsciousness again.

He had lain thus about half an hour when the solitary figure of a bent old man passed along the street, carrying a tin lantern which cast a circular pattern of its punched holes on the ground about him as he went along. Luckily for Robert that this old man happened to come along that street at that particular moment, for the cold wind and muddy filth had chilled all his body save one lukewarm spot, which death's frozen fingers were searching for even then. Happily, too, that the yellow disk of light reached wide enough round so as to show the awful sight to the dim, old eyes of the man. He saw, and let out a yell which brought two other men to the spot. Together they picked up the body, searched for signs of life, and finding none, were about to drop the body and flee when a policeman appeared. After the old man had told all that he knew concerning the tragedy, the policeman held the light so that its rays fell full on the young man's face. With a mutual cry they all started forward, searching the face of the man on the ground.

"Robert Drew, as I'm alive!"

"But it can't be," said the old man who found him. They looked again. Robert Drew it proved to be—but in what a plight! They thought it a case of robbery, never connecting the young man with drunkenness.

The policeman then searched the body for signs of violence. In the search he found the whisky bottle, emptied of two thirds its contents. Then he knew. To make sure, he bent over the young man—down close to his frozen lips. The unmistakable odor clung to them.

Silently the men lifted the half frozen body and bore it away. The policeman swore an oath and spat on the sidewalk.

Down College Street they turned—on toward the Drews' residence. Once one of the men sneered: "It's whisky and women that has brought young Drew to this. I knew it would come soon or late—a chip off the old block."

"Shut up!" thundered the old man who carried the lantern. "If you say aught against John Drew's son, I'll wallup the life out o' yer! There's something else back of this. I know the boy and his father, too."

. . . .

The little sitting-room in the Drews' home was comfortable on this wild, wintry night. The faithful old housekeeper had been asleep fully two hours. Nobody knew just when John Drew was accustomed to retire—indeed, the housekeeper had her suspicions as to whether he retired at all some nights. It seemed to be his delight to sit musing by the fire far into the night. At times he seemed particularly lonely. She knew in what direction his longing lay. She missed the lad herself. The first days after his absence she couldn't help but wander about the rooms, and her motherly old heart always warmed at the sight of any article that belonged to him.

"Such a dear, big-hearted lad he is, and I miss his jolly ways," she said. "Pity his mother was not here to see how capable he looked as he marched away from the old homestead that mornin', out into the world to scratch for himself."

To-night old Janet had retired early and was fast asleep when John Drew came home. Replenishing the fire, he settled himself for his accustomed reverie. A sense of peace stole over him as he warmed himself and listened to the chilly winds outside. The firelight shed an appropriate glory around the room. It seemed to caress his hair, now showing the first signs of old age. By now he had grown somewhat accustomed to the longing in his heart, and had settled himself for the task of making a last desperate effort in the strenuous but not unpleasant task of making money and saving it against his son's wedding day. He planned to make that dowry as gracious as possible. His days were full of hard work, but he cared not, so long as he was successful. Each day's end was always crowned by the sweetest of all—the hours of cheerful musing and pleasant memories that he spent by his fireside. Always his fancies could create some bright dream of happiness for his son and his wife and little children. For himself he wanted little—just peace and quiet for his old age.

So in these chaste and warm affections, humble wishes, and honest toil for some useful end, he found health for his mind and quiet for his heart, the prospect of happy old age, and, fairest hope of all—the hope of heaven.

As the clock struck twelve he entered into a sort of doze. Slowly the figures in the room grew indistinct, fading into pictures in the air, and then to fainter outlines, while the firelight glimmered on the walls of the room, bringing to relief strange shadows which took the shape of evil, mocking demons.

O the slight tissue of his dreams could no more preserve him from the stern approach of misfortune than a robe of cobweb could repel the wintry blast outside!

Suddenly he felt a chilliness—not of the body, but a strange shivering, a foolish dread of looking behind him. It was no wonder; for at that moment he heard the tread of many feet mounting his front steps. When the doorbell rang it sent a chill of apprehensive horror to his soul. With a mighty force he took hold of himself.

"Fool that I am! to shrink like a haunted criminal because someone rings my doorbell at midnight! Perhaps it's Robert—come on the eleven-thirty!" The thought lent wings to his feet. In a moment he had opened the door. A broad smile of welcome was on his face. But it was upon the visage of old Josiah Brown that his benevolent smile was cast. John Drew, quickly recovering his shock of disappointment, opened the door wider in order that his late visitor might enter out of the cold and bitter night. As he did so he caught sight of the silent procession which stood under the shelter of his veranda. A stream of light fell upon a limp object which they held among them. It took the shape of a man—dead perhaps; or severely wounded. "It is someone in trouble seeking shelter at the nearest residence," thought John Drew.

"We'd better hurry, or the young man might peg out. He's half frozen," sounded a gruff voice. Old Josiah Brown stammered out something about Mr. Robert and an accident, while the men proceeded to pass into the hall. Still the poor father did not know, and stood looking at them like one in a dream might gaze upon a passing spectral vision.

That man which they carried was like Robert! Yet it could not be—unless he had met with some accident on the way home. Half crazed with apprehension, he snatched the hat away which covered the face. Robert! What did it mean?

Old Josiah, seeing John Drew's miserable state, caught him by the arm, saying: "Don't you understand? There's been an accident of some kind—robbery perhaps. Mr. Robert was found on Subway Street, in a gutter—unconscious. He had been lying there for some time, sir, for he was well-nigh froze to death when I found 'im, sir. Better call in a medicine man 't once't, sir."

John Drew darted over to the body, which lay smoking by the hearth as the warmth began to melt the sleet on the frozen clothing.

Down on his knees went John Drew, and began to remove the wet, muddy garments, then to rub the frozen limbs of his son. Vigorously and in a sort of frenzy he applied himself to his task.

Once as he bent his ear to the young man's breast he thought he caught the faint odor of—no, no, it couldn't be that—and he worked the harder.

Old Janet, now thoroughly aroused by the noise and strange occurrences, fetched warm blankets, clean linen, and soon Robert was wrapped from head to foot.

When Robert did open his eyes he looked up at the face above him—looked long, as if his dazed brain could not grasp the situation. Then a glorious light leaped into his eyes. He smiled and whispered, "Pater!" Then again, "I'm sick—sick, Pater." The warm fire seemed to make him worse. His stomach seemed as if it would turn wrong-side out. He began to heave. Just then the doctor entered. He went over to where the young man lay, a look of incredulity on his face when he saw who the patient was. His skilled nostrils detected the strong odor which filled the room.

"Whisky!" he exclaimed under his breath. The policeman smiled.

"Robert," said the father, coming forward, "tell Doctor Morris what has happened."

While he bent over Robert, he smelled the odor of whisky, too, but attributed its presence to any of the others, never thinking of Robert as its possible origin. The young man attempted to speak, but a paroxysm of coughing seized him and he grasped his side in an agony of pain.

"Don't try it now," said the kind doctor. "There is a mystery here," he said, turning to the policeman.

"Not much as I can see," said that person addressed. "I was present when the young man was found. He's simply drunk! Look in his coat pocket and see the empty bottle."

"Robert drunk! You lie!" It came from John Drew, who had been listening in amazement to the dialogue which was being carried on by these two. "Never!" he cried vehemently, as with one powerful stroke he cleared the space around his son, and bent to search the muddy garments himself. In one of the pockets his trembling hand came in contact with something hard—a bottle! He drew it out, trembling all over as he held it to the light. It was two thirds empty!

"O God!" The cry was like the last exclamation wrung from a creature on the inquisition rack of torture. It was terrible! The men who heard it were chilled by that awful, despairing cry.

Gasping for articulate speech, a wild imprecation left John Drew's lips without his realizing his own utterance. He was giddy and faint; his temples throbbed heavily; the blood rushed to his brain— the table, the chairs, the bed on which his son lay rushed round and round in dark, whirling rings. All at once his throat filled with a cold suffocation; tears flooded his eyes, and he broke into a loud sob of fiercest agony as he fell upon his knees beside the bed.

Robert gazed from one to the other in mute wonder—not able to comprehend anything at all. Surely he was not going to die—yet he felt very ill—worse than he had ever felt before. That must be the case; the doctor must have told the pater that he was going to die, or he wouldn't act like that.

WHO WAS RESPONSIBLE? 37

The pain in his side was terrible. How he wanted to rise and comfort his father! but he could not talk for coughing.

"F-father," at last he managed to whisper, "don't grieve so."

"How can you ask me not to grieve after seeing you lying before me as you are—drunk! Ah! I'd rather they tell me that you are dying!"

"Am I not going to die, father? What have they told you?"

"Son!" exclaimed the father, a faint hope entering his breast, "tell them they lie! Tell them you have not been drinking this!" He held up the bottle in pitiful, shaking hands.

Robert looked at it, then said: "Why, yes, Pater, I drank all but what you see in the bottle. I—I was so chilly and wretched—and—and the stuff is fine for medical uses." Robert spoke with great effort.

"But, my son, you knew the effects of alcohol—what a base deceiver it is! You read that in your books."

"But, father, I—I'm no habitual—drunk-ard! This is the first—I've ever tak-en. I find it great for that purpose."

The father groaned aloud. "My God! I should have warned my boy—my innocent, unsuspecting boy!"

"I—I'm so—sorry I drank it—father, since it grieves you s-so. I am sure I shall never touch it again—no, never—if it pains you—so." He writhed in the terrible pain which grasped him. A fit of violent coughing seized him again. The doctor advised absolute quiet: the policeman withdrew.

For three days Robert was very near death's door, but on the fourth day was better—a fact which delighted his father's soul. He rarely ever left the bedside, and the strong affection between these two was beautiful to see. The faithful old housekeeper also hovered over her "blessed young man" like a mother hen hovers over her brood. In about a week Robert began to convalesce.

One night about eleven o'clock Robert suddenly awoke out of a troubled sleep, in which he dreamed that he was seized with a great thirst and had drunk gallon after gallon of water without allaying that thirst. The fire burned low in the grate; the wind outside whistled frigidly. Robert, shivering, drew his warm blankets about him. Suddenly he realized that he was in truth very thirsty. Not wishing to disturb anyone, he slipped quietly out of bed, went over to the little table across the room in hopes of finding a drink. Janet always kept a pitcherful of fresh water on the table; but to-night it was empty. He was about to scamper back to his bed when he spied the whisky bottle standing among the vials of medicine. What cruel fate had made Janet place it there when she should have hurled it out of the window?

The invalid stood looking at this bottle in wonder; for it was liquor he craved—not water. An almost uncontrollable longing for it filled his throat. He wanted to feel its delicious fire on his palate.

"I'll just taste it," he said, uncorking the bottle. It had a delicious odor, which the young man liked immensely. He glanced guiltily toward the door, then took one draught, smacked his lips, then took another. This time he emptied the bottle.

WHO WAS RESPONSIBLE? 39

Like a guilty rogue he slunk back to bed. Again that mysterious, delightful sensation fused his brain. He felt jolly; and he wanted to laugh, laugh, laugh—and talk! The world seemed full of dreamy fancies. His thoughts turned to Miss Grace. A mighty passion sent feverish blood coursing through his veins. He thought of her in dumb, rapt ecstasy while she, fair siren in white robes with bosom full and bare—she with her wicked, laughing eyes and jewel-wreathed tresses and sensuous shape, was beautiful wanton enough for Robert's eyes. She seemed to float about him in lambent wreaths of exquisitely brilliant colors.

O! A most wretched evil is alcohol, for its greatest mission is that of transforming pure, chaste ideals, true felicities, into voluptuous thinking and sensuous longing. It distorts and renders hideous that which is the best, the holiest—the sublime crucible in which is consummated the fusion of man and woman—love. It makes men drink and dream, dance and caper in a fool's paradise. It encourages writers and dramatists to pen obscenities, the painter to paint repulsive nudities. It causes the public man to talk loud inanities. It makes women practice wanton wiles.

All of a sudden Robert's foolish brain formed the cunning idea of hiding the empty bottle. He must not leave it where the Pater or Janet would find it empty. This would never do, for that would destroy all hopes of securing more of the stimulant. "I must hide it—hide it," he kept repeating, foolishly. He staggered to the table, seized the bottle and raised it to his lips in order to get the few remaining drops of the precious liquid. Then he crept back to his bed. That subtle flavor clung to his palate—that insidious fluid had already crept drop by drop through his veins.

There had been a slow but sure transfusion of the strange and deadly fire into his blood, which once absorbed, must cling to him forever. The draught to-night had given the devil time to finish his work, which had its beginning in the first glass of wine taken at that high-class social entertainment, the Kings' banquet. It had given the devil time to finish his work of consuming virtue, conjuring up vice, and turning an honest man into a liar, a feeling heart to stone, and making of a man a fiend!

Robert's desire to talk aloud was replaced by the cunning idea of secrecy. He tucked his head under the covers and delighted in his wild, delirious thoughts of Miss Grace. This fantastic dreaming continued for some time; but finally he dropped into a troubled sleep, and the next morning awoke quite depressed and languid. He attributed this feeling to his need of more alcoholic stimulant, and later in the day began to formulate plans which would enable him to procure more without anyone's knowledge. Before night he had that plan all cunningly laid, and proceeded to send an order to Croggs. The faithful old Janet had never questioned anything Robert did, so he knew that he could give her the letter to post, with the assurance that the dear old soul would not stop until she had carried out his orders.

Early that night he said to his father: "Go, Pater—get some rest. I'm all right now, and shall be strong and well in a day or so." His father tucked him in with unusually tender hands, and before he

WHO WAS RESPONSIBLE? 41

left, dropped on his knees beside the bed, evoking the mercies of heaven for grace which alone could sustain in keeping his son from the evil influence of whisky. Robert was deeply touched. The sight of his father's bowed head in prayer for his safety caused Robert's heart to melt down in remorse, and a great tenderness and love filled his soul for his only parent, who had been both mother and father to him. This sweet influence dwelt with him and kept him from making his order that night.

The next morning he awoke with the same feeling of excessive thirst. It was the fatal thirst for whisky! He took the empty bottle from its hiding place, and the delicate whiff of odor intensified his longing, hardening the tender fibers of his heart once more. Robert made up his mind to make just one order, believing that as soon as he should become strong and well he could abjure the passion without difficulty. He reasoned that on account of his excessive weakness and nervousness, he needed support in the form of a stimulant.

Robert was ignorant of the fact that the moral power of resistance decreases with each repetition of the dose. He conjured himself into believing that his father's idea concerning alcohol was largely prejudice. He, Robert, could prove that he could take it as a medicine and when he no longer needed it, he could easily let it alone.

It was a fine morning. The air outside was cold and bracing. The naked trees stood grim and tall and unbending in the sunlight. A few stray birds twittered near Robert's window. These same birds had visited his window many a time, and always had their boldness rewarded by generous supplies of crumbs and clean, sweet chops. But this morning they twittered in vain. A shaft of sunlight streamed clear across Robert's room. It revealed and illumined millions of tiny particles of matter. How often had Robert as a child lain awake for hours watching this same shaft of light, so wonderfully peopled with mysterious little bodies, which frolicked—pitching headlong, turning over and over in the sunlight, then suddenly disappearing. It always made him think of the countless millions of souls invisible to the human eye, and which the light of immortality alone could reveal. He used to lie there as long as possible —thinking of his mother, wondering how he was going to know her among the other souls.

This morning while he lay there watching the light, his thoughts turned into the same channel as of old, and he wondered if his mother knew what he was about to do.

His father's room was just across the hall from his. When the house was built, Robert was only six years old, and they had arranged the rooms that way so that he and his father could lie in bed and see each other the very first thing in the morning, and talk across the hall to each other. This had been a sweet custom of theirs when Robert was a little lad. This same custom had grown into his young manhood.

While he lay looking at the sunlight and thinking about his mother, the door, left slightly ajar, opened wider so that Robert was able to see his father sitting at his desk, busily engaged in writing. The desk was strewn with papers; he looked fatigued and careworn.

WHO WAS RESPONSIBLE? 43

For one brief second Robert's conscience smote him. His father's fine, placid, yet weary face roused in him a struggling passion of regret and remorse. It was a mere flash of pain, for the very devil of craving filled his throat. That consuming thirst for the stimulant seized him—shutting out all tender sentiments.

"Pshaw!" he said, "there is no need for this weak sentiment—it is not at all a matter for compunction." As soon as he heard the last echo of his father's departing footsteps he got out of bed, seated himself at his desk and wrote Croggs an order for whisky. The letter indicated a strong wish for absolute secrecy. The devil within him bore witness that Croggs would not fail him in the matter of concealment.

Sure enough, a few days after that, he was the recipient of a package which, to all appearances, was a package of books. No one thought of it being aught else save books.

On the day of the arrival Robert was in a state of feverish excitement. He tried hard to appear calm, but inwardly raged to open his package. He stifled the peevishness and impatience which arose in response to Janet's tender, motherly concern. He hungered to be alone with his secret. For the first time in his life he wanted his father's absence.

At first opportunity he broke the seal in his room behind a locked door. At sight of the sparkling fluid a million demons broke loose. He wanted to drink all of it at once, but cunning saved him from this error. "A little at a time," he said, and held the bottle to his lips. He got only one great gulp, when he heard Janet's footsteps in the hall. He heard her stop at his door, turn the knob, and heard her grunt of disappointment at finding the door locked.

"In a minute, Janet," she heard her "blessed young man" say, and waited patiently. Robert darted about with devilish haste, tucking the parcel from sight. "Damn it!" he muttered thickly as he scrambled to bed without unlocking the door.

"I'll come again, Bobbie," he heard Janet say, and inwardly swore because she had called him by the old pet name. "Confound! Why can't they let a fellow grow up sometime!" "No—come on in now, Janet," he said, calmly.

"How can I come in when the door is locked?" And old Janet laughed.

Robert unlocked the door and Janet came in, bringing a tray of tempting food. But Robert did not want the food—the steaming broth and crisp brown toast had no attraction for him. The crave for drink consumed every other want. More than the hunger after bread—more than the frenzy of love, this poison hunger overpowers every other instinct.

He waved the food aside with a show of irritability that he could not conceal. This was a thing quite new to the eyes of old Janet. She wondered what had come over her "blessed young man." Something had embittered and crossed his once sweet nature, she knew. She soon left the room, but to Robert's complete dismay, returned after having been gone only about five minutes. This time she brought a cup of hot cocoa.

"Here, drink this, Bobsy, dear," she crooned; "drink this, my honey. It will make Janet's young man strong—drink it for Janet, my honey-child," she begged in soft, sweet tones, which in the old days would have settled the thing at once. He would have gulped anything just to please her.

Now he hated her foolish, baby talk, and wanted her out of his sight. But Janet lingered—going here and there, fixing things a bit before Daddy Drew should come home. Robert, in his eagerness for her to begone, hated her.

Terrors! She was nearing its hiding place. Hell! had discovered it! Robert felt it to be so, although he did not turn his head. Janet's long pause and hoarse grunt were significant enough.

Poor Janet picked up the bottle and looked at it. She did not utter a word—just gave an involuntary grunt of fear and horror. "Heavens have mercy upon us!" she inwardly groaned, and she quickly thrust the bottle back into its hiding place. Her limbs seemed to age ten years. She tottered feebly toward the door without a word.

They both heard the front door softly close—heard the quick steps of John Drew hurrying to the bedside of his beloved son.

"God!" said Robert in wild desperation, "Janet must not tell father. I'll kill her first!"

"Janet!"

The woman turned. Robert sat up in bed. There was a sinister look in his eyes of fire which caused poor old Janet's heart to wither in her bosom. She read his meaning, even though he had only called her name.

John Drew hastened onward. Quick as the old woman's limbs would allow, she pushed the package further away from sight, then took up the tray and, sitting on the edge of the bed, she commenced to say, without a single catch in her voice: "There now, Janet's 'blessed young man,' drink this. It will be havin' you runnin' everywhere in no time."

A second later the father entered, and smiled to see her thus mothering his son.

"I am much better—thanks to Janet's dinner," he beamed into his father's inquiring eyes. At the first opportunity Janet left the room. She had barely reached the door when her feeble old limbs gave way. She managed to totter to her room, where she dropped into a chair and for a long time her body shook with silent weeping.

Janet had been connected with the family so long. She knew the history of all the Drews—knew the poor young mother's struggle to keep John Drew from filling a drunkard's grave—knew that this struggle and the birth of Robert had brought about the hapless young woman's early death. Old Janet had watched the perfect love which existed between father and son, and hoped that the father's heroic struggle against strong drink might be bountifully rewarded in the perfect manhood of the son.

Old Janet had faithfully adhered to her duty in helping John Drew to give Robert a careful training. Both of them used the utmost caution in regard to their mutual fear.

The cruel truth had been thrust upon her, that the curse which they feared most had descended upon Robert in spite of all their caution. "Oh, my poor baby! My poor, dear little Bobs! My poor, God-forsaken 'blessed young man'!" she wailed, rocking herself to and fro in her misery

WHO WAS RESPONSIBLE?

All that evening Robert's father lingered near, reading to him and telling him stories—like he used to amuse little Robert of old. All during this time the appetite for the poison stimulant burned in Robert's throat.

"To-night—to-night I shall have it at all cost," he said to himself. It was twelve o'clock that night before the opportunity came. John Drew and Janet had retired. As soon as Robert felt sure of safety, he slunk out of bed and slipped his precious package from its place.

"At last!" he said, "at last!" He gloated triumphantly as he eyed the bottle—eyed it with a half scared exhilaration a man feels who takes a chance and is quite sure he'll not have another chance if he loses that one. He became desperate—nothing must hinder him now. He felt that he could shoot the first person that interrupted him.

Anyone looking in upon Robert at that moment would have been greatly shocked to see him thus transformed. His once firm lips drooped; his jaws sagged; his once splendid body was gaunt and haggard. There was a wicked glint in his eyes, and his long, bony fingers trembled as he raised the bottle to his lips in one long draught.

"Ah!" he said, smacking his lips. "Ah!—let anyone disturb me now."

He threw back his head and another stream of fire poured down his throat. This time the bottle was half empty. Being weakened because of undue excitement, Robert sank panting to a chair, looking wildly around the room as if he feared some hidden menace in the shadows. Then he threw back his head and laughed softly. He continued to drink and to gloat until intoxication began to mount to his brain. Again the deadly poison crept through his veins, and he began to lapse into the delirium of intoxication. He raised the bottle to his lips again—it was empty!

Muttering foolishly, he rose to get back to bed without thinking to hide the traces of his guilt this time. The empty bottle fell to the floor with a slightly ringing thud. Robert took no heed as he reeled toward the bed. He was still muttering foolishly when he reached it. Instead of smuggling beneath the warm covers, he fell asleep upon top of them all, in a deep drunken stupor.

Outside the night was chill and raw, and rendered boisterous by a gale of wind which whistled along the streets. It had ceased to rain, and the high wind had shifted to the north and was bitterly cold. The fire having now burned low in the grate, gradually brightened and threw flickering shadows upon the walls and ceiling of the still chamber. Strange shadows seemed to dance in weird, wild mockery around the prostrate figure lying there on the bed and outside the covers.

Once the young man was aroused by the chilliness which crept all about his body. He stared above him; for in his fancy—was it fancy?—a shadowy figure had glided out from the semi-darkness and stood by his bedside. It laid a finger upon his scintillating heart, while the index finger of the other hand, gleaming in the darkness, pointed upwards to a mysterious fate. Robert's lips moved to form the word, "Mother!"

Thus he lay for hours until a terrible cough seemed to rend his chest. Something broke loose and blood issued from his mouth and nose. Suddenly John Drew awoke with a start. He had been having an awful dream. His first thought was of Robert. He sprang out of bed and rushed to the room across the hall— to find a sight which froze his blood in his veins. He picked up the empty bottle and stared from it to the wreck upon the bed, with a strained and startled gaze of a brave man wounded to the death. His body aged and trembled. He bore the aspect of an aged man stricken with palsy. His heart, all his hopes—his very life—rent asunder! Down, down, nearer and nearer to the floor he sank—dumb misery and unutterable woe in his dim eyes. The blow was too much for him. It struck him to the very ground.

"Robert!" he cried as he went down, "you kill me!"

What a spectacle our hollow, deceitful, brutal world must present to a higher and nobler order of beings, if cognizant of the struggle, the strife, and baseness and misery of this mundane sphere! What a wretched fool is man to allow such a miserable indulgence as drink to ruin homes by bringing youth down to degradation, and hoary hairs to a grave of dishonor and shame!

For three days Robert lingered in the throes of untold suffering. He had contracted pneumonia. The careful nursing of poor old Janet and the heart-broken father availed little. During those last days the humble pleading in the sufferer's eyes as he looked at his father was enough to melt a heart of stone. Robert knew that his father had discovered his secret, and his eyes followed him everywhere, pleading—beseeching forgiveness.

Crazed with grief, John Drew watched by the bedside through all the hours of crucial suffering. He had not many days to watch before death entered the still chamber—and Robert Drew was no more.

Friends came and went all the next day while the body of Robert Drew lay in state. Every heart was touched, and many were the tears shed in sympathy with the bereaved parent and old Janet. All over the house there brooded the majestic stillness of sorrowing humanity, bound in breathless silence by a common spell.

Sick to the very dregs of misery, John Drew raved for days in feverish agony—agony that was blind, desperate, hopeless, helpless, and cureless! O! that horrible time! O! those dreary, wild, dark days and nights of utter loss and blank wretchedness! —that frightful space of torment in which every nerve in his body seemed torn and wrenched by that terrible grief! How he lived through it one cannot tell. His friends did not wonder that he came through it with somewhat unbalanced mind. When the frenzy of it wore itself out at last, he grew calm with that dreadful calmness of stupefaction and exhaustion. During this time he never saw anyone— never went out of the house, but kept himself shut in—alone with all his bitter sorrow.

CHAPTER IV

ONE night John Drew paced the floor of his lonely room—quick, restless pacing, which betokens an almost frenzied condition of mind on the verge of committing some desperate deed. For the last day or so he had acted that way, as if he was trying to make up his mind to a contemplated suicide. He paused in his rapid walking to open the drawer of his desk. He drew out a revolver, eyed it furtively, slipped it back into its place, and resumed his pacing again. A large, splendid photograph of Robert hung on the wall. This photograph had been made only a few months before his graduation. His father had often looked upon it with special pride. John went over to it and gazed silently upon the handsome, perfect contour of the face. When he turned abruptly away there was something in his eyes which would have alarmed an observer. His jaws were set in grim, dogged determination. At last his mind was made up to whatever he had contemplated doing. He removed the revolver from the drawer, chuckling softly as its evil gleam matched the light which burned in his eyes.

Whatever he had made up his mind to do, he must do it at once! John Drew had been wandering for many days, aimlessly, hopelessly, without consecutive idea, coherent thought, or plan of action; without the faintest inspiration or suggestion of a manner of escape from the bewildering torment of his grief, without even the power to conceive or the will to execute a plan out of the dumb misery which gripped his heart. While he gazed upon the photograph of his unfortunate offspring, his mind had suddenly seized the terrible idea which in his unbalanced, frenzied condition of mind seemed the only retribution that would soothe his hurt and much wronged heart—murder!

He would seek the fellow who sold his son the poison, and make him pay for the dastardly deed with his blood. He would never rest until he had placed that man beyond the power to ruin other innocents. The world would be better off without him.

At that moment Croggs, in his rum shop at New Gate, had no dreams that the name and address on the label of that fatal bottle of whisky would be the means of pointing him out as a criminal, instead of fulfilling the innocent function of increasing his trade.

Having only a few moments in which to catch the early train going out to New Gate, John Drew thrust a few things into a bag, slipped the gun into his pocket, and dashed out of the house in almost an instant.

It had begun to snow, so lightly at first that it seemed a mere brush of some viewless insect upon the cheek; but by the time he reached the station, he went in out of a swarm of whirling flakes, blinded and whitened. By the time the snow had covered the streets, the train had started on its way to New Gate, carrying John Drew as one of its passengers.

The snow fell all that night, with fierce gusts of wind that moaned in the chimney of that house of sorrow which John Drew had just vacated. It moaned and sorely troubled the sleep of poor, faithful old Janet. While the wind howled, the snow softly precipitated a spotless mantle of merciful obliteration over John Drew's departing footprints.

Day was just beginning to break when he reached New Gate. On account of the early hour and the inclemency of the weather, there were few people astir. As John Drew walked down the familiar streets of New Gate, a fierce onset of wind caught him savagely and stirred his blood into action. He turned towards Croggs's saloon, walking rapidly and undeviatingly on to escape observation. Almost before he was aware of it he was entering Croggs's. There was no other customer—a fact which pleased John Drew, for he wanted the man all to himself.

With a good-natured smile he walked up to the counter, demanded a drink, and laid down a bill. Croggs's eyes twinkled as he noted the careless indifference with which this customer handled his money. It savored of abundance. He handed the decanter to John, which he took with as much ease and confidence as he could assume. The hesitancy and tremble of his hand was unnoticed by Croggs, who continued to beam across the counter at the "early bird with the dough."

John Drew eyed the sparkling fluid amidst a tumult of rage. Suddenly some strange, intuitive knowledge seemed to warn Croggs—a creeping sensation at the nape of his neck, a strange quivering of his muscles—something. He shot a keen glance at John, thence toward a drawer in which a revolver was concealed. All at once John Drew took on an aspect of wily cunning. He leaned one elbow on the counter in an easy, confidential manner and asked, "Business on a boom, eh?"

"Well, purty good, purty good," said Croggs.

"When the weather is like this you have an increase of trade—huh?"

"Yes, yes. You see, they must have spirits to keep their blood hot. Nothing like it to keep out cold—prevent grippe."

"Young men drop in continually and get a glass to drive out the shivers." John Drew fixed the barkeeper with a searching glance.

"Sure they do—nothing like the stuff for that," said Croggs.

"Sometimes they are innocent young men who have never had a drink—innocents who have been carefully reared in ignorance of whisky and its evil effects; and the first glass, at your suggestion, is the beginning of their ruin. You urge them when they are reluctant—timid and green."

"Sure! They, every mother's son of them, always act upon my suggestion, and are none the worse for it," answered Croggs boastfully.

John Drew's eyes narrowed perceptibly.

"Why should they come here, then, if not to buy or beg a drink?" said Croggs, noticing the rising heat in his customer's eyes.

"They might chance to come in—just drop in with a friend, perhaps."

"They ought to know what they want or don't want—it is none of my business. I sell it to whoever I can. I'm not here to reform men, but to sell whisky to any fool who wants it."

Croggs was entirely ignorant that he was sealing his doom with his bully words.

"I guess you find it a pleasant job indeed—this taking advantage of fools!" Such a sudden fury lit up John Drew's eyes that Croggs involuntarily recoiled.

"A few weeks ago a youth as ignorant of alcohol as a girl stopped in here with a chum of his. He was ill, and on his way home to his father—that father who would have given his life to prevent the steps which the young man took. You took advantage of his ignorance, urged him to drink, then sold him more. That fatal first drink was the beginning of his ruin. You finished the work by filling an order for another quart. Your damned work was as sure as hell! My boy now fills a drunkard's grave, and you —beast that you are—you are responsible for his death!"

John Drew towered above the barkeeper, who cringed in astonished fear. In his eyes there lay a look of cowardice and guilt. He remembered the incident well, and had even planned further temptation for the unsuspecting youth.

Croggs was afraid. Terror clutched at his quaking heart, for there was no mistaking the stranger's murderous intention. He tried to assume an air of indifference. He turned as if to attend to other matters of more importance; but that feeling of deadly fear crept at the nape of his neck. His moments were numbered! This was no situation to trifle and parley with. He turned and found himself staring into the deadly barrel of John Drew's revolver. Already the finger was quivering to pull the trigger which would send Croggs to instant doom. God! Would nothing interfere—would no one come in! A cry would be useless. The arm which held the weapon was as steady as an arm of steel.

"Nothing but your life! Your life must pay for my son's ruin and death!"

"Merciful heavens! The man must be mad!" thought Croggs. Would not the merciful hand of God stay the deed which would rip his soul from his body and hurl it quaking and all unprepared before its Maker?

John Drew's teeth bared in a snarl of rage. He was madly enjoying this cowardly dog's torture. But suddenly, in the midst of his triumph, an image formed itself in his brain—the pure, spotless image of his wife. Just when he was about to pull the trigger, lo! it seemed that he was about to empty the contents of the revolver into the naked breast of his own wife —Robert's mother!

He lowered the weapon, and Croggs saw the look of murder miraculously turned to wonder and amazement. Poor Croggs breathed at last, and wiped his forehead, on which there clung great drops of cold perspiration. He knew that he had looked death square in the face. He did not know what invisible force had intervened. It was enough that the moment had passed and he was still alive. He began to beg for mercy. "Lord, man! Don't you see that this is my living? I've got to sell whisky—there's no other way. How could I know that it was going to cause the young man's death? Everybody in this town buys whisky here at my little shop. I'm not to blame for your son's death."

"If you are not, pray who, then?" The vision of Alice had vanished just in time for John to catch Croggs's last words. "Who then?" he repeated.

"Why, the one who gave me license to sell whisky—I suppose. There are other saloons—the town's full of them. Kill me, and the work goes on, while you gain nothing but bloody hands and the gallows. If you would find the real perpetrator of this crime, seek the one who issues license to sell liquors."

John Drew could not deny the truth of Croggs's statement.

There was a sound of shuffling feet outside; then three men entered the barroom. Greatly relieved, Croggs proceeded to wait upon them. Though somewhat reassured, he was yet afraid of the sinister look on John Drew's face as he watched and waited.

Croggs turned—only for an instant it seemed—but when he again sought the face of his tormentor, he was gone!

John Drew hastened from the saloon and turned down an obscure alley, out of sight. When the excited Croggs and the three rushed to the door, he was nowhere to be seen. As soon as he felt sure that he had made good his escape, he stopped in order to collect his shattered senses. He was nearly insane. The thoughts which coursed through his brain were vague and incredulous thoughts which utterly darkened all his capacity for reasoning out the tragedy of the situation. In the midst of it all he kept thinking of his boy—his glorious, manly Robert—ruthlessly destroyed by man's folly and weakness.

"Surely there shall be an atonement!" he cried. "If not, then there is something wrong in the system of creation—a flaw in the universe, and God himself cannot be perfect!" He gazed about him at the dazzling mantle of snow which covered the heaps of filth and rags, shook his head dazedly, perplexed and baffled at the inexplicable cause of things. His temples throbbed. He felt a strange dizziness about his head. Then he remembered that he had not slept in twenty-four hours, nor eaten anything. He shook himself to be assured that he dreamed not. He looked at his hands as if to find an indelible bloodstain upon them. Had he accomplished what he had come here to do? Somehow the accomplishment of the deed seemed half way between reality and fancy. He drew the revolver from his pocket and found that no bullet had been fired. He heaved a sigh, whether of relief or regret, he knew not.

Suddenly a longing for rest took possession of him. He needed warmth: he was so cold. He must move on or freeze.

John Drew stumbled on through the snow to the end of the alley. He had no strength to go farther, but threw himself dejectedly down upon the cleanly swept steps of the little cottage which stood there alone. He took no cognizance as to whether it was occupied or empty. He had been there only a little while when the door opened; and great was his surprise to find the visage of old Tom Greely framed therein. He had known old Greely from childhood. Many a time had he sought refuge from showers of hostile missiles by running into the house of old Tom Greely.

WHO WAS RESPONSIBLE?

How strange that fate should send him there now—a place of refuge from his tortured mind! The sight of this old friend served to restore his equilibrium more than anything else.

John Drew was placed comfortably by a warm fire and bidden to rest while a simple meal was served. He made a great effort to become his natural self, and was successful to a great extent. After a good night's rest he was able to think more clearly. Already the actions of the previous day seemed a hideous dream. He looked at his hands, and there arose a feeling of thanksgiving that they were as yet unstained by human blood. Yesterday his plot of crime was the uppermost thing in his mind. The greatest wish of his heart was to strike the death-blow of revenge, but to-day he rejoiced to find his hands still clean of crime.

Men often overestimate their capacity for evil. They may often take steps which lead to the crime, impelled by the same sort of mental action as in working out a mathematical problem, yet be powerless with compunction at the final moment.

The joy which came over John Drew when he discovered his failure in committing the murder far surpassed the savage joy of revenge, however complete. He, the father, must take care lest he fall lower than the son. After all, Robert had committed no great crime. He had sinned against the stern law of nature and she had made him pay the price—as nature will ever do to those who break her laws. Robert had only fallen an easy victim to the snares set daily by society at large, for not a day passed but that some form of alcoholics was served upon the tables of the poor as well as the rich. Even a great majority of the clergymen warmed their blood with it every raw morning. Numerous physicians prescribed it. No wonder that his innocent Robert had become a victim. John Drew was able to reason in this manner, and with this ability to reason there dawned a new purpose—that of giving his life for a nobler gain than revenge.

. . . .

In the meantime, Miss Grace King, in her home of pomp and splendor, had undergone as strange and as interesting a transition as can be imagined. Spoiled and petted though she was, there were many splendid traits in this young girl's make-up which, once developed, would make her a noble woman. Having traveled a great deal, she had seen a lot of society, had noted its frivolousness and lack of sincerity in many instances; and although she had often entered society with all the coquetry of a natural flirt, there was deep down in her woman's heart an undercurrent desire for true love and happiness.

Once when Miss Grace was barely seventeen she had come near losing her heart upon a Spanish violinist of great skill. Her quick and keen intellect soon discovered the man's perfidy; but her disappointment had been so great that for months she gave herself over to reckless abandon and frivolity. Up to the time she had met Robert, she had not quite recovered. She still tried to harden her heart against love, telling herself that no man was honorable and few women virtuous.

Her attitude toward young Drew was nothing new. And she was elated over the complete novelty of the situation. It was not long, however, before the real condition of affairs asserted itself in a way which puzzled Miss Grace herself. She did not at first define her own feelings. Before she was aware of it, she began to thrill with pleasure whenever she caught Robert's burning glances. The young man's clean ideas, chaste thoughts, and high regard for womanhood fascinated and charmed her. She had met many men and had acquired the method of ascertaining their true character largely by their conversation. It is easy to judge the young man whose aspirations are pure and high, by their conversation. By this same method it is easy to judge the youth who reads much and discriminately, who finds his associates among the exemplary. Evil habits, low aims, and inferior manhood are nearly always disclosed in the conversation of the individual.

By this method Miss Grace had gained a knowledge of Robert's intelligence, purity, nobleness of purpose, and true manliness.

It charmed her soul in spite of herself.

On the very night that Robert wrote his last little note to her, she invited several of her friends to tea, including Robert, just for the purpose of having him near her. When she received the note which Robert wrote telling her of his illness and prospective journey, she felt a greater disappointment than she had ever felt in all her life. The whole entertainment was completely spoiled for her. When it was over, she fled to her room in a tumult of feeling which she could not account for. She sat staring into space— wondering at the strange, sweet emotion which stirred her soul. Those who had called Miss King a heartless flirt would have formed a different opinion of her now if they had beheld her sitting there in the pale moonlight, her face suffused with a sweet, rich blush of a soul first awakening to the glorious and mysterious dawn of love, for at last the haughty Grace King loved!

Her love made her glorious. Not only had the face of her become softened and beautiful—she had become idealized. As three April days are enough for certain trees to put on a covering of flowers, so a few moments had been enough for her to put on a new mantle of beauty.

We sometimes see people cold and hard who seem to awaken, pass suddenly from frigidity and become all at once splendid, prodigal, and magnificent. So it was with Grace King. But alas! poor girl, she did not know that the most terrible disappointment was to come to her. She did not know that in a few days the angel of death would be knocking at the door of her lover—a knock which could not be denied. On the eve of her newfound joy she was destined to be cast into the deepest gulf of black despair.

The news came to her, without the slightest warning, like an eagle sweeping down out of a clear, blue sky snatches an unsuspecting victim in talons of unavoidable destruction. The news smote her a cruel blow. The world, so gloriously splendid only a little while before, became black and gloomy. For hours she lay beneath the stony weight of it, bruised, crushed, and broken. She walked about the house with tottering, faltering footsteps of an aged dame, her face grown old and haggard, the bloom of youth

WHO WAS RESPONSIBLE?

and beauty fading under the stony despair which settled over her countenance. Her parents and friends wondered what had befallen the once brilliant young woman. They never dreamed of connecting her condition with the reported illness and death of young Drew.

On the morning of John Drew's departure to New Gate, a heavily veiled young woman stepped off the train at Hollyville—a young woman upon whom had befallen the utmost sorrow, that of yielding up her first and one great love of her womanhood to the corruption of the grave. The few who saw her standing over the grave of Robert Drew thought her some relative who had arrived too late for the funeral.

Grace King knew as she stood there that this sacred spot contained the body of the one man to whom she had given the crowning love of her womanhood. She had found out all the particulars concerning her lover's death, and she thought of all now as she stood there so utterly alone. She was by no means blind to the part which she herself had played in the tragedy. She realized with shame and great remorse that in her sinful recklessness she had helped to lay the foundation of her loved one's destruction.

In deepest contrition she bowed her head in silent prayer: "O God, let me not rest until this greatest curse of mankind shall be annihilated, and the country free from this evil which has so cruelly slain my newborn happiness." While she prayed there seemed to be a choir of angels singing in her ears. She raised her face toward heaven, and there was indeed a light in her eyes and hope in her soul.

CHAPTER V

LARRIMORE, the city clerk, sat busily engaged at his desk when a stranger entered. Something in the man's eyes attracted his attention at once. The stranger was John Drew, who did not hesitate but made known the purpose of his coming immediately. Straight to the heart of his mission he plunged, saying:

"My son, the light of my eyes, the idol of my heart, lies dead, and you are responsible for it! Tell me, why do you issue license to sell whisky, which means death to so many people, complete ruin for so many homes—which makes men lower than the insect which breeds in the mold?"

Larrimore sprang to his feet in complete astonishment. "You are mistaken," he cried. "I have caused no man to die! I do not know the man of whom you speak!"

"Then it was not you who issued Croggs' license to sell whisky?"

"It is I, for truth," said Larrimore; "but, my friend, I have no grudge against any man. I have only been doing what I've been commanded to do—my duty. I am simply a servant carrying out the instructions of higher authority. The city council is responsible for the licenses I issue. It is my duty to sell license to all applicants. I have nothing to do with the right and wrong of it. If your son became a whisky fiend, it is his affair, not mine!"

The heart of John Drew weakened. During all those years of frequenting saloons, and with all his wisdom concerning whisky and its evil influence, he had never taken thought as to who was responsible for it, having always looked upon the barkeeper as a sort of irresisting devil and the sole parent of alcoholics. The sole cry of the reformers had always been: "Shun the barkeeper and his whisky." He stared at Larrimore while slowly it dawned upon him that the man was right. Since the barkeeper had (justly, it seemed) disclaimed the responsibility, and the city clerk had done the same with equal speciousness, it slowly dawned upon John Drew that he must seek further.

"When may I meet this council?"

"Let's see. There's a meeting to-night," answered Larrimore.

After John Drew had departed, Larrimore shook his head doubtfully, saying, "Some nutty, that."

That night the august assembly known as the city council—makers of laws or ordinances, regulators of public force, raters of city taxation, orderers of the issues of bonds, and constructors of public works, and makers of appropriations for public purpose—had a visitor in the person of John Drew. It was certainly a matter of serious import that brought him before that body of most experienced and self-contained citizens of New Gate.

He put on as serious air as his beating heart would allow, knowing that if he hoped to bring about a successful accomplishment of his plans, he must avoid all show of undue emotion—must not appear to be a madman or a crank. These men must be made to see the cruelty of allowing such a fatal proceeding as the free sale of liquor.

Therefore when the time came, his voice fraught with a deep earnestness, he told the story of his suffering and irretrievable loss—a story which could not fail to touch the hearts of all who listened to it.

"Gentlemen," he asked at the close of his narrative, "who is responsible for my son's death? I thought the responsibility rested with Croggs, the saloonkeeper who sold my boy the whisky; and had it not been for the timely intervention of Providence, Croggs would now be sleeping the sleep from which no man waketh. Croggs proved his innocence—that is, he convinced me that he is not directly responsible since he has been authorized by the city clerk to sell intoxicants to all who want them. His argument was logical; but when I had an interview with Larrimore, he also shifted the responsibility.

" 'The city council is responsible for the license which I issue,' he says—a statement which is also true—therefore I knew that I must look to you to exterminate this evil. Were I the only one that has suffered, I would make no complaint: but I speak in behalf of the thousands who suffer with me; the thousands who are yet to suffer on account of this evil: for as long as intoxicants are sold over the counter, vice and crime and untold suffering are bound to stalk abroad in the land. I feel that the rights of every human being are as sacred as my own. There are hundreds of others who have beloved ones, upon whom they lavish their whole life's love, hopes, and ambitions. Think of the number of these doting ones who are doomed to disappointment because those loved ones fall victims to accursed drink. Shall you men stand by and see the evil work go on without raising a hand to stop it?—or, worse still—will you continue to take part in it, you who grant the barkeeper the privilege to sell intoxicants—will you do nothing? When I looked upon the face of my beloved son, cold in death, and realized the utter loss upon all that I had prided myself, I was mad with grief: sick to the very dregs of misery, hopeless, helpless—raging! I came here to kill Croggs; but he—wily wretch though he is—he is not responsible for the laws which you gentlemen make and enforce. Could you not make better laws?—laws that would prohibit the sale of alcohol, for instance? Think of your own sons. The time will come when civilized man will feel that the rights of every living creature are as sacred as his own. Anything short of this cannot be perfect civilization. Think of the millions destroyed not only in body but in soul by the ravages of alcohol! Their untimely death is a tragedy that we must abate."

At the beginning of John Drew's speech the board had listened with somewhat amused tolerance, then with a rising interest, and finally at the end there was not one among them who remained untouched. Among them there was one who was more impressed than the others; for he, too, was the father of a son who filled a drunkard's grave. Fortunately this one was Mr. Anderson, the most influential member of the board.

"Fellow citizen," Mr. Anderson said in reply to John Drew, "I am in deep sympathy with the grievous hurt you bear. I feel sure that all who have heard your story are in sympathy with you. Before I say what I must say ultimately, be it understood that

I am bitterly against the use of alcoholics—I suppose we all are. And I cannot leave unexpressed my natural perception of what is just and right. All that you have said is true. The naked truth has been demonstrated in thousands of instances, in close proximity to every one of us; but on the other hand, have you, who bear this grievous wrong, thought of our position in regard to prohibition? The sale of liquor is an important factor in the advancement of this or any other town. In the first place, it would be unwise for this town to enact prohibitory laws while the other neighboring towns permit the sale of liquor. I can point you to several towns where such laws have been enacted—Bloomington, for instance—it is a town which was once very progressive, but which now owes its deterioration to its prohibitory law. There is little hope for Bloomington so long as the surrounding cities keep open saloons. On the other hand, Tiny Town, only a distance of ten miles from Bloomington, prospers and flourishes under the wet measure. I am stating these facts, Mr. Drew, in order to show you how prohibition may be harmful to a city or town rather than beneficial. A dry city within a wet State is at a great disadvantage on account of rival prosperity of neighboring cities that are not dry. Mr. Drew, this is a matter which the State should settle, not the city. I hope that I have made my reason plain —why it is not wise for us to enact prohibitory laws for New Gate. However, the cause which you advocate is certainly a worthy one, and if you are persistent enough to carry the matter before the State Legislature, I promise you my support."

Bitter disappointment on account of this repeated shift of responsibility took possession of John Drew's heart at first, then slowly this feeling began to ebb—slowly it dawned upon him that the purpose for which he had come to New Gate was not to take the life of one man in revenge for his son's death, but to save the lives of thousands by removing the evil cause of their destruction.

He had a private interview with Mr. Anderson, and expressed his determination to take the matter before the State legislature. Mr. Anderson again pledged his support.

One morning, a few days later, Mr. Anderson sat in his office pondering over the situation in which he found himself placed, when a young lady was announced. Miss Grace King, her color heightened by a rapid walk against a frigid wind, entered the office. There was a lack of the accustomed breeziness about her. Her uncle noticed this as he took her hands and looked deep into her clouded eyes.

The natural Grace was always so full of sunshine and withal such a merry twinkle in her eyes that no wonder her uncle noticed the change. He refrained from questioning her, however, knowing that whatever the trouble was, she would be certain to confide in him.

Sitting by the fire, she seemed to forget his presence, and her thoughts were evidently heavy and gloomy.

Whatever it is, he mused, it is the biggest thing that has ever come into her life. Something very serious is troubling the child, no doubt of that. Grace troubled and old—why, it is preposterous!—

yet that clouded brow, that sad droop of her lovely shoulders—that black dress! Her uncle started in alarm as he noted the last suggestion of deep, unfathomable sorrow. "They're all wearing black nowadays," he reflected. Whatever it was, he wished with all his heart that she would reveal it. He was plunged into deepest concern when he saw two bright, big tears hang on her lids a moment, then splash upon her folded hands. The ice was broken. In wild abandon of grief, Grace threw herself upon her uncle's bosom and gave vent to a passion of tears.

"Oh uncle, I'm the most miserable creature on the globe!" she wailed. "My very heart is broken!"

"There, there," he soothed; then waited.

In passionate words which tore at her listener's heart-strings, Miss Grace told the story of her love and loss—every minute detail from beginning to end, not sparing her own part in the tragedy. When she had finished, her uncle knew that her woman's love—the love that comes to every woman but once in life—had been given too late.

The thought overwhelmed him with tender sympathy and pity that to this child, as dear to him as a daughter, there should come such a monstrous grief. He was utterly at a loss how to comfort her. In the presence of such overwhelming, sacred grief he was awed and silent. Tenderly he stroked her bowed head and mingled his tears with hers, praying that God would give her strength to bear this crowning sorrow of her life. They stood silent until she became calmer, then he gently placed her in a chair and waited for whatever else she had to tell.

Outside the wind swept around the corner of the house in frigid fury. Miss Grace shivered and clung to her uncle. She felt cold—and alone. Suddenly the half-burnt logs in the fireplace tumbled together, and then the flames leaped up anew—and crackled.

Mr. Anderson's thoughts reverted to that other story. "How strangely similar," he said quietly. Then he said to Miss Grace, "You haven't told me his name, dear child."

"Robert Drew," she whispered softly.

"Robert Drew?—John Drew's son—of Hollyville?"

"You knew him, uncle?" she asked, wistful as a child.

"Knew him?—er—no—not before to-day. I learned of him to-day in a very singular way. Grace, darling, the death of that young man has caused me to enter into a great undertaking." Then he told her the father's story, and finally of his promised support. "Grace," he said, "the story of that young man touched me deeper than anybody knew. And now, since it is the story that is nearest and dearest to your heart, so it becomes of first importance to me. I shall leave no stone unturned till I shall have done all that is within my power to obliterate the cause which has brought such a lasting sorrow upon your head, and which, if allowed to continue, is destined to bring sorrow upon so many others."

"Oh, uncle! God is just and wise. That was my mission here to-day. The hope of securing your aid in this great undertaking, which I myself have resolved to take up, brought me here to-day. I am so ignorant in affairs of this kind; but I knew you would help me: you have never denied me anything." Then for a brief space they sat silent, each deep in the thought and feeling of the moment.

The deeper the feeling, the less demonstrative will be the expression of it.

Finally Miss Grace spoke again: "Do you think the undertaking most difficult, dear uncle?"

"Aye, little one—very much so. The thing is possible with a very improbable outlook. However, we will do our best—nothing short of our best. A man is especially and divinely fortunate, not when his conditions are easy, but when they are such that they evoke the very best that is within him, even if they provoke him to nobleness and sting him to strength. Any condition is fortunate that kindles his enthusiasm and inspires his will. I am glad to be instrumental in this work, for I, too, have a just cause for hating intoxicants, as you well know."

Again there was silence. Miss Grace remembered well the sad fate of her only cousin and playfellow. They had been like brother and sister until the awful drink habit had caught the young man in its clutches and hurled him to ruin and despair.

The painful silence was broken when her uncle looked at his watch and said: "I am to have a visitor this morning, my dear. Would you care to remain and meet John Drew—Robert's father? Or perhaps you'd rather not just now."

"I'll meet him now, uncle," said Miss Grace. Already his steps sounded in the hall. When John Drew entered, he noticed the deep embarrassment of the strange and lovely young woman, and wondered who she was.

"Mr. Drew, this is Miss Grace King, my niece," said her uncle. John Drew expressed his delight at meeting the young lady, but became somewhat perturbed when several minutes passed and still she did not depart. He secretly wished her a thousand miles away so that he and Mr. Anderson could be free to discuss their all-important topic.

To Miss Grace the resemblance of this man to Robert was striking. She began to wonder how she could make this man know that her love for his son was no light infatuation.

"Sit down," said Mr. Anderson—and straightway he began to lay his plans before John Drew. "I have a friend, a boyhood chum, who is a member of the legislature. I think he will be willing to draft a bill for us. He is one of my closest friends; was a special friend of mine when I was a lad. He loved my boy. I know that he will do all within his power for us. His influence is marked, and if anyone can be successful in getting an anti-liquor bill passed, he can."

"Then let us communicate with him at once and start about this work. My heart is full of it. I can do nothing but plan it day and night." John Drew caught the eager look on Miss Grace's face just then, and quickly curbed his excessive vehemence.

"We must go at this in a sensible way if we wish to be successful," said Mr. Anderson, thoughtfully.

"Grace, dear, our plan is to have my friend Howard draft this anti-liquor bill and present it to the legislature. He will, I am very certain, urge its consideration, doing everything in his power to create waves of sentiment that will influence its getting passed."

Seeing the look of wonderment on John Drew's face as he thus freely conversed with Miss Grace, Mr. Anderson thought it best to reveal the young woman's delicate relation to the matter.

"Mr. Drew," he said, changing the subject somewhat, "did it ever occur to you that your son might have left a young love somewhere to secretly mourn away her youth because of that young man's untimely death? Such has been the case. A young girl whose soul is as white as an angel's gave her love to your son, and although he loved her and declared his love, he died before he could make her his wife. That young woman, like yourself, has resolved to devote the rest of her life to the prohibition cause. That young woman is as dear to me as a daughter. So you see why the accomplishment of this work is almost as important to me as it is to you."

John Drew looked at the young woman in astonishment. This, then, was the Grace King, daughter of Raymond King, the spendthrift. He had known Raymond King all his life, but was not aware that he had a daughter until sometime before Robert's illness he had heard it whispered that Raymond King's daughter had become infatuated with his son Robert; but since Robert had never mentioned the matter to him, he had discredited the rumor altogether. It was no doubt, and no wonder then, that Robert had been lured into habits of intemperance. He loved this girl, daughter of a man whose entire house reeked with alcoholic drinks. It was a natural revulsion of feeling as he looked at Miss Grace. Under that gaze, which was not altogether kindly, the poor young woman cringed. She knew that there was a certain amount of guilt connected with her love. She thought she read a verdict of condemnation in that burning glance of Robert's father. She cowered for a moment; but that great, deep love for Robert surged her soul. It gave her courage. She took a step toward John Drew, her head held high in queenly beauty, her bosom heaved under the tumult which stirred her soul.

"I love him!" she cried; "I will always love him! For this reason I shall devote the best that is within me to the temperance cause. No one shall do more towards purifying society, ridding it from alcohol's venom sting, than I shall do. I know alcohol's subtle power. I know youth's weaknesses. Trust me to do much towards remedying the evil that alcohol has brought to so many homes."

John Drew's heart was touched—was melted by her words. The hard feeling against her softened. After all, it was not his to judge her. She loved Robert, and since Robert had loved her, she must be all that a good woman should be. He went to her, took one of her little hands in his and reverently kissed it. Turning to Mr. Anderson, he said reverently: "Happy man to have won the love of such a maiden."

Miss Grace's uncle took her other hand, and the two men found themselves with the same vow, that each would do his utmost in wiping out the curse which was destined to rob so many other women of their lovers and their husbands.

. . . .

The interview with Mr. Howard was not very encouraging to our friends at first. He did not manifest, in the beginning, the enthusiasm that they had hoped for.

"It is a preposterous idea," he said, "to hope to rid the State of alcohol in a short time. Then, too, I was not elected from a prohibition platform, as you know, and for me to ally myself with prohibition, it might injure my political future."

"But think what a great benefit to humanity you would render should you be successful in getting the bill passed. You would stop a traffic which injures everyone in each community of the State by disturbing public order, by endangering personal safety, by demoralizing legitimate productive industries, and by cursing the homes on which, in the last analysis, a nation is built, and on which its future citizens receive their bent toward virtue. Think what it would mean to you to be able to prevent this injury, positive and enormous, to the State as a whole and to every individual in it. Does your fear of political injury outweigh your interest in humanity? Is it not enough to make you blush with shame when you realize that you are a member of the legislature which legalizes such a traffic, protects it with its courts, its police, its militia if necessary—nay, may even summon any citizen to take up arms in its defense? This is an opportunity for you to win for yourself as great glory as your future hopes could wish. A prohibitory law effectively enforced would serve to improve the character and lives of so many people. Saloonkeepers of the State would be forced to go into some decent business, which would make them and their wives and children better. Many a young man who has been subjected to temptation and has just started out on the road to ruin would be saved by a law shutting up the saloons. Two thirds of the arrests made are for drunkenness. We cannot honor a Government which legalizes saloons, making men immoral by law. We must have a law that will shield and protect the young, the habit-bound and the helpless. Howard, the ultimate good accomplished by such a law will surpass your most sanguine dreams."

After listening quietly to what was being said, Mr. Howard spoke: "Success in this undertaking, as I see it, is very improbable. There is no doubt that nearly every member of the legislature looks upon saloonkeeping as a legitimate business. They will object on the account of the effect of a prohibitory law on the revenue of the State. Many of them hold that the liquor traffic has a natural right to exist, and that prohibition is opposed to personal liberty. They advance the argument that because one man out of ten becomes a drunkard and makes a fool of himself, there is no reason that the other nine should be deprived of the pleasure of drink."

"But you are able to meet such argument with good, sound reasoning," said Mr. Anderson. "So far as revenue is concerned, the saloon must pick the pockets of the poor to pour a thin golden stream of revenue. The man who thinks the saloon helps him to pay his taxes is in sad error. You can readily make it clear that saloonkeeping is not a legitimate business but a crime. Business is a service for profit; saloonkeeping is a profit without service.

If a man spends his money at the grocer's he has a supply of provisions in his pantry. If he deposits it in the bank he has a bank account to his credit. But if he spends his money at a saloon he has nothing to show for it but a brutal temper. Business is for public good, but crime leaves one the victim and the other the victor. The sale of liquor, therefore, is not a business but a crime against the man, the church, and the State. Those who think the liquor traffic has a natural right to exist are also in great error. There is no such thing as a natural right to commit wrong; nor should there be a legal right to injure society. Consideration of the public welfare overshadows the rights of the individual. On this account the so-called personal liberty argument in behalf of alcoholic drinks loses its force. The drink traffic of any State should be suppressed if the public welfare demands its suppression. Any condition that threatens and menaces society should be suppressed. In this way, Howard, you can meet these objections to prohibition impressively, I am sure. Come, give me your promise to do your best toward the passing of this much-needed law. Given a prohibitory law in the State, men like yourself can bring on a reign of righteousness that will do honor to your name forever."

Mr. Anderson extended an irresistible hand, and Mr. Howard grasped it in a heart clasp.

What the passing of that bill meant to John Drew, no one knew but himself. He hated alcohol as he hated no other substance in all creation. There could be no rest for him till he could see the entire State rid of it forever.

WHO WAS RESPONSIBLE? 79

Miss Grace realized the responsibility which rested upon her, and the part she must take in the accomplishment of their undertaking. Knowing this, she resolved to do her best loyally and cheerfully, and suffer herself to feel no anxiety and fear. "My time and destiny are in God's hands," she said. "He has assigned me my place; he will direct my paths; he will accept my efforts if they be faithful."

And they were faithful. For a woman of Miss Grace's social standing to assume the rôle of leadership of a temperance movement is neither an easy task nor a very pleasant one. The fact that she was Raymond King's daughter had its disadvantages for her. The general statement that Miss Grace King had turned moralist and headed a temperance movement was discredited by most of her friends and viewed askance by several of them. The fact of her parentage had its effect in another channel. Having been a natural social favorite, she had little trouble in getting an audience when she wanted one. In spite of all handicap, she worked wisely and well. There seemed to be some inward wisdom working within her. She never took the wrong step; but every movement of hers was a carefully laid plan—worked out methods of handling the situation. Each effort was crowned with success.

Miss Grace at once became a member of the Woman's Christian Temperance Union. Heretofore she had looked with absolute indifference upon the work which this great society is accomplishing. Her constant study and increasing knowledge of the work done by that society opened her eyes. The knowledge imbibed a new determination within her: it created a hope of what she might be able to do if allied with this great union. She took pride in reading the glowing accounts of its varied achievements in the uplifting of humanity. And well she might, for the great Woman's Christian Temperance Union, during the forty-two years of its existence, has done a great deal more for society than the average citizen realizes. In fact, few of the best informed are aware of the great work which it has accomplished. It has worked silently but very effectively. Besides the aggressive warfare it has waged against the alcohol evil, it has been instrumental in having many States enact laws prohibiting the sale of tobacco to minors; laws raising the age of consent and providing for better protection for women and girls. In this way it has accomplished much for the promotion of social purity.

Miss Grace organized a local Woman's Christian Temperance Union and the effect of that movement was satisfactory. The women, reluctant at first, soon responded with enthusiasm. Miss Grace rented an office in one of the most attractive buildings in the city, furnished rooms at her own expense, purchased literature—the best that could be procured—literature that would stimulate their interest in the prohibition movement, and at the same time was of educational value. The importance of prohibition as an educational factor was not minimized by any means. The work accomplished by Miss Grace during those days and weeks and months will ever be remembered by New Gate.

Mr. Anderson observed all Miss Grace's movements with a great deal of pride. He admired her patience, gentleness, sweetness, and unfailing energy;

he even found himself renewed and invigorated and inspired by the higher spirituality of her—spirituality which is the power that displaces falsehood with truth, selfishness with generosity, and transforms the hard, cold, designing, worldly minx to a tender, sweet-souled, divine woman.

Her love and interest in her work brought such a degree of pleasure to Miss Grace that it served to purify, strengthen, and beautify her nature. There was never a time that she was idle. Her life and work gave her such a mental impetus that it filled her with a sense of both surprise and pleasure. She could hold an audience spellbound in her temperance lectures. It seemed that each thought expressed stirred her to fuller forms of expression—full and rich and deep, and never failed to arouse the interest of the least of her hearers.

At home and alone in her beautiful room, after some of those effective meetings, she often reviewed the events of the last few months of her life and then a consciousness of growth and change would occur to her. She felt as though some distinct boundary line had been passed, and realized that forces which she had not been conscious of possessing had been aroused. Hitherto the grooves of her life had been all too easy and careless. Thought, action, controlling power had been extended, it is true, but on matters where the mechanical part was easily arranged, and all that had been required of her was the executive faculty, which it is easy enough to employ with every facility at hand. Her life as a socialist had been entirely too light, too easy to bring out the best that was within her.

Now all that was changed. The problem of this new life and undertaking dealt with the stern realities. She had to awaken to many things: that nothing worth while is accomplished without great labor; that in order to realize one's hopes one must begin, live, aspire, realize the best ideal of the moment, and every earnest effort should lead the way to greater achievement.

Often her thoughts reverted to that short period of her life which marked its turning point—that wonderful, vibrating, palpitating starlight time of her awakening, against the memory of which there was always her careless flirtation; then the marvelous but gentle leading of God's hand. How short a time ago something akin to despair had seemed to belong to her lover's death! Something of that, of course, remained—would always be a grief to be borne, like any other visitation from the hand which is the Father's despite its discipline.

CHAPTER VI

ONE afternoon, after a very busy morning, Miss Grace decided to get a bit of recreation by taking a little pleasure trip of a few hours' duration. She wanted to be alone and quiet, therefore she chose to go away out beyond the extremity of the car line which ran past her home—"West End" they called it—the borderland of woods and hills and valleys. West End afforded a wealth of picturesque landscape, fresh air, and sunshine. The view of the landscape from the window all along she knew would be pleasing and refreshing.

It was a fine day: the temperature springlike, the air cool but delightfully bracing. Exquisite and indefinable indeed was the charm of the early evening, exhilarating alike to mind and body, communicating its ineffable buoyancy to the young lady's somewhat jaded energies; and for a creature so responsive as Miss Grace to resist its influence was impossible. Her spirits rose like mercury: the journey before her assumed the promise of one abounding in possibilities of interest and pleasure.

The trees, still naked, were nevertheless restful to look at. Such hidden promise in their millions of branches—promise of abundant life and beauty, sure of fulfillment. The fields, low hills, and woodlands, stretching away into the distance, were fairly magical in color—color which seemed to her a more delicate, ethereal, divine thing than she had ever seen or imagined before. Rounding a curve about two miles beyond the city's limit brought her into full view of the city she had left behind. Here and there at various distances apart rose the graceful campaniles of distant churches. The sunlight glittered on magnificent architecture, and bathed the low, wooded parks in dreamlike beauty. Miss Grace felt her senses thrilled by the spell of the association—uniting the wild freshness of nature with the charm of civilization.

At the end of the car line she got off the car and aimlessly followed a little path which led up into the woods. The air was so fine, the sunshine so bright, that she found herself worked up into a transport of joy. She was glad that she had chosen this for her route. Out here she could be alone—away from the din of the city—to wander where she pleased. Little birds twittered among the naked branches as she walked on up the narrow path. She walked slowly, quite content to listen to their suggestive prattle. Her brain was wondrously quick to catch the promise of hope which they told of—the promise of spring and little warm nests full of darling young birds. Now and then she paused as if to better understand their chatter, then sauntered on up the path, trying as she went to understand something of the hushed and spiritual beauty of the land and the silent woods.

Two great, naked trees whispered mysteriously and mingled their sighs with the warbling of the little birds. There was no living soul to be seen as yet. That hour of solemn quietude and rest seemed all for her and her alone. She continued to walk on up the path until at a sudden turn she leaned forward in breathless surprise, for she found herself only a few yards from a queer little hut. The thin spiral of blue smoke issuing from the rickety chimney told plainly that there were inmates. Miss Grace had never known anything about the life of the lowly. She had never entertained a thought concerning the lives of the ragged waifs who helped to make up the number of inhabitants of the city. Moved by a strange impulse, she went up to the house and knocked at the door, wondering in the same instant what she was going to say when her summons was answered.

A few moments passed in fruitless expectancy, then she knocked again, more loudly this time. Suddenly there was a slight shuffling sound, and then another sound of objects falling on the floor. Then she heard the soft footfalls of someone coming to the door. It was opened only a little way, just enough for Miss Grace to catch a glimpse of two piercing, wondering, half-frightened eyes of a child. A little boy regarded her in silence without opening the door any wider, then, reassured by the stranger's smile, he slowly opened it wider and stood looking at Miss Grace in open-eyed amazement.

"You live here?" asked Miss Grace sweetly.

"Yes, my lady," answered the boy, still regarding her in wonder. "Will you please—er—come in?" he asked presently in a little voice breathless with awe. The intelligence which marked the child's speech surprised the young lady very much. She had always associated coarseness and ignorance with peasant life.

She followed the boy into the cabin, the interior of which was of the very poorest, but scrupulously neat and clean. That the little family which resided there was composed of people of gentle manners Miss Grace never for a moment doubted. She began to talk freely with her little, bashful host, soon gaining his confidence by her simple questions concerning his woodland surroundings.

He was soon telling her some of the wonderful secrets of his favorite haunts. He told her of many nooky paths and quiet corners down under the trees by the edge of the brook, where one might bask for whole hours in happy solitude—a solitude so complete that one might easily imagine himself miles and miles away from any city. "Often and often do I wander there," he told her, "stopping under the sweet, cool shade to read some favorite book, or giving myself to pleasant day-dreaming and air-castle building. "You just ought to see the brook," he continued; "it makes a musical, rushing and gurgling sound as it flows along." He told her how the moonbeams silvered the trees above it and transformed its waters to a sparkling stream of light. Then he told her of another dell where a little spring bubbled. "In the summer the bush creepers make a tangled tapestry around it, and crimson and blue wild flowers form dew-beaded chalices above it. Squirrels leap and frisk in the leafy boughs above; a few feet below it the tallest ferns grow," he said in this thrilly, poetic treble.

While the boy talked, Miss Grace noted his striking personality. She felt a thrill whenever he turned upon her his beautiful eyes—eyes habitually earnest and grave in expression, and holding in their brave, brown depths a sweet, childlike reliance and dependency; eyes with a certain deprecating droop as if the child had known the bitterest sorrow, yet eyes which seemed to say, "I am truthful; I am born a gentleman."

Just in front of him, on a shabby table, there lay a book worn and ragged about the edges. Several others lay upon the floor. It was the sound of books dropping on the floor that she had heard while she stood outside the door awaiting admittance.

Miss Grace stooped and picked up one which lay near her. She gave a slight gasp of surprise when she read the title. "Plutarch's Lives" in a home like this seemed incredible.

Suddenly the door was darkened by the entrance of a woman, who did not try to conceal her look of surprise at the presence of a stranger. The little host rose hastily, saying, "Mother, dearest, this is Miss—" he hesitated, remembering that he had not yet learned his fair visitor's name.

"Miss King," said Miss Grace, smiling one of her dazzling smiles, which never failed to warm the coldest heart.

"I am delighted to meet you and your little son," she said in half apology for her strange and unusual presence in this house.

The touch of hauteur which at first marked the woman's bearing melted away and she beamed a mother's smile of welcome as she attributed this lovely young woman's presence to the fact of some secret intimacy with her little son. He was always making friends—that little son of hers.

Miss Grace took in the woman's personality at a glance, and was convinced of her gentle breeding.

Hers was a personality which mere words of description here cannot give justice. Her rare combination of gentle dignity with profound force, of a set resoluteness of purpose with a philosophical patience, her physical equipoise, even in the mere details of her simple dress, indicated a certain aristocratic exclusiveness. She somehow gave to Miss Grace the presentment of a queen who by the irony of circumstance was exiled in this lonely cabin of the woods—this solitary cabin of such pauperish mien. From the crown of her proud head to the soles of her shapely feet, she gave distinct evidence of gentle breeding.

Miss Grace's bearing—quite innocent of any prying curiosity or priggishness—soon evoked a spirit of friendliness and hospitality. "Jean," said the mother, addressing her little son, "bring the lady some of your nice brown nuts. The yield of nuts this year has been unusual," she said to Miss Grace, "and I have been fortunate in finding a ready sale for them. Jean and I have been especially proud of that fact since it has enabled us to buy another one of Jean's favorite books."

"Does your little son read those?" asked Miss Grace, pointing to the volumes of "Plutarch's Lives," Scott's "Lady of the Lake," and Hawthorne's "Twice-told Tales."

"O yes, and it is remarkable how appreciative he is. He has such quick perception. My little Jean has a passion for books. I cannot keep him supplied." Her voice and smile were so frank and pleasant, so free from the previous restraint, yet so respectful, so gentle and womanly, so tender in her praise of her son, that Miss Grace found her own

WHO WAS RESPONSIBLE? 89

heart glowing. While they talked, Jean returned, bringing a bag of the greatest, brownest, most perfect pecans she had ever seen.

"O, thank you, thank you—what perfect beauties!" she said; and Jean's little heart glowed.

Miss Grace had spent an hour in the little cabin before she realized that the perfect evening was drawing to a close. In the midst of their happy chatter she received a sudden suggestion of coming night, and she also noticed that the mother's attitude toward her became mitigated with a certain uneasy apprehension which she could not conceal. She kept turning her eyes toward the door as if she expected someone. A certain fear crept into the eyes of little Jean. He gathered all his books and put them away. Over the mother's face there seemed to creep an expression of suffering. Miss Grace felt an oppression in the air, and wishing to avoid further intrusion, she arose to go.

She went swiftly to Jean, bent and kissed his high forehead which bore such a strong mark of intelligence; thanked him again for his rich gift—longing to slip a shining gold piece into the little hand. But thinking it might wound the little donor's pride to offer him gold for his generous gift, she thought of another plan and turned to say a parting word to Jean's mother.

"I shall see to it that Jean gets all the books he wants—may I?" she said, as she went towards the door.

"A-rr-r—books—blamed—b-books! I'll burn hell out of 'em!"

Both women started and looked toward the door. Rage, humiliation, fear, scorn—all struggled to gain supremacy in this mother's face.

Jean sprang up, his two small fists clinched in anger as he confronted the red-eyed brute-man who staggered into the room. It was his drunken father! Miss Grace fell back against the wall—astounded. She could not have received a greater shock if a lion had walked in at the door.

The drunken man made one stride toward the rigid, defiant form of his little son. Suddenly the mother hurled her body with all force against him— a blow which sent him crashing to the floor, knocking his head against the table as he fell. Miss Grace stared at this tragedy in frozen horror. All at once the woman turned to her:

"Go!" she said, "this is no place for you!"

Miss Grace moved swiftly out of the door and fled down the narrow road. The evening had lengthened into early twilight. She heard the plaintive, sad-sweet melody of the wood dove.

While she was hurrying along toward the street car, she heard the rapid approach of footsteps in pursuit. She started to run faster, but thought of little Jean and turned to look back without checking her pace. It was Jean's mother. Her beautiful face was pale and melancholy, her lovely eyes moist with recent tears; an expression of troubled passion lurked within their depths. What a piteous look she gave the wondering Miss Grace! What speechless sorrow swam suddenly into her lovely eyes! She strove to speak, but her lips only trembled. The tears began to rain down her cheeks. Her tears, the sincere outflow of a pure woman's grief, fell like dew upon the younger woman's heart, and for the moment Miss Grace was stricken with sympathy.

"Oh, I do hope you can forgive me—forgive us, you beautiful creature!" she said between her violent sobs. "It was such a cruel blow to our happy little meeting—his coming in like that and threatening Jean—my little Jean! O, why did you ever come to our little cabin of sorrow? Forgive me for detaining you," she said, forcing herself to calmness. "I simply could not bear to have you leave without knowing something of our unhappy life—without warning you never to come again so long as my husband continues to drink as he does."

Miss Grace started involuntarily. That brute the husband of this queen—the father of little Jean —impossible!

"It is true," the poor mother moaned, as if answering Miss Grace's thought. "He is my unhappy husband—my little Jean's father. He was a good man once. He was honest, intelligent, upright, and a gentleman. He came from one of the best families, and was a man of great promise until he took to drink. He began his downward career a few months after our little Jean was born. His many friends induced him to join their fashionable clubs. He was so frank and open-hearted that they all loved him. He soon became a social favorite, falling in with all their ways, drank beer and whisky, and gambled. He continued to go on in this way until finally I awoke to the terrible truth that I was a drunkard's wife—too late! He went from bad to worse. All we possessed was soon swallowed up in drink. Unable to bear the shame and the humiliation, I induced him to move here—away from my former friends—to see if I could cure him of the awful habit. I have only succeeded in seeing ourselves reduced to abject poverty, with no hopes of his recovery. Were it not for poor little Jean, I could commit suicide. Jean is my only hope of happiness in this life—my one ray of sunshine. He is an unusual child—precocious to the point of genius. If I can only succeed in keeping him from following in the footsteps of his poor father, he will be a wonderful man some day. Now you have learned our sad story, and for my son's sake I will ask you to please think kindly of us—Jean and me, especially Jean. Your coming to us in our poor cabin was like having a visitor from another world. Our grateful hearts shall never forget you. Jean will dream of you night and day; the memory of you will be an inspiration to him. Now good-bye forever, sweet young woman. May God bless you always!" With those words she turned and hurried back along the narrow road to her lonely home of sorrow, shame, and patient endurance.

Miss Grace's journey to her own home was a sad one. She could never forget the poor mother's story and little Jean's danger. Little Jean had impressed her deeply. Here was a lad peculiarly endowed with personal power. What a magnificent specimen of manhood this youth promised; what infinite possibilities beckoned him onward! What a sublime spectacle it would be to watch this youth going straight to his goal—working his way up through difficulties, surmounting every obstacle, encountering dangers—but never turning his eye from the goal! How beautiful was that mother's love! What a pity if this good woman's life should never be restored to its original height from which it had been so cruelly dethroned by alcohol! That possibility lay in the son's future attainments. It lay within his power to finish the wreck or to rebuild it into an elegant mansion. How Miss Grace adored the mother for cultivating her son's æsthetic faculties! It was evident that she had taught him to find in the landscape, the valley, the hills, the fields, the meadows, the flowers, the laughing brook which ran back of their house, riches that no money could buy—beauties that enchant the angels. How good the fact that she was teaching him every day to see them, appreciate them, to read their message, and to respond to their affinity! Surely this mother's beautiful patience, love, and endurance would have its reward. Surely—O God! surely the idolized little Jean would not one day become like his father—a physiological hulk wrecked on passion's seas and fit only for a danger signal to warn others. Surely this lad of such wonderful promise, and this beautiful, refined mother, were not destined to perish like lovely flowers plucked by the hand of a grim destroyer. Yet this thing, terrible as it seemed, was a probable possibility as long as alcohol flowed freely in the land. A vision of another little boy that had once been—her beloved Robert—rose before her. That young man, so beautifully endowed with manly qualities, in spite of his father's utmost caution, had fallen a victim to alcohol. No, there was no sure hope of escape for the little Jean. Under the prevailing circumstances only a miracle could save him. But Miss Grace resolved that, if the proud mother would allow, she would aid largely in creating a chance for the boy.

A degree of sadness crept into Miss Grace's heart as she awoke to the sad realization of all the splendid opportunities which she had lost—opportunities for helping the struggling, ambitious poor to work their way to success. She thought of the many glorious hours she had ruthlessly wasted in frivolous pastime; the riches spent in useless pleasure—riches which might have helped some youth of promise—like little Jean. Her heart ached with pain when she thought of how those two, the mother and son, had to grapple with hardships, wrestle with poverty, in order to buy a book for Jean's hungry little soul. He would never starve for books again so long as she had a penny. She shuddered again when she thought of the awful danger in which he stood. Something must be done to save him. It could be done and it must be done. Alcohol must no longer continue to rob the world of its children of genius.

It was a very determined young woman who stepped off the car in the gathering dusk and ascended the elegant steps of her home. Henceforth nothing should daunt her courage. She felt that if she had a thousand lives to give, she would gladly surrender them all to the work of destroying the evil which threatened little Jean, and thousands of others like him. Now in her thought of active work for the good of humanity, all seemed to be moving toward peace; and Miss Grace could almost hear her lover's voice bidding her to be of good cheer and go on with the work which lay so plainly before her.

CHAPTER VII

AT last the time came for the attempt at passing the all-important bill. The day—the very hour arrived. The bill had been formulated by Mr. Howard and started out on its interesting and intricate course through which all bills must pass before they are enacted.

It was referred to a committee for its critical consideration. Many of the enemies of the cause hoped that it would never be recorded; but through the influence of Mr. Howard, the bill was reported with the recommendation that "It do pass." It was then set as the special order for Thursday—three days hence.

The site of the State capitol was beautiful. It was built upon a gradual summit, from which there was a charming panoramic view of the whole neighborhood.

Thursday dawned—a fine day, with plenty of sunshine; an Italian sky above, and the air so clear and bright on every side made the handsome walls of the capitol glitter in such dazzling splendor that it hurt the eyes.

In obedience to the summons of the three ardent workers for the prohibition cause, there was a general gathering of rank, wealth, and beauty; and the doors of the capitol had never given admittance to more numerous guests than on that particular occasion. Without any extravagance of eulogy, the spectacle must be termed splendid. The most beautiful sight of all was the turnout of the Woman's Christian Temperance Union. There came representatives from all over the State. They came wearing their badges of white ribbon, and their merry eyes twinkled in excitement born of expectancy and hope. Their cheeks were brought into full bloom by the clear, frosty air.

The day was uncommonly fine—being a day which stood on the borderland between winter and spring. The air was just cold enough to be bracing, and lent its aid in making the whole aspect of the stirring citizens cheerful and full of hope. They heeded not the cold, for the air was so intensely clear and dry and bright that the temperature was not only endurable but delicious. Finally, when they occupied every space in the galleries, everybody seemed intensely interested and hopeful in the outcome of the prohibition bill.

John Drew, all his faculties stretched to a dangerous tension, sat near Miss King. His brain was a chamber of conflicting emotions. He sat tense, his hands clinched as if he would be ready to grapple with some foe. Miss Grace and her uncle never dreamed of the state of excitement their companion was in. Had they been cognizant of that fact they would have been somewhat alarmed for his safety.

Miss Grace herself was calm, confident, and hopeful. She had done her best loyally and cheerfully, suffering herself to feel no anxiety or fear. "My time and destiny are in God's hands," was her constant thought. "He has assigned me my place; he will direct my paths; he will accept my efforts if they be faithful."

The hour arrived. After devotion and the House had been declared ready for business, Mr. Howard immediately called for a reading of the bill. After it had been read, he made a short speech in which he gave logical reasons why this bill should be written in the statute books of the State. Then a general debate commenced. The ardor and enthusiasm manifested soon reached its height; the outlook for the passage of the bill seemed favorable. The weak-kneed arguments advanced by those who opposed State prohibition were met with denunciation and sound reasoning by the friends of prohibition—such arguments as these: "The liquor traffic has a natural right to exist"; "It is opposed to personal liberty"; "Prohibiton don't prohibit" (a statement which is as faulty in logic as it is in grammar); "Saloonkeeping is a legitimate business," etc. Some even advanced the argument that prohibition attempts to remove temptation from men, while God's plan is to permit temptation to exist in order to strengthen man's moral power, therefore prohibition is not in accord with God's method (as if man must take sides with the devil in order to prove the Lord a true prophet). "You can't make a man good by law," another asserted.

"But we have made men bad by law," was the answer. "The purpose of a prohibitory law is not to make the drunkard moral and the saloonkeeper virtuous, but it is to protect the public against wrong-doing. The supposition of any criminal law is that it should have a restraining influence among men. No doubt there is a good deal less of crime in the State than there would be if we had no criminal code.

By so much are men made better by means of law. A good prohibition law enforced would serve to protect the community against crime. Every community has this right to protect itself. You assert that we cannot make men moral by law: we assert that we certainly ought to stop making men immoral by law, for that is what we do when we tolerate laws which allow citizens to procure poisons which we know will destroy every vestige of morality in man."

"It is a bad thing to have laws that are not enforced," said another. "After all, a prohibitory law will not keep liquor out of the State. It will find its way anyhow and set up in the form of blind tigers."

"You make the assertion that it is a bad thing to have laws that are not enforced," came the answer; "we assert that it is a worse thing to have laws that decent people cannot respect; enactments which, instead of reflecting the sentiments of the best classes, only mark the level of morality among the lowest and vilest. Shall we put into our statute books only laws that can be enforced without difficulty? Whenever we discover an existing evil that is particularly favored by thieves, robbers, and all classes of criminals, something that will make trouble if we try to enforce laws that will prohibit it, should we legalize the thing, encourage it, promote and protect it in spite of the mischief it will do among men? No! Then we ought not to assume that attitude toward the sale of liquor. There is no menace to society more dangerous than the saloon. It is more dangerous than the gambling house; it is more dangerous than counterfeiting—more dangerous than any other evil in existence now placed under the ban of law.

Liquor is an evil that demoralizes everybody it touches from the time it issues from the distillery until it empties into the hell of death, dishonor, and crime. Think of the suicides, the insanity, the abject poverty, ignorance, and destitution all over the State. Think of the little naked children clinging to the sunken breasts of starved, cringing mothers, made cowards on account of dastardly husbands. Think of the talented men of genius, whose fine brains have been wrecked by the devil's agent—alcohol. It behooves us to be consistent and treat liquor selling as we treat any other dangerous evil—itself the most dangerous of all, because it has for its accursed merchandise men and women and their unborn children."

In this manner rival sentiment passed until the enthusiasm reached its height. Fortune seemed to smile in favor of prohibition. But there was one present who had not spoken. Pearson was an aged, gray-haired member of the legislature—a man whose influence was remarkable—a fact due to his age and experience. Hitherto he had been silent, listening to their arguments with a great deal of interest. Now he arose in all the calm dignity of his bearing and made some remarks which decided the fate of the anti-liquor bill almost instantly.

"In making the State dry," he said, "we will be doing it a much greater injury than benefit. We will succeed in checking the State's progress in a large measure—cutting off revenue, transferring our trade —and yet only leaving a very small clean spot on the liquor map. If a State prohibition law is passed, it faces a hostile attitude on the part of the Federal

Government in many particulars. The regulation of interstate commerce belongs to the national Government. A dry State cannot prevent other States shipping liquor into its territory. You are all aware of the fact that internal revenue collectors—representatives of the national Government—do issue license to sell liquor in dry States. The friends of prohibition will accomplish a greater work—the most effective work, and, as I see it, the only effective work—by ridding the nation of this evil. Let the Government, in which it is most largely vested, destroy it. Upon the Federal Government rests the responsibility of this traffic's red-handed crimes. Make the nation dry, and you will not only bring about complete prohibition, but you accomplish it without disturbing the State's commercial equilibrium."

John Drew had listened to the discussion, his heart buoyed up with hope one moment only to be followed by the next moment pregnant with uncomfortable doubts and presentiments. Toward the last he became uplifted again—so much so that his heart sang in his bosom. He even sat there looking down the vista of future years, seeing their untiring efforts crowned with success. He saw himself walking in the midst of it, happy and content all the rest of his life—happy in the glorious compensation for his son's death: a condition which not only gave him peace, but afforded a wellspring of joy to thousands. He beheld himself in a happy old age, gliding on through peace and prosperity to a last and holy reward, in which he would gain Robert, Alice, and everlasting life.

WHO WAS RESPONSIBLE? 101

This ecstasy of thought carried him to the very pinnacle of hope—then the words of Pearson cast him back down—down to despair. As he hung upon Pearson's words, his intuition warned him that this man had blocked the way of the State prohibition law almost completely. Before Pearson ended his speech—before the vote was taken even, John Drew knew that all was lost. Suddenly he stopped up his ears, but in sheer fascination removed his fingers just in time to catch the words: "Let that Government in which it is most largely vested destroy it. Upon the Federal Government rests the responsibility of the traffic's red-handed crimes."

John Drew shuddered. An involuntary groan escaped his lips; his hands clinched themselves in stonelike rigidity. "My God!" he cried, "who is responsible?"

The vote was taken: prohibition was defeated.

John Drew never quite realized when or how he reached his room. All the old, pent-up grief and hurt which his hope of victory had kept quelled during the campaign now burst loose with redoubled force. All the terrible misery, the madness, the reckless despair crushed him with a greater force than ever.

He went and sat in a chair by the window. The sunlight streamed in upon him as if it strove to melt the heart fast turning to stone. "Is there a God—actually a God?" he cried. "Yes; but a cruel, unforgiving, awful Being—and he, in all his omnipotence has set himself against me—one poor, miserable soul! He whose proud will evolves the universe. He has arrayed his mighty forces of heaven and hell against one miserable atom of his own creation, and the titanic wheels of life, time, and eternity are all whirling into motion to grind me, a poor worm, down to destruction! Why? Simply because of the fulfillment of that terrible promise—'Visiting the iniquities of the fathers upon the children unto the third and fourth generation.' God! What infinite pains he has taken to destroy me! My last hope—my last avenue to peace—gone!"

At that moment of John Drew's despair, Grace King and her uncle were engaged in a conference in which they formulated plans destined to plant hope once more in that heart of utter despondency.

As soon as possible, Miss Grace hastened to find John Drew. As she drew near to his lodging, her heart quivered with apprehension and fear of danger to her friend. Her steps sounded upon the threshold, and John Drew started as if he feared some fresh and final stroke from the hand of the Almighty—a final punishment avenging his profane thoughts of a moment ago. Without looking around, he sat quaking—expectant. A tender hand was laid upon his shoulder, a sweet voice which he had learned to recognize and to love came from the tender soul of Miss Grace: "Don't grieve so, dear friend; all is not lost—indeed, not so."

What was it she was saying? All not lost! How was that?

"We have been defeated in this only to make a bigger attempt. A brighter hope—the most glorious of all—lies before us. It is the hope for the greatest, most everlasting victory of all—national prohibition."

While John Drew listened, slowly the tension of

his nerves relaxed. A scalding moisture of unfalling tears blinded his eyes. He turned his face upward and looked at Miss Grace for the first time since her coming. As he looked up at her, the sunshine glittered on two great drops, as large as a child's tear.

Miss Grace was moved with tenderest compassion. Grief, disappointment, and sorrow had made this once strong man almost as helpless as a child. He regarded her with the wistfulness of a little child. She saw the dawn of a new interest in his eyes. She noted how white his hair had become during the last few months. She noticed how his hands shook: how weak he seemed, and helpless.

But she could not guess how her words planted new hope in his heart. How he loved her for giving him this hope! It was not false hope, either, and slowly his half-dazed brain comprehended her meaning. This, then, was God's mysterious plan of bringing about a greater achievement. It was indeed a new hope—the brightest ever.

Miss Grace was beautiful—comely and quiet, as if all her emotions had been subdued to the peaceful tenor of her life. Another step sounded upon the threshold, and Anderson entered. The sight of him gave John Drew even more assurance. Together the three talked and planned until the daylight lengthened into evening. This rejuvenated interest wrought wonders toward restoring John Drew's mind to equilibrium.

"Now let us walk somewhere in the evening sunlight," he said to Miss Grace, after their conference was over and Mr. Anderson had departed. "Exercise, fresh air, and sunshine are what I need."

As they walked down the street there was a singular contrast in their two figures: he dark and picturesque, one who had battled with the world, whom all suns had shone upon, and whom all winds had blown in a varied course; yet their faces, all unlike as they were, had an expression not so alien—a glow of kindred feeling flashed outward, born of one common interest. John Drew felt inspired by her patience and untiring energy. If this slip of a girl could bear up so bravely, why could not he? For her sake he must make a strenuous effort to overcome those periods of unreasoning madness. "We will fight this evil with all our might," he said to her; "neither shall we be at peace until we see this country free of its poison. Our country's prosperity and glory shall be our reward. There shall be no more brutal homes for young wives; no more shall the homecoming of the drunken wretch assassinate joy and murder happiness in that sanctuary of love—the home. Better homes shall mean better citizens; and out from ideal homes shall come ideal men who shall hold the highest offices of this country. May God give us strength to fight—to tear down the temple of Bacchus and lay the foundation of the magnificent temple of righteousness, wherein, with appropriate rites, there will be celebrated the religion of humanity! Little girl, we shall see it—you and I." John Drew had spoken more to himself than to Miss Grace; but now he turned to her and said: "I am glad you are interested as you are. Had it not been for your kindly words of hope, I would now be in the deepest, darkest despair. Nobody knows what the loss of Robert is to me. He was all I had to live for—the center around which my life revolved. His happiness was the aim of my life. The love of him made up for everything else that I had lost. I loved him with a passion such as the angels know. His childhood was my sunshine— my springtime of life. All that I had missed in my own boyhood was made up for in Robert's.

"Robert was a perfect child and youth. I often wondered at God's mercy in choosing me for the father of such a son—then I'd remember that he was Alice's son, too; that he was the offspring of her great love for me. I could never feel myself worthy of such a wife as Alice and such a son as Robert. God was indeed merciful: my life, which could never have survived the loss of my young wife, was brightened and blessed by this perfect son of hers. My love for him helped me through all the long, dark years which followed—helped me when I needed help most, helped me not to lose sight of God! His young manhood was perfect and was my glory. Do you wonder then that I bear an everlasting hatred to the thing that wrecked his life? I shall never be content until alcohol be slaughtered in his stronghold. Your serene, confident, and hopeful energy serves to magnetize one's will and draw power toward one."

"Triumph of success comes not to doubt and disbelief," said Miss Grace softly. "It comes to sunny expectation, eager purpose, and to noble and generous aspiration. O, I have never regretted for one moment the step I have taken. I thank you for your faith and utmost confidence in me. O, I am so glad that I did not go all through my life with a selfish, purposeless heart. I am glad that my soul had its awakening, even though it took sorrow to awaken it."

They walked on down the street slowly and in silence then. There was little need of words. These two had so much in common. When they had thus walked in silence for a few blocks, Miss Grace spoke: "How fortunate for us to have secured the co-operation of Mr. Pearson, of the legislature. He is a man of marked influence—and a gentleman. It was through his influence that we failed to-day, yet he afterwards destroyed all our bitter feelings against him by declaring his willingness to render all the aid in his power, should we make an attempt at national prohibition. He showed us wherein the task of getting a national prohibition bill passed is an enormous one, due to the fact that the world has not been prejudiced enough against alcohol.

" 'It is apt to be set aside as an issue of minor importance. Perhaps we may not be able to accomplish much for a long time,' he told us."

Miss Grace paused, then continued: "If this should be so—using the words of Catherine of Russia, 'I beg you take courage; the brave soul can mend even disaster.' "

Miss Grace had been acquainted with Robert's father only a few months, but her intuition told her that he would need such advice often. His mind and heart, wrenched and torn as they had been by grief and disappointment, were on the verge of breakdown.

He answered not a word, but turned his eyes upon her—a gaze that was eloquent and deep in gratitude and admiration. He thought he had never seen her

WHO WAS RESPONSIBLE? 107

so glorious. Her beauty was like the noonday sun—it made him glad, it made him resolute, it imbibed him with new courage. This woman of Robert's choice was not only very beautiful, but very intelligent. For a woman to be wise and at the same time womanly is to wield a tremendous influence which may be felt for good in the lives of generations to come.

Time passed. Weeks lengthened into months, and the months slipped by until a whole year had passed. In the meantime the advocates for national prohibition made preparations for their ultimate effort. The first step they took was to confer with members of Congress who were from their State. Unfortunately, each senator and representative absolutely refused to take the initiative in introducing a national prohibition bill before Congress. Their main reason was, that prohibition was not in their party platform. Each of them feared that such a measure might mean his political assassination.

Let me beg of my readers not to be too harsh in their judgment and dub these men as cowards because they feared political injury. Remember that self-preservation is the first law of nature. It takes a hero to brave any kind of danger.

But in providing heroes in time of crisis, America has been most fortunate. In the dark days of the new Republic, when a hero was needed to lead the untrained soldiers against the British troops—there was a Washington. When that great curse, human slavery, threatened to rend the American Government asunder, there was a Lincoln to avert the disaster.

108 WHO WAS RESPONSIBLE?

Nor did the friends of national prohibition have to wait long to find a champion for their cause. In an adjoining State there resided a man who had already startled the world with his daring and patriotism when he, an officer in the American navy, at the risk of his own life, braved the perils of the sea and the deadly fire of the enemy in order to render his country a service which should always live in the hearts of a grateful people. By this brave deed he had already sprung into nobility, worth, and service.

For months the heroic deeds of this man had been on the lips of every American. He was now a member of Congress, a representative from his State, and his voice had often been heard in Congress in favor of social and political purity. He was also known to be a friend to the temperance cause. Miss Grace had recently heard him deliver an eloquent speech before the Woman's National Temperance Union. In this speech he had declared himself in favor of national prohibition. She had never before heard words used as such powerful weapons in the denunciation of wrong and the exposition of fraud. His scathing denunciation of alcohol had made a deep impression upon her.

After they had failed to secure the consent of the congressmen from their own State, they became somewhat baffled; but Miss Grace, remembering the eloquent speech from the noted hero of the State of G——, remarked: "If we only possessed claim enough upon the friendship of Mr. Gibson of the State of G—— to approach him with this proposition, I feel sure that we would be successful. But perhaps it would not be just to ask him to hazard his political

WHO WAS RESPONSIBLE?

future by serving us, since he is not a representative from our State."

"But Mr. Gibson is a personal friend of mine," said Mr. Pearson. "I've known him ever since he was a child. His father was my boyhood chum. Gibson is not the man to fear political death or any other death when he feels that the sacrifice is for the cause of righteousness."

They communicated with Mr. Gibson as soon as time permitted, and received the very encouraging information that he would gladly serve them—in fact, was himself planning to prepare a bill to be presented at the next session of Congress.

CHAPTER VIII

ONE week before the time of that session of Congress in which the national prohibition bill was to be introduced, John Drew went to Washington. His impatience to be there got the better of him. Not that he cared for the city itself, but he had an indescribable longing to get in sight of the National Capitol wherein in a very few days a bill was to begin its intricate journey. Whether the outcome would be favorable or not, John Drew could not tell. He was only sure of the intense longing in his heart, the burning wish which seemed to consume his soul.

It was in the month of December and very cold. The day of John Drew's arrival in the city of Washington was bright and crisp and exceedingly cold. At first sight of the city an indescribable thrill passed all over his body. It was the mingling of a thrill and a chill, and it made him shiver. His intense eagerness to see the Capitol was childish. Presently when he stood in full view of the magnificent building, a glow of delight overspread his whole countenance. He had a perfect view from where he stood. It impressed him as a very fine building indeed, placed as it ought to be upon a noble and commanding eminence, from which one could have a splendid bird's-eye view of all the adjacent surroundings.

John Drew gazed long and earnestly upon that great structure wherein only a few days hence he hoped to realize the greatest wish of his heart. He had yet to view the interior; but just now the ex-

WHO WAS RESPONSIBLE?

terior was quite enough. His imagination penetrated the magnificent walls and handsome pillars of stone and created impressions of the live pillars of the great Capitol. His imagination pictured this public body, an assembly of men bound together in the sacred names of Liberty and Freedom—a body of men who applied themselves in this new century to correct some of the vices of the old, to purify the avenues of public life, pave the dishonest, dirty ways to position and power; and who made laws for the common good of mankind. He saw among them intelligence and refinement; the true, honest, patriot heart of America—men of highest character and great abilities; men who stood hand in hand, shoulder to shoulder for the benefit and progress of their country.

Seeing this vision, John Drew smiled a most gracious and benevolent smile upon the great Capitol. Reluctantly he turned his face toward the city. To him it represented the whole country. His gaze became fixed upon its mass of buildings, while again his imagination penetrated the walls of brick and stone, and conjured visions of the lives of the inmates. From every chimney the blue smoke curled upward in the frosty air like incense from the altar of domestic peace. In every home he beheld Bacchus lying dead—his evil cup shattered into a thousand fragments. On every hearth he saw bright fires crackling—fires that cast ruddy lights upon glowing children, offsprings of healthy, temperate parents. Their childish laughter filled his soul with symphonies, soft and sweet—laughter which fills the eyes with light and the heart with joy, laughter which catches, holds, and glorifies all the tears of grief.

In every home he saw Queen Love—the morning and the evening star—shedding her radiance upon the parent and the child—Love, the mother of beauty, the mother of melody, the builder of every hope, the kindler of every fire on every hearth—Love that makes earth heaven and men gods. And there was an ache of joy in John Drew's heart, for the whole of the horizon was filled with glory and all the air was filled with wings.

With this twin vision in his soul, John Drew went on his journey to the hotel where he was to abide until that day should come when that dignified and decorous body of Congress should confirm his hopes and send him forth along the long-sought avenue to peace. The evening of his first day in Washington came to a happy close. Midnight and sleep blotted out those happy thoughts and visions, and John Drew slept the peaceful sleep of a tired child.

For the first day or two after his arrival the city provided many objects of interest which kept him well occupied. On the third day there occurred an incident which, trivial as it seemed to everybody else, caused such a turmoil of feeling to arise in the heart of John Drew that it threatened to shatter all his glorious dreams of the future. When he took his place at the table for dinner, he noticed the presence of a strange gentleman of striking appearance at the table opposite his own. This table was set for one, and an expression of expectancy lighted up the face of the head waiter—who himself brought a bottle of most carefully decanted red wine, examining the delicate color through the fine glass with the air of a great connoisseur.

WHO WAS RESPONSIBLE?

To a less casual observer the man's appearance would have been less marked. He was a man of about forty-five perhaps, carefully dressed—a superb figure, with a strong face and eyes of gray velvet, lighted at times with curious little steel points. A very attractive and gentlemanly person to an ordinary observer; but somehow the man caught and held John Drew's attention in a magnetic grasp. John Drew also noticed the obsequiousness of the waiters, who passed everything to the dignified servant, to be placed before the gentleman by his hand. After the red wine had been poured into his glass, the gentleman lifted it up to the light to see the clear ruby, then swallowed a single gulp, and nodded his approval to the waiter, who stood anxiously waiting his verdict the while.

John Drew watched every movement of the strange gentleman—watched without knowing why: saw him finish his fourth glass of wine, and seeing, shuddered. But why should he shudder? Wine had been served daily—though perhaps not such expensive sort—ever since he had been there at the hotel. Why should not this man take it? Why not?

It was not until after the stranger had finished his meal and had passed out that John Drew had the question answered for him, by learning the identity of the man. "It is Senator B——, of K——," he was informed.

Senator B——. One of that chosen number! John Drew almost rushed out the door into the open. It was a miserable day—chilly and raw, a damp mist falling, cold and wintry. John Drew had seen a very ordinary thing—a senator partaking of alcoholics—

that was all; but when he reached the cold pavement he seemed to feel the ground tremble beneath his feet. The cold mist shivered his frame: fear gripped his heart—vague and terrible.

But that was not all he was to see. Other members of the legislative body arrived. Several of them drank freely of alcoholic drinks—expensive wine and beer.

John Drew watched the actions of these men as a child might watch and wonder at the deeds of some worshiped hero, suddenly caught in the act of doing those things which he himself had been forbidden to do. He watched, fascinated—struck with horror.

When Miss Grace and her uncle reached Washington, they found him in a peculiar state of mind which neither was able to fathom. They could not account for the wistful, childish expression in his eyes. The groping, searching way he had was puzzling. They were unable to analyze the peculiar expression which came over his face whenever he was thrown into the presence of any member of that distinguished body.

Miss Grace observed all this with a secret dread, fearing that John Drew's mind might give way under the strain. She strove with all her might to divert his attention as much as possible by going about the city, visiting places of interest, pointing out to him many interesting curios and mementos of historic events. After such jaunts he would always seem to be restored almost to normality—at least he tried hard to make a brave showing before his friends. But in his room, alone, he would pace the floor for hours until he would almost fall from exhaustion.

WHO WAS RESPONSIBLE? 115

After that he would go to his bed to sleep and dream, sometimes of turbulent waters and violent earthquakes—then again he would dream of a vast assembly where sat many legislators, who uttered coarse threats, who passed words and even blows such as drunken men deal upon each other; men who practiced despicable trickery against one another, and engaged in dishonest faction in its utmost depraved and unblushing form.

Those first days of Congress' session were very anxious ones for John Drew. Even Pearson, Anderson, and Miss Grace found their blood tingling with intense excitement. But never in the history of his life had John Drew passed through such an ordeal of hope and despair.

At last the day came—then the very hour, when the Gibson bill for national prohibition, prohibiting the sale, manufacture, transportation, exportation, and importation for sale of intoxicating liquors for beverage purposes not only in the United States, but in all territory subject to the United States, was presented and voted upon in the House of Representatives. It was on the 23d of December, a day remembered ever afterwards by the friends of national prohibition.

The vote was taken; but those who were in favor of national prohibition were in the minority. The enemies to the cause, using principally the States' rights theory as a bulwark against national prohibition, had won.

But in spite of the fact that the Gibson bill had been defeated, the vote in Congress showed a great triumph for the national prohibition movement, 386

116   WHO WAS RESPONSIBLE?

of the 433 members of the House declared themselves on the Gibson resolution for constitutional prohibition. The significance of the action was striking. The vote in favor of the amendment, according to statistics, was 197 to 189 against, making a majority of only eight of those voting.

But perhaps more striking than the bare majority of the membership voting is the fact that seventeen State delegations voted solidly for prohibition, and twelve were for it by a majority vote. Only eight States voted solidly against prohibition, and only nine additional States gave a majority against.

In view of the fact that only thirty-six States are needed to ratify a constitutional amendment providing for national prohibition, the significance of the action which placed the congressional delegation of twenty-nine commonwealths out of forty-eight behind the Gibson bill is very striking.

"This achievement far surpasses my expectation," said Mr. Pearson. "It makes me believe that the liquor traffic in America is doomed beyond doubt. Another such glorious achievement and the victory is won. The States' rights theory will be comparatively easy to overpower. There is nothing more insincere than the statement that national prohibition will violate the doctrine of States' rights."

Suddenly they thought of John Drew. A simultaneous spasm of alarm passed over each of their faces. Without another word they hastened to his apartment, where they hoped to find him and give him comfort. With heart almost sick with misgiving, Miss Grace led the way upstairs to his room. There they found him in a most pitiful state. The look of despair on his face was touching indeed. A great wave of pity swept the tender heart of Miss Grace.

"O, my dear, my dear!" she murmured as she knelt by his chair and stroked his trembling hands. "You must not give way like this. Try, O try hard not to give way! Don't you see that it could not all be accomplished at once? There must be time—a long time, perhaps, and the victory will be more complete. Do you realize just what this one single effort of ours has done? Tell him, uncle—tell him just how much ground we have covered."

All the while the two men talked, John Drew sat still—his eyes dilated, his breath coming and going quickly, but saying not a word. Any man of more rational mind would have rejoiced in the achievements of the day. Miss Grace and the others sought wildly for words of comfort, striving to show him the folly of giving up in despair, now that they had accomplished so much and the future looked so bright.

But John Drew made no response whatever to their cheering words. This alarming attitude of his made it evident that a physician was needed at once.

But there was no real healing for John Drew. His hurts had gone too deep. His passionate heart, ever secretly brooding on the grief he had borne, had caused his mind to weaken and to almost give way.

. . . .

All was still in the bedchamber at Hollyville where John Drew lay—faded, weary, and still. Weeks had passed; but with him their progress had been scarcely noticed. He had lived in a sort of semi-

118 WHO WAS RESPONSIBLE?

somnolence—a state of stupid, dull indifferentism as to what went on around him. A sort of dream-daze, wherein hazy recollections, dubious wonderments, vague speculations hovered to and fro without his clearly perceiving their drift or meaning. He was not in any pain—but was calm with the dreadful calmness of stupefaction and exhaustion. His once splendid body had worn to emaciation. His eyes were large and eloquent of calm despair, born of defeat.

Miss Grace rarely left his bedside, but sat waiting for what she knew must come soon. She wanted to be near when the soul of John Drew, the patient long-sufferer, should enter into that mysterious Beyond.

One evening—the last that John Drew spent on earth—Miss Grace sat quietly by the window in the invalid's room looking out over the landscape of barren fields and hills. The sun had sunk low in the west, its slanting rays streamed in the window under the half-lowered shade and reached across to the bed where the sick man lay. Miss Grace had not observed that it shone full on his face.

From the window one could always have a perfect view of the setting sun. Away in the distance, and rising above all the suburban housetops, there was a long range of hills. Many a time had Robert stood there watching the perfect disk of fire as it slipped slowly behind these hills out of sight.

All was quiet—and John Drew lay watching the sun's dazzling, blinding splendor as it sank lower and lower. The light did not seem to affect his eyes in the least, and there was a rapt expression on his face. Suddenly Miss Grace looked around and started up in reproach at her neglect—hastily reaching to pull down the shade and shut the offending sunlight from the sick man's eyes.

"Please do not!" John Drew's voice was strikingly clear and distinct in spite of his weakness. Miss Grace stood transfixed at the divine expression of his face as he watched with unblinking eyes the sun as it went down. Somehow she knew that John Drew was at last fulfilling his day and was passing away just as the sun was passing. The whole room was lit up with a holy radiance—not of earth, but of heaven—as the sun sank steadily, slowly, round and shining, without a single cloud in the horizon—beautiful as she had never seen it before. The air was so clear that she could note the very instant that it touched the horizon. Slowly it journeyed down to its setting, lower and lower still.

All of a sudden John Drew stretched out his arms and cried in a clear, triumphant voice: "Alice—Robert—Christ!"

Of the sun there remained a crescent, a line, a sparkle of light, then the sun was gone—and at that very moment John Drew entered into eternity.

The death of John Drew was a shock to Hollyville, and to New Gate especially. Everyone who resided in those two towns had become acquainted with his sad story. By some he was regarded as a crank: but others knew that he suffered a real grief.

The next day after his death the newspapers of Hollyville and of New Gate gave brief accounts of his career, and a detailed account of that part which related to the death of his son, and the effect of young Drew's death upon the father. The account in the New Gate paper told how the parent, crazed by grief after his son's death, visited Croggs's saloon with vengeance uppermost in his mind. But the saloonkeeper pleaded that he was not the guilty one. Pointing to his license, he maintained that if wrong had been done, those who commissioned him must be guilty. Drew then went to the city clerk, the city council, the State's legislature, and finally carried the matter before the national Congress—each of which disclaimed the responsibility: the city claiming that this matter should be referred to the State; the State, that it should be referred to the Federal Government, and Congress claimed that national prohibition would violate the doctrine of States' rights, that it is a matter which the States should settle themselves.

These conflicting contentions on the part of the lawmaking bodies, from the city council to the National Congress; the perpetual shifting of responsibility for the great alcoholic evil, together with his recent bereavement, wrought so heavily upon his failing strength that he succumbed beneath the burden, which was too heavy to bear. "Thus ended the life of one of the most respected citizens of Hollyville."

In the *Sentinel* of Hollyville there appeared the following editorial, under the caption of

"Who Is Responsible?"

"The *Sentinel* desires its readers to answer the above question—each for himself. We will state the facts in John Drew's case as they were presented to us:

"About thirty years ago there moved to Hollyville, from an adjoining county, a man and his wife. The woman was young, beautiful, and accomplished. The man was a descendant of one of the best and oldest families in the State. But through heredity and environment he was in great danger of becoming a drunkard. In order to avoid this, his wife induced him to move to this county, which, as you know, was the first county in the State to go dry by local option. These two made their home here in Hollyville and the man became engaged in the mercantile business, afterward becoming one of the most successful merchants of the town. This man was none other than John Drew, son of the well-known Colonel Hamilton Drew, of New Gate. In less than two years after their coming to Hollyville, the young wife died in giving birth to their first child—a boy. John Drew quite naturally bestowed all his affection upon his child. As this boy grew, the father was scrupulously careful about his training, seeing to it that he received not only the proper intellectual training, but the proper physical and moral instruction as well. In the careful training which the lad received the question of alcoholics was omitted altogether. The father had, as he thought, a good reason for this. The boy was heir to the inherited tendency to drunkenness; and the father, fearing to arouse the boy's curiosity—with a great amount of which he was especially endowed—he thought it best to omit the subject of alcoholics altogether. This may have been a sad error; but it was thought to be the best policy.

In this manner the son grew to young manhood

WHO WAS RESPONSIBLE?

with practically no knowledge concerning the great, impending evil. He finished his college course in Hollyville College a few months before he was twenty-one years old. He graduated with honors, and was not only the idol of his father's heart, but was the pride of all Hollyville.

"Shortly after he had finished his course in school, he accepted a position in New Gate, the former home of his father. Here, through a combination of circumstances, he learned to drink; and drink led to his death, for it was while under the influence of whisky that he was exposed to excessive cold weather, the result of which exposure caused him to contract a fatal illness which resulted in his death. The story of that young man's death is the saddest that has ever occurred in the history of Hollyville.

"The terrible idea of revenge—murder—took possession of the grief-crazed father, and led him to seek the man who sold his son the poison, and to make him pay for the deed with his own life.

"But when confronted by the irate father, the saloonkeeper lost no time in showing him the commission or license which he had obtained at the City Hall. 'The city clerk,' he pleaded, 'is the one who is responsible.'

"John Drew visited the city clerk, who in turn pleaded that he was only a servant of the city government. After hearing the city clerk's story, John Drew decided to give up the idea of revenge, and resolved to dedicate both his time and his fortune to the work of ridding the State entirely of this evil.

"His attention had been directed to the city coun-

WHO WAS RESPONSIBLE? 123

cil by the city clerk, but this body disclaimed all responsibility, and directed him to the State legislature.

"The State legislature said that the responsibility for the liquor traffic rested with the National Government. Then John Drew, with certain other sympathizers, took the matter before the United States Congress. But Congress claimed that prohibition is a matter which the States should settle.

"Then John Drew lost all hope. Disappointed, discouraged, unable to longer endure the strain, he died, leaving the whisky evil still in the country—the mystery still unraveled.

"There has always been a tendency for people to disclaim responsibility for public evils. Perhaps in countries where the government exists for the benefit of the royal families; where the expressed will of a king is the only law, everybody except the king himself can claim immunity from responsibility: but in a Republic like ours, where the government is of the people, for the people, and by the people, it is quite different.

"But it is not our purpose to accuse. We leave to our readers to say who is responsible for this liquor evil—who is responsible for that recent tragedy which wrecked the lives of that honest, industrious father and that beloved son.

"To be candid and just, although it is humiliating to do so, we must claim a part of the responsibility as our own. The *Sentinel* has always been an advocate of prohibition: but after saloons had been driven from Hollyville and Marshall County, we regarded our task as finished. In this we were mistaken. The press is largely responsible for the death of thousands of young men who fill drunkards' graves, and for a great deal of the ignorance, poverty, and suffering throughout this country—yes, we are responsible. Now, since God has given us light to see our duty, we pray him to give us strength to discharge it."

The above editorial, read by hundreds of people, had its effect. It was the aim of the editor to set the minds of his readers pondering the liquor situation, and in this he was successful.

The minister of St. Mark's Church, in Hollyville, and who was the pastor of the two deceased, read the editorial, and felt that a great measure of the responsibility rested upon him. Although he had often availed himself of the opportunity of denouncing the liquor evil from his pulpit, he knew that he had not done his whole duty. He had not done his very best in pledging the youth and populace of his own parish to do their utmost toward the elimination of alcohol from their own homes and the homes of their various friends.

When he thought of how he had neglected so glorious an opportunity, he felt ashamed—and with this there came a resolution to henceforth make his pulpit the freest forum from which his voice should constantly ring in denunciation of alcohol.

Doctor Morris, the family physician of the Drews, after reading the editorial, and after reviewing the pathetic actions of his half-demented patient during the last year of his life, found it impossible to sleep that night. Every time he closed his eyes, that

WHO WAS RESPONSIBLE ?

question, "Who is responsible?" would force itself upon him in such a tormenting and accusing way that he began to feel very like a fugitive from justice who is being sought to answer some serious charge. The fact is, Doctor Morris was being arraigned before the bar of his own conscience; and the indictment was: "Thou art responsible for the conditions which led to young Drew's death." So strong was the evidence in the form of what appeared to Doctor Morris as neglect of professional and official duties, that he was oppressed with a sense of guilt.

Doctor Morris had served as a city and county health officer, and was at this time a member of the State board of health. He was regarded as a very efficient officer—aggressive in the fight for better sanitary conditions, untiring in his efforts toward the eradication of preventable diseases. Upon the suggestion of the board of health the legislature had enacted laws seeking to protect the people from those diseases supposed to be caused by flies, rats, the bites of rabid animals, mosquitoes, etc. But not one word of warning against the diseases caused by alcohol had ever been issued by him or any other member of the board. Why should alcohol enjoy such immunity from the attack of the guardians of the State?

No one knew better than Doctor Morris of the different forms of mental and nervous diseases due to the use of alcohol. He was fully cognizant of the fact that the majority of the inmates of the insane hospital, almshouses, and sanitariums, suffering from the different mental and nervous psychoses, are primarily victims of alcohol.

"There is no doubt about it, Doctor Morris," he

said, addressing himself as he rose to a sitting posture in his bed, "you are in a large measure guilty, not only of the death of young Drew and many others, but you are equally responsible for the conditions in which the inmates of the insane asylum yonder is found—responsible, quite responsible," he repeated. "It is quite evident that I am guilty of a neglect of duty that I am not only under obligation to perform, but a duty for which I am being paid to perform. The task of ridding the State of the saloon is primarily the work of the medical profession." That night Doctor Morris got consolation only by making the resolution to bring the matter up at the next meeting of the board of health. He would induce the board to suggest a State-wide prohibition law as a health measure. He also decided to prepare a paper to be read before the next session of the State Medical Association on the subject, "INEBRIETY AS A DISEASE." He would perhaps be invited to read it also before the American Medical Association. "I will not rest," he said, "until not only my State but my country shall be free from alcoholism."

The next morning after the editorial appeared in the *Sentinel*, Mr. Douglas, secretary and executive officer of united charities of New Gate, on reaching his office, met a strange visitor—a man attired in the garb of a workman. He presented the aspect of an engineer, a fireman—or perhaps a blacksmith. It was evident that he had been and was even then suffering great mental anguish. Mr. Douglas thought that his visitor was a poor man, without employment —a man who had sickness or perhaps death in his family, and was there for the purpose of seeking aid.

WHO WAS RESPONSIBLE? 127

"What can I do for you?" asked Mr. Douglas.

"I want to ask a favor of you," was the visitor's reply.

"I know that," said Mr. Douglas somewhat impatiently; "but what do you want?"

"I want to leave $1,500 with you, which I want you to accept; and in the name of the trustees of this institution, the titles to two tenement houses on Fifth Street. The income from the rent of these houses, together with this $1,500, I want you to use for the relief of destitute families of drunkards, including orphans and widows of drunkards."

This stranger was none other than Croggs—the Croggs whom we formerly knew as the saloonkeeper. He was now employed in a blacksmith's shop. Croggs gave up his barroom business shortly after his experience with John Drew. Until then he had not thought very seriously on the comparative merits of the different professions or of the different forms of business. He had never studied political economy. He had been brought up in a saloon. His father had been a saloonkeeper, and at his father's death he of course came into possession of the business by inheritance.

Croggs heretofore had never stopped to think of where he would be listed in the catalogue of laborers —whether he would be classed as a productive or as a non-productive laborer. He had not considered whether it was right or wrong to conduct a saloon. It was not until after his interview with John Drew that he realized the fact that the wealth of the community was not increased by his labor, but, on the other hand, his business served to incapacitate real productive laborers. He could not remember ever having made anybody happy, but had spent his whole life spreading misery and wretchedness. At first Croggs tried to console himself by saying that society permitted the saloon—seemed to demand it—why should he care? But somehow Croggs never did become reconciled to his liquor dispensation again. He had, as I think most individuals have, an innate desire to be useful. Being now thoroughly convinced that he was engaged in a business which was worse than useless, he decided to sell out. This he did, and secured employment in a blacksmith's shop. Here he put forth every effort to master the trade. When he had made an inventory of his resources, Croggs found that he was worth $1,500 in cash, and had two tenement houses which would yield him an income of not less than thirty dollars a month. He first decided that he would put this away in reserve against a rainy day, but after reading the editorial, "Who Is Responsible?" in the Hollyville *Sentinel* and realizing the part which he had played in that tragedy—and in hundreds of others—he decided on another use for the little fortune which he had laid up for himself.

Said he: "Others may have been indirectly responsible for young Drew's death, but I am directly responsible. I sold him the poison which ended his life. I am responsible for hundreds of widows and thousands of fatherless children. My whisky and my beer have washed away a great deal more happiness than my little fortune can ever replace. But this is the very best that I can do toward righting the wrong that I have done."

WHO WAS RESPONSIBLE?

In this act was not Croggs bringing forth fruits meet for repentance? The true penitent is not only sorry for his wrongdoings. He resolves to turn away from them; nor does he stop there, but tries to correct as much as possible the wrong which he has committed.

Our sympathy goes out to Robert Drew and his father, to little Jean and his unhappy mother—all victims of one of America's institutions, the saloon; but how many are in sympathy with Croggs? Is he not also a victim of the same institution? No doubt, many men like Croggs, who have within them the possibilities which would have developed them into useful men, benefactors of mankind, ornaments to the human race, had not circumstances and environment forced them to become agents of destruction.

In her room at New Gate, Miss Grace King read the editorial with thought and feeling too deep for words. How vividly it brought back to her memories of the years now passed—memories of all that was lost to her; memories of their short struggle, and memories of that last day of John Drew's life.

Overwhelmed, she laid the paper aside, rose and walked over to the window. Resting her head against the casement, she looked out. The wonderful witchery of the solemn night wove its spell around her. Great, glittering stars clustered in the heavens. A crescent moon swung high in the eastern sky and threw a weird light along the marble palace next door, and down on the dark evergreen trees of her own garden—on the lilac bush, snow-powdered with splendid, fragrant bloom.

130 WHO WAS RESPONSIBLE?

In that wan, mysterious, and melancholy light New Gate was sleeping. Miss Grace's thoughts wandered down the little path to the cabin where she had gotten her first glimpse of lowly life. She wondered how the lonely inmates fared—if all was well with Jean and his beautiful, sad-eyed mother. Her heart beat in tenderest sympathy with those two victims of misfortune and bitter sorrow. She shuddered when she thought of all the two must have had to undergo since her visit to them. Thoughts of the poor, wretched father filled her with pity. Pitiful indeed was the story of that once good life now wrecked by alcohol. How numerous were the stories of others all over the city—all over the country, and would continue so long as that chief curtailer of human happiness was allowed to exist.

As Miss Grace looked out over the slumbering city her heart groaned. But her brave spirit was not one which brooded long in morbid fancies. With penetrating, clairvoyant vision she looked down the vista of coming years (let us hope the distance was not far) and saw the people of her beloved country come into national prohibition as their rightful heritage from the diligent sowing, the faithful prayers, the many sacrifices of the friends of the prohibition cause.

In this new condition she saw millions of young people coming out of schools and colleges, standing on the threshold of actual life, their high ideals and glorious visions unthreatened by alcohol's curse, their hearts full of hope and big with promise, in no danger of alcohol's fatal germ being spread throughout their whole natures, inoculating their ambitions

WHO WAS RESPONSIBLE? 131

with its vicious virus, causing the high moral standard to drop—warping and wrenching the whole nature out of its legitimate orbit. The mind of the young would be left free to develop in its natural manner; eyes unblurred by poison, left free to discover opportunities everywhere; ears of sympathy would be attuned to the cries of those who are perishing for the want of assistance; open hearts, which would not want for worthy objects upon which to bestow their gifts; willing hands, which would never lack for noble work to do.

She saw the hands of progress touch the villages, the towns, the cities—the whole country; for all those places formerly occupied by saloons would be displaced by business of worthy character. Under the new condition she saw her country waxing bounteous in wealth—gloriously bountiful in its production of efficient manhood and perfect womanhood.

To consecrate her life to the work which should bring about a realization of this mental vision seemed to Miss Grace at that moment a mission far grander than the conquest of empires, and infinitely more to be desired than the crown and heritage of Solomon.

The night wore on while she planned her work for the coming years. While her brain was at work, she walked back and forth with slow, uncertain steps, like one who, peering at distant objects, sees nothing close at hand. Her beautiful face was pale and fixed —not flushed with the gush of enthusiasm, like the jets of a violent flame, but calm and fixed and full of thought—thought that was a crystallized and consecrated purpose.

WHO WAS RESPONSIBLE?

At last, when the feeble light of the sinking moon admonished her that the night was growing old, she stopped again to look out over the slumbering city—her heart no longer light, careless, and free, but burdened with grave responsibility.

Miss Grace knew deep down in her heart that the disreputable rum-hole or saloon in the cheaper districts of the city is not the chief place which is responsible for the creation of the "drunken sot"; but it is at the so-called respectable bar, the fashionable rooms at these big hotels, the cafés at men's clubs, the harmless beverages always served at social gatherings in the homes of respectable people—these are the places that are really responsible for the wrecks that are "drunken sots." They invariably get the beginning of their downfall at one or all of these high places before, in the end, they are seen frequenting the low saloons.

The history of nearly every drunkard may be traced back to the first glass in one or the other of these places. Few men ever become habitual drunkards by being induced to take their first drink at a saloon. The first step is taken perhaps in the home, where only a harmless glass of wine is served; or the iniquitous cocktail at the club or café, or in the fashionable bar. The truth, that in these high places is where the big evil lies, forced itself upon Miss Grace.

"Ah!" she said in mournful tones of deep regret, "the greatest responsibility rests upon society. The civilization which begot this evil must destroy it or else be forever branded with the scarlet letter of its own crime."

WHO WAS RESPONSIBLE? 133

Being firmly convinced of this, she saw clearly the long, stony path in which she must henceforth choose to labor.

While she stood there her lips moved in prayer: "Be pleased, O God, to make me a fit instrument for thy work; sanctify my heart; quicken and enlighten my mind; let me be endowed with patience, perseverance, and unwavering faith; of all things, let me labor with an eye single to thy glory. Let me not labor for any worldly applause, but for the sole purpose of bringing about righteousness upon this earth. O, my Father, crown my efforts with success in thine own good time—thou knowest best."

The still, solemn splendor of the night spoke to her soul; and out from the depth of the starlit sky there seemed to come a sacred voice which soothed her anxious spirit: "Let not your heart be troubled, neither let it be afraid."

Calm and hopeful now, Miss Grace retired to her rest. Nothing broke the sweet repose which settled upon her quiet spirit. She slept on until out of the whitening east the new day rose, radiant in bridal garments, wearing a single gleaming star upon its pearly brow. Then the sky flushed and the hilltops glowed, and the abundant sunshine streamed over the world once more—streamed over the world in glorious promise of a new fulfillment.

The first rays flashed into Miss Grace's room, falling warm and bright upon her closed eyelids, kissing them to wakefulness and the golden radiance of a new day.

CHAPTER IX

ON a beautiful day in July, several years after the death of John Drew, Miss Grace King stood on deck of a great liner which plowed her way up the English channel. For many weeks she had been on a tour about the country. Feeling that a recluse life would give her only partial glimpses of that part of humanity whom she wished to help, she had decided to spend several months in travel, for the special purpose of making a study of peasant life. Her chief purpose in doing this was to gain a thorough knowledge concerning the effects of alcoholism upon the peasants. Having done extensive travel about the United States, she was now about to spend a few weeks in Europe for the same purpose.

As the great liner plowed her way up that historic strip of water toward the Hook of Holland, Miss Grace was struck with the extraordinary spectacle presented to her eyes. The channel was crowded with vessels, ranging from the tiniest submarine to the most ponderous dreadnought. In the narrowest part of the strait, between Calais and Dover, there lay a long line of torpedo boats, gunboats, light cruisers, and destroyers. Unanchored, they extended an unbroken front, like a regiment of cavalry. It was the British fleet, the main line of defense and offense of the empire. As the liner made her way through those floating forts of steel, those who stood on her deck saw in that display only a pageant of peace. The warm sun shone in splendor upon the

WHO WAS RESPONSIBLE?

spectacle, and the sea slipped past the great liner with a swish of molten gold, while the sky overhead was blue with a hue which can hardly be described.

It was the birthday of King George of England, and the main feature of the celebration was the mobilization and review of the British fleet, the pride of the nation.

It was a spectacle which caught and held the eyes of all the voyagers; but none of those who watched that peaceful scene suspected or even dreamed that in the background of this beautiful picture of pomp and splendor there already lurked the grim brute-visage of war—immediate war, which would involve all Europe and eventually the whole world.

A few days later, at The Hague, wherein is situated the Temple of Peace, while she with other tourists wandered through that magnificent structure of international harmony which the munificence of an American millionaire has given to the world, they had no dreams that at that very moment the ambition of an imperial nation was operating to plunge the world into the most hideous war that has ever been known to civilization.

However, those happy holiday makers were not destined to remain long in ignorance, for not many days passed before they caught rumors of war and were warned to return to America immediately.

August 1st, a few days after Miss Grace's arrival at New Gate, marked the beginning of the world's struggle, when Germany declared war upon Russia. The reader knows that for a period of five months the world looked in wonder upon that nation's almost uninterrupted success; and looked in horror upon that period of France's greatest peril, and Belgium's supreme agony. We know also that, so far as America's relation in the struggle was concerned, it looked at first upon the European nations' strife with somewhat indifferent eyes; but as the struggle progressed, America began to watch with increasing abhorrence and amazement those methods of war employed by the imperial German government—methods which gave evidence more and more of that government's character and aim.

Soon the time came when American citizens, sailing on American ships, under American flags, were slain by German submarines in absolute and vicious disregard of a nation's rights. Then indeed did America awake to the appalling fact that not only was the freedom of the European nations menaced, but the rights, the liberty of every democratic nation was imperiled by the purpose of these people to rule the world.

We know further that at last America, thoroughly aroused from its dream of peace, becoming fully awake to the dangers which threatened all those sacred ideals for which democracy stands, arose in splendid determination that absolutism must go down in defeat.

So great a national cause naturally evoked the patriotic service of every true American. For a short period the prohibition cause became somewhat obscure before the more vital questions which agitated the country. All America became absorbed in the one great task of winning the war for humanity.

Opportunity for patriotic service rapped upon all doors, from the richest to the poorest. It fell to the

WHO WAS RESPONSIBLE? 137

lot of some to make munitions; others, to run ships and railroads; others, to work in the mines and in the forests; others, to plant, cultivate, and harvest, and still others, to fight on land and sea.

Miss Grace King, being a true daughter of America, at once began to take inventory of herself to see what service she could offer that would prove most beneficial to her country.

The most important thing in life is bread, the primeval struggle being always to appease hunger. To the American housewife was consigned the great business of economy. On this one task of the American woman seemed to hang the fate of humanity. Knowing this fact, the housewives arose as a single unit in the great task of conserving the nation's food.

Miss Grace, regarding food conservation as the woman's vital problem, at once formed the determination to do her utmost along that line. Having made up her mind as to the work she intended to do, she plunged into it with religious enthusiasm. After first offering her services to the Woman's Committee, Counsel of Defense, she began to take infinite care in acquainting herself with every possible means of conserving food. She organized a Woman's Home Committee at New Gate, canning clubs and various other clubs of patriotic origin, and began work in real earnest.

The women of New Gate, witnessing the patriotic zeal of Miss Grace, were determined not to be outdone by her; therefore it was not long before every woman in the city, of whatever station, became enamored with the idea of "doing her bit." The season of play and lightsome mood was over for the woman force at New Gate; the time for sterner thought and vital action had come. Even those most prosperous ones, who had all their lives basked in their conditions of ease, selfishness, and self-complacency, became patriotic to the point of self-denial and personal sacrifice.

During those times New Gate underwent a sort of transformation. The influence of the women's committees penetrated every home, and the spirit, finally taken up by adjoining cities and towns, soon became spread over a vast territory in the South.

In this strenuous time of worldwide strife and turmoil, it seems that the only institution in America which remained deaf to all appeals of patriotism, and which continued to ally with the enemies against those subjects vitally related to the successful prosecuting of the nation's war, was the selfish, unscrupulous liquor traffic. This fact caught the attention of Miss Grace and stirred all her dormant hatred against this curse of the American people. She observed with jealous hatred the continued work of this ruthless industry, took strict notice of the vast amount of the nation's much needed food which it consumed.

"Uncle," she remarked to her kinsman one day, "the desire to continue the fight for national prohibition has been woven into the very warp and woof of my life. I am drawn to it by the irresistible force of my everlasting hatred against alcohol."

She was standing by the window, looking out over the smoking factories, past the thick masses of buildings, over and beyond the restless surge and grind of the city's traffic, to the lovely hills and woods, where nestled the tiny hut of her friends, Jean and his beautiful, sad-eyed mother. She was silent, thinking of the little family, and of her own blighted hopes. Her fond uncle looked up at her and was moved with compassion. The girl seemed to radiate a new beauty. As he looked at her he thought he had never seen a more perfect profile, nor a countenance that expressed such a beautiful blending of wistful longing, of patient fortitude, and saintly resignation. Hers was the face of a madonna after the crucifixion—pathetic in its lonely sorrow, but inspiring in its spiritual strength and holy in its purity and depth of character. Her beauty was of the kind which is revealed only in the faces of those who have been fortunate enough to have experienced the one grand passion to the utmost bounds of the human capacity—all its exquisite joy, all its exquisite pain, all its tenderness, all its cruelties, all its high idealism, all its broken hopes. This young woman, in that one brief period of her awakened love, from the time that she had opened her eyes that first dazzling instant and the spirit of unbridled, irresistible youth had burned brightly and had completely captivated young Drew, had felt love's keenest delight, its most stinging pain; had sounded its profoundest depths, and found it of a quality that is as sublime as it is human.

Her uncle knew that this great love had proved a blessing to her, for it had been the means of transforming his beloved kinswoman into the being who stood before him now—a woman of broadest sympathies and great kindness of heart. How he wished her mother, his only sister, might have been like her!

140 WHO WAS RESPONSIBLE?

Turning her glorious eyes, brimful of hidden purpose, upon him, she said: "Uncle, the Government tells us, and rightly, that saving is a patriotic duty. During these strenuous times every living thing in the United States is feeling the pressure of economy. Increased taxation, the high price of food and clothing, the need of aiding America's soldiers in their self-sacrifice, the complete disarrangement of ordinary industrial and commercial conditions, have made rigid economy necessary. But bearing this yoke of economy gives a sort of pleasure, because we feel that we are doing it for the grand purpose of making all the people and all the resources of the country supremely effective in this fight for humanity. The Federal Department of Agriculture is urging the increase of food production. The United States Food Commissioner is busily engaged in its effort to conserve and control the consumption of food. The food that America saves will go far toward winning the war. The American housewives realize this and are everywhere striving to steer their domestic crafts to the port of wartime economy. In response to the Federal Department of Agriculture, the farmers all over the country are making special efforts to produce full crops from every acre under tillage in the United States. War gardens are being planted, canning clubs organized—all for the purpose of taking care of the nation's food. But there is no doubt that with all our efforts to economize, the food situation, as the months shall advance, is going to become most critical. Proper economy makes it our duty to cut out every expenditure that does not definitely contribute toward American efficiency.

WHO WAS RESPONSIBLE? 141

But while all this patriotic response to the request of the authorities is going on, does it seem just and fair that our Federal Government should allow any traffic to exist which persists in manufacturing the nation's much needed food into a poison which robs the country of its efficient manhood and patriotic womanhood, and which continues to strike bread from the lips of our men, women, and children?

"I have been making a special effort to estimate the amount of food which this ruthless traffic is consuming while we are struggling along with our great problem of economy. Of the principal grain crops of the United States, barley, wheat, rye, corn, and oats, it is estimated that the liquor traffic uses annually 2.25 per cent: the grain destroyed by being converted into liquor, if conserved, will save 11,000,000 loaves of bread a day. The brewing of beer alone destroys from fifty to sixty million bushels of grain—and the farmers are urged to produce more grain!"

"There is no doubt about it, Grace, my daughter," said her uncle; "the loss of the liquor industry would mean a tremendous gain in foodstuffs. The prohibitionists are not blind to the fact of this great waste, and are already urging the adoption of national prohibition as a war measure."

"If national prohibition is adopted now, it will be adopted as a war measure exclusively, I suppose," said Miss Grace, thoughtfully.

"No doubt this will be the case," said her uncle. "The Anti-Saloon League deems it unwise to press any further prohibition proposal that might delay the passage of any other important issues. They believe that the operation of emergency war prohibition will so prepare the public for permanent prohibition that the amendment will easily become operative. And Grace, dear, I think this is a wise step—no doubt, the best step, because, on account of the inevitable strain upon the Government, the attempts of the prohibitionists to force the adoption of permanent prohibition at present would not be good political strategy or statesmanship."

After a long silence, Miss Grace spoke again: "Uncle, I'm wondering what can be done to focus the attention of our Federal Government upon the fact that in this huge, unparalleled job of winning the war, this agent of destruction to both physical and moral forces ought no longer be tolerated; that it is the height of folly to continue to maintain under its protection this oppressive trade, this greatest enemy to America. I wonder what I, a lone woman, can do. If I were only a man!"

"Grace, dear, whatever a woman of your character wishes to do for the welfare of a community or a nation, if she does it with the zeal and religious enthusiasm which you have manifested in all that you have already done, will be far-reaching in its influence. I believe you have the will and the courage to do all that is within your power. Continue to do as you have always done, and ask God to bless every effort you may put forth."

One evening Miss Grace walked back and forth in her elegant library, her thought concentrated upon a manuscript which she was preparing. The room lent its charm to her queenly figure as she moved amid its efficient spaciousness like a goddess within

WHO WAS RESPONSIBLE? 143

her habitual temple. There came a timid knock at her door, and she opened it to find Jean of the cabin standing there.

Miss Grace could not avoid remarking the ashen pallor and troubled expression of the boy's face. "What is the matter, child? You look as if you are either ill or dreadfully fatigued. How is the dear mother?" she asked, drawing the boy to a chair and looking anxiously into his wistful face, while she tenderly stroked back the glossy hair from his high forehead. This youth had become very dear to her, like a young brother. Jean's lips trembled, and Miss Grace waited

"My poor father is dead," he said simply, and a great tear stood in each eye. Miss Grace's tender heart was deeply moved. She kissed the boy, whose soft eyes held much misery. Suddenly she left his side and for a long time stood looking out the library window. The sun was just going down behind a fleecy cloud-mountain: great rays of scarlet shot up from its silver rim, while lurid beams of light streamed down toward the horizon. Vacantly her eyes rested on this glorious picture, but its splendor passed away unheeded, for she was looking far beyond the western gates of day and seeing a ghastly, distorted face turned up toward heaven—a coffined corpse ready for its last resting place of dishonor and shame. A slight movement of the bereaved lad roused her and she turned to him again. There was an inner light from her soul shining in her eyes, a look tender, loving, and kind in their clear depths as she drew the boy's head against her breast.

Suddenly she thought of the poor mother alone

144 WHO WAS RESPONSIBLE?

with all her deep misery, and bade the boy come with her at once to their little hut. So they hastened to her, whose proud head was bowed almost to the earth under the weight of its grief, loneliness, and shame. The man had met his death in a tragic, dishonorable way, and the poor, proud wife, thus so sorrowfully humiliated, oppressed with an intolerable sense of desolation and isolation, had sat all day, her aching head pressed close against the window— silent and awed by the terrible loneliness which surrounded her. All through the long hours of the day she had sat there unmoved, like a statue. Interminable seemed the dreary day to her son, who, unable to longer bear the sight of his mother's stony grief, stole away to find his beloved Miss Grace.

The day finally drew to a close and still the poor woman sat there until the red light of day died in the west, and until a young moon hung her crescent among the treetops and the stars flashed out thick and fast. Softly the door opened and Miss Grace and Jean entered.

The young woman drew the bowed head of the older woman to her breast, letting it rest there while she strove to soothe the troubled heart with words of love and comfort. She felt strangely drawn to this mother and child. Out of her own heart there seemed to issue an electric chain of sympathy.

Outside, God's changeless stars looked down upon that lonely cabin where alcohol's cruel hand had added one more crime to its enormous list; one more example of manhood destroyed, another character debauched, the wreck of love and happiness to another one of America's homes. A deep stillness reigned, broken only by the stifled sobbing of the child. The crescent moon swung low over the treetops and threw a weird light down on the cabin with its dead and bereaved ones. Presently through that wan, mysterious, and melancholy light a bell sounded from a distant section of the city.

Gradually Miss Grace's troubled spirit revived and the light of reason pointed further along the stony path before her. Mechanically her hands caressed the bowed head upon her breast, while her countenance became eloquent with determination and with humble gratitude to God for giving her wisdom to choose that path, with grace and courage and strength to pursue it.

"O, my Father!" she whispered, "bless the work which thy servant is doing. Endow me with wisdom and strength to do whatever I can to help lead the way to my country's future peace and happiness."

A few days after the quiet funeral of Jean's father, Miss Grace set out to her uncle's home on a mission of love. It was one of those rare afternoons in September when summer, conscious that her reign is ended, with a final exultant effort brings together all her gorgeous colors and decks the world in regal pomp and short-lived splendor. The shade trees all along the streets stood thus splendidly arrayed, while a strong, steady southern breeze caught the leaves which had fallen and whirled them here and there in a mad, merry dance. Hosts of gay children tripped merrily home from school, and it was a delightful picture to see them darting here and there in pursuit of some scarlet pinnated beauty which, bewitched with an elfin spirit of wickedness, whirled away at the very moment when the dimpled fingers thought them secure and fast. As Miss Grace hurried along, the sight of the ruddy-faced boys and girls heightened her determination to be successful in her mission, for it pertained to the future welfare of her little friend. Success in what she had undertaken meant an opportunity for his development and education, at the same time protection from future misfortune. The boy should have a chance to rise above the humiliating station in which society's curse had placed him —a chance to climb up beyond the reach of that subtle menace which threatened to destroy him. A divine smile lit up the young woman's face in the satisfaction of knowing that she was adding another effort to her list of trying to help the struggling poor to better environment, and in so doing repairing her own wrongs to society during that period of her reckless, thoughtless girlhood. O, what a blessed thing it is to feel that you are doing some good in the world: how dim in contrast does the light of sinful pleasure shine to the divine light of usefulness —helping somebody to find life and opportunities in which to grow to perfection!

She found her uncle alone. With a smile of welcome he came to greet her, who, ever since the death of his only son, followed shortly after by the death of his beloved wife, had been the only means of bringing sunshine into his lonely home. He had always loved this daughter of his only sister with a fatherly devotion. From the time that she could toddle she had been a favorite in his home. The dear wife, having no daughter of her own, had lavished a motherly affection upon this child, who often seemed to prefer their home to her own. And the son of theirs, who through the influence of alcohol had wrung their hearts with grief and bitter disappointment, had been her playfellow all through her childhood and girlhood. After the uncle was deprived of both his nearest and dearest, he naturally turned to Grace for sunshine, love, and comfort.

"How is my daughter getting on with her work?" he asked, smiling genially upon her.

"O, famously, uncle. But there is another very important matter which brings me here to-day—a request which I want you to grant me, uncle." She paused, assuming an air of gravity, while her uncle waited expectantly with the air of a doting father who is ever ready to listen to the request of an idolized son—a request which, even before the asking, the father knows he is going to grant.

"Uncle, suppose the opportunity should come to you to take as a protégé a boy of great promise, of rare intellectual ability—but who is a child of very unfortunate circumstances. Would you do it?"

"Well, that depends, my dear. I shouldn't like to become responsible for the future of a child of a criminal or a drunkard. If the child is the offspring of clean, honest, but poor parents, I shouldn't hesitate to take the responsibility, but—"

"Suppose, uncle, the boy's father is a victim of drink—a misfortune which may be acquired, you know, through a combination of circumstances of which the poor victim may not be altogether to blame. What then?"

Since her uncle vouchsafed no answer, she continued: "I have never told you about a lad—a family whom I learned to know a few years ago, just after the sad incident at Hollyville, uncle. Since then I've watched this boy, to see his fine nature struggling through the most pitiable conditions in its attempt to come into its rightful heritage of beautiful, efficient young manhood. I have rendered him all the assistance I could without wounding their pride. His mother would accept no further aid than that of providing books for the boy's education. Not that she is a woman who is inculcated with antipathetical ideas regarding people of wealth and high social standing, but she is just one of those women who is too proud to beg and too independent to complain or lament. She is a very remarkable woman, uncle—one of those rare creatures one often discovers here and there among the extremely poor, a woman who naturally carries herself with an air of conscious self-respect which her shabby dress cannot hide, nor a robe of silk could not enhance."

"And the father?"

"The father? O, uncle, another one of those debauched characters, a most wretched victim of alcohol, a poor, wretched fellow who, under the influence of that diabolical curse, has dragged into the very dust the name of—Jean Richter."

"Jean Richter! Grace, my daughter, what is this you are asking of me? What! Take Jean Richter's son under my roof as my protégé? The very idea is preposterous!"

WHO WAS RESPONSIBLE? 149

Mr. Anderson arose and began pacing the floor. He knew that this strange request of his niece's was no idle one. But believing that the young woman's great love for humanity and sympathy for the unfortunate and suffering ones had prompted her in this charitable idea, he felt that he must be gentle with her. His restless agitation did not arise from mental debate as to whether he would grant her request, because it never occurred to him to grant it. But his mind was puzzled as to a best method of refusal without hurting her. He was convinced that observation of the misery of these people and the hope that she might be instrumental in relieving it had determined her course.

Presently he stopped in front of the fireplace and leaned his great form against the mantel. The blood throbbed in Miss Grace's heart while she sat waiting.

Instantly the answer had sprung to Mr. Anderson's lips, but he had checked it in order to acquaint her with its negative in the gentlest manner. If she had been anybody else, he would have brought down his fist upon the table with a most emphatic "No!"

At last he came and sat beside her while he said: "Grace, dearest, do not ask me to do that which my reason will not permit. I have seen many phases of human nature, and watched the development of many characters, and have found that the law of heredity is strong—sure. Think of what I have already suffered from the hand of this terrible evil. Grace, this is asking too much of me. The fatal outcome for the boy is inevitable on account of the law of heredity. If my own son with his honest parentage did not escape, what can I hope for this boy, born with the fatal thirst woven into the very warp and woof of his life? Suppose I should learn to love him, as undoubtedly I would if he is the rare character you say he is. Another disappointment would kill me. You don't wish me to undergo such another ordeal as the first. Grace, my dear, nothing could save the boy from a drunkard's ruin. Experience has taught me that the fate of the inebriate is hopeless. In spite of what this boy's mother is, think what his father was—think, Grace!"

"But, uncle," the young woman pleaded, "I'll admit that Richter was a man of the very lowest type; but was he always so? His wife tells me that he was from one of the best families. He became what he was after Jean was born. Can you hold him exactly responsible for the deeds done under the influence of alcohol? The thing for which I hold him responsible is for allowing himself to take those first drinks, which he knew would perpetuate into debauchery and crime. He ought to be held responsible for his first yielding to temptation, especially if he was wise concerning alcohol's evil effects. He merits punishment for deliberately surrendering his will and intelligence to the drink habit, thus accepting the chance to commit grave crimes. But in the end his own responsibility, as with all drunkards, vanishes and he became a victim of license issued under the sanction of a supreme government.

"I believe that this boy, given the proper environment, will develop into splendid manhood, of which the nation will one day be proud. He certainly shows marked evidence of his blessed faculties: whether they are of maternal or paternal origin, we are not able to say, nor should it matter. The fact that he possesses them is sufficient. I am sure, uncle, that here, within the pure atmosphere of your home, you will witness the perfect unfolding of this boy's great abilities into usefulness and power, as the sun unfolds into beauty and fragrance the tender petals of a flower."

Mr. Anderson was not unmoved by the young woman's pleading, nor insensible to her logic.

"But, Grace, darling, think of that other life no less promising perhaps—I do not say this to wound you," he said, quickly observing the look of pain which passed over her face—"but I mention it as a sort of reminder, you know. The chances of escape for children born under the best environment are little enough; what could you hope for this child, born with the inherited tendency toward inebriety?"

"Uncle, I do not believe that the appetite for liquor is inherited. This, I know, is contrary to the general belief. I do believe that there is inherited a predisposition to such weakness, so that if the child of drunken parents gains access to alcohol, the appetite is much more rapidly developed than would be with the child of abstaining parents. I verily believe that if the child with the bad heritage abstains absolutely, he will never crave liquor. I do not believe that the appetite for liquor is a natural demand. Naturally the physical being rebels against the first drink of any alcoholic beverages. I have seen (and I blush with shame to say it) green youths sicken with the first drink, many of whom could be traced to drunken parentage. O uncle! I know to my great shame that it is through the social instinct, through very natural and healthy impulses, that an appetite is engendered, which in turn pays such dividends of ruin to its victim. It makes me shudder to think of how much responsibility lies at my own door for having lured young and innocent men on to the formation of this most disgraceful habit. It is a sin for which I shall give the service of all the rest of my life in atonement. With most young men the habit of drinking liquor originates in social pressure, and the habit is the result of persistent social temptation. Of course, after the habit has once been acquired it is exceedingly probable that the drunkard will continue the practice in order to satisfy the appetite. Once the habit takes possession, alcohol becomes the master and man becomes the slave. After all, the great question, 'Who Is Responsible?' is not a hard one to answer. The false friends of society who bombard the tender youth with alcoholic drinks could answer the question if they would; the wily barkeeper, who picks the pockets of the poor, robs men of their money and honor, who ruthlessly commits crime against the man, the home, the church, the State, and the country, could answer the question. The members of our Federal Government who refuse to enact a law against drunkenness, and allow alcohol to continue to dispense its evil effects throughout the entire population, could answer the question. This boy's father was no more born a drunkard than you or I. His wife tells me that he was once an honest, respectable gentleman. I feel a deep conviction that if we can rescue this boy from the curse of this sin which threatens his life, we will be rendering our country a service which will be long remembered. The effort is certainly worth while, uncle, and you will agree with me when you learn to know the lad. Give him a trial for my sake, dearest uncle. I will be responsible for his conduct. If he shows the slightest tendency to deteriorate morally, I'll see to it that he is speedily removed from your home."

"Grace, I may seem to be hard—brutal, but I fear that I must be obstinate in this. I couldn't have Richter's boy here! Think of all his being in my home would involve—a host of low kinfolks hanging around—"

"There are no kinfolks but his mother, uncle, and you need fear nothing from that proud, reserved woman."

"You don't know, Grace, what these people of her class will do if you give them a chance. You had better keep them at a greater distance yourself. A certain kind of charity work among them, such as donating funds for the improvement of their school facilities, or for community improvement would be all right; but actually taking them up with all their rags and filth and dirt into your very arms is quite another matter. I'll give these people money—no, I can't think of having Richter's son here!"

Raising her face, Miss Grace looked steadfastly at her uncle, and pain, compassion, dread, and misery filled her soft eyes. The stout heart melted. He had never refused her anything; and she had never asked for anything unreasonable. It seemed that she had never desired anything half so much as that he should befriend Richter's son. Her heart was set upon succoring this child, and he knew it would be no easy matter to dissuade her from her purpose. Her tremulous, compassionate face showed how very earnest was her wish; and should he refuse to grant it, she would resort to some other means.

Without another word, Miss Grace arose, drew on her gloves, and started toward the door.

Unable to bear the sight of her disappointment and grief, her uncle laid a detaining hand upon her shoulder, saying: "Very well, Grace, I will let you persuade me in this, though it is against my better judgment. Remember, you have asked me to do a difficult thing. Everybody around here knows Jean Richter, and his son's lot is going to be a hard one. I wonder if you are doing the best thing for the boy, after all."

"I have thought of how hard it would be for him at school, therefore I think best to provide for his private education," said Miss Grace.

"Very well. I think this would be the best for all concerned. I'll give the lad employment here in the office, and the salary which I pay him will help support his mother. If the boy proves worthy—well, the future will tell."

"O uncle!" said the grateful Miss Grace, "I can never love you enough for doing this for my little friend. I am sure that you will never regret doing this for him."

"I am doing this for your sake, Grace; but you must bear in mind that life is a long series of disappointments. The failure to meet with your own ideals both in private affairs and in the affairs of the nation is sore disappointment. But such things are inevitable; you must make up your mind to them."

CHAPTER X

ALL was very quiet in the little cabin under the hills. Early dusk and twilight dimly revealed two figures huddled close and silent by the low window. They had been sitting there for hours—the mother holding the form of her darling boy close up against her heart as if she feared that death's cruel hand might tear him from her side. Now and then her body quivered as if in pain. Perhaps she was thinking of the long, weary years of sorrow which stretched out before them—years of crucial suffering and perhaps unfilled hopes. How to support herself and boy was a problem which she must face. Drink had swallowed up almost their last penny. To secure employment that would pay enough to support them both and provide for Jean's education would be almost impossible. It seemed that her husband's dishonesty and crime had blocked every avenue. Jean, suddenly peering up through the semi-darkness into his mother's face, thought he saw tears in her eyes. Very sadly he watched the sweet, sad face with its light of love and devotion; and with his desire to see her happy, free from care, and in perfect safety; with his manly longing to shield her from danger and suffering, his heart was made to feel an anxiety far beyond his years. Presently he laid a timid hand upon her cheek and said, "It is such a blessed thing to love, isn't it, mother?"

A fierce, almost jealous love clutched at the mother's heart.

WHO WAS RESPONSIBLE?

"I am glad, mother, that I'm big enough to work for you. I shall go over to New Gate and find employment at once—to-morrow."

Mrs. Richter shuddered involuntarily. Life had brought some fair things for her boy in the last few years, in spite of the terror which had constantly hung over them. She had managed in some way to keep things as cheerful as possible, taking infinite care in teaching him to find beauty and sunshine in life in spite of the gloom which overshadowed them. The woods, the fields, the hills, ever abounding in nature's wealth of treasures and pleasures, had been the means of keeping this mother and child above the life of utter despair. Then, at the very time he needed it most, God had sent Jean a new friend, Miss Grace King, from the city. The beautiful friendship between these two had broadened and deepened until the mother had at last consented to allow the young woman to provide books which the hungry soul of her boy needed so. No further aid would she accept, jealously guarding as her own the task of feeding and clothing his precious growing young body.

But now—accepting any aid, or any notice even, from the beautiful young woman, after everything happening as it did, seemed imposition and ingratitude. If she only had somewhere else to go in order to begin again, perhaps her lot would be easier.

"I am sure there is somebody over at New Gate who wants a boy," Jean went on. "We shall not need much—just you and I, mother—you know—now. And we can save so much—now. We won't have to leave here, shall we, mother?" There was

WHO WAS RESPONSIBLE? 157

a sort of pleading in his voice which the mother-heart understood. In spite of his father's cruelty and drinking, the boy's life here had been his happiest. He was by nature a child with the homing instinct. To him this little hut was home and he loved it passionately. The mother understood her boy's longing for the hills, the woods, the little spring with the tangled tapestry around it, the friendly squirrels which frisked and leaped among the boughs above his head, the rabbits hopping unafraid in the tall, cool grass and fallen leaves, the gossiping birds, and all the other forms of animal life; his deep longing for mother earth and country life—the life that gives vitality, stamina, courage, and all those other qualities which make for happy boyhood. There was nothing about her boy that this mother did not understand. Suddenly the firm resolve that he should have his wish took possession of her. All at once she was able to glory in the fact that she was to give him at least his soul's desire to remain in the country, in the midst of mother nature's perpetual miracle, where he could not open his eyes without seeing a more magnificent picture than Raphael or Michael Angelo could have created in a lifetime—pictures not only beautiful but perfect, breathing, and throbbing with life.

In this the mother-heart was wise, for during those few years there in the country he had already acquired a rich amount of that superior stamina and mental caliber that makes the stuff which rises to the top in all vocations of life. He already possessed a peculiar quality of superiority which would later be a powerful factor in the shaping of a nation's destiny perhaps. There was within him a sufficient hunger for knowledge that would stimulate him to self-education. He was ever athirst for learning, having a peculiar yearning to know the history of men and women who had made a nation, to know the history of his country, and above all, he had that all-absorbent ambition to be somebody in the world. At that moment the heart of this mother, coming into full realization of the bigness of her charge, arose out of her condition of perplexity and doubt, and stood ready to take up her burden.

She began by first setting the house in order—making those thousand little touches of taste that were needed to drive the darkness out of the corners and the stiffness and gloom out of the house. She cleaned and polished the dim lamp, cooked a simple and appetizing supper, and sat down with her boy to a table spread with a snow-white linen cloth.

Jean, with a peculiar understanding of his mother's sudden show of bravery, looked at her across the table with eyes which worshiped, eloquent with promise of fulfillment.

They chatted pleasantly over their frugal meal until a knock on the door caused a look of fright to leap into Mrs. Richter's eyes. Instantly both mother and son leaped to their feet.

Again the knock.

Jean started forward, but the mother sprang ahead of him, and instinctively putting herself in front of her child, she opened the door.

"Miss Grace!" Jean sprang forward, his young face beaming his pleasure while with due courtesy he greeted his beloved lady.

"Come in, uncle!" called out Miss Grace to the waiting gentleman outside. The light faded from the faces of both mother and son when they saw Lawyer Anderson. A vague fear filled Mrs. Richter's breast, while complete wonder overwhelmed the child.

"Mrs. Richter, this is my uncle, Lawyer Anderson."

With her characteristic regal dignity, Mrs. Richter greeted Lawyer Anderson, never for a moment losing sight of the fact that the gentleman's keen eyes were in constant scrutiny of her young son.

One glance at the youth, whose magnetic personality was intangible, had sent a peculiar thrill through the man's heart, causing him to experience a sense of relief, as if a great weight which pressed upon him had been suddenly removed. Miss Grace's perceptive genius quickly understood the apprehension in the mother's eyes, so, very tactfully, she made known to her the object of their visit. Lawyer Anderson also explained to her the kind of work he would give her son, for which he promised to pay a liberal salary, to be increased as the boy's efficiency should merit such. He also made known his intention of providing for Jean's private education. Gradually the mother's fear and timidity vanished and she was able to converse with ease and confidence, while her heart swelled with gratitude to these two good people whom God had sent in the very hour of her sorest need. The fact that she would have her boy with her during those hours when he would not be at work was very pleasing to her.

Miss Grace, with her wonderful understanding of human nature, did not think of urging removal from their quiet cabin home, but was already laying secret plans to help this noble woman to make this humble spot a home—a sanctuary of love, filled with that subtle and powerful spirit which affords inspiration to the heart, comfort and contentment to the restless spirit.

"What is your opinion of my friends?" asked Miss Grace, as they pursued their way home.

"They are unusual," said her uncle, thoughtfully. "The boy has great ability, which is strikingly revealed in his charming personality.

"And the mother?"

"She is very beautiful and queenly."

"So beautiful," said Miss Grace, "that one would dread to think of her leaving that quiet country home where she can be so sheltered from the cruel unkindness of the foolish society people here within New Gate. And she is as good as she is beautiful, yet there is about her nothing stiff and narrow or what you might call Puritanic, except it be the purity of her heart and life. I would be the last to take her away from her quiet, simple manner of living. Her greatest ambition is to see Jean properly educated; and she shall have her heart's desire, uncle."

Mr. Anderson watched with some curiosity the process of Jean's development. For the first few weeks his employer left him very much to himself, exacting implicit obedience, but taking care to issue but few commands. He also established and increased his influence over him by showing interest in all his concerns, and at times treating him with

WHO WAS RESPONSIBLE? 161

affection, which bound the boy to him as nothing else could have done.

Jean was awed by the great wisdom of his employer, and fascinated by his brilliant conversation, in which he was not yet able to take part, for he was as yet only in that pleasant borderland where, with suspended judgment and ready observation, it was his part to listen and learn and study, and to hold his tongue, regarding it as a positive duty to keep his own opinions to himself, or when questioned, to put them forward with all due modesty and confession of ignorance. This trait of his endeared him to Mr. Anderson all the more; and that gentleman was never so happy as when the boy began to rely less on books and more on him for interest and companionship.

Many weeks passed: still the hearts and hands of America's patriotic sons and daughters applied diligently to the task of adhering strictly to every command from Washington pertaining to the economy of time, labor, money, or food. In the meantime America's curse kept up its ruthless waste, snatching its loaf of bread a day from 15,000,000 American families and handing them in exchange complete ruin to both body and soul, while at the same time it continued to gloat over the swiftness and certainty with which it would wreck the whole land: continued to mock at the hollow hope of the American people for democracy in truth—for peace, happiness, and freedom for themselves and their children when the nation's struggle should be at an end.

All during these times Jean continued to grow

more and more in both physical and mental strength. As even in their sports children seem to be aware of the events which agitate the outer world, so in the quiet of his life of employment and study Jean could not fail to be aware of the great national struggle going on, nor could he fail to take keen interest in it. Life seemed to grow bigger, and he became growingly conscious that there was much indeed to learn. He had come into the realization that there is a living history which can be daily and hourly studied—a history in which we all have a share, our infinitesimal yet priceless share of influence and responsibility.

Therefore the lad was very watchful lest he should do something that might in the least destroy the beautiful confidence which his dearly loved Miss Grace and her uncle placed in him. Not that he was one of those pale, soft, girlish youths with a long face and mushy timidity, which is disgusting; but he was a strong, vigorous, natural country boy, full of self-reliance, energy, and grit, sound judgment and pure nature, which recoiled from anything that weakens, impairs, or pollutes the human mind and body.

Somehow he felt a secret consciousness that he was in a great measure contributing to Miss Grace's effort in providing the reading public with facts taken directly from life—facts which could not fail to show what great possibilities there are for Young America, provided the country can be rid of those polluting evils of society, the greatest of which is alcohol.

In this he was correct, for he was indeed the inspirer of all that was best and true in her writings.

His exalted sense of truth and right, his strict adherence to all that was noble, and marked abhorrence for the ignoble, were her strongest incitement. With her hand clasped in the warm, strong hand of this son of lowly birth but most exalted principle, she was able to put into her articles knowledge of facts exemplified. Through him she was able to throttle the furies whose accursed fingers clutched at Young America in order to destroy.

Mr. Anderson watched with increasing interest and pride the unconscious growth and development of both his loved ones. He was aware of the immense pleasure which his niece found in her work of usefulness. She was forever busy, working in the various well-organized clubs, in the church, in everything which pertained to the improvement of the city. All during those weeks in which she worked so assiduously, so efficiently, she was unconsciously drawing from the faithfulness of her work, from the grand spirit which she carried into it, the high purpose which emanated from her in its performance, a recompense so munificent that her countenance lost a great amount of its wistful longing for all that she had lost in life—those joys which might have been. Her work constantly enabled her to gain in much valuable experience, in fine training, in increased efficiency, in splendid discipline, in self-expression, and in the strengthening of her beautiful character. From time to time newspaper articles appeared in most glowing praise of this young woman's work and beautiful patriotic spirit.

One afternoon Miss Grace was busily engaged in looking over a great stack of registration cards for the Woman's Home Committee—Council of National Defense. There was a smile of satisfaction upon her face as she noted the great number of these cards signed by the patriotic women of the city. A ray of sunshine stole through the fluttering curtain and made golden ripples upon the floor. Upon the table there lay a magazine—a special copy of an American periodical renowned for the lofty tone of its articles, the asperity of its criticisms, the wholesomeness and cleanliness of its fiction. Within this copy there was an article written by Miss Grace. This article, which was the first of hers to be published in this magazine, had been read with avidity by people all over the country. In it she had aimed an effective blow at alcoholism.

Presently, the cards finished, she settled herself in her comfortable "thinking chair," as she called it, and surrendered herself to a few moments of reverie. Such moments were almost invariably spent in working out some plan or perfecting some philanthropic scheme, or mental scrutiny of a charitable project. But this evening her mind dwelt upon recent occurrences which marked rapid progress toward the secret goal of her heart's desire—national prohibition.

Within the last few months America had learned the lesson that alcohol could not be tolerated among the men who were engaged in the death struggle for liberty. This lesson no doubt had been doubly enforced by America having witnessed the spectacle of Russia abolishing vodga, France suppressing absinthe, and England grappling with its beer problem. The lesson had been enforced to the extent that the

WHO WAS RESPONSIBLE? 165

people of America agreed with the Government in its decision to make it a punishable offense to sell liquor to the soldiers. And now the constant cry of the prohibitionists to down the liquor interest and save the nation's grain made it imperative that Congress consider a bill which would make it unlawful for any person, firm, or corporation to use in the manufacture of any intoxicating liquor for beverage purpose any perishable or non-perishable feeds, foods, or food materials.

As Miss Grace reviewed the summary of the advance toward the overthrow of her most hated enemy, suddenly a glory illumined the future. The vision caught and held her in a fascinating reverie in which she beheld much of the world's darkness dispelled by sunshine, sorrow dispelled by happiness, that which is base and low and deceitful displaced by the lofty and the true; those things which breed filth and unrighteousness displaced by those things which beget cleanliness and righteousness: the fathers of little children returned from haunts of vice and crime, back to the shrine of prayer at their own hearthstone; womanhood, the glory of America, made divine by the halo of faithful wifehood and sacred motherhood; manhood, the pride of America, purified and exalted by strength of intellect and depth of moral character; youth, the hope of America, vigorous, superbly equipped with physical and mental strength which characterizes the youth who is destined to do great and worthy things in the world—youth endowed with great beauty, not superficial beauty, but heart beauty, soul beauty, which marks the spirit of kindness, helpfulness, and unselfishness—youth, possessed with character of the superior sort which develops into undefiled manhood and womanhood.

Thus Miss Grace beheld the future in a dazzling glory which lured and charmed. Reluctant to part from the vision, she sat and dreamed on until evening and mellow sunset filled the world with a last glory ere the darkness set in. A knock on the door startled her from her reverie. What could be more pleasant than a visit from her uncle and Jean. There was a certain youthfulness about her uncle as he came into the room. This pleased the young lady very much, and she marked the growing friendship between the man and boy with increasing interest and pleasure. Their friendship proved of immense benefit to both. Under her uncle's guidance Jean was growing rapidly, both mentally and physically, and to a keen observer nothing is more fascinating than to watch this sort of growth. In the anxieties of the national struggles at that time Mr. Anderson was able to interest himself keenly through the frequent contact with a young, fresh, vigorous mind feeling its way into greater things.

The evening was most pleasantly spent. Her uncle and Jean's visit to her home being of limited frequency made those visits all the more pleasurable. They usually came together at those times when Miss Grace's parents were absent, for neither of the two proud people could become quite reconciled to their daughter's and brother's intimacy with "common folks," as they called Jean and his mother.

CHAPTER XI

THE advance toward national prohibition was destined to make another stride in a very short while. As soon as the law was passed making it a punishable offense to sell liquor to the soldiers, the prohibitionist commenced to urge the fact that what is bad for the soldiers is bad for all American citizens, whether they are soldiers or not. Once started in this direction, the whole temperance force combined to keep up the agitation, nor did they languish in the least until Congress passed a resolution embodying an amendment to the Constitution which, if ratified by the separate States, would prohibit the manufacture, sale, transportation, importation, or exportation of all alcoholic beverages. The Constitution itself provided that such an amendment must be ratified by three-fourths of the States by legislative action, and the congressional amendment gave them seven years in which to make this ratification, stating that the amendment should take effect one year after its ratification.

At last the great issue was transferred from Congress and made to become an issue on which the people should have an opportunity to express their will. Although the passing of this amendment marked one of the most effective legislative actions in the whole history of the temperance movement, it served to create a new issue which would bring to exercise the will and mind of the American people to their fullest extent.

The passing of such an amendment raised a new issue in every one of the forty-eight States.

"Uncle," said Miss Grace one day while they were discussing the subject, "this places a double duty upon us—brings us face to face with both our enemies, imposing upon the American people a double duty which means: conducting the forty-eight campaigns on prohibition, and seeing the war against Germany victorious."

"There is one thing which may aid in this twofold duty," said her uncle, thoughtfully; "if the States can be made to see in the ratification of the amendment an opportunity to aid in the war, they can also be made to see that promptness in ratification is essential to that end."

"This is the great work which must be done," said the young woman, earnestly. "As the thing stands now, national prohibition is not effective in the least, for such a resolution does not close a single saloon, nor does it render the sale of liquor illegal. O, uncle! Somebody's got to fight this thing to a finish. I'm certainly going to do my part."

"It is going to be a great fight, my daughter—one that will require statesmanship and leadership of the very highest order, to be able to carry on the prohibition amendment campaign and at the same time refrain from detracting the people's interest from their great duty of helping to terminate this war successfully."

"I believe, uncle, that our State can be made the very first to ratify the amendment."

"You are thinking chiefly of New Gate and the rapid stride she has made toward high idealism; but remember that New Gate is but a very small portion of the State."

"Yes, I do remember that, uncle, but I also realize that her influence is vastly more far-reaching than her territory. How is Jean these days?" she asked, remembering that she had not seen the lad in several days.

"That boy has no equal. I am proud of him, Grace. A father could not be more proud."

"Anyone looking at that handsome boy, bearing all the marks of good parentage, with those strong features and that refined and sensitive nature, would never dream that his father was who he was, would they?" asked Miss Grace. "It is for his sake and all like him that I am determined to keep up this fight for national prohibiton complete."

During all these years the editor of the Hollyville *Sentinel*, who, immediately after the death of John Drew, wrote the editorial, "Who Is Responsible?" had adhered strictly to his promise that so long as the liquor evil should exist in America he would never fail to use the columns of his paper in denunciation of it. Numerous and forceful had been those articles, in which the author took the most radical stand in favor of prohibition. Therefore, when the prohibition amendment was passed, and his State was the very first to ratify it, he could not help but feel a secret satisfaction in the knowledge that he had been most faithful to his promise. He also had the secret belief that the relentless fight which he had carried on through his paper was largely responsible for the prompt ratification by his State.

There was great rejoicing over the State's action,

and the pages of the *Sentinel* were eloquent in praise of the people for taking the lead in the final stride for national prohibition. The *Sentinel* paid special tribute to the faithful activity of the pastor of the church where the Drews had worshiped. Since the death of John Drew, this minister had striven to make his entire church a solidified, active, aggressive, and obedient unit in the warfare on intemperance. He had been most successful in this attempt, for total abstinence in its membership had been the result.

To Dr. Morris, the old family physician of the Drews, it also paid a glowing tribute for the manner in which he had faithfully established the facts that, contrary to the general belief, alcohol has a very small place in medicine: that alcohol when taken into the system acts as a definite poison to the brain and other tissues, and that the effects of this poison are directly or indirectly responsible for the greater portion of the insane, epileptic, feeble-minded, and many other forms of mental, moral, and physical degeneracy: that either as a food or as a drug, alcohol is of no service, and that it is a virulent poison which should be placed on the list with arsenic, mercury, and other dangerous drugs, and that a system of legislation should be enacted whereby the sale and use of alcohol should be prevented and prohibited.

Although their State had been the first to ratify the amendment, the prohibitionists of Hollyville did not consider their work ended. They realized that they had only made a very effective beginning in the fight. Therefore, for the purpose of discussing plans which might prove beneficial in conducting a further campaign, they appointed a meeting, to which they invited Lawyer Anderson, Miss Grace King, and several others from New Gate and other towns and cities.

"Our safety lies in going forward," wrote the editor of the *Sentinel*. "If we stop now, we stand in danger of losing all we have gained."

The day before Miss Grace was to leave for Hollyville was so beautiful that she decided to run out to Peace Villa (the name which Jean had given their dear home up in the woods) and see Mrs. Richter. The faintest trace of approaching spring was in the air, and as she went along the path she thought of that very first day, years ago, when her wandering footsteps had led her to discover the little hut and its interesting family. She recalled how the cabin had sprung into view at the sudden turn of the road a few yards ahead. Her heart leaped in exultation when she thought of what that turn in the road would reveal to her to-day. She quickened her pace in order to gain sight of the house, and at the proper angle it leaped into view and seemed to beckon her with a triumphant smile of welcome.

"It is perfect!" she breathed while she stood watching it nestled there among clinging vines and hardy shrubbery—amidst a sort of peaceful repose which seemed ever to rest like a benediction upon it.

An intense desire burned within her heart—a deep yearning for a house like that, on the edge of something that was grand and close to nature—something wonderful yet real.

"Spring in such a house would be divine," she whispered. "Spring—a husband and little children to toddle in the dear little path cutting its way so cleanly through the velvet grass—children to romp on the level stretch of lawn at the foot of the sloping background of low hills and graceful trees."

She could almost see the riot of color in the darling garden in front of the house—a profusion of yellow jonquils, crocuses, violets, and lilacs; and sweet, sweet roses; the hundreds of little wild beauties upon the lawns; the gleam of white dogwood blossoms among the trees in the background. With a little catch of breath she suddenly clasped one hand over her left side to soothe the ache of longing in her heart, then went on up to the house.

Joy swept over her when the door opened and Jean's beautiful mother stood there with a smile of welcome. "O, if more dear mothers could be like that!" was Miss Grace's inward thought, and she looked lovingly at this woman so beautifully endowed with purity, intelligence, simplicity of manner, and dignity of bearing—in fact, was all that a perfect mother should be. What a wonderful woman—to have maintained her loveliness, her superior intelligence in spite of the wilderness of trials through which she had struggled; who had not allowed poverty nor social standing to paralyze her ambition to improve herself in every way she could, so that now she was able to surround her home with an atmosphere of refinement, culture, and purity.

"I was expecting you to-day," she said in her charming, soft voice. "Jean is away just now—off down yonder somewhere," she continued, pointing toward a long stretch of deep, cool woods. "Spring is in the air, and he's sure to find the first violet—he always does."

"I wonder if there's any place on earth half so beautiful as this," said Miss Grace, as she went about from room to room and noted the exquisite taste which made the whole interior of the house a sort of alluring personality. The place was indeed lovely—not with the cold, soulless elegance abounding in high-priced furniture, fine paintings, rare collections of art in the form of artful nudities; but clean, chaste, simple elegance, such as intelligence and refinement can impart to the most humble cabin —a radiance of beauty which a rich and noble spirit will cast over the humblest home, regardless to situation—a perfection which the upholsterer and decorator can never approach.

A deep thankfulness filled the young woman's heart. She felt that having restored peace and happiness to this good woman was a sort of reparation for some of those thoughtless, frivolous actions of her own girlhood. What a blessed thing it was to be able to bring sunshine instead of shadows to the lives of people!

Miss Grace was very proud of Jean, loving him as a young brother. Indeed, the youth was one to be proud of and worthy of anybody's love and admiration. Everybody liked him who knew him. The people of New Gate had almost abandoned the habit of looking at him askance because of his lowly birth. They liked him because he was original and not quite like the rest of the world: fresh and unspoiled, superior in intellect, but void of the smallest particle of conceit. Many of them were sometimes amazed how he would dexterously avoid doing anything which was low and mean, and how he religiously strove to merit the goodwill, confidence, and approval of his employer, whom he reverenced; and how above all he loved Miss Grace King and adored his sweet mother.

In spite of Jean's youth, he had already begun to show keen interest in the affairs of the nation. His interest in political events was growing so keen and strong that it was no longer possible to remain silent. When he returned from his ramble in the woods and found his beloved Miss Grace there with his mother, the fact pleased him very much. But there was an air of perplexed gravity about the boy which Miss Grace did not fail to notice. Perhaps his passion for books and reading was being overindulged.

"Jean, what are you reading these days?" she asked, noticing the magazine he had in his hand and had evidently been reading.

He handed it to her, saying as he did so: "Miss Grace, this is a very great country in which we live. I'm intensely interested in the splendid spirit of devotion and self-sacrifice the people of this country are exhibiting in this time of national trial. It makes me regret that I am not more advanced in years so that I might have a hand in my country's fight for humanity and right."

"My son has been regretting his years very much of late," said Mrs. Richter. "He, like the rest of us, is very anxious to 'do his bit.' He has already bought a Liberty Bond, and now his patriotic young

WHO WAS RESPONSIBLE? 175

soul is seeking broader avenues of usefulness to his country."

Miss Grace went to the dear boy and, placing both her hands on his broad young shoulders, said: "Jean, dear, you are doing more for your country than you realize. Every day you are making yourself an example of what young America should be. Every day of your life you are paying a magnificent compliment to America's effort to produce ideal, capable, efficient men, who are to hold the highest places in the future—men whose principles of right, honest, lofty idealism shall create a new era when this war is ended. You are demonstrating to the world what sober America can be. Ah! be satisfied that in this you are 'doing your bit'!"

The young woman was not mistaken in saying this, for the coming years would prove the truth of her statement, when this boy, born under the curse of America's greatest evil, but liberated and reared in the blessed atmosphere of sobriety and purity, should become a man of whom America would be most proud because of being able to boast of him as one of the grandest combinations of heart, conscience, and brain beneath her flag. And it would become the proud boast of New Gate that this leader of men, whose spotless character had become the dowry of the nation, snatched the name of Jean Richter, which alcohol trailed in the dust, and made of it a name ever to be remembered, loved, and honored.

The meeting at Hollyville proved to be most interesting. It was well attended by prohibitionists from all over the State, and many from adjoining States. In all the Southland there has never been a more effective meeting of its kind. It proved to be most beneficial in that it gave those who attended the opportunity to form into an effective unit for the grand purpose of making a final and successful warfare against the liquor industry in America.

A few weeks after this meeting there appeared in one of the leading magazines of the country an article written by Miss Grace King. This article, in which her purest thought, her holiest aspirations, her grandest and noblest spirit of patriotism were expressed, was prized by the prohibitionists of America as among the most effective factors in the final victory.

Ruthlessly she assaulted America's pet, soft-footed, velvet-masked folly of society, demanding that all intelligent Christian citizens pause in their headlong career, then decide once for all whether a God-fearing nation, under the white banner of the Christian religion, would further tolerate this mortal enemy of peace and order, this despoiler of all that is best in man.

The following paragraphs of her article made a fitting and effective closing:

"The time has come at last when the great question, 'WHO IS RESPONSIBLE FOR THE LIQUOR EVIL?' hangs in letters of scarlet before the eyes of every American citizen, and the long-standing issue must be settled once for all—NOW!

"The world no longer remains blind to facts concerning alcohol—facts too often vindicated by living examples, and facts which have been proven beyond doubt. The world knows that greater calamities are inflicted on mankind by intemperance than by any other scourge. Facts to prove this have been discovered, reported, and established beyond all controversy.

"For these, if for no other reasons, the American people must eradicate this evil; and, in view of the fact that no attempt to regulate it has been successful, the only thing which remains to be done is to eradicate the evil, root and branch. For so long as it exists, all classes are in danger of becoming its victims. It is an evil genius which may bring the most exalted down to wallow in filth and rags.

"But there are still other reasons why America should no longer tolerate the liquor evil. Our country is at war: the eternal principles of justice, freedom, and right—those sacred ideals upon which America was founded—are in jeopardy. It is a holy heritage that we have been called upon to defend. America is now in the struggle which means life or death: every American is facing the supreme test— the test of souls and brains. The genius that does not enlist for victory is treason. Wealth that is not funded for the great cause is spurious. Every American who is not giving the very best of every ability for the purpose of winning this victory for humanity is disloyal. Every American mother who shrinks from allowing her son to shoulder arms in defense of freedom and honor is a coward. Every expenditure that does not contribute to the nation's task of winning the war is CRIMINAL! Any industry that steels itself against these facts, and steals those vitals which give life and strength to the men who are engaged in the fight for justice and clean hopes of freedom and equal rights for all men is a THIEF and ROBBER!

"The cost of the liquor industry to the American people may be divided into two broad streams of waste. Money spent for intoxicating drinks is lost—being money spent with no profit received. The poverty, crime, insanity, and idiocy, which is the loss of America's efficiency and lives, is an unpardonable, irretrievable loss. Statistics show that the expenditure at retail for intoxicating drinks in the course of one year in the United States is estimated at from $124,607,519 to $2,290,000,000.

"This black-handed dealing with the American people has been going on for many years, and these facts represent money received by that traffic and that which is worse than no value returned. Think of the enormous price we have had to pay for maintaining so corrupt and oppressive trade. This foolish indulgence on the part of Christian men and women must cease!

"Then, too, O Americans! behind this great problem of winning the war for humanity and liberty stands the greater problem of preparing America for freedom. Liberty stands at the risk of being grossly misunderstood by the masses, who will attach the narrowest definition to the term. America must take care lest, treading upon the heels of victory, there shall come other forms of oppression; and to-day there exists no greater form of menace within all America's boundary than alcoholism.

"There is nothing that has brought more corruption into politics than alcohol. Now is the time to pave the way, so that in the efficiency of govern-

WHO WAS RESPONSIBLE? 179

mental administration, America may stand unsurpassed: so that this country may be a land of limitless resources wherein every boy and girl under her floating colors may have equal chance to reach the topmost round of the ladder of prosperity, power, and honor. Then, and not until then, will America be restored to its original great spirit of unity and Christian brotherhood. If we would make this country worth living in when the war is over and victory is ours, let the people decide—let the States ratify the amendment. This thing must be done if we hope to purify these avenues of peace. If drunkenness interferes with efficiency in war, will it not interfere with efficiency in peace? When the war is ended and the nation's soldiers return from the perils which they have been called upon to face on land and on sea, let them not return to find that alcoholism with its mighty power stands waiting with new opportunities to debauch and destroy that which love and pride and self-sacrifice have won for them.

"There are some who deny the evil which alcohol has wrought, and claim that the sale of it should not be suppressed because of interfering with the personal rights of the individual. The 'personal rights' plea is perhaps the strongest argument advanced by the anti-prohibitionists. The 'personal rights' plea is not only weak but portrays a selfishness that any true American would be ashamed of. The consideration of public welfare overshadows the rights of an individual. Any man who puts himself in a position to injure others in any way ought to be punished. Any industry or traffic which menaces society should be suppressed.

180 WHO WAS RESPONSIBLE?

"Is there one who questions the right of the Government to prescribe wheatless days and meatless days, and to actually restrict our diet in order that our own and allied soldiers should be benefited? Do you stand up and contend that, in spite of our soldiers' needs, you will not comply with the country's request because it interferes with your individual rights? Such an argument is just as reasonable as the 'personal rights' plea of the anti-prohibitionists.

"For the sake of humanity we are engaged in a great international struggle, and, for the sake of humanity, we are also engaged in a national struggle. I pray that every American will cease the selfish clamor for individual rights long enough to listen to the appeal that humanity is making to you. Hear the cries of the children in the tenement districts of nearly every large city in this country: they cry for food, clothing, and shelter; they are children whose fathers believe in exercising their personal rights to the extent that the greater portion of their money goes for drink instead of food and raiment.

"Hear the cry of the widow, who prays not only for the protection of her country from absolutism, but prays for the protection of her boy from that most dreaded curse, ALCOHOL.

"This is the supreme hour; we stand face to face with the Liquor Demon! Strike the fatal blow now, lest in the years to come we find our chaste hopes of liberty and freedom dragged at the chariot wheels of BACCHUS, god of WINE!"

The future! Who can tell what to-morrow may bring forth? New and better conditions are bound to be formed out of this enormous caldron in which twenty nations are commingled. When we look down the vista of the coming years, what a glory breaks upon the vision! In it we see national prohibition made sure and secure through the ratification of the amendment. Further, we see the nations' crises passed and the triumph of democracy over autocracy. We see America's sons returning from the battlefields rejoicing in the victory for liberty. And we see those valiant soldiers who have waged the long warfare for temperance rejoicing in the fact that they have won for America national prohibition as a crowning glory and a richest blessing!

THE END.

SERMONS IN STONES

By Maggie Fullilove

Evelyn leaned out of the window, looking down on the little fixed moons—the street lamps. There they stood, anchored in the night, solemn and regular. How limited they stretched! How motionless! Like her own life, they always shone on the same patch of ground—little, dim, insignificant lights. The thought filled her with dreariness. A little later she raised her eyes to the real moon rioting through the clouds. Every hour it looked down upon new lands on its ceaseless march around the world. That was what her life should be like. That was how she had planned it—until she met Lionel.

They had been class-mates at college, had graduated together. Opportunity had held out to her a richer choice. The one rival of his—the only one who had really counted—was the son of a rich man, and resided in a large city. But, being a true daughter of nature, she had answered the call of her heart and married Lionel, the farmer. He loved her with a strong true passion that would not be quelled and would not be denied. In spite of herself, she loved him in return and married him—and he had brought her *here*. It didn't seem fair. She was young; life was calling—full, broad life— while she sat in this little hole of a place, like these stationary street lamps, when her ambition secretly craved to be like that striding moon up there.

It was the first time in their four months of wedded love that a cloud dimmed their sky of perfect happiness. She had talent, no doubt of that. Her own inward craving told her that writing was her vocation. While at college, she had been told that journalism was her particular gift. She had written several small articles of merit. Unfortunately, fate had cast her lot in this obscure, one-horse village, where there was nothing to give inspiration, nothing to even suggest a story.

The people with whom she came in daily contact were all ordinary, homey people. They were all simple, ignorant folk—a slow-living, slow-changing, hard-working but kindly, good-natured and sociable set, content to jog along in the same old primitive manner of their forefathers.

Over there by the little low-roof church, there squatted a small rickety school-house where all the young people learned their *a-b, ab's* and *h-a, ha's* in the old way, grew into their teens, thumped silly little love notes to each other, graduated, then marched into the little church and got married, and settled down to the same humdrum way of living as their parents had done before them. Nothing romantic about that, eh?

Evelyn had made several attempts to write, but she lacked inspiration. There seemed nothing in all the little village to write about. Her knowledge of the outside world was sadly limited. She had seen practically none of the world, having come from a little village herself, where she was born and had spent all her early girlhood. There was no romance for her in this small place—no poetry, no inspiration; everything dry, nerve-racking prose, from the little school-house with its stony playground and bare interior to the poor little place of worship with its solemn faces and its long-meter hymns.

The only extraordinary person in the whole place who wanted to do the big things of life was herself—she knew it, and longed to get at her desires in some way. Lionel, she realized, was superior in his station to the others. He was the finest, most thrifty young farmer in the whole country round. It seemed strange to her how very adapted to his work he was. He was tall, broad and rustic, and fitted well into the landscape of field and forest and fence. She had tried so hard to make herself a part of his life and his interests, but somehow the thing seemed impossible.

She craved the bigger things of life. She wanted to write, and must write; but her surroundings afforded no inspiration. Once, since she had begun house-keeping, she had written a pathetic little story which her little crippled neighbor had inspired; but she felt that the great outside world did not want that, so she laid it away and waited for something bigger.

Her days were continually haunted by dreams of the city, aristocratic people and high society. She was constantly haunted by dreams of the distant sea—dreams of the mighty ocean. She had the idea that true inspiration would come to her if she could see the white-winged ships which ply the waters of the Pacific. She had her visions of tall men in dripping oil-skins, weathering the storms of the Atlantic—men who viewed the wonders of the great deep; who fetched up trophies from the bottom of the ocean; men who sailed the seas and had actually stood among the historic and famous places of the old countries—not stolid-eyed, bent-back, lazy-going men like those she had been accustomed to seeing.

She had in her possession a pink sea-shell which her roommate at college had given her. She pressed this to her ear many times and wondered if the sea sounded like that—a low, ceaseless murmur; or was it an intermittent roar, that threatens while it intrigues the soul? How she could weave a story if she might have the sea for a back-ground!

Or she could visit some of the places of renown—could actually stand among the famous ruins of Melrose Abbey and Kenilworth. There alone in that sacred spot, amid the graves of the illustrious dead, what surges of feeling would fill her soul! It would seem as if she were on the border land between the spirit world and this—as if it would be a simple matter for those spirit forms to appear. She imagined that she could almost hear the prayers and chants of the ancient worshippers at their altars.

What if she could visit Abbotsford, the home of Sir Walter Scott—"A Romance in Stone," as it is said to be; a house which contains curios and interesting mementos of great men and events, the place which inspired Scott to write his Waverly Novels and the Lady of the Lake. Then, too, not far away, she could visit Dryburg Abbey, where the great novelist is buried.

Or if she could go to Florence, Italy; visit the Uffizi Gallery, one of the finest collections of art in the world; or the house of Elizabeth Barrett Browning, near the Philli Palace in Florence; or the house of Michael Angelo on the Via Ghibellina; or the house where Dante was born—the sight of these places and others of like renown would stir her soul to the height of producing something great. Evelyn was hungry—hungry for big life—hungry for the inspiration that she knew would come to her in that far-away, grand life.

She had her visions of the city—the great, glowing, immense, wonderful, throbbing city, with its millions of people—fine aristocratic heirs to millions, beautiful young people who dwelt in ease and comfort, surrounded with love and romance. These were the people who could create heroes and heroines—not the ordinary, home-spun folk like the buxom, large-footed girls and boys of her home place. It took something big, something out of the ordinary, to make a story; something far away like the sea, something tantalizing—unreal! She wanted, above all, to write a love story, a real big love story with a thrill to it.

Why not write her own?

The idea came to Evelyn as she sat there looking out at the dim street lamps. Their's had been a love match, if it was just ordinary. She could let their wealth of love be the heart of the story and draw on her imagination for the mystery, the romance and the poetry that had been lacking. He had wooed her somewhat in the manner of the cave-man; looked upon her, loved her, wanted her with a passion that would not be denied—had literally carried her off—his woman, his mate.

She could no more resist his magnetic attraction, could no more resist the deep response which arose in every fiber of her being, than the little flowers can resist the warm and tender kiss of the sunshine. Her man was adorable and her love for him was big enough for any story. She would make the attempt, would succeed, the story would sell, and they would have a chance for a bigger life.

The next day she began to write.

Outside the air was scented with the breath of rejoicing, budding trees, the damp smell of newly-ploughed earth, and abundant growing new life. She sat by the window, staring with unseeing eyes at the blue sky which looked down the meadow filled with new butter-cups of gold, and forget-me-nots which reflected the blue. She did not see that patch of green woods halfway up the hillside where the brooklet raced and bubbled. At last she had hit upon the right thing, she thought. She would write something with a thrill to it—something that would stir the heart. She wrote nearly all the morning, stopping just long enough to serve the poorly prepared mid-day meal.

Evening in Evelyn's little village is glorious! As the evening becomes far advanced, there is a faint decline in the soft brightness of the sky overhead, for the sun is setting. This is a time when the sun lends full value to the inspiration of man. It is especially true in rural places where there is a whole unbroken expanse of sky, not contaminated with the dust and smoke of the city. The whole western heaven stands out in all its beauty, while the sun softly colors the lovely clouds. The most inferior structure is luminous in the glorious light. The window-panes of Evelyn's little house shine in glory. Finally, when the sun drops behind the horizon, with its glowing colors like the flaming fires of a forge, it is enough to fill the heart with wonder and awe. It gilds all in a last glory of triumph, the sky so brilliant that one can hardly define the line of horizon. There in full view of Evelyn's house, where the sun has disappeared, the sky is now orange, then slowly the orange fades away and another immensity spreads out. The glory of night is about to extend over the firmament its melancholy charm.

Night in Evelyn's valley is inspiration in itself. There is such a wealth of sky, studded with those myriad words which have so long attracted man's attention and filled his mind with wonder and awe. Unconscious of all this passing beauty, Evelyn wrote until it became almost too dark for her to see.

Her husband came in, bringing his enormous appetite, sharpened by a hard day's toil. Instead of a nice warm supper of crisp bacon and steaming coffee, he found a cold stove, unwashed dinner dishes and no supper. He was naturally good-natured, but when a man is hungry, his temperament is very uncertain. To come in from a hard day's labor in the fields and find no supper, not even a fire in the stove, was not in keeping with that well-known, heart-warming song, "There Is No Place Like Home." He had done a big day's work and was tired and starved.

Their four months of wedded life had been very happy ones, for here in this small place she had been all his. He was not entirely ignorant concerning her secret desire to write. That had been the one shadow over them, the one cloud which hung dark and menacing over their happiness, this secret longing of hers for a wider scope. She could always foil his ardor by the merest hint at their narrow existence. But, fine-hearted fellow that he was, he was anxious for her to win her laurels in the world of letters. He knew she was of a poetic nature—a fine, extraordinary being—and he entertained the hope that the time would come when he could afford her much travel. But there existed an under-current of foreboding and anxiety whenever he thought about her career. Somehow it seemed to come between them. He wanted her all to himself—for a while longer, anyway.

Therefore, when he came in and found her engaged in writing, he was all unprepared and received a shock, especially when he found things left undone. If the beginning had brought about such a neglect of things, before long there might be a complete upheaval of all their domestic affairs. Evelyn had not as yet shown any extra skill in house-keeping, but he had been patient, hoping that her fine brain would learn in time. Now that she had begun writing, would she ever learn? Lionel groaned.

The lamp was lit and spilled a halo around Evelyn's dark head, piled high with masses of thick, shining black hair. One of her quick-thinking moods was on her. He had seen her write like that when they were in school together. She could not get her words down on paper fast enough. Whatever she was writing, it had her in its mesmeric spell.

She raised vague eyes to him, nodded abstractedly and kept on with her rapid writing. When they were in school together, he had loved her for this power of concentration. It showed her superiority above the others. She was a darling, a wonder, who intrigued and delighted him by her willful cleverness. But now—O Lord! This time he groaned aloud. Evelyn heard and came down to earth.

"Oh, dear man, I have prepared no sustenance, and you must be ravenous after your strenuous labor in the fields," she said, not having quite shaken off her poetic spell. "Just you wait a bit, though, I'll have a decoction bubbling in a sixtieth part of an hour."

She snatched up an unwashed coffee pot, put in too much coffee, poured in too much water, and set it upon the cold stove to boil.
"Oh dear me! No conflagration!"
She ran over to the wood-box and became almost distracted at finding it empty. Then out into the dark she plunged, nearly knocking her sense out against a post which the darkness hid from view. It seemed an age before she could find an ax to split kindling with. She fretted babyishly and wondered why her husband did not come to her aid—but, of course, he was tired, poor dear. She groped about in the dark until she found a piece of plank and chopped it, then dashed into the house and built a fire. Her husband ate of the poorly-cooked food, drank the muddy coffee and inwardly groaned. But Evelyn was so very sweet in her big effort that he couldn't help loving her. Yet he hoped that this writing mood of her's wouldn't last long.

The next day Evelyn was up with the birds—all eagerness to be at her writing again. The breakfast was no improvement on the supper of the night before. She flung things about like one possessed. As soon as her husband had finished his poor meal, he started off to his work. There was a cloud on his brow which Evelyn failed to see. Her head was too full of the love story—the story with the thrill to it.

The sun rose, flooding the whole valley with a soft, misty, golden radiance.

Morning in Evelyn's valley is divine. The brilliant air makes everything, the trees, flowers and little blades of grass, appear vivid and startling. The hills, the forests, the glades, with sharpened outlines, stand eloquently clear, as though one looked at them in a crystal sphere. The rising sun is nothing less than divine as it lights everything with a golden glow.

This morning it shone upon people who went to and fro along the streets—common-place, home-spun, simple-hearted folk—as if it would illumine their rustic aspect and turn them into kings and princes. Now and then the sweet air was disturbed by the loud guffaw of a good-natured jester, or the braying of a donkey—both of which sounds usually grated on the fine ears of Evelyn the dreamer. But this morning she was insensible to it all; her vision was peopled with the dream-folk of her imaginary world.

She had no trouble in creating a heroine for her story. It began with a word-picture of her. She was very beautiful, of course, had willowy grace—a slim narcissus, altogether charming and lovely, with her pale and wistful and child-like expression; eyes dark and large, full of subtle charm, fringed with dark lashes beneath penciled brows; and hair like a blue-black cloud, trailing across the rich brownness of her forehead; cheeks soft, smooth, fresh and brown as ripe nuts in autumn. She was small—so dainty, so fragile, yet as vividly glowing with her soft, warm lips and charming voice—a creature whose beauty was altogether dangerous.

Her hero was tall, swarthy and strong, exceedingly handsome, irresistible—and loved her heroine madly. "He first saw her in a lovely city park." Here she had to pause. She didn't know whether to place them in a city park or at the seashore. The sea seemed so far—so remote. Flowers grew in parks—millions of them—and she had seen flowers—thousands and thousands of them—in their wild, free beauty and harmonious arrangement, the like of which no man's hand had been able to accomplish. But the desire to reach out for the blessings, the grand things which she did not have, had Evelyn in its grasp.

"It was in a lovely city park where the youthful lovers met." She followed this with a clumsy, unreal description of something she had never seen; for she had never visited the city in all her life. Her nearest approach to city life was that which she had lived in her college town—a comparatively small place. There her entire surroundings had been distinctly rural. She then attempted to weave around the two young people her own love story—her's and Lionel's.

A week passed and still she wrote. During that week of intense concentration, her house suffered a sad neglect. Her husband suffered most. Everything seemed jumbled together, meals were forgotten, floors went unswept from day to day. The kitchen was fearful! Pots and pans lay topsy-turvy in greasy silence. Hunks of burned bread disgraced the greasy shelves. The house, both inside and out, was just the opposite of cleanliness and order. The natural beauty of the yard was completely obliterated by heaps of rubbish and filth. People who came to visit Evelyn these days met a dreamy-eyed, bedraggled, unkempt young woman, who was not even civil enough to exchange words with.

"Lionel's wife is a stuck-up young piece," they said among themselves. And they were very much disappointed; for they all adored Lionel, having loved, petted and pampered him all his days.

Lionel, whose patience was about worn to a frazzle, went about the house like one distracted—fearing to breathe or cough lest he break into her thoughts and spoil the wonderful story. He, too, had caught the spirit of the thing, although he suffered greatly. He kept buoyed up with the feeling that success was at their door. The story must be great, since his Evelyn was creating it. Conditions were terrible, but it would soon be over, he thought.

Late in the night when from sheer fatigue she did stop writing, they would build air-castles out of the money which the story would bring. They would go away to the city and live a grand life—have many servants to do the drudgery of house-keeping—and Evelyn would write, write, write—and the money would flow.

At last, the story reached its close. They sent it away and waited—sure that such a story couldn't be refused.

Evelyn could no more settle herself to house-keeping after the story had been finished than she could beforehand. Something had gone wrong. She hated the dirty dishes, hated the dirty, smirky floors, loathed the greasy pots and pans—utterly despised to cook, and showed her dislike by such cooking as was enough to nauseate the dog.

Her husband, poor fellow, grew thinner and thinner. He found no joy in his work and little pleasure in his home. He had hoped that as soon as the story would have been finished, he would have his Evelyn back again; but somehow, she seemed farther away than ever.

Everything went bad and was indeed on the brink of a climax when—*the story was returned!* A neat little card of rejection was enclosed from the editors. Evelyn read this card over and over again—paralyzed with disappointment.

As soon as Lionel came in she ran to him, placed the returned manuscript in his hands and fell upon his shoulder. Then before she knew it, she found herself sobbing frantically in his arms; not gentle weeping which is becoming to so many women, but eye-reddening, handkerchief-soaking, body-racking sobs. Her story, had it been meritorious, might have been sold elsewhere, as you know; but Evelyn did not know this; and it was well that she did not, because the real reason for its rejection was on account of its faultiness. It would no doubt have met the same fate had she submitted it to a hundred magazines.

Lionel drew her close to his big, warm body; held her tightly in his strong, hungry arms; soothed and petted her, rubbing his cheek against her hair, repeating phrases of comfort, interspersing them with red-blooded, virile curses at fate and the universe—then ending all with a fervent "Thank God!"

In an instant her anger blazed—then flamed into white heat.

"What!" she cried, furious, "you are glad it is back—glad it failed? You are cruel; cruel!" she screamed.

He took the trembling, passionate creature in his strong arms.

"I thank God," he said deeply and tenderly, "not because you have failed, dearest, but because you have come back to my arms. Think how long it has been since you have allowed me to hold you in my arms like this. Why, Evelyn, I'm starved both in body and in spirit. Thank God," he added under his breath, "this writing foolishness is over."

He was filled with compassion, nevertheless, when he saw how shaken and really disappointed she was. With the tender hands of a mother, he undressed her and put her to bed just as if she had been a little tired girl. She would be herself again soon, he knew. And he secretly hoped that she would leave off writing for a while, at least.

After she had fallen asleep, he sat down in silent meditation, his heart gloomy with thoughts of his young wife's troubles.

"Poor little Evelyn," he said again and again. He remembered the empty wood-box and got up to fill it. Outside the stars shone blurred in a murky sky. He looked up at them and smiled bitterly.

Evelyn did not awake until about nine o'clock the next day. The sun shone brightly. Its warm rays pierced the kitchen curtains and fell upon the filthy floor. She found the remains of a breakfast which her husband had attempted to cook. The house smelled of burned grease and made her almost sick. The stove, laden with sticky, smutty, unwashed pans and spits, was quite cold. On the table in the dining room, dirty dishes contained bits of spoiled food. On top of a pile of nasty plates, there lay her manuscript—the story with a thrill to it. The sight of it made her angry. She snatched it up and crammed it into the waste basket. She then remembered that she had had no breakfast. It took some time to remove the dirty vessels and kindle a fire in the stove. After it began to burn, the odor of grease and filth, which began to melt and then to burn, was nauseating almost beyond endurance.

By force of habit she opened the oven in search of dishes which might be placed in there and in danger of being burned. There was a surprise for her. A plate contained rice with gravy over it, two flat, blistered biscuits and a thick slice of bacon. Lionel had left that for her breakfast. The sight of it, the thought of his big loving heart, the thought of her sad neglect of her young husband these many days, smote her heart with remorse. She looked around her, and for the first time in many days saw what a mess she had made of things. What must Lionel think of her!

But Evelyn was no coward. She was the offspring of brave, stout-hearted farmer parents whom nothing daunted. She began to see what a failure she had made in this, her supreme duty. Seeing this, she made up her mind to set things right again. Lionel must be made to see that she had not made an utter failure in everything.

But the problem which confronted her at present was where to begin. There were so many disordered angles. For a while she stood stiffly inert in the midst of it all. Then pride, self-reliance, determination, came trooping to her relief. She would not be beaten—would not tarry another minute in the midst of such desolation.

She hurled an angry look at the greasy floor, the smoking stove, the walls draped in disgraceful, spider-webby drapings. Startled by the new spell upon her, all at once she beheld a vision. She saw the dismal rooms transformed by such alchemy as only the hands of a woman can achieve. She saw the dust, grease and disorder vanish and the whole place made sweet and clean. Swiftly, lest her dream vanish, she hurried to her room. From somewhere in the dresser drawer, she snatched a blue gingham apron with broad, housewifely strings. She tied it on exultantly. Never before had she felt such a glorious feeling of capability and strength which came with the tying on of the blue gingham apron.

She tackled the stove first. Dinner must be gotten. She rattled the stove lids and experienced a new triumph when the fire roared cheerily up the chimney and the kettle began to hum and sing. She flew out to the garden and came back bringing her arms full of crisp mustard greens, new onions and tender, scarlet radishes. What a dinner she was going to have!

Back and forth—back and forth—she went, sweeping, dusting, setting things in order, cleaning, polishing; the song and fine purpose in her heart lent wings to her feet. She did not realize how much she was accomplishing in so little time. Why it was a joy—a joy instead of a drudgery!

Then her husband came. He came into a place transformed—a sweet, cheery kitchen, a dining room where a snowy cloth graced the table, and a bowl of wild violets perfumed and smiled. The clean, white curtain at the window fluttered merrily in the breeze. The table was set for two, and the odor from the delicious dinner filled his nostrils. Evelyn had never before shown such skill in cooking. It was wonderful! He looked about for a participant in the miracle, but there was no one but Evelyn—she had done it all. He stared at the vision before him. The realization that it was no dream caught him by the throat with strangling gladness. He didn't say a word just at first—just beamed his surprised joy out of his beloved eyes.

Lionel's joy and appreciation of what she had done, the great love and admiration which shone in his eyes, was quite enough for her. It would last a lifetime.

After dinner, Lionel went back to his work with a lighter heart than he had carried for many a day. He had nothing more to fear. Evelyn had learned her lesson.

But he was very much mistaken if he thought that Evelyn had given up writing. A brand new idea came to her as she washed the dinner dishes. As soon as the last one had been put away, the floor swept clean, the chairs pushed to their places, the new tins polished and hung in their places, she hastened to get her pencil and pad, sat down in the kitchen amidst the brightly polished tins, and waited for inspiration. It came!

The shining stove, the clean shelves, the spotless cupboard, the glittering tins—all whispered it in her ear. The teakettle, now rid of its coat of grease and soot, sputtered and sang—

"Are you in earnest? Seize this very minute!
What you can do, or think you can, begin it!"

The coffee pot took it up: "Begin it! Begin it!" And she began—
"When you have a number of disagreeable duties to perform, always do the most disagreeable first."

Then followed paragraph after paragraph of good, wholesome, instructive ideas on how it is possible to make house-keeping a pleasure—how to make suitable and sensible arrangements in the home so as to insure an economy of time and labor, and at the same time afford a pleasing and gratifying effect to the eye; how to beautify the rural home; suitable and serviceable furniture; helps toward securing cleanliness and order from the back-yard to the parlor.

She did not finish the article all in one day, nor in a week; but it required many weeks to finish it. During this time she worked the thing out with mathematical precision. Nor did she neglect her other duties—no, indeed! The careful and skillful manipulation of her daily routine of duties made it possible to work out the theme.

By the time the manuscript was complete, Evelyn's little house was a wonder in itself. She had made it a place of such extraordinary perfection, that it was the center of attraction for all the inhabitants of the village.

"Why don't you send the big, practical idea to some magazine, dear?" suggested her husband. "It may be the means of helping thousands of tired, worn-out housewives all over the country."

Therefore, with the one idea of contributing something useful to the greatest business in the world—house-keeping—Evelyn sent the article to one of the leading magazines, hoping that its acceptance and publication might be the means of rendering aid to thousands of women, especially those of rural districts, who found house-keeping a drudgery rather than a pleasure. Evelyn had found out herself that the reason for so many supercilious ideas concerning house-keeping, and the reason so many find it a drudgery, is because there are so many who do not know *how* to do it.

She sent it, not simply for its pecuniary value, but with the hope that it might be the means of perpetuating love and sunshine, and bringing greater life into the small rural homes.

This unselfish purpose of hers had its reward; for some time later, she sat with Lionel in one of their immaculate rooms, holding in her hand, not only a check which the magazine had sent her in exchange for the manuscript, but also held a letter from the editors, stating that they would be glad to examine more articles of like nature.

The happiness which Evelyn experienced was great and deep. She felt that she had contributed largely to the working out and perfecting of one among the greatest ideas in the world. When she had written her first story, she had chosen for its subject, *Love*—the greatest theme on earth and in Heaven. But in choosing and working out her second theme, she had selected that which goes towards making love and happiness and home more perfect. In doing that, she had shown the greatest manifestation of love—*Service*.

Evelyn hardly dared to speak, so great was the joy in the victory she had achieved and the lesson she had learned. For Evelyn had learned a great lesson. Her heart no longer slept insensible to the beauty all around her.

Outdoors she could hear the faint tinkle, tinkle of a cowbell. From the low trees just back of the garden there came a sound of much lively chirping. It told the blessing of love—of springtime. The flowers listened and blossomed at the call of the unseen Orpheus. The air was laden with misty melodies—songs of love that proclaim the eternal reign of Mother Earth. It is a time when Orpheus calls—his notes waken and bring the flowers into full bloom. A sprouting twig proclaims the fullness of life.

In the distance, outlined against the horizon, Evelyn sees the trees of a young forest. The trees expand with vigor, their young leaves outlined against the sky. The sap has risen in the trees and now takes part in the great festival of Spring. The wonderful charm of the whole scene consists in the differences of light and shade of the harmonious blending of delicate colors. For where the tender young green strives to predominate, it is tenderly tempered by the glistening, whitish-brown of the bursting buds and the shadowy darkness of the naked branches.

The very soul of meditation dwells in this forest. These beautiful trees garbed hardly a fortnight, proclaim the majesty of youth in nature. At the foot of the steps there is a verdant carpet sown with little stars. It stretches out towards a lane; for there is a lane leading down to the forest, which seems an avenue of enchantment. The slanting rays of the sun strikes the trees and the grass. Over the lane bluish shadows play. These little dashes of blue among the grass are forget-me-nots. Far down at the end of the lane, Evelyn thinks she sees happiness; but it is not only there in the distance, it is close—all about the young wedded lovers—it is everywhere. The marvel of it all!

As Evelyn sits there enthralled in the rapture of her first victory, there stirs in her a faint sign, mysterious and startling—a sign which every woman understands who has drunk deep of the cup of love and is fruitful. With it there comes a thrill which Evelyn has never felt before.

Suddenly she sees the lawn peopled with childish faces, their sweet voices mingled with the birds, their little hands filled with forget-me-nots, their little voices calling to her for admiration of their beauty. They are her children—hers and Lionel's.

Then Evelyn's heart overflows with tender emotion as she gazes wonderingly at Lionel—her big, strong lover-husband. Somehow she does not wish to reveal her secret just yet. For a little while, let it be hers—and God's.

Pointing towards the distant hills, Evelyn said: "See, out yonder lies inspiration, as well as here at my feet. What treasures I had overlooked! This little house is a corner of happiness, a corner of eternity. Here thoughts can thrive and worship. Here I have found the secret of true love and happiness. Here and out there in that valley I may have everything. The great things of life are not the exceptional things but the beauties of everyday which I did not stop to notice. These vast treasures within my grasp, which I neglected and did not even touch—they are the things that count. Here in my own little house, I am in touch with life—abundant life. What more can I want than this tenderness which surrounds me everywhere—this ever-varying Nature which says so much to me—this atmosphere which envelopes me?

"It was Lord Houghton who said:

'The best things are nearest—breath in your nostrils, light in your eyes, flowers at your feet, duties at your hand, the path of God just before you. Then do not grasp at the stars but do life's plain common work as it comes, certain that daily duties and daily bread are the sweetest things of life.'

"How very mistaken I was to seek inspiration only in the distance. Just think! It was pots and pans that gave me a true knowledge of life and taught my soul the gracious lesson of submission. That writer spoke truly who said:

"For there are sermons in stones,
Books in running brooks,
And Good in everything."

LOVE VS. GOLD.
By Raleigh James Johnson.
The man who has the money is
The man who can repose
Upon the doway flower beds of ease:
But he that has a heart to love
Yet just a single rose
Can shake the golden fruit from blissful trees.

NAVY BLUE VELVET

By Maggie Fullilove

(A brilliant, spicy story of a woman who liked pretty things to wear and what she did to get them. It's a hum-dinger. In this month and next month's.)

Kensington's, the leading dry goods store of the little town, was beautiful that day. Garlands of tinted leaves festooned the show windows and hung in elaborate clusters above the counters, along the walls, and suspended from the ceiling overhead.

Little Mrs. Harding turned her footsteps in that direction. She loved beauty in any form, and the little town afforded so little beauty to her hungry soul. Suddenly she stepped before the gorgeous window and stared in unfeigned admiration at the beautiful creation encased there. It was a stunning suit, one of the smartest models of the season—an uncommonly handsome suit, rarely seen in the show windows of small towns. It was made of fine quality velvet. The coat was made with a fashionable cape collar, edged with black seal fur. Mrs. Harding adored the fur trimmings; they conveyed such an air of warmth and comfort. The dress was navy blue—her favorite color for winter wear. She loved all shades of blue, and always made an attempt to purchase a navy blue suit for winter, but never quite accomplished it. Her purse never allowed one of the quality she desired; so she went without, year after year, with the longing in her heart never satisfied.

Here, before her eyes, was the dress she had always longed for. She gazed upon it with hungry eyes—that graceful, flaring coat made beautiful and complete with a row of adorable fur, rich and black around the bottom of it; the handsome collar which could be turned up at the neck in the new Shakespeare effect—that was the dress of her dreams. She glued her eyes upon it, unheeding the string of women who filed past her.

As she gazed, she clutched her purse, which held every cent in the world she owned—fifty dollars. She was on her way then to deposit it in the Citizen's Bank in her own name. It was the first real money she could call—really call—her own. A wild desire seized her—a desire to possess this dress if she had to spend her last cent for it. She looked at it with undisguised fascination, then went inside the store.

"The dress in the window—the navy blue one with the fur trimmings—how much?" She asked the sales-lady timidly.

"Ah, that?" the little woman answered. "Very pretty dress indeed! Latest thing from New York."

"But how much is it?" asked Mrs. Harding with a touch of impatience.

"That one with the black fur trimmings?—navy blue—good color you know, just the shade for you. Of course you could wear most anything with those eyes and that hair of yours," she rattled on flatteringly; she knew her business.

"But you haven't told me how much?"

"The price of that dress? Now really you would be surprised at the price of that dress. Such a beauty you know—the very newest thing! That color now—"

"Please tell me the price," Mrs. Harding almost pleaded.

"Why, just think of it—that dress—only fifty dollars! Small sum, isn't it, for so elaborate a dress? Almost like giving it away."

Mrs. Harding gasped! It would take every cent of her money to pay for it. "Let's try it on."

Already the woman had taken the dress from its place in the window and was holding it temptingly before her. Mrs. Harding put out her hand and the soft touch of it went straight to her heart. She followed the woman to the dressing-room in the back of the store, and stood like one in a dream, while deft fingers fitted the dress upon her. The effect was astonishing! Mrs. Harding stared incredulously at the lovely little figure framed in the mirror. Could that be herself—that beautiful woman?

How she loved the darling fullness of the coat, falling in graceful, flaring ripples. The sleeves, too, were lovely—flared with fur trimmings. She listened to the praise of the other woman in charmed excitement. Fifty dollars! All the money in the world she possessed. But she just could not refuse that dress. What if she did need so many other things—many things for the children and for the home. Hadn't she always needed? Wouldn't she always need? She had always denied herself for others. Her girlhood had been pinched and self-denying, too. She had had so few pretty things which a young girl so loves—never being able to afford even a bright new ribbon for her hair. All through her girlhood, she had gone, scrimping and saving, doing without. Then, finally, when she married, it was for love in a cottage. Her young husband was one of those hardworking sort, economizing almost to the point of stinginess. He had been born in poverty, reared in poverty, and had struggled through his school life—strung to his last notch in order to meet his bills. This ceaseless struggle developed him into one of those men who will go almost naked in order to save money; one who will wear rags sooner than break a certain sum and buy himself a suit of clothes; one of those none-of-anybody's-business-what-I-wear sort; who will go with baggy-kneed breeches in order to save the presser's bill. This quality of his was, no doubt, a sort of virtue while he struggled through school, but now, since he had gained a fair footing on the road to wealth, it had become a sort of vice. Mrs. Harding had fallen in with all his plans—going shabby, scrimping and saving every nickel. All through the term of child-bearing, Mrs. Harding had been most faithful to her duty. She never hired a maid for any of the five, but attended her babies all by herself in order to save the maid's wages. She managed by skillful economizing to keep them decently clothed, going almost naked herself in order to accomplish it. She had proven her readiness to fall in with all his plans so well, that Mr. Harding had accepted the situation as a matter of course, and saw her meanly clad from day to day without compunction; with never a thought that underneath her shabby, out-of-style clothes, there beat a heart which longed for pretty things, hungered for dainty silks and soft muslins.

To him—

"Life was a meat and bread affair:
Stout clothes and heavy shoes to wear."

To her it meant that and more. She loved a little beauty thrown in here and there. While she hoed the turnips, she would have liked to rest her eyes upon a bed of glowing verbenas, stately hollyhocks, gorgeous hyacinths, scarlet geraniums; or stop to admire and to pluck a rose from a tall, hardy rose bush; or she would have found great joy in turning from the strong, not altogether agreeable smell of onions, to inhale the sweet odor of modest violets. Once, in early spring, Mr. Harding came upon her as she spaded a patch of ground in one remote corner of their small garden.

"What, Margaret, planting mustard? I shall have a man here to plow the garden tomorrow so you can plant everything. We shall need plenty of vegetables—times are so hard. Can't you wait till after tomorrow? Your seed will grow so much better in well cultivated ground."

"But I—I'm not going to plant mustard. I—I just thought I'd make a little bed in this corner, away from everything else, you know, to—to plant—er flowers in."

"Flowers!" His tone was full of surprise and rebuke.

"Now you know, wife, that we can't have any ground for foolishness! We need every bit of our ground for vegetables! We must have things to eat; we can't eat flowers."

"But we can admire them and smell them," she said weakly.

"Admire and smell, indeed! That won't make you fat, will it? I'd rather have cabbage than roses; an onion smells better to me than a violet."

"I'd rather have roses, sometimes," she said, but meekly put down the spade. She walked away, hurt—her lips trembling on the verge of tears, like a disappointed child's. She never tried to have flowers again—not in the garden. A few buckets contained plants—wild fern and geraniums, which promptly died at first freeze.

Now that the children had grown big enough to go to school, she had found some time to work for herself. Day and night she had toiled, saving every penny until the sum had reached fifty dollars.

Foolish woman, she thought, to go and spend it all on one dress!

"Why, you are beautiful, deary," the other woman said in coaxing, soft tones. Mrs. Harding beamed! She was beautiful and she knew it.

Quick! She must decide at once!

"Yes, I'll take it," she said. "No, don't send it; I'll take it with me."

Like a guilty creature, she slipped into her home and hid the precious package from sight. What would Mr. Harding think of her, she wondered. She became terribly frightened when she thought of the fact that he would regard her as a perfect little fool as soon as he found out what she had done with her money. He had planned its future disposal so differently, too. "Put it in the bank," he had told her. "Next spring we will buy some shoats, or some fruit trees to start a little orchard. That money will go a long way, I tell you." "Oh, dear! I am a selfish, weak fool, poor me!"

But the touch of the soft velvet beneath her fingers thrilled her.

One evening, when all the rest of the family was away, she slipped the dress out from it's hiding place, arrayed herself in it and stood looking in the mirror. Suddenly it occurred to her that she had nowhere to go to wear it. If she should wear it to church the neighbors would stare at her in incredulous wonder. She simply could not walk up their little church aisle with that dress on. She was not a member of any of their swell clubs, and she never had dressed like that on the streets.

"Oh, I have been foolish indeed!" she wailed. "Now I guess you're satisfied, you silly creature," she told herself.

With heart withering in her bosom, she slipped off the rich velvet, folded it carefully, with sudden decision. She would take it back, tell the woman something, get her money back and common sense as well.

She started up guiltily as the door burst open; but it was only Edwin, home from school.

"Where's Margaret?" she asked, relieved but agitated.

"She's coming on, mother. She stopped a while with Nelly to look at the posters of that new opera that's coming. It's going to be a stunner!"

"Edwin, don't use slang."

"Well, a corker then." Edwin simply could not think of any word that would express his idea about the opera like "corker" and "stunner."

"Mother, why don't you go to the opera some time—you and father and us?"

Why not, indeed! Mrs. Harding gasped at the idea. Mr. Harding wouldn't think of allowing such a thing. To him, it would be the height of folly to throw away money on such foolishness. She wouldn't dare mention such a thing to Mr. Harding. She remembered the severe rebuke he gave her once, on that account. It was after their second child was born. The little town was in a flutter of expectation over a coming theatrical event. The play was to be one of those high class moral plays. Mrs. Harding had read the story and knew it to be clean, wholesome and worth seeing. One day after a critical survey of the pictured posters, being fully convinced as to the high moral standard of the play, she timidly mentioned it to Mr. Harding, saying: "It would be so nice, dear, if we could go." "What!" he thundered, "we go to a theater! Are you crazy? You talk like a foolish woman. Never will I throw away money on that kind of nonsense—understand that, woman."

Mrs. Harding had never glanced at a poster since. It was evident that Mr. Harding did not care for such things.

"We don't attend operas," she told Edwin. "Father doesn't care for them. Now run along," she said, to avoid further questioning.

—his quiet, demure, self-denying little woman. Her whole clean, pure, quiet life ought to have told him better.

Reasoning in this wise, he found himself worked up into a transport of remorse. He wanted to go to her at once and beg her pardon, but he found himself cowering at the thought of her spirit. Those cruel things he had said must have gone deep. He did not mistake that hurt, outraged anger in her eyes. He hardly knew what to do. Finally he consoled himself by dodging behind the silly thought that "women are so unreasonable." Still he did not know what to do. His mind was all chaos.

"Well I'll be hanged!" was all the conclusion he was able to reach, after about three hours of chaotic thinking. "Small-hearted cur am I," he said just before going off to sleep. "Well, we'll see."

The next day he furtively watched Mrs. Harding out of the tail of his eye. She was as calm as usual, and went about her duties with the same, quiet precision. He didn't dare make mention of last night's quarrel. The whole unpleasant affair seemed like an ugly dream. He was baffled, hardly knowing how to act or what to expect. If he had seen a drayman carrying off Margaret's trunk, he would have known just what to do and say. But before this calm, clear-eyed woman, he could do nothing. He couldn't just go up to her and say, "Well, you are going to stay, after last night's affair? You're a brick!" For her part, she seemed calm enough, only she carried herself with a certain queenly dignity which he had not noted before. Perhaps she meant to stay and buy herself dresses and "fol-de-rols," and go to theaters as often as she liked. That must be the meaning of the new dare-devil-may-care attitude she had assumed.

"Well, we shall see about that," he said.

One day, about a month later, Mr. Harding slipped all unobserved into his wife's room. When he came out he carried a book under his arm—a thick catalogue of New York styles. As soon as he had gained his own room, he laid the book upon the table and proceeded to turn the pages. He had often seen her busy with one of those books. Several different ones always came at the beginning of each season. He found many turned-down pages—mostly at children's clothes. Under several garments, he found marked. "For Edwin," "For Margaret," "For Tom," etc. He turned the leaves until he came to the fur sets—warm, soft and attractive. Under one particular set, he saw marked, "for me," in Margaret's hand writing. It stared at him in a sort of childish appeal. The picture-woman wearing it looked just about as Margaret would look in that particular set of furs. The set was marked eighteen dollars—ten for the cape and eight for the muff. Mr. Harding sat looking at this a long time. There was a twinkle in his eyes. He knew very little about women's clothes, but he knew Margaret must have liked this set, or she would not have written "for me" under it.

Some time later they sat together—he looking over the daily paper, while she was busy at her darning. Up to this time, not one word had been said concerning that eventful night. He had always avoided any allusion to it and so had she. The children had been rushed off to school, so all the house was quiet. Presently there was a rumble of wheels at the door, and the express wagon left a big flat package for Mrs. Harding. Mr. Harding buried his face in the daily, completely absorbed in some article. Mrs. Harding examined the address on the outside of the package to make sure that there had been no mistake. Her first impulse was to take it to her room; but no, she had resolved never to do anything suspicious again. Therefore she laid the package upon the table and cut the string with trembling fingers. She carefully lifted the lid and there lay the very fur set of her latest New York Styles, come to life.

"Oh!" she said, when she had found her breath. "Who, who could have done th—this?" Mr. Harding, peeping over the paper, thought he had never seen her so beautiful, with that divine expression on her face.

"Who on earth could have done it!" she kept repeating. "Who? Who?"

All the time, he was hidden behind that paper reading intently. Suddenly, she went to him, and taking hold of both his big hands which still held the paper, she peeped over at him.

"Oh! It was you!" she cried. "You! You darling!"

Then she did the strangest thing—so he thought. She dropped on her knees, buried her face in the folds of his sleeve and wept as if her heart would break. He made several awkward attempts to quiet her, but she wept all the more. "There, there now," he soothed. "I'll send it back if you don't want it!"

"Oh! It is not that!" she managed to say. "I'm just so hap-happy!" Still she sobbed.

"I have been a blundering, old idiot," he managed to say as soon as she was calm enough to hear him. Forgive me, Margaret."

"Forgive you! Oh, it is I who should come crawling on my knees to you for pardon. I was a poor, weak fool! I have put that dress away and will never wear it again—not even look at it without feeling like a fool! I don't know what was the matter with me. I shall always hate navy blue dresses. I shall sell that one—get rid of it in some way."

"You shall do no such thing, you shall wear it, my dear woman, and as many others like it as I can afford. You are charming in it! I didn't dream that you—why you're just like my little honey-moon wife. You're beautiful. There, there, don't cry again!"

"You and I will both go out more together. I shan't have my little woman traipsing around at twelve o'clock in the night—alone. I am still opposed to attending low-down, dirty trash at these theatres; but whenever there's something worth while, we'll see it together. By-the-way, Margaret, I've bought that vacant lot adjoining ours. We'll raise every kind of vegetable that grows. There'll be room enough for corn, peas, potatoes, peanuts, pumpkins, onions, cabbage—every thing! You and the children can have all the front half of the old garden—for flowers. Raise as many roses, violets, and kerthantmi-ums as you like."

"Chrysanthemums dear," whispered happy Mrs. Harding from somewhere near the lapel of his coat.

THE PRECURSOR OF THE DAWN

By Maggie Fullilove

Author of "Navy Blue Velvet", "Sermons in Stones", etc.

His moment of extreme darkness had come. Instead of the illustrious career which he had mapped out for himself, he found that misfortune and disappointments crowded about him so fast that now he was engulfed in a darkness from which he could see no deliverance. Heretofore he had been buoyed up by his hunger for greatness, his self-confidence, and self-sufficiency; but now, where was it all?—lost in the gulf of defeat.

He had successfully passed through many a moment of darkness, but this last struggle bowed him almost completely to the earth. It seemed that all his efforts, all his self-denial, had been swallowed up in this final disappointment. He saw his hopes dashed to the ground, his ambition crushed to nought. His whole life's plan lay a shattered wreck at his feet, and he could do nothing. He could never hope to enter into the life of his dreams or accomplish all that he planned. The fabric of his self-confidence was shattered to fragments as if shaken by a mighty earthquake, and the ruin was indeed great. All seemed irreparably thrown away in this last failure. He bowed his head in the agony of this grief; the darkness wrapt him in silent gloom.

He was alone, yet not alone; for out of the impending gloom, the Devil came and stood beside him. Pointing towards a bottle of whiskey on the opposite table, the Devil bent low over the bowed head and whispered, "Drink,—find forgetfulness in one bottle of the delightful fluid."

The Precursor of the Dawn

Raising his head, the crushed youth looked steadily at the unopened bottle upon the table. Such an easy matter, he thought, to blot out this bitterness with the feelings of joy which this liquid would give! How he blessed the hand of his friend who had so kindly given it to him. This friend of his was a prominent young man of great and varied talents which he had carefully cultivated. But alas, the drink habit had set its seal upon his brow. He had carelessly taken the first drink, perhaps, then another and yet another, until now his prominent position, his high social standing, his family happiness and all his fine moral sensibilities were on the brink of ruin. Never had he admitted to himself that he was a drunkard. He tried to console himself with the belief that he was only taking it moderately when in truth he was fast becoming a slave to the habit, unfit for the association of decent people.

This friend had pressed the bottle of whiskey upon the youth, saying, "Take it. It is the best thing in the world to drown your troubles in. One bottle of that will make you forget that sorrow exists."

"I have never stood in greater need of it than now," argued the youth, as with an unsteady hand he poured out a glassful of the sparkling fluid and raised it slowly to his lips. But deep down in his heart there stirred some holier influence. He saw himself yielding to this one drink, then another and still another until all his lofty thoughts, his high aims and even his moral ideals should be dragged down to a low-level, evil-minded, diseased-brained wreck, the companion of riotous men too low for the association of brutes.

One by one, men who had fallen victims to this accursed drink came before his vision; men endowed with great intelligence and who otherwise would have been great leaders, men greatly needed, because of their superior abilities and great social influence, to use their lives in bringing about righteousness upon the earth.

He recalled one man, a very promising minister, who had given himself almost entirely up to the alcoholic habit. He had been a man of excellent moral character and amiable disposition. Finally, it was discovered to the dismay of his friends that he was falling into the habit of intemperance. No entreaties of those nearest and dearest to him availed to stop his dreadful course. At length, he was forced to give up his pulpit and sank down to the depths to which only a drunkard can sink.

The youth knew of prominent lawyers and eminent physicians whose lives would have been prosperous and useful were it not that whiskey had been allowed to gain so fast a hold upon them that they stood among the unfortunates, on the brink of ruin.

It seems that the drink demon seeks those who are best fitted for doing good to humanity and cuts off the hopes of their useful lives by destroying all those fine ideals and good qualities in them.

The Devil, seeing the youth hesitate, bent over and whispered, "You need not be a drunkard. Drink moderately like your friend. No one need ever know. Drink it secretly in your own home and among respectable people. All up-to-date people drink moderately. Drink just enough to make you forget your troubles."

Once again the youth raised the glass to his lips. The fumes filled his nostrils. It was a most delicious odor, so pleasant that he took a deep breath in order to completely fill his lungs with it. The inherited tendency again! He had had this experience once before when quite a boy. One day he had happened upon a small glass which had contained the liquor. He put it to his childish lips and the odor and taste of the few remaining drops had been good, oh so good! But it happened that on the very same evening he saw "Drunken Bill," the terror of the village, reeling along the streets, cursing and raving like a madman. When he was told that whiskey had caused this man's condition, the child vowed that he would never drink one drop again. Until now, he had faithfully kept that vow.

Once more he found the odor delicious, and the whole bottleful was in his own possession. But stay,—again the Holy Spirit speaks, "Touch not, O youth. There is evil in it from which there is no returning, for—

"Step by step, it leads its victim
To the verge of dread despair;
Hurls him over the brink of ruin,
Laughs,—and leaves him there."

He saw a mental picture of himself and what would be his fate should he yield. He saw himself after becoming a moderate drinker, a central figure around whom a crowd of youths gathered and listened to his smart speech tainted with unclean ideas. He saw himself watching with scientific interest the mental and moral deterioration of his young men associates and taking pride in helping them on to their downfall.

Again he was the center of the group,—a youth who loved to argue falsely, to mock at virtue, to jeer at faith and to instill morbid sentiments into the minds of the youths who listened to him; one who played off sparkling witticisms against purity and cared not whether women are faithful or men honorable, thus killing all his high sentiments one by one; and when a noble thought or a fine idea presented itself, springing at its throat and strangling it before it had time to breathe, making himself believe that nobler thoughts and fine ideas are the laughing stock of the present age, and that the stupid dreamers who indulge in them are made the dupes of the times.

And further, he saw himself finally developing into a complete moral wreck, a reeling drunkard, bereft forever of all honor, all hope of self respect. Then what would become of that fine resolution which he had made beside the death bed of that beloved mother; that mother who had known so little of the joys of life, and who had drawn her last breath without ever gazing above poverty and want. He remembered how he had vowed that he should one day make her name illustrious. He knew that unless her sons and daughters should become worthy men and women her life would have been lived for naught. He knew that it was left with them whether they should cause the name she bore to be honored or dragged in the dust.

Yet another vow had he made which was this: that when that young woman he adored should give her life and her virgin purity into his keeping she would find him worthy of the charge. Rising to the full height of his splendid physical manhood, the youth poised the glass in the air for a moment, then sent it crashing to the floor, shattering it into a thousand fragments.

"Away with thee, thou worker of iniquity; thou fiery symbol of hell, thou thief of virtue and honor, murderer of every good thing in man, I know thee.

"Thou art an agent of the Devil, the most subtle of all his agents. I have seen thee drag down a friend of mine,—a companion of my boyhood, a noble youth, 'ere thou didst rob him. Thou thief! Thou didst cast him into the gutter and fetch him from his purse and his good name. Thou didst steal from him that Godgiven boon, will power, so that he now piteously but helplessly seeks his own destruction. Away with thee forever!"

Dropping into the chair, the youth spent his rage in a storm of scalding tears.

The tempter receded. As soon as this passion was quelled, he advanced again, however, and whispered over the bowed head, "Suicide."

The idea appealed to the youth and he looked about for means of taking his own life. From the window he looked down into the darkness at the cold white pavement below. What an easy matter to throw himself from the window,—a crushed skull, a maimed body, and all would be over. But deep down in his heart a voice whispered the one word, "Coward."

He sank into the chair and once more buried his face in his hands. In this hour of great darkness the youth cried out in all the anguish of his soul, "God has forgotten me! He has hidden His face from me!"

Though he knew it not, in this complete overthrow, this utter ruin of all that he had so laboriously constructed, this loss of all that he had prided himself upon, lay the very first step to a new and higher and holier life; for death must ever come before resurrection and the break down of self before the manifestation of God's power.

His moment of extreme darkness was the precursor of the dawn; the dawn of a new day in which he should awake and find that the work of his great manhood should be done to the glory of God rather than for the gratification of selfish motives.

Little did this youth know that this last terrible disappointment was the first means that God was using to remove the barrier between him and his Master, to strip him of self-complacency and to teach him that if he were ever to win the battle, it was God who must fight it through him.

He did not know that it was God's means of teaching him the great life's lesson of the surrender of the human will to the divine. He was a thorough believer in the Divine Creator of all things, but he had erred in depending too strongly upon his own power to bring things to pass.

God needed this youth so bountifully endowed with ability, so strong in will power to resist temptations, for the further establishment of His kingdom upon earth. The desolate youth wept bitter tears in his present weakness.

But there is no tear wrung from the human aching heart but that it may become a part of the sufferings of Christ. He took upon himself the sorrow as well as the sins of humanity, that when sorrow is put upon us it is in order that He may bring us into fellowship with Him who is the great High Priest in the Temple of Sorrow.

As the youth sat bowed in his grief, he listened to the voice of the Holy One telling him that no life can be successful save that life which is lived to the glory of God. It was in this hour that he learned his utter dependence upon his Saviour. As soon as he realized this, a strange deep joy welled up in his heart in the midst of his sorrow,—a bright gleam of sunshine shone through the riven cloud. He would not despair but go on believing that God has not forgotten.

He felt that God had fought his first great battle within him when he had in this hour of great need helped him to resist the temper. He felt that even this present obstacles which now seemed to block the way so completely would somehow be removed.

"I will arise, place my hand in the strong one of my Saviour and trust in God as Moses did, let the way be ever so dark; and perhaps in time, it shall come to pass that my life shall surpass even my longings, not maybe, in the line of that longing, but as it pleaseth God. And in those hours of great temptation, I shall not forget that Christ himself was tempted. Neither shall I forget that Christ commanded the tempter to get behind him—

"Lord God of Hosts, be with us yet,
Lest we forget—lest we forget."

SWEET PEAS BETWEEN

A NEW SERIAL

By Maggie Fullilove

Author of "Navy Blue Velvet", "Pass It On", "Precursor of the Dawn", "Sermons in Stone" etc.

The Woolworths and the Days were neighbors. They lived side by side, only an open wire fence about five feet high between them. Unfortunately they were not on friendly terms. That happy relationship which should exist between people who live at such close proximity was totally lacking.

The unhappy condition had been brought about in this manner. Mrs. Day's little daughter, Aurora, and Mrs. Woolworth's little son, Benny, had a quarrel. They had had numerous quarrels previous to this, of course, but fortunately those trivial disagreements had occurred away from the observation of the parents, and had always ended in happy terms of peace before either of those parents knew anything about them.

The two children had grown up together from earliest infancy, had become good comrades in their their earliest childhood, and understanding each other thoroughly, they were left free to roam the wood-lot together, were never segregated and allowed to meet and play only under the surveillance of their elders, but played together all day long in happy innocence. Benny, being the older of the two, had tended and protected his little playmate ever since tho first time he awoke to the knowledge of her dependence upon him. He never failed in his duty, never failed to stand up in

Sweet Peas Between

defense of the little, chubby, dimpled darling whose every crinkly curl he adored. Even in her childish fits of anger he never raised his hand to strike her—not until he reached the age of twelve and she the age of ten, did he strike her. And that one blow was the cause of the quarrel which severed the friendship of the two families for many years.

The incident occurred just before the time for spring gardening. The quarrel was only about two weeks old when one bright, sunny morning, Mrs. Day, armed with spade and accompanied by her little daughter, who carried rake and hoe, marched into the front yard (nearly all of which they used for flower garden) and preceeded to make preparation to plant their early flowers. Mrs. Woolworth and Mrs. Day both adored flowers and flower culture. Their activities in their gardens were most untiring, and a pageant of beauty began with the Crocuses in March and kept up, with unabated fervor, until the last Chrysanthemum in late Fall. Side by side they always worked, vying with each other, in very friendly manner to see who could make the best productions. The first of May always found them particularly assiduous in their efforts, and by the end of the month, their gardens were the envy of the neighborhood, and remained a blaze of color all through the summer season. All through the early weeks of Spring their yards screamed in bright blossoms of almost every flowering shrub adapted to the climate. The Lilac, Syringa, the Spiracea Opuli folia, with its clusters of snowy blossoms and the Cydenia—all were dashes of red, and white and purple; the Wistaria and the sweet Honeysuckle adorned the trellises. All these having chosen the month of May for their glory, gave way to the June blossoms. The Suetzua, the brilliant Wigelia, the Japanese Snowball, the Hydrangea, the sweet Jasmine emblazoned the yard all through July and August; then September, October and November gave place to Cosmos, Dahlias, Asters, Gladioli and the queen of Fall flowers, the Chrysanthemum. Running all through the warm season, the yards were bright with roses of every hue, their borders were resplendent with drifts of Snow-Pinks, gay Peonies, and Hollyhocks, Sweet breathed Day Lillies, brilliant Poppies, Larkspur, Phlox, Iris and all the year's train of the old time, hardly flowers, which, while natural and restful in general effect, their beauty was ever varying and appealing.

That day was perfect and flooded with warm sunshine, and Mrs. Day and daughter commenced to dig the ground, then to plant the flowers. The fresh earth smelled so delicious, its inviting odor reached Mrs. Woolworth in her kitchen. Straightway she stepped to her door and called "Benn-ee! Benn-ee!" Not many minutes passed before she and Benny, well armed with garden tools, went forth on another planting mission, in their own front yard. She and Benny spaded and planted and dug until their yard rivaled that of Mrs. Day in the fragrance of it's upturned earth.

By that time, Mrs. Day had planted all her beds—all except the long one over by her neighbor's fence. Gripping her spade determinedly she commenced on that. All the previous years those beds afforded a splendid rivalry in their production of bedding plants; but now, from the way Mrs. Day jerked her hoe it was plainly evident that a new idea possessed her.

As soon as she had prepared the ground she dispatched her little daughter off on a secret mission. That young lady soon returned holding in her restless little hand, five ten-cent packages of sweet peas. Mrs. Day and her daughter were busy all the rest of the afternoon enriching the bed with well rotted manure, and pulverizing the ground. The sun sink-low in the west, hung big and red over Mrs. Woolworth's green house, when Mrs. Day opened a trench in the rich bed and deposited all her sweet peas. With an exultant finality which plainly said, "That'll fix her," she covered them over, shot a glance at the incorrigible Benny, who hung near in curiosity, picked up all her implements, and strode around the house, the dimpled, excited Aurora following closely in her wake. That proud young lady, just before she turned the corner out of sight, stopped, faced about, shot out her little red tongue at the staring, curious Benny, then switched herself out of sight.

The next morning, Mrs. Day was roused by the echo of Mrs. Woolworth's hoe. It came from the long bed which ran parallel to her's along side their barrier fence. Consumed with curiosity to know what her neighbor was planting, Mrs. Day cautiously raised her curtain and peeped out. There stood Mrs. Woolworth engaged in the act of digging and enriching a long, suspicious trench. Suddenly Mrs. Day staggered back in angry surprise as Benny came whistling in the gate bringing five ten-cent packages of sweet peas, which he delivered to his mother.

Mrs. Day watched Mrs. Woolworth drop the seeds into the fertilized trench with motherly caution. It was simply too much to rival her's; and this time it would not be friendly but hostile rivalry.

Days passed. The rains descended, and the sun shone warm and bright upon both beds alike, causing the seeds in each row to germinate; then one morning, just after a refreshing rain, the plants of both rows raised their tender heads above the sod and commenced to grow in real earnest. For many weeks both rows continued to grow and then to bloom. Throughout the whole term of blooming, nobody could pass without stopping from sheer admiration. They were the center of attraction, the envy and despair of all the little beauty-loving children who peeped through the front fence and hungered after one, wee, small blossom to pin upon their persons.

The two women, each religiously followed the directions laid down for successful sweet pea culture, viz., *Trench deeply; manure liberally; plant early; stake quickly; water freely; dispod promptly.*

On account of their strict adherence to the above rules, no garden yielded a finer supply of blossoms than did this double row of sweet peas. As the years passed, Aurora lengthened from chubby, round-faced childhood to maidenhood of great promise in physical beauty as well as intellectual attainments. Benny Woolworth, also grown into his teens, gave promise to vigorous strength and exceptional young manhood.

Soon after the family quarrel each child had been sent away to a distant city in which the educational advantages were excellent. The change in their lives had come about in this way,—Mrs. Woolworth's sister, a lady of considerable wealth, while on a visit to Benny's mother, was greatly impressed with her promising little nephew, and after considerable amount of persuasion induced Benny's mother to let her take him away to her home.

Sweet Peas Between

Mrs. Woolworth, thinking that sending Benny off to school was an accomplishment far superior to any which Mrs. Day could ever hope to reach, consented to let Benny go. It was a step which proved one of especial benefit to Benny; for his doting aunt took great pride in her nehpew's ability, and spared neither pains nor money in giving the lad the very best educational advantages.

Mrs. Day, unable to endure this flaunting victory over her, at once began to lay plans for her daughter's education. Determined not to be beaten, she searched most diligently for means of getting even. Her only hope lay in a half brother of hers, who resided in the far north, and from whom she had received no tidings for a number of years. She wrote him at once, then awaited his answer with fretful impatience. As fate would have it, she received a message from him, a message which proved very favorable; for in it, he informed her of his prosperous condition. Mrs. Day hastily wrote him, begging him to pay a visit to his only sister whom he had not seen for so long.

This letter was answered by the appearance of the gentleman himself. To Mrs. Woolworth's consternation and surprise, he departed after a short week's visit, carrying the star-eyed, excited, little niece with him.

With the passing of the years Benny Woolworth developed into splendid young manhood; likewise Aurora Day, situated in another and far distant city, blossomed into beautiful and accomplished young womanhood.

Year after year rolled by until fifteen years had passed, before either of the mothers realized the fact. During all these years they still remained on unfriendly terms. The feeling had been constantly stimulated from time to time by one hostile action then another. During this time both the son and the daughter had finished their courses in school. Benny had written several popular novels and bade fair to become one of the most popular writers of the day.

One evening in early June, Mrs. Woolworth read a letter from Benny, stating that one week from the day on which his letter had been penned he would come home to spend a month or two—perhaps all summer at the old home.

During the fifteen years of his absence he had returned home only a few times, and each visit had been cut very short. He had not seen Aurora on any of those visits; for Aurora's visits to her mother had been quite as infrequent as his and always occurred at different times to his.

After Mrs. Woolworth read her son's letter, she jumped up and down in her excessive rejoicing. When a strong impulse seized her to run and tell Mrs. Day. She almost forgot at that blissful moment that they were enemies. The sight of Mrs. Day in her own yard, busily engaged in tying up some rosebushes, heavy with bloom, brought Mrs. Woolworth back to her nonsenses. So, instead of announcing the good news to her neighbor, Mrs. Woolworth seized a hoe and commenced to dig with strong, vigorous strokes, plants that needed no digging; and to tie up bushes that stood in no need of support.

Mrs. Woolworth's actions greatly annoyed Mrs. Day; but she continued to work at her own flower garden in silent earnestness until nearly nightfall. Likewise did Mrs. Woolworth work with hers, and there was a song in her heart, a buoyancy in her steps, a sparkle in her eye, all of which Mrs. Day's sidelong glance did not fail to detect.

Mrs. Woolworth's jubilant actions caused all the pent up anger in Mrs. Day's heart to flame anew. This anger was greatly incited by the fact that just before sundown, Mrs. Louise Devoto, the wealthiest lady in the town, had stopped at Mrs. Woolworth's gate, actually descended from her wonderful car and purchased an enormous bouquet of roses. Mrs. Day listened to every word the lady said in praise of her neighbor's exquisite display of flowers, and that distinguished lady fairly went wild over the sweet peas getting as a reward, a generous supply of the blossoms thrown in with the roses. Mrs. Day's jealous heart failed to catch the looks and words of admiration which the lady cast in the direction of her own fair yard.

After Mrs. Devoto's departure, the happy, bubbling Mrs. Woolworth's house rang with song accompanied by the echo of busy footsteps. "Something's sure to happen," thought Mrs. Day, as she made a feeble attempt to fling back to her neighbor a similar attitude of gayety.

One morning the mystery was solved as a carriage rolled up to Mrs. Woolworth's gate and a decidedly handsome, tall, broadshouldered, cleanshaven young man rushed into the outstretched arms of the smiling, weeping Mrs. Woolworth. The meeting between these two was very touching. It caused even Mrs. Day to glow when she saw how the tall, strong stranger clasped the woman in his arms.

Who can that be, wondered the peeping Mrs. Day, as she adjusted her position to a better view. Presently, as the two unconsciously turned their faces in her direction, she gave a start of surprised recognition.

Benny Woolworth—that handsome! that distinguished! How incredible! She had never dreamed it possible for her neighbor's son to develop into such a striking personality as that. She had to admit that he was decidedly fine looking. "Took it after his father," compromised Mrs. Day. "Richard Woolworth did claim the honor of being the handsomest man in town. Pity poor Richard didn't live to give the son of his a better bringing up."

She had little idea concerning Benny's real accomplishments. She watched Benny from behind drawn shades the next day, as he sat out under the big tree in his mother's perfect garden. To her he was the personification of idleness. But in truth, his great mind was deeply engaged in creating ideas for his new novel.

The surroundings were perfect. His mother's little home and garden afforded enough real beauty for any artist or dreamer. The young author was delighted beyond words, and entertained in his heart the secret hope that there he would find sufficient inspiration for his masterpiece—here in this perfect little heaven.

With real capacity and a liking for his work, this young man was certainly making a name for himself. To his friends he was a sort of paradox. His many friends, who had yet to learn his moods, wondered at his choosing to live all summer in this little house with its scrap of a garden, rather than at the spacious dwelling of his wealthy aunt.

"He must in truth adore the little mother of his." They did not know that solitude was the thing Woolworth's heart craved most. His was one of those rare natures that at times will go miles to seek absolute solitude, and yet he was an excellent companion—had many friends who felt for him that affectionate distrust which is almost always inspired by those who are prone to fits and starts of work and play, conviviality and loneliness.

Benny was like that. He could romp and frolic and tumble on the grass like a huge kitten for hours at a time on some days, then suddenly drop to the very depths of solitude and even moroseness. During those times he would be hardly fit to keep company with his collie.

Mrs. Day continued to watch young Woolworth walking in idleness as she thought, among the shrubbery of his mother's garden or among the trees of the wood lot. He seldom had company, seldom went out for any length of time. He spent most of his hours at home with his mother, or in long rambles quite alone.

One evening, about two weeks after Benny's arrival, Mrs. Day, peeping from her window, got a scene which set her heart to beating rapidly. It was a very simple but beautiful scene—tea on Mrs. Woolworth's lawn. A table was spread with a snowy cloth. The immaculate Benny, handsomer than ever, sat at the table with the most lovely and most distinguished young women and men of the town.

The three young ladies were Dulcie Devoto, the elegant Mrs. Devoto's niece, Alice Wilcox, daughter of the noted financier, Thaddeus Wilcox, and Felice Middleton, whose vivid beauty and charm, instead of wealth had won her a place among the "big folk" of the town.

Never before had Mrs. Day seen Mrs. Woolworth look so girlish and happy. She smiled upon the ladies, was at her best as hostess, beamed upon her son with open admiration. The whole scene filled Mrs. Day's heart with jealousy, while at the same time it caused the birth of a new idea.

Shaking her fist in the direction of the party, she left the window and sat down to her desk to write. A whole week passed before her letter was answered; but the favorable answer which it did bring sent Mrs. Day about the house on winged feet. She was never so happy in all her life. It was positively evident that she expected a guest. Her already clean house was cleaned anew, and polished until everything shone.

Flowers perfumed every corner, and on the day of the arrival of the guest, the house shone resplendent. The morning was perfect. The sky was tinted with the tenderest morning blush; and the sun was just rising as the carriage rolled up to Mrs. Day's gate. This time it was Mrs. Woolworth who peeped from behind her drawn curtain; and what she saw caused her eyes to open wide in one fixed stare.

✦ ✦ ✦ ✦

THE SYNOPSIS

AND THIS IS WHAT HAPPENED IN THE FIRST INSTALLMENT

The Woolworths and the Days were neighbors, but owing to a quarrel between Mrs. Woolworth's twelve-year-old son, Benny, and Mrs. Day's ten-year-old daughter, Aurora, the were no longer friendly.

Both families took great pride in their flower gardens and previous to the quarrel had vied in friendly fashion to see who could grow the prettiest flowers. After the quarrel, however, Mrs. Day decides that she must do something extraordinary in the way of gardening. Therefore she plants sweet peas along the fence between the two yards in such a manner that when they are fully grown they will form a 'spite dence' between the two yards. Mrs. Woolworth, not to be outdone plants more peas on her side of the fence.

Soon after the quarrel, Mrs. Woolworth's sister, a lady of considerable wealth, visits Benny's mother, and becomes so impressed with the lad that she takes him home with her in order that he might have the advantages of city life and a college education.

Mrs. Day, not to be outdone by her neighbor, persuades her brother to take Aurora to live with him, in order that she, too, might have the best education advantages.

Fifteen years pass, and they are still unfriendly.

Benny, who has become a famous author, comes home to spend the summer with his mother. She surrounds him with the wealthiest and most beautiful young people in town, but they do not seem to impress him very favorably and he spends most of his time in solitude.

Mrs. Day is jealous because her neighbor's son has grown so handsome and because of his popularity with the "big" folk of the town, sends for her own daughter. Aurora comes to spend a few weeks with her mother.

✦ ✦ ✦ ✦

Sweet Peas Between

A young lady, as lovely as the dawn itself, stepped from the handsome carriage and flew into Mrs. Day's greedy arms.

As soon as the first happy greeting was over, the young woman went all about the splendid garden admiring the flowers, her young face glowing. She made a lively picture with her wide hat almost falling off, showing all her ripply masses of black-brown hair brushed smoothly back from her perfect forehead. She wore a simple traveling frock of gray material, which fitted her perfectly, showing her graceful shape to the best advantage. As she stood there, her large eyes sparkling, and the young blood flushing through her clear, smooth cheeks, Mrs. Woolworth thought her the prettiest girl she had ever seen. Who on earth could she be? A bubbling outburst from the glorious creature gave Mrs. Woolworth the answer.

"Oh, mother," exclaimed the girl, "what a beautiful little heaven of a place you have here! You have so many lovely flowers! I can hardly realize that I once lived here."

It was Mrs. Woolworth's turn to fall back in surprise. "Aurora Day, as I'm alive! It can't be—that beautiful girl!" But Aurora Day it was, whose fresh beauty and girlish charm were destined to work wonders in this place.

Later in the day Benny Woolworth sat out under the tree in his mother's garden. He held a volume of Shakespeare in his hand and was reading "Romeo and Juliet." There is a time, a very sweet time too, when to every young mind, the play of plays, the poem of poems is Romeo and Juliet.

It was a warm June morning, breathless, soundless—a perfect day for quietness and dreams. Sometimes a bee came buzzing through the roses, in and away again, like some happy thought. Nothing else was stirring; not a single bird seemed to be seen or heard except that now and then he could hear the cooing of the wood dove among the trees in the woodland meadow—a low, tender voice which made him think of a mother's lullaby over a cradled child; or of two lovers clasped heart to heart, soul to soul, in the sweet embrace of love.

Aurora Day, with a pair of large scissors in her hand, tripped lightly over to the row of sweet peas to cut a supply of blossoms for herself. She had cut off only a few when she thought of Mrs.

Sweet Peas Between

Woolworth and little Benny of long ago. The sight of the other row of peas in the other yard reminded her.

"Well of all the ridiculous things—the most!" she exclaimed in half-amused, incredulous amazement. "All these years!" Soon after Aurora's arrival she had asked if Mrs. Woolworth lived next door. Her mother had answered in the affirmative without mentioning Benny. In cutting the flowers she took care not to cut a single one of the other row, which, on account of the open wire fence between, mingled their blossoms together in very beautiful and friendly fashion. Aurora noticed this and wondered how Mrs. Woolworth and her mother could live side by side all these years and not be friends. The thought made her feel very sad. Judging from her mother's short answer to her when she had inquired after Mrs. Woolworth, she knew it must be so. The fact seemed to the lovely young woman both sad and ridiculous.

Clip, clip, went her scissors as she filled her soft brown arms with blowing blossoms. All at once she saw him—the young man sitting under the tree lost in thought.

Women's eyes have a way of seeing all things at once instead of one thing at a time. She saw that he was very handsome in that suit of gray. His great length as he stretched himself in full view, his striking unusual intellect, his eyes, dark and dreamy, his satiny skin, of rich dark hue, his abundant hair brushed back from his adorable forehead—all these she took in at a single glance; then in a flash she knew it was Benny, her old play mate of years before. Her heart quickened; she started to slip away, but changed her mind. She would like very much to speak to Benny. She wondered if he remembered her. She wondered whether by fixing her eyes on him, she could make him turn and see her. Just then he did turn and did see her, and instantly his face lighted up. She smiled back at him. Why shouldn't she? They did not hate each other. That foolish feeling which existed between their parents was altogether absurd.

But it was rather startling to her to find how her heart beat. She lapsed into natural womanly vanity. She wondered if he liked her dress; was her hair fixed becomingly? Did it ripple and shine as she knew it could shine? She toyed with a gorgeous sweet pea blossom and did not look at him again until she heard his voice close to her, saying, "How-do-you-do?" across the fence and flowers. Then his large, smooth hand reached over to her and she grasped it in her own little warm impetuous one. "Miss Day?" he asked and answered the question all in one.

"Yes, Mr. Woolworth," she answered, smiling at him.

As she smiled, his heart quickened. Her youth and beauty charmed him: the fact that he was once her playfellow, thrilled him; the magic of her smile filled him with wonder.

At that moment Mrs. Day, peeping from her window, said to herself, "That will never do."

Mrs. Woolworth, likewise peeping from her window, said to herself, "I must be careful."

Later in the day, as Benny strode through the woodland grove alone, his thoughts were full of the wonderful creature who had once played, leaped and frolicked with him under those very trees. Strange he had not thought of this little playmate before now. He found it hard to associate this tall, glorious creature with the frolicksome, wilful, little dimpled spitfire, with bare, brown legs like exclamation points, short chubby, swift little feet, big, black eyes, often blue-black with anger during their childish quarrels, a round—very round face, her short curly hair, no longer than *that*, which her mother kept pinched up tightly in disgusting little makebelieve plaits, tied with a ribbon, red or some other vivid color. He remembered having thought her the nicest playmate—just tomboyish enough to be a good companion; just girlish enough to inspire in him the honor of being a good companion; just disagreeable and wilful enough, yet lovable enough, to keep him alternating between love and dislike. He loved her enough to fight to the very inch of his life on some days, then again he would run away from her in order to keep from slapping her flaming, round face—a thing which he never was guilty of until the day of that final quarrel. The unpardonable act had been committed in plain view of her mother's window, and had brought on that perpetual warfare between his mother and hers. Benny was seized with a sudden desire to visit all their old haunts. He wondered why he had not thought of them before. First he sought the little pool down in the hollow of the woods, where her chubby brown toes had so often paddled and spattered and splashed water and mud up to her dimpled knees; where she had so often launched the toy boats he made for her.

There he found the pool gone dry and in the place where it had been, ferns grew rank and tall; but just above, there leaned a sapling, little bigger than it had been when he bent it down for her horsey. How well he remembered her little flying skirts as she

"Went up and down to London Town,
Going over, arriving never,
On the road to London Town."

All at once his heart went soft and tender, and he bent and kissed the rough bark of the little bent tree, now stiff with the years.

Then he thought of their little play-house, the cave house he had made for her. It used to be up under the hill. His heart gave a curious bound as he neared the place. But there he found instead of the cave, a deep, dark sink-hole, occupied by an enormous spider with her colony of young.

Among the leaves near by, he found the head of a china doll that had been her baby. He picked this up and put it in his pocket.

Then down the hollow he plunged—down there where he used to set traps. The young, green woods bore no evidence of his former rambles; but afforded much fragrant, cool shade.

Benny lay himself down under the shade and dreamed of success. In his dreams he saw the woman whom he wanted to share it with him. He commenced to be glad that he had come here; for his coming held something, though obscure as yet, more valuable than all else in the world. He rejoiced that he had come here with his heart untouched. He knew now why God had endowed him with the power to preserve his perfect manhood—chaste from the secret sins of the world.

He was thankful that there were no past sins like a scarlet blot to stain his coming greatness; that there were no memories of evil living to arise now like hideous aspects, to mouth and gibber at him, threatening his new born hopes. He had met many beautiful, accomplished women, but had remained heart free—his manhood unplunged. He was glad it was so, now that he knew that

"Cupid's well aimed, fatal dart
At last had pierced his sleeping heart."

The arrow had been borne on the wings of that first sweet smile across the sweet pea hedge. The fact of their parent's quarrel never worried him in the least: indeed it appeared to him a perfectly foolish trifle.

The next day the penetrating eyes of Mrs. Woolworth did not fail to observe the change which had come over her son. Why was that strange wonderful new glow upon his face; that infinite depth of softness in his eyes as he looked constantly toward the Days' home? Although she asked herself these questions, she sensed the cause. These facts made her hate Mrs. Day and Aurora all the more. She became to be foolishly wicked as to accuse the two of wily cunning, of setting traps to ensnare her son. "He is much too good for the common, little pretty minx," she said.

Being aware of her son's unusual ability she naturally thought him the greatest person in the world. This thought enhanced the value of herself in her own estimation. From her vainglorious height she began to look down upon Mrs. Day and her daughter as far beneath her and her son; therefore she became determined that her son shouldn't fall in love with this common girl.

Every day she brought to her home as many of the "big folk" as she could, hoping to turn Benny's attention to them; but he was bored by their ceaseless, nonsensical chatter, and often sought refuge down under the hill near the spider's cave, or under the cool trees which had so often shaded him and Aurora when they were children.

Five whole days passed and he did not see Aurora. He began to wonder why she kept herself so completely out of sight. He would sit for hours gazing toward the house which sheltered her. When he failed to see her all that time his heart began to fear. Surely she had not gone away without speaking to him again—surely. The thought made him shake. He did not know—did not dream that Mrs. Woolworth, in a blind rage because of what Aurora had done for her son; unable to forgive Mrs. Day for bringing the girl there, led on to desperation because of her son's utter lack of enthusiasm over her distinguished guests with which she constantly surrounded him, had written Mrs. Day a letter in which she informed her of their knowledge concerning the trickery being practiced—the trap which she and her girl had set for her son. She ended the letter by stating that she didn't expect any more from such common folk, and that it was a mere waste of time to think that her son would marry a common girl like Aurora with scarcely any education to her credit.

Mrs. Day naturally flew into an unholy rage when she read this insulting missive, and it took all her daughter's force to keep her from marching over at once in order to effect an immediate settlement. "It's only his mother," Aurora pleaded. "I dare say he doesn't know a thing about it. The best way is to utterly ignore the whole unpleasant, disgusting affair." By much coaxing and begging she induced her mother to keep calm, at least until she could return to her uncle's. "I shall have nothing more to say to the gentleman," she promised with a certain ache in her heart.

Therefore Aurora decided to cut her visit short and return in three days to her uncle's house, never to visit Fair View again as long as the Woolworths lived next door.

As much as her heart longed to, she never allowed another meeting with Benny—not of her own choosing. On the day before the time set for her departure she was seized with a desire to visit the old haunts of her happy childhood—haunts that she had almost forgotten. She did not remember them nearly so well as Benny Woolworth did.

Benny found her sitting beside the old cave, near the home of the big mother spider. She sat there watching the great insect, lost in thought. What she was thinking at that moment, Benny would have given worlds to know. He carried the loved volume of Shakespeare in his hand. The story of Romeo and Juliet had become the poem of poems to him now.

Making a slight noise so as not to frighten her, he advanced. She looked up perfectly calm as if she had expected him to come. Her eyes did not fall from his and a look of purest beauty welled in them. Seeing the volume of Shakespeare she reached for it. She adored Shakespeare.

Benny, overwhelmed by his good fortune, settled himself beside her. The beauty of the place, the golden sunlight streaming through the fresh green lent an added charm to her—already more lovely than any other woman he knew. Benny watched her shapely fingers turn the pages of his book, thinking as he watched, "What better heroine can be found on earth than this nut-brown maiden of my childhood."

He listened to her voice as she spoke of the great poet, and its soft richness of tone thrilled him. "I perceive that you are a lover of Shakespeare," she said. "It is no wonder; for he is everybody's favorite. This homage is due largely to the fact that he is a cosmopolitan writer. He, so far as touches our earthly horizon, is ubiquitous. One marked characteristic of his is, he was so uniformly truthful. In his delineation of character he was always accurate. His penetrative genius never erred in his logical sequence of character."

"What about fair Ophelia?" asked her listener, delighted to hear her intelligent interpretation of his beloved poet. "Shakespeare paints her as pure as air, altogether faultless. Certainly from any standpoint her conduct is irreproachable; yet as soon as she becomes insane, she sings unclean songs, salacious suggestions fall from her lips, suggestions which she never uttered in her sanity. Is there no fallacy in his delineation of character there?"

"No," said Aurora. Leaning toward him, she regarded him in silence a few moments, then continued, "—thoughts are like the interior of rooms with closed shutters. They cannot be seen. We tell our thoughts or we keep them hidden according to our desire to secretiveness. Speech is not always a full index to thought; and it was Shakespeare's aim to point out that fair Ophelia, lovelorn and neglected; fair Ophelia whose every word and conduct had been exceptional—this same seemingly perfect creature, cherished thoughts not meet for maidenhood, and in the secret recesses of her heart, thought voluptuousness. I know no greater example of accuracy in character delineation than this!"

While Aurora spoke she mechanically turned the leaves of the book. Suddenly she raised her eyes, and whether she gazed past him or straight at him, he could not tell. He was unable to penetrate their marvelous depths as she said: "The lover is Shakespeare's main thesis: and his lovers, both men and women, never violate the proprieties of love. 'In 'All's Well That Ends

Well,' Helena is a true phase of womanhood. Even in those days of general infidelity and lordship of man, woman had power of self-sacrifice and religious self-denial in love. Many of the great writers of today are different to the old writers in that respect. A great many of our modern writers are so very weak in their production of women characters. Take Mr. Allan Worth, who is attracting the attention of the literary world. I am sure you have read his novels—the latest and best of which is, 'The Master.'" Aurora was quite unmindful of the slight start which Benny Woolworth gave at the mention of his pseudonym. He quickly regained his self-control, however, and listened intensely for what she might have to say concerning his greatest book.

"We must admit," she continued, "that he has framed some mighty men, tragic or melodramatic sometimes, somber always, but men of bulk and character. Daniel, in 'The Master,' is a creation sufficient to make his readers conceive him as immortal. And Dod Peterson is real, manly, mighty, self-mastering and self-surrendering. In all Mr. Worth's works, all his men are giants; but his women do not satisfy. They are weak, even foolish, entirely too sentimental—do not possess enough real womanhood! Mary Atwood is very interesting, but quite unsatisfactory. She doesn't seem to know her duty; or if she does, fails to adhere to it. May Allison, although she grips the reader's attention and holds it all through to the end, is to my idea a silly creature, with no depth of character. Evidently the writer has met no real women—or—"

"That is the condition," Benny cut in.

"Or if he has, he failed to understand them," she continued as if he had not spoken. "Victor Hugo, the greatest creater of heroes, who fashioned a hero, Jean Valjean, after the likeness of Jesus—even his women are unsatisfactory. It seems that no man had greater skill and inclination to create heroes than Victor Hugo. All his books are biographies of heroism of one type or another. No book of his is heroless—why could he not have created a like heroine?"

"Was not Cossette a heroine?" asked Benny.

"I have no patience with Cossette. Her selfishness is not to be condoned. Her contrition and her tears were delayed too long. Fantine was a heroine, though not altogether satisfactory—

Fantine, with mother love omnipotent; Fantine with her dead face turned toward the door, looking even in death, for her child. The same is true of Eponine; for in her is shown the miracle of woman's love."

Aurora continued to turn the leaves of the book. Suddenly her face lit up with delightful little ripples like sunshine across water touched by the breeze.

"Of all poets," she said, "Shakespeare is the richest in material of simile. He thought in pictures—pictures which never failed to make the dull eye bright. What is more delightful than this?

'Night's candles are burnt out and jocund day
Stands tiptoe on the misty mountain top.'

Then what evokes a smile more quickly than this:

'Oh I am stabbed with laughter.'

Indeed Shakespeare is never remorseful. Dante is a picture of melancholy, Tennyson is perpetual melancholy, Aeschylus is a poet whose face is never lit with smiles, but Shakespeare, although a writer of tragedy, is a laughing poet. He weeps, but always a smile breaks through his weeping, and he turns from the grave of tragedy with laughter in his eyes.

"Ah! Shakespeare is entirely too massive to be discussed in an hour. I can never say enough in praise of him." She closed the book and started to rise to her feet.

"Do not go!" he cried in breathless admiration of her. He had thought her beautiful before, but now he thought her divine. Even her ruthless criticism of his own book heightened his admiration of her.

"But it is imperative that I go," she said laughing, as she quoted another one of Shakespeare's similes, "'We burn daylight,' I go away tomorrow," she said, sobering at once. He gasped. "So soon! You must not!" He put his hand on her shoulder to keep her in place, and her blood raced in her veins at the contact. All the time she kept saying to herself, "I must not let him see that I care:

I must not let him see!" She did not speak a word—did not feel at that moment, capable of speech for he was looking at her with the strangest expression in his eyes—a glint of steel; yet mingled with something infinitely tender. She met his glance unwaveringly for an instant, then looked away past him without veiling her eyes—a look full of baffling mystery.

"Please, I must go," she said, arming herself against him with coldness. Instantly he cleared the path which led up the hill to her mother's house. As she passed him a dazzling smile broke over her exquisite features, and she held out to him her impulsive little hand, saying:

"I've enjoyed this half hour with you, my old play fellow. I had almost forgotten Benny Woolworth and the delightful path which led to our playhouse. But you see I did find the cave-house you made for me—inhabited by that big black spider. I wonder how long she has lived there with her host of spider-children?" Aurora gave a queer little smile. Suddenly she drew her hand from his, darted away up the path and was soon lost among the tender green.

Benny, left alone, sat down upon a patch of green tuft. The warm sunlight shone upon his head intensifying that look of wonder and tenderness in his eyes. Previous to this his chief aim in life had been to attain success, sure and glorious. Now he knew that he could never reach the goal unless he reached it with this woman by his side. Up to this time he had entertained little thought concerning woman and marriage, devoting his whole time to fitting himself for his life's work; now this girl was teaching him of woman's subtle influence over man—how necessary she is to him in every walk of life. To the charms of this woman Benny fell a willing victim. That supreme hour which comes to every man and to every woman once in a lifetime had come to him. In matters of this kind, the strongest, the most logical have their moments of fainting.

Benny spent all the rest of the afternoon in aimless rambling about the woods. Every leaf, every flower seemed to fill him with thoughts of her. He must see her again,—would see her again. No power on earth must hinder. That quarrel between his mother and hers was but a little thing. He had not asked permission to call, she had not given him time, but this he meant to do as soon as he should see her again. Then Benny remembered that she would go away on the morrow. The thought worried him greatly.

He strode to and fro among the trees, tramping down hundreds of little flowers beneath his feet and heeded it not. She had not acted as if she cared very much for him, and yet—

Benny found himself wandering on toward his mother's house—perhaps she might be wandering in the garden. Aurora was not in the garden—was nowhere in sight. He hung about the garden until long after nightfall, hoping to catch a glimpse of her; but no soft footsteps disturbed the dewdrops which hung on the tender grass of the quiet garden.

About eleven o'clock that night, Benny, in a restless mood, came out of the house and walked down toward the grove. In certain moods men turn insensibly towards any space where nature rules, where the sky is free to the eye, and one feels the broad companionship of primitive forces. A man wants no company when he is in love—he cares for nobody save the one whom he adores.

Benny paused beneath a widespread oak and looked up at the stars. Now and then he drew a deep breath of the unstirring air and smiled without knowing that he smiled. His restlessness of a few hours before had given place to patience. He felt that all things would come out right. He would see Aurora before she went away, at all hazards.

A sweetish sensation beset his heart, a kind of quavering lightness was in his limbs. He shut his eyes for a moment out of sheer joy, and he saw a face—*her* face. He sat down frog-fashion on one of the projecting roots of a tree, gazing upwards like one in a trance, the smile coming and going on his lips. Then he rose to his feet again; that feeling of extraordinary lightness was still in his limbs; still that face floated before his vision,—its perfect regularity, its beautiful intelligence, its dark, smiling eyes full of subtle tenderness and charm; its soft brown skin, which must be velvety and fragrant like the petals of a rose; its mouth—ah its mouth, full and ripe. The thought of what her sweet, soft lips held for him made him stagger.

Sweet Peas Between

There was no beauty so compelling as hers; no mind so brilliant, no intellect so sympathetic as hers. He adored the sweep of the black-brown hair across her soft forehead. There was something in her whole make-up, an emination, an expression, a turn of her soft neck, an indwelling grace, a something which he could not analyze, something that appealed to him; that turned and touched him to the very depth, something that would not let him alone, something that was so fierce and sweet that it pained yet was the source of excessive joy. It wouldn't let him rest, nor did he desire that it should.

She was right in her saying that he didn't know women. In truth he hadn't ever known one like her. No wonder the women of his novels had been only commonplace. In her he could redeem that weakness in his novels.

He rose to go back to the house, still in that exquisite rapture so new and possessing. Before going into the house he walked out into his mother's garden. That lady was asleep and knew nothing of her son's wanderings.

✦ ✦ ✦ ✦

THE SYNOPSIS

AND THIS IS WHAT HAPPENED IN THE PRECEDING INSTALLMENTS

The Woolworths and the Days were neighbors, but owing to a quarrel between Mrs. Woolworth's twelve-year-old son, Benny, and Mrs. Day's ten-year-old daughter, Aurora, the were no longer friendly.

Both families took great pride in their flower gardens and previous to the quarrel had vied in friendly fashion to see who could grow the prettiest flowers. After the quarrel, however, Mrs. Day decides that she must do something extraordinary in the way of gardening. Therefore she plants sweet peas along the fence between the two yards in such a manner that when they are fully grown they will form a 'spite fence' between the two yards. Mrs. Woolworth, not to be outdone plants more peas on her side of the fence.

Soon after the quarrel, Mrs. Woolworth's sister, a lady of considerable wealth, visits Benny's mother, and becomes so impressed with the lad that she takes him home with her in order that he might have the advantages of city life and a college education.

Mrs. Day, not to be outdone by her neighbor, persuades her brother to take Aurora to live with him, in order that she, too, might have the best education advantages.

Fifteen years pass, and they are still unfriendly.

Benny, who has become a famous author, comes home to spend the summer with his mother. She surrounds him with the wealthiest and most beautiful young people in town, but they do not seem to impress him very favorably and he spends most of his time in solitude.

Mrs. Day is jealous because her neighbor's son has grown so handsome and because of his popularity with the "big" folk of the town, sends for her own daughter. Aurora comes to spend a few weeks with her mother.

Shortly after her arrival, Aurora asks her mother concerning the Woolworths. Her mother tells her that they still live next door, but the two families are still on unfriendly terms. Later the two young people renew friendship much to each mother's consternation. Mrs. Woolworth writes an anonymous letter to Aurora telling her that her son would not marry a common girl—like Aurora. Aurora decided to cut her visit short and return to her uncle's never to visit her mother's house again as long as the Woolworth's are living next door.

Late that night, Benny Woolworth, restless and unable to sleep, wanders in the garden in hopes of catching a glimpse of Aurora. Towards midnight he decides that she must have retired for the night and turns to go into the house, when he catches a glimpse of something white in the moonlight.

✦ ✦ ✦ ✦

Suddenly his heart leaped! Was that a gleam of white among the shrubbery? It was. Stealthily he crept toward the barrier fence, his heart beating loudly in his bosom. The ghost-like figure came nearer. It stood at arm's length from him, just across the fence of fragrant blossoms. Benny feared to breathe lest he should frighten her. It was Aurora, the darling of his soul!

The night was warm and heavily scented with the mingled odor from the flowers of both gardens. Aurora stopped close to the row of sweet peas, and burying her nose in the blossoms, she was visited by a memory of her first sight of Benny, stretched at full length under the great oak; and then only that evening of such delight and disillusionment, down under the hill by the spider's cave that had once been their little house—the cave-house he had made for her in the days of their happy childhood.

She wished with all her soul that their parents had not had that foolish quarrel. It would be a delight to go over the old places together; to travel again in those dear paths wherein their feet had so often trod.

With sudden impetuosity—a sweet characteristic of her's—she placed one little soft hand over her heart as if to quiet its too rapid beating. Benny Woolworth on the other side of the fence, could endure no more. His instinct told him that her thoughts were of him.

"Aurora," he whispered softly, like the sweet echo on a summer breeze. She heard and swift as a fawn, she darted back toward the house. Benny grew desperate. *"Aurora!"* he cried, "it is I—Benny!" He stretched out his arms across the blossoms, all the time assuring her that it was no one to do her harm.

"Oh, you frightened me so!" she said, coming toward him.

"Did I Love—Aurora—pardon me! I didn't mean to do it!

"Come closer, don't be afraid. You see I cannot rest until I tell you what has happened to me—to us, I mean. Oh Aurora, I love you—I want you, I must have you for my wife! I cannot endure life without you! Success is nothing—fame is nothing—nothing without your love. These few hours with you have taught me what ideal womanhood is. You were right this evening when you said that I—that is—Worth hadn't seen the ideal woman. He had not until he met you!—er—I mean to say that I am the author of those miserable stories which fail to depict the ideal woman."

"You!" she cried, "Oh Benny Woolworth—you! What a beast I've been!"

"No, no, by far the grandest, the dearest woman on earth—the woman I must have for my wife, the woman for whom I've kept my manhood chaste and unplumbed until this hour!" His arms still stretched toward him across the barrier fence. All at once she ran forward, and he caught her in his arms and kissed her lips as he would never stop. It was their first kiss—the kiss which joined their souls in one long blissful union. Suddenly she drew herself from his arms. Her lovely face grew ashen, and she fell against the fence, her lips still quivering from the magic thrills of that kiss, her eyes very dark as she looked at him distraught, drunk on the bliss of the moment.

The odor from the crushed blossoms was almost too sweet. Her childish impetuosity asserted itself again, and she held out both her arms toward him again, as if the world lay beyond that fence; but as swiftly she dropped them upon the fence and buried her face in them. A sob came up in her throat, that seemed to rend her body. He reached over, touching her with timid touches of despair; but she wept on, unheeding his anxious voice.

Benny could no longer endure her sobbing. With one wild leap he cleared the fence and gathered her in his arms, demanding to know the cause of her troubles as his right. "Is it because of the old trouble between our parents?" he asked, seeing that she hesitated. She looked up smiling through her tears. "Oh it is ridiculous!" she cried—"yet very serious—more serious than you think—perhaps." Benny's heart rejoiced to know it was only that. "Leave the matter to me," he said, "'All's Well That Ends Well,' you know," he laughed, and trembled in his joy.

Before he let her go, he drew her to the little seat over behind the lilacs, where they used to tumble and frolic when they were children. He told her of his secret hopes and ambitions, and she, feeling quite ashamed of her criticism of his great stories, tried hard to apologize. "That criticism is worth everything to me," he assured her.

Then they entered into their sweet love making. The darkness was dear to them. The heavens studded with stars smiled upon them, and there was a thrill in the immense mystery of the universe, as their souls communed. At that hour of love those two beings composed of every chastity and innocence, were resplen-

Sweet Peas Between

dent to each other in the darkness. The little garden seemed to them a sacred place. All the flowers opened about them and proffered them their insense; they too, opened their souls and poured them forth to the lovers; the lustrous, vigorous vegetation trembled full of sap and intoxication and thrilled to hear their whispered words of love. Those whisperings were like the gentle cooing of the wood doves.

For one hour they sat together in the darkness, fascinating each other in the shadow, their hearts murmuring, whispering under the immense liberation of stars which filled the sky. In that happy hour the white soul of Benny dazzled the spotless soul of Aurora. It was that first embrace of two virginities in the ideal—a wonderful hour when ecstacy, not passion, reigned supreme.

Benny was altogether charmed by Aurora's voice. It was like a tender love song in his ears. Everything she said came from the tender instincts of her pure heart. Nobody knew how to say things so profoundly sweet as Aurora. Sweetness and depth characterized all her expressions. To Benny her whole person was artlessness, transparency, candor and radiance. "How very appropriate is her name," thought Benny. To him this woman was a condescension of auroral light in womanly form.

To Aurora, Benny was lord, king,—master of her soul. She worshiped him.

Reluctantly they bade each other a sweet goodnight. She went into her mother's house to retire and dream of him; while he went to his room, not to sleep but to work on his new novel in which woman should reign supreme. All was very still, and the solitude was what the young author wanted most. He worked on till three o'clock—just coming dawn. He possessed one of those constitutions that can do that sort of thing and take no harm from it. Indeed he worked best, and accomplished most in such spurts of vigorous, inspired concentration. When at last he did retire, it was to dream of Aurora, the queen of his soul.

The next day Aurora, fresh as the morning, went all about the house singing like a soft throated oriole. Her mother remarked: "You're awfully gay, Honey, on the morning you must leave your mother to her loneliness."

[239]

"But I'm not going, Mother darling," and snatching her mother about the waist, Aurora whirled her in a mad caper about the room. "Not—go-ing—what?" gasped her mother, all out of breath.

"Not until Benny Woolworth bids me," the young girl answered with the merriest twinkle in her eyes.

Her mother stopped short and stared at her daughter as if that young lady was suddenly bereft of her senses. *"Benny Woolworth! What has he to do with it, pray?"*

"Everything! We are to be married: I go away when he goes—where he takes me; or stay with him over there—wherever he chooses to stay."

Without another word, poor Mrs. Day dropped into a chair. It was like seeing her daughter slain before her very eyes. Unable to endure more she buried her face in her hands and commenced to sob. Aurora flew to her. "There, there, Mother mine! Did I hurt you, Mumsie darling?" Perceiving her mother's real distress, her voice took a tone of deepest tenderness. "Mother, darling, I'm so sorry I hurt—don't weep, mother, my sweet." Then she said softly:

"Our love is so very wonderful, Mother. I went into your perfect little garden: he was over there in his mother's garden. He saw me, was thinking of me—was all the time loving me with all his splendid soul. He told me he loved me, and I—I woke to the fact that I loved him. I think I have loved Benny Woolworth all my life, Mother."

The mother raised her tear-stained face and stared at her daughter—a pitiless, merciless stare of cold contempt, before which Aurora shrank as if from a blow. "So this is what I brought you here for, is it?—to go traipsing about in my garden at midnight with worthless, lazy, idlesome dudes!"

"Mother!" The girl's hands flew to her mother's lips in order to stop the foolish words. Mrs. Day, in her anger, snatched the hand away. "I've suffered enough at the hands of that woman and her son. In bringing you here, I've only cut off my nose to spite my face, it seems. But listen, Aurora Day, listen to me, you go away from here this morning—understand?"

Aurora stood up every inch of her queenly height, fixed her dark, beautiful eyes a full minute upon the woman who gave her birth. The flaming indignation which had sprung up at first, slowly changed to patient tolerance. Her mother must learn her lesson—must learn that a quarrel so groundless as that which had happened so long ago could not rob her of her happiness and crowning love of her life,—must learn that the daughter which she sheltered was no longer a child, but a woman, having a woman's capabilities, a woman's mind and desires. She turned and slowly left the room without a single word. Mrs. Day was baffled. She did not know her own daughter. She had not reckoned on Aurora's intelligence in the matter. Almost at the same moment the same kind of drama was being carried on in the home of the Woolworths.

Benny, in spite of having worked nearly all night, rose early. His mind was so filled with thoughts of Aurora that he could think of little else. To be alone with his thoughts, he strode out toward the sacred spot down in the woods where they had spent such a perfect half hour together the day before. He had not gone far before he heard the breakfast bell. "Now is a good time to tell Mother." he said, as he retraced his steps. Somehow the task did not savor of pleasantness. "Better to have it done with at once," he said to himself.

"Mother,"—he plunged into the subject as that benign lady beamed upon him from her place at the head of the snowy table—"Mother, the pearl, the very jewel of womanhood has promised to be my wife."

His mother, thinking that he meant Alicia Devoto, because he had mentioned pearls and jewels, clapped her hands in astonished glee, saying: "Oh how utterly grand! Alicia is a fine girl—is worth her weight in gold."

"Alicia!" cried Benny, "*Aurora Day* has promised to be my wife."

"Aurora Day!" Mrs. Woolworth screamed the name as she threw up both her hands like one that is shot.

"It's a trick! a scheme!" she screamed. "That girl and her mother are nothing but designing women!"

"*Mother!*" Her son's voice thundered a command of silence. Mrs. Woolworth paused only a moment, then burst out with vehemence. "That woman and her girl have done nothing but 'tit-for-tat' me ever since I knew them. I won't stand it! I'll tell her to her head that I won't have her for a daughter-in-law!"

"Mother!" again the son spoke his command. "Are you a sane woman?" he asked in as calm a voice as he could command. "If so, then listen to me. By the honor, the reverence which I bear you, I ask you to speak naught against the woman who only last night promised to be my wife. Mother, you are in gravest error concerning Miss Day and her mother. Miss Day is the purest, the fairest flower of womanhood. Mere words cannot do her justice. I love her with all my soul, and I beg you, mother—because I love you, and revere you as my only parent—never to speak ill concerning the woman I love better than my life."

Mrs. Woolworth's knees shook and she crumbled into her chair. She never could withstand Benny's pleadings. This time it was no childish pleading for a coin with which to buy some cherished toy; but a deep pleading, born of self-respect and respect for his mother—a pleading which said plainly: "Do not drive me to violence against my own mother in order to defend the woman I love; for I will defend her regardless of circumstances."

Mrs. Woolworth began to whimper. "Mother," said Benny, laying a tender hand upon his mother's head in which many streaks of gray hairs shown. "I've always regarded the quarrel between you and Mrs. Day as the most ridiculous thing I ever heard of. Why can't you be friends? You've kept up this perfectly foolish quarrel for a great number of years. I don't understand how two sensible people can indulge in such utter nonsense. Why not be sensible and make up with Mrs. Day? She is an admirable woman. It's just foolish, stubborn pride that keeps you two from being excellent friends and neighbors. Let's see, what was the origin of the quarrel, Mother, I've quite forgotten."

"How *can* you forget? flashed his mother. "She struck you three times, simply because you slapped that impudent hus—"

"Mother! Yes, I do remember now. I was a dastardly coward enough to strike that dear, little child's face when I should have kissed her little cheek instead."

"Well, she and I caused you two to become enemies by this quarrel in which I slapped her face; now we will be the cause of bringing about a complete reconciliation; for last night in her mother's garden we declared our love, and I—" here his voice grew low, sweet and reverent—"Mother, I kissed her."

A few minutes later, Aurora, armed with a pair of scissors, came out into her mother's garden to cut flowers. Clip, clip went her scissors, as she cut off scores of long-stemmed roses. The morning was perfect, and she knew that life held many such fair mornings for her. Her white dress intensified by a dash of blue ribbon at her belt, fell in graceful folds just above her ankles. Her wealth of shining hair rippled above her forehead. The morning breeze had brought the faintest flush to her face; her large dark eyes, soft as dove's shone with light; her sweet lips were parted in keen enjoyment.

It was thus Benny Woolworth found her and was abashed by the beauty of her expression as he went toward her. "Aurora," he said, his voice scarce above a whisper,—"I am the happiest man alive, and of all men, the most fortunate. The love of a pure, divine woman like you is a treasure above price." She held a great bunch of freshly cut sweet peas in her hand, the basket at her feet was filled with glowing, long-stemmed roses. The beautiful picture she made—a woman whose beauty all soft glowing and alluring as it was, yet radiated purity, modesty and goodness, filled him with awe.

At that moment a pair of eyes slyly peeped from the windows of Mrs. Woolworth's and Mrs. Day's homes respectively, and what they saw turned the tide of hostile current that had been flowing in one direction for fifteen years. A moment later the locked gate between the two back yards clicked and Mrs. Woolworth stole softly through.

"Please may I have that bunch of sweet peas, dearest," said Benny Woolworth, merely for the sole purpose of touching her hand in the transaction. Aurora held them out obediently, and Benny seized the hand, blossoms and all and crushed them against his breast.

At this moment two pairs of eyes peeped from Mrs. Day's window and as Mrs. Woolworth's son gathered Mrs. Day's daughter in his arms, the two older people turned away.

Suddenly Mrs. Woolworth held out her arms. The next instant, the two heads, both of them were streaked with gray, mingled together in a long, friendly embrace.

Sweet Peas Between

Outside the two happy lovers resumed their sweet task of cutting the long-stemmed magnificent blossoms from the double row of sweet peas,—rows which hatred and hostility of the past years had labeled as *Sweet Peas Between;* but which the magic power of love had transformed for all the coming years into the bright, glowing symbol of *Sweet Peas Between.*

THE RESENTMENT

BY
MARY ETTA SPENCER

PRINTED BY
A. M. E. Book Concern
631 Pine Street
Phila., Pa.

DEC -5 1921

©CI.A630580

DEDICATED TO THE MEMORY OF MY
MOTHER FROM WHOM I DERIVED
MY LITERARY TALENT, AND
TO THE GROWING BOYS
AND GIRLS OF
MY RACE

THE AUTHOR'S PURPOSE

It is not my desire to write this book merely to show my ability to write or to win fame as a writer, but that I may write some little something that would inspire some boy or girl of my race to be willing to endure struggle, to become a man or woman of worth by refusing to stay on the ground floor, and thereby be classed as a "good-for-nothing," by willingness to do hard and honest labor, by doing well whatever task is assigned you, by unselfish deeds, by preservation of virtue, by alienation of vice, by determining your course, and if that course proves right, let nothing turn you from it; that determination backed by will-power and sticking to it through thick and thin.

MARY ETTA SPENCER.

CONTENTS

Little Silas 7- 13

The Awakening 15- 26

At Work in Earnest 27- 54

Seeing City Life 55- 73

"Net" Determines Her Course 74- 84

Step by Step 85-101

"I Shall Not Always Be Called A
   Nigger" 103-118

Obstacles 119-141

Two Great Events 143-173

Let Me Build My House By The
   Side of The Road and Be A
   Friend to Man 175-192

The Reward 193-208

Two Great Men Meet 209-216

CHAPTER I.

LITTLE SILAS

"Come on, come on there, boy, you must think you are owner of half this county instead of being a good-for-nothing "nigger." Come, hurry up, we have got lots of work to do today, with the sun two hours high already. And, by the way, a gentleman, a Mr. Walker, will be here today. He is one of the richest ranchmen in the West. Don't for goodness sake, forget your manners, and please remember to take off your hat to him. He is a great man, and your kind must honor him," said Mr. Baxter with a twinkle in his eye.

Mr. Baxter was a wealthy white Southern farmer. He was talking to Silas Miller, a little colored boy.

Silas had been hired to Mr. Baxter by his father about a year before our story begins. He was then a boy barely fourteen years old, small and delicate for his age. His mother died when he was twelve years old, leaving four children—Silas being the oldest. Two years later, his father married again.

It was the custom in the rural districts of the South for parents to hire their children out as soon as they were old enough to do a little work for small sums of money, monthly; and, very often, for food and clothing only. Silas, not being so strong, was not put to work so soon, but his father hired him to Mr. Baxter when he was fourteen years old, to do light work. Poor little fellow; at first he was so lonely, there being no children there. He missed the merry fun-making of his little brothers and sister.

He was made to sleep over the kitchen stairs, away from the other part of the house. He would have died from fright had he not believed in God. On entering the dark room (he was not allowed to have a light because they were afraid he would set the house afire through carelessness), he would kneel beside the bed and ask God to send "Mamma" to stay with him. Such childish faith! In the next few moments he would be in dreamland.

Humble and poor as they were at home, this child would have given worlds (had they been his to give) to have remained with them.

He was permitted to go home two Sundays in each month. He looked forward to these days as the happiest days of his young life.

Silas had lived here over a year, amidst luxury and wealth. He did not have to work hard, yet little consideration was shown him, the fact being he was only a Negro boy.

At work, he was a little slow, but what he did was well done. Silas is an unusually bright and quick-witted boy, and I doubt whether he shall be contented to work as a laborer for other farmers long. Of course, we don't want him to know what we think of him; it would make him feel important, yet we all love him and would hate to part with him," said Mr. Baxter in speaking of him to his friends.

Little did Mr. Baxter know that he had said the words that, in years to come, would make Silas Miller one of the richest and most independent men of his race.

While at work that morning, hot tears ran down Silas' face, his heart ached. "Why must I be reminded every day that I am a Negro, I try so hard to do what is right?

But, it is always "Nigger." He looked at his dark, brown-skinned hands and wondered why God made some white and others black. Stamping his foot upon the ground, he said, "But there is one thing certain, I shall not always be called a 'nigger,' I am going to be a business man, and men will take their hats off—well, we'll take our hats off to each other."

Dinner over, Mrs. Baxter asked her husband to let Silas stay and help her. She wanted him to motor to town with her and then help with the supper. Silas was elated because he was very anxious to see this man that they all seemed so excited about.

Dressed in his Sunday clothes, with a white straw hat and a black tie, he was a picture, in spite of his color.

"Now, Silas, don't forget to take off your hat and say, 'Good afternoon, sir,'" said Mrs. Baxter for the twentieth time since they started. "Yes'm," replied Silas slowly, wishing that she could think of something to talk about besides the taking off of hats.

They arrived in town just as the train steamed into the station. Mrs. Baxter stood upon the platform scanning every face as the passengers descended from the train. "At length," she exclaimed. "Oh, there he

THE RESENTMENT

is." Walking up to a tall, well-groomed man, "How do you do, Mr. Walker?"

"Well, well, Mrs. Baxter, I'm fine, thank you; how are you, and all of the family?" he asked as he shook her hand.

"Very well," replied Mrs. Baxter, smiling. During this conversation Silas stood looking; he saw a fine example of a successful business man. His forty-odd years rested lightly upon his shoulders. His gray hair gave decidedly a touch of distinction to his appearance. He was an alert, progressive ranchman from a Western State. Silas admired this stately, refined looking man, and hoped with all his heart that he would not use the word "nigger." He stood with hat in hand waiting and wishing that he would speak to him. He felt slighted at not being noticed when Mrs. Baxter said, "Come, Mr. Walker, my car is over here," pointing to a beautiful car a short distance away.

Mr. Walker had not noticed that the boy was with them until they reached the car, and saw Silas struggling to lift his heavy baggage into the car. "Hello there, little fellow; are you with us?"

"Yes, sir," Silas answered, his hat still in his hand.

Seeing that the baggage was far too

THE RESENTMENT

heavy for his child strength, he said, "Don't, child, don't! Let me help you."

"I can get it in, sir, if you give me time." Silas was afraid of being called "good-for-nothing" before this great man.

"Yes, my child, I shall have to give you ten years, I'm afraid, you get hold of that end," pointing to the lighter side, "and I will take this end; now, both together."

Then Mr. Walker did what few colored boys of the South had seen a white man do. He took the little brown hands into his soft, white ones with their glittering diamonds, shook them and asked, "What is your name?"

"Silas Miller, sir."

"Well, Silas, I am indeed glad to know you." The child did not know what to say, but he did the right thing—he smiled and bowed his head, then he put on his hat.

As they motored home, Silas wondered if Jesus was any nicer than this man. Mrs. Baxter also saw that Mr. Walker was different from the men of the South, but said nothing.

That night they sat down to a real Southern supper of fried chicken and waffles. As Silas served the supper, he could not help noticing Mr. Walker's cultured and refined manner. Each time he whe served, he said "Thank you," or bowed his head. "Ain't he grand?" thought Silas, "I do hope he will stay two whole weeks."

Silas got up early the next morning and by ten o'clock had all of his work done. Mr. Baxter wondered what had come over the boy. "He worked well before, but now he is a wonder," he said to his wife.

THE AWAKENING
CHAPTER II.

The second day of Mr. Walker's stay he motored with Mr. Baxter to visit different farmers. Silas was overjoyed at being permitted to go with them. He enjoyed hearing the Westerner talk of his ranch, his cattle and the beautiful mansion he had built for his wife and Ethel, their only daughter. He did not let one word escape his ears.

The following Sunday was his day off, but he asked Mrs. Baxter if she wanted him to stay and help her with the dinner. She was delighted, but did not know what to make of Silas, as he was always so anxious to go home. The fact was, Silas wanted to get a chance to talk with Mr. Walker. How he hoped against hope that Mr. Walker would remain at the farm that day.

Sunday came, work done early, but poor Silas was very much disappointed. Mr.

THE RESENTMENT

Walker had been invited out after dinner, so Silas slept part of the afternoon and afterwards sat on one end of the front porch with his head resting in his hands, thinking what a big dunce he had been to have remained away from home. He did not know what a treat was in store for him. They had returned while he was sleeping. As the unexpected happens when we least expect it, so Silas was delighed when he saw Mr. Walker come out on the porch. "Well, Silas, why so quiet? I missed you so much this afternoon. I wished we could have taken you with us, but the car was filled, but you shall go with us tomorrow. Did you go home today?"

"No, sir, I stayed and helped Mrs. Baxter."

"That was fine."

Before Mr. Walker had time to say more, he was joined by Mr. Baxter and others. No one told Silas to go, so he remained where he was.

Years afterwards, Silas said it was the crowning day of his boyhood.

Yes," said Mr. Walker, after a long talk with the other men on business and how they got their various starts in life. "Yes," he said, and drew a long breath which was

THE RESENTMENT

almost a sigh—as if it hurt to recall past years: "There were so many weary years in my life, I would often wonder if it were better to die than to struggle so hard, but I stuck to it."

Mr. Walker told how he had been left an orphan and at the age of eight, bound out to people who were so cruel to him; how he had worked ten long years without a dollar's pay—only food and clothing. "If one can call one cheap suit, a pair of heavy boots and two suits of underwear to be worn the entire year, clothes," he added. "In summer, I went barefooted and half naked." Silas' eyes were wide open. "Ten years! Good gracious, why, I would never get any clothes if I had to work ten years for them," he thought.

"How well I remember," continued Mr. Walker. "There was a big circus coming to town, and for weeks all the boys of the neighborhood had looked forward to this day. I had never been to a circus, or a picnic or anything, so I made up my mind to go, too. When I asked one of the boys what it would cost, and he said 'fifty cents,' my heart sank. I had never had fifty cents in my life. The boys, seeing such a distressful look on my face, asked what was the matter. I told them I had no money. They told me to ask Mr. Jones, the man with whom I lived, for it. I told them I was afraid. They called me a 'sissy' and other mean names. I waited until the day of the circus. During the morning I asked Mr. Jones if he would let me have fifty cents to go to the circus in the afternoon. If I had asked him for his heart he could not have thought it any worse. Fifty cents! Why, he thought I was insane. He knocked me down, then kicked me, and called me terrible names. I answered him back for the first time in my life, and there followed the hottest words I have ever spoken. I had always been quite an obedient boy, but that day I was almost besides myself. That disappointment was too great for me.

"I wanted to die, but instead, I went to bed and slept all the afternoon. I awoke, feeling better. I had decided that it was the last day I would ever work for him. As I ate supper that night, I said, 'This is the last meal I shall ever eat here.'

"Next day being Sunday, I got up early and got through with the milking. Then, instead of going to breakfast, I went upstairs and tied up what few things I had in a small bundle. Mr. Jones sat at the table eating as I passed through the dining room. When he saw me, he asked, more tenderly than I had ever remembered hearing him speak. 'Well, Jack, I suppose you are moving today?"

"Yes, sir,' I said, 'I have a human heart and feelings; I am no longer a boy; I start, today, to make my way in this world; I must live as well as you.' Mr. Jones thought for a moment, then said, 'What have you got to start with, young man?' (sneeringly). 'Two hands and will-power, sir.'

"Taking his wallet from his pocket, he drew forth ten dollars and pushed it towards me, saying, 'There is ten dollars, take it and buy a little common sense.' Taking the money, I flung it back to him, telling him that he needed it more than I did.

"Well, Mister, I wish you good luck with your two hands and will-power," chinned in Mrs. Jones. ' You better stay here while you are here, 'cause you ain't goin' to be runnin' back here after you once go; you don't know that you are eating your white bread.'

"I shall never trouble you, Mrs. Jones; I may come to see you, some time."

"Well, be sure that you don't need help when you come."

"I would rather starve than to ask help from you." With these words, I left the house a free boy.

"Until that day, I had almost been a helpless boy, but as I left that farm, I felt the responsibility of manhood. I walked about fifteen miles to a little town called Rocksville; there I met a farmer who was in need of a hand. He promised to give me ten dollars a month, which was considered good wages for a young fellow, at that time. I worked there for three years. During that time, I bought a little calf, and when it was old enough, Mr. Snithers sold it for me for five dollars. You can picture my joy. I really thought I was rich. I put the money with some I had saved and bought two more. Seeing my determination to get on, Mr. Snithers let me raise cows on shares—he taking a third of all that were raised.

"At the end of the third year I had saved two hundred and fifty dollars. I attended the district school during the winter months and had learned to read and write well. I took special interest in arithmetic, for I realized that this subject was most important to a business man. Having success in raising these cattle stimulated my determination to become a cattle rancher. With this point in view, I left Mr. Snithers and went West, and there hired to one of the largest cattle raisers in the State of Wyoming. I lived there four years, learning the business. I had my ups and downs and would often say, 'At the end of this week I shall leave and learn something easier.' Then I would think of the years I had struggled. If I gave up, now, it would mean wasted time and possibly lost opportunity. So, I toiled on and on. I bought fifty acres of land and saved enough money to start business on a small scale.

"It was just four years and six months from the day I arrived in the West until I started in business for myself.

"Fortune seemed in my favor. With help and encouragement from the other ranchmen, I gained rapidly. I adopted the habit of not getting too deeply in debt; if so, I worked hard and paid it off as soon as possible. Soon, I became what they all called a shrewd business man. After two years—how well I remember—one day an old ranchman came to me and said, 'Walker, you are getting along fine, but you haven't started right.' I looked at him astonishedly, and asked what was wrong.

"Whole lot is wrong," with a smile.

THE RESENTMENT

"I did not understand, but stood looking at him, trying to fathom his meaning. 'Well, boy, you ain't got the jewel here."
"The jewel, the jewel?" I exclaimed.
"No, you ain't got no gal."
We both laughed heartily.
"Now,' he said, slapping me on the back, "you look 'round here and get married to some good gal and you will be all right."
"I took his advice and a year later was married to one of the best girls of the West. I have given that advice to many other young men. Get married to the right girl while you are young—better than diamonds. Today I am a wealthy man, a happy husband and a proud father; but it was through Resentment to a long-standing injustice that I found my path to success."

All enjoyed hearing Mr. Walker's story —how he battled his way from a penniless country boy to position and wealth; but no one enjoyed it more than Silas Miller, who sat unseen and unheard. All that was said was food for his hungry soul.

Mr. Walker talked long into the evening of his investments and other interesting things. There was no egotism in his talk, only plain, every-day facts.

That night, when all were fast asleep,

THE RESENTMENT

Silas lay awake far into the night. He had heard the great Westerner talk and had determined to become a great man, too. But he did not know what to do. He thought of raising chickens, of horses and sheep; but, as hard as he thought, things did not seem to plan out right. Just as he had about given up thinking, he thought of hogs. "There," he said to himself, "I shall become a 'hog ranchman.'" With this thought uppermost in his childish mind, he fell asleep.

During that week, Silas racked his brain with plan after plan, but, small as they were, they were the foundation of his future work.

The next Sunday a proud and happy boy wended his footsteps homeward, a boy full of hope and ambition. It was pleasing to see how much he had learned from Mr. Walker in such a short time. When he entered the house that day he was a new Silas; the other children did not know what to make of him. Taking off his hat, he called, "Good morning, papa and mamma," and, after speaking to his sister and brothers, he asked how they all had been getting along. "I stayed at the farm my day off two weeks ago. It seems like a year since I last saw you all."

"Think you better stay there your Sunday off, next time, and learn more airs," said his mischievous sister, Nett.

Silas felt a little hurt at this unexpected remark. He had tried so hard to be nice and had hoped the others would see it.

Poor little fellow, he did not know that these children were not able to grasp his meaning so quickly.

It was rather amusing at dinner to the children, with Silas saying, "I thank you" and "Please pass this," or "May I have a glass of water." Yet, as funny as it seemed, they soon began to imitate him.

After dinner, Silas called his father and said, "Papa, I want to talk with you awhile."

"Well, son, what is it?"

"I want to start in business for myself, next year. I'm not going to work all my life for folks to be called a 'nigger,' and he laughed at."

At first Mr. Miller was inclined to laugh, but, seeing the child was so much in earnest, he said, "Well, Silas, what are you going to do?"

"I had thought that I —, or you and I would raise hogs, papa; don't you think we could?"

"Silas, I think that is a capital idea, but

THE RESENTMENT

I am going to let you depend on yourself; you can have that acre of ground at the end of the wheat field. Then I shall let you have all of your wages from now on. That is all I can do. You must manage your own business. I am only a hard-working man and know little or nothing of business."

Silas was pleased. He nearly hugged the life out of his father, and went back to work a happier boy.

There was still more happiness in store for him. As he was working Monday morning, Mr. Walker came out into the yard to watch him feed the chickens. "Good morning, Silas; you certainly are an industrious boy. You will make a splendid young man. What do you intend to do when you grow up?" he asked.

"I am going to raise hogs, sir, and I'm not going to wait until I grow up—I'm going to start now."

"Good, I say, boy, you have the right idea. When do you think you shall start?"

"Next month, sir."

Placing his hands upon Silas' shoulder, Mr. Walker said, "You have determined your course. Unless it proves wrong, let nothing turn you from it. Remember, my boy, great men whom the world honors to-day, did not make their way in one single leap, but step by step. You may encounter many difficulties on the way, but with determination, you can overcome all things." Putting a ten dollar bill in his hand, he continued, "I give you this to help you to get a little start, but, remember, Silas, the ability to become a successful man will not depend upon what others give you, but upon the man within you. It will mean many hours of hard work and much sacrifice of pleasure, but stick to it. I am leaving here in a few days, but shall carry you in my mind always. I hope to have you as a visitor at my home, some day."

With this encouragement, Silas began his life's work.

CHAPTER III.

AT WORK IN EARNEST

The following weeks were great ones for Silas Miller. Mr. and Mrs. Baxter said he grew over night from a playful boy to a strong, thinking man. Mr. Walker had lighted the torch to Silas' ambition and it had burned briskly.

A month had passed since Mr. Walker's visit. One day Mr. Baxter was astonished when Silas walked up to him and asked him how much did he want for the six little pigs that he had in a separate pen with their mother.

"Well, Silas, I hadn't thought much about them; they are quite young, yet, to take away from their mother. Did some of the farmers ask you how much I wanted for them?"

"No, sir, I want to buy them."

"You want to buy them? Why, they are too young to kill for camp-meeting."

"I don't want them to eat (impatiently); I want to buy them to raise, myself."

THE RESENTMENT

"Hump," said Mr. Baxter; he did not know what else to say, he was so surprised.

"How much do you want for them?" continued Silas, anxiously.

Mr. Baxter rubbed his head and thought for a moment, then said, "Well, Silas, I will sell them to you for twenty dollars."

Poor Silas was surprised that they should cost so much, but he quickly survived the shock and asked, "How much do you want down?"

"Not less than half, Silas."

His face beamed with joy as he said, "All right, Mr. Baxter, I shall take them."

"When will you pay me the money?" asked Mr. Baxter, a little puzzled.

"I have it now, sir."

"Very well, then, you can make the payment today, if you wish."

Silas started to give Mr. Baxter the ten dollars, then he asked, "Mr. Baxter, shall we go to the house and sign papers?"

"Y-yes, Silas, that's the way to do business," he answered, looking at the boy out of the corner of his eye, and thinking what a bright little chap he was.

In the house, Mr. Baxter and Silas sat down to a table and made out the necessary papers. This incident brought the little

THE RESENTMENT

black boy and the white man nearer together than any other thing had.

From that day, though Silas was still a Negro boy, Mr. Baxter began to see him from a different view-point. He was ready to give him as much encouragement as had done the great Westerner, but in a different way, because it would take more than a few days to make this Southern-born man see that this child, created by the same God as he, had the same right to opportunities and privileges as the white man, yet, this was the beginning, and, already this step had brought forth great consideration.

He told Silas he could let the pigs remain in his field and that would save him the cost of buying food for them. Thinking for a while, Silas then asked how much he would charge for their board.

"Why, nothig at all, Silas."

"Will you write that on a piece of paper for me? Then I will be better satisfied."

"Why, Silas, can't you take my word?" said Mr. Baxter, a little hurt that Silas did not trust him as did most colored people.

"Yes, sir, I trust you, but nobody hears the bargain between us."

"I must say, Silas, you are starting right;

I shall do as you ask, then there will be no trouble."

When Silas went home the next day he had off, he could hardly wait, he was so anxious to tell of his purchase. He found **his father walking around, looking over his** truck patches. "Hello, there, Pa; bet you can't guess something?"

"No, not unless you are going crazy; I certainly thought something had happened the way you were racing against time or dust. I don't know which—when I first **spied you.**" They both laughed.

"No, dad, I ain't crazy, I'm all filled up with joy. I bought six little pigs and their mother."

"You don't mean it, Si!"

"Yes, sir, and I have them half paid for, already."

"Well, you can have all you make to finish the payment. I won't bar the door of opportunity against you by taking your money, as long as I can posisbly do without it. You just go right on, I am sure you will do the right thing. Si, you were your mother's heart; she was so fond of you. For her sake, I should like to see you prosper."

The children crowded around and looked with childish pride at their brother, Si, who

THE RESENTMENT 31

had learned so many "airs" and was going into the pig-raising business.

"Why, Si, you're getting to be just wonderful," said Nett, who was never lost for something to say."

"Thank you," he answered, without paying the least attention to her bantering remark. Seeing this, Nett abandoned her plot to tease.

Months passed quickly by. Silas worked hard during the day and studied at night. He had made it a rule to study each night before going to bed. (Mrs. Baxter permitted him to have a light in his room with the promise that he would be very careful with it.) He was astonished to see how swiftly he improved by this method.

One of the things that pleased Mr. Baxter was, as anxious as Silas was about his own business, he never neglected to do his duty towards his employer. In this Mr. Baxter encouraged him very much by saying, "You will certainly be a successful business man, you put both self and love into your daily work; no man can fail who does this." These words were worth hundreds of dollars to this boy.

At the end of six months, Silas paid the last dollar that he owed Mr. Baxter and became the owner of the pigs. Can you, dear reader, imagine the joy that swept through the heart of this young boy when Mr. Baxter said, "Silas Miller, you deserve to be the owner of a hundred pigs, so faithfully have you worked, and in less than six months you are entirely out of debt? That is right, keep as far from debt as you possibly can."

"Yes, sir, that is what Mr. Walker said he did," answered Silas.

"Did Mr. Walker tell you that?"

"No, sir, not exactly, but he said it was the best way."

This was the first time that Mr. Baxter noticed that Silas was drafting a pattern. "Whoever follows in the footsteps of Mr. Walker will become a conscientious, successful man, I can say that much."

"Silas, I am afraid that we Southerners have been made to look upon your race as though it was just to exist, but Mr. Walker sees it differently. It will take many years for the people of the South to come to this knowledge, but, nevertheless, we shall gradually awaken to it." Silas bowed his head as he usually did when he did not know just what was right to answer.

A few days later Silas drove his litter of

THE RESENTMENT 33

pigs home. "Look, Papa," he cried as he came into the yard, "ain't they grand?" Before his father could get to the door, Nett exclaimed, "Good gracious, Pa, it's Si with his gang of pigs." "You hush, Miss Nett, or I shall box your ears," said Mr. Miller.

The little pigs started to squeal very loud as they came into the strange yard; they were tired and hungry.

Nett, with her little hands on her hips and her large, brown eyes rolled upwards, said in a very exciting manner, "I know them pigs squealing shall get on my nerves and there shall be no living around here with me."

"For goodness sake, Nett, who cares for your nerves?" said John, a younger brother. "You can stay anywhere that suits them."

Their father, hearing this conversation, commanded them to hush. They all quickly obeyed.

While Nett was mischievous, she was also very kindhearted and industrious, and was the first to offer her assistance to care for the pigs. She started to work in the early morning, as Silas had left them in her care, his father being too busy and away from home most of the time.

After feeding them their dinner, she got a piece of an old box top, sat on the ground, and printed in large letters: STOP, LOOK AND LISTEN. A WHOLE LOT OF PIGS FOR SALE—HIGH BRED, ALL KINDS AND KOLORS. CALL AT OUNCE. PLEASE PAY CASH.

She was nearly frightened to death when a farmer drove up to the house. He called several times before Mrs. Miller heard him. She went out to see what he wanted and was nearly shocked out of her wits when he asked to see the pigs they had for sale. He also asked how much they wanted for them and of what stock they were.

Mrs. Miller stood with her mouth partly open, hardly knowing what to say. "Who'se got any pigs for sale?"

"Why I thought you had; I saw a large sign in the back lot near the main road, reading: 'Pigs for sale.' "

"I don't know anything at all about it; our Si bought a sow and its litter some time ago, but I understand he had calculated on raising them." The stranger had hardly finished talking when another farmer stopped to ask the same question. Nett had seen and heard the men and had taken refuge behind the barn, so no one could tell where she was, neither did anyone know who put the sign up in the back lot. "Well, I am going down

THE RESENTMENT 35

to see what kind of a sign that is. If Si was going to sell the pigs I think it was as much as he could say the same and not have me standing here like a fool with a hundred farmers a riding here asking me about pigs and what stock they are, as if I knew the pedigree of pigs," said Mrs. Miller, perplexed.

Mrs. Miller started for the lot, but Nett had stolen from her hiding place and removed the sign, so, when she got there, no sign was in sight. She stood and looked as far as her eyes could see, then said, "They certainly must be seeing things, there ain't no signs here, and the next old dunce that stops here and asks me about pigs for sale, I'm going to give him a piece of my mind." But no more called.

Nett felt rather shaky about her mischievous prank and stayed away all of the afternoon, fearing a scolding from her stepmother. She did not go to the house, but towards evening, went to meet her father and told him what she had done to help Si sell his pigs. "Why, Nett," he said, "I don't know as Si wants to sell his pigs yet; not until spring, if he sells them at all."

"I put up a sign and when some men stopped and asked about them, I took it down.

I thought I had better wait until you came."

"I am glad you did; Si will tell us what he wants us to do, then we will help him as best we can." Nett was overjoyed when her father did not scold her.

Mrs. Miller told her husband of the strange calls during the day and he explained to her what Nett had told him.

The next month being December, it is an old custom in the South for hired men to work from the first of March to the twenty-fourth of December; this day, they all leave firesides with their families until spring again. After the holidays, Silas began to plan for the coming year. He did not care to work for Mr. Baxter again unless he consented to give him more money. This, Mr. Baxter did not see as being necessary and Mrs. Baxter added that his kind had worked for her father for nothing. "Yes'm, but that was fifty years ago. Do you think that my people could live in a progressive country, in a progressive age, and not grasp the progressive spirit?" asked Silas, in a reproachful manner.

"Yes, Silas, you quote that which is true, with that spirit you will get on even if you do not work for us."

They both really liked Silas and hated to

THE RESENTMENT

see him leave them, but could not think of paying him more money.

It was New Year's Day. Silas sat reading the "Ad" column in a Philadelphia newspaper; at last he came to this ad: "Boy wanted to help on farm; must have previous knowledge of farm work and care of hogs; Southern colored boy preferred. Reference required." Reading it over to his father, he asked his opinion. Mr. Miller said little, but told him to go over to Mr. Price, his teacher, and ask him to help him to answer it. The letter was written and mailed. Each day Silas looked anxiously for the rural mail carrier. It was nearly two weeks before the long-looked-for letter came. The man not only answered the letter, but stated that he would refund his fare as soon as he arrived; that he did not want him until spring, and if this was satisfactory to him, he would not look for anyone else. He was willing to give the wages Silas asked for and said that if he proved to be a good hand, he would raise him after two months, five dollars more.

When Silas read this letter he was elated. In plainer words, he was wild with joy.

"Isn't this great, Papa?"

"Yes, Si, it is fine," said Mr. Miller slowly,

38   THE RESENTMENT

"but I kinder hate to see you go so far away from us."

"But, Papa, it will only be for a little while, you know how anxious I am to get started and it will take me so long with the small wages I get here."

"But, son," his strong voice quavering, "I'm afraid when you once get away, and get a glimpse of city life, and Northern freedom, you will forget both us and your business."

"No, Papa, I want you to trust me and pray that God will direct me. Papa, you know they say you can get a broader knowledge of life and business in the North where you come in closer touch with both races. It will help me so much and prepare me to battle with the problems of the business world."

His father thought a while, then said: "I guess you are right, Si, as I said at first I would not put stumbling blocks in your pathway; I shall keep my promise; you may go. What are you going to do this winter?"

"I'm going to school; I must know a lot to be a good business man."

"Very well, that's a good plan."

School opened on the second of January. Two weeks later Silas started. Nett and

THE RESENTMENT

little John had started, and they were proud that Silas was going, too. That morning, while all were preparing for school, Nett asked Silas who was going to care for the pigs while he was away.

"I was going to ask you, Nett. I know you will do your best. Of course Papa will help you."

Nett opened her eyes wide and trying to look astonished, asked, "Who, me?"

"Yes, Nett, you. No one would take care of them better than you."

Nett was really pleased to know that her brother would trust her with his pigs, and Silas knew this. "Well, if I must, I shall," she said, tossing her head on the side, and scampering away to the mirror to see if she had grown taller over night.

"For the love of Mike, come on, we shall have to start to raise *looking glasses*, if Nett continues to plaster herself up before that one all of the time. No one can get a chance to see, for her," said little John.

"Good night, Moses; we shall soon have an orator in the family if John keeps on making such fine speeches."

"Children, stop quarreling and get off to school at once or you'll be late!" said their mother.

News had spread quickly concerning Silas' plans. When he walked into the school room, that morning, a number of boys were standing around the stove. As soon as they saw him, some started to squeal as loud as they could—imitating hogs. Others grunted and still others got down and walked around on their hands and feet.

Earl Green asked how many pigs could he buy, as he wanted two dozen at once. Silas felt hurt at these sneers and remarks. He was nearly in tears when Nett came to his rescue, saying, "Don't let the boys tease you, Si, they will be sniggling and working for other men when you will be your own boss."

At this remark, many hushed, others laughed louder. It did not matter much now to Si—Nett was in sympathy with him, and he cared little what others thought or said.

When Mr. Price came in a few minutes later, he went forward and shook Silas' hand, saying, "I am glad to see you here. You know you are nearly through the eighth grade, and I am sure you can finish in two months if you try hard. I am also glad to learn of your success in securing the position you wrote for. We shall be sorry to lose

THE RESENTMENT 41

you, but glad to know that you are making such a good start."

Silas was much beloved by his schoolmates, but they were a little jealous of his determination to become a business man.

Let us stop here a moment and say for the sake of some boys and girls, that envy and hatred are two enemies that rots the very souls of men. They who hate their comrades because they possess the ability to become more successful than themselves, have within them souls that have no magnetic personality. They are hopeless and make shiftless men and women. They are the ones that fill the courts, the jails, the reform schools, the homes for the incorrigibles. But if they possess lifting qualities and help others, they are also lifted. It is also true with many as they succeed in life: they makes enemies instead of gaining friends.

The two months in school passed quickly for Silas. He studied hard, but at play, he was foremost in all sports. On the twenty-eighth of February, he said good-bye to his schoolmates and took farewell leave of the rural district school where he had spent most of the joys and sorrows of his childhood. These he was leaving behind him to take his place in the wide world; to share, as had others, the struggles and disappointments to win fame, honors or successes or whatever Fate had in store for him.

The following evening, Mr. Price asked Silas to come to his home. Never was he more surprised when he walked into that house that night; all of his schoolmates greeted him; it was a surprise party.

Seated around a beautiful table, twenty-eight boys listened to their teacher. Mr. Price took for his subject "Unselfish Encouragement." He talked until their young, undeveloped minds seemed at length to grasp his meaning. At the conclusion each boy stood with his left foot upon his chair, and with lighted candles in their right hands, held high above their heads, and pledged in thunderous voices these words: "Silas Miller, we, your comrades and schoolmates, light your pathway through the darkest hours and wish you all the success that mortal man can obtain in this world. Our hearts and hopes are all with thee."

"It is just one of the things I want you to always remember, Silas," said Mr. Price.

The sneers and curt remarks of the boys were all forgiven and forgotten; there was not a boy who was not sorry to see him go.

THE RESENTMENT

The memory of that party, the handshakes and good-byes, Silas Miller carried with him to his grave.

Silas' leaving home was the gossip for general discussion in the community.

Aunt Mollie Noble, widely known as the "newscarrier," and who never forgot to voice her opinion of the same, called on Sister Maria Dudley, Sunday, after church.

"Good marnin, Sis Maria, how is yo' today?"

"Only tol'rable, Aunt Mollie, come in!"

Aunt Molly stepped in almost out of breath. Sitting down on the first chair she came to, she said: "Ah jest came ovah for a little while after church, I thought I would stay 'ntil Sunday schule stahts."

"Sho, Honey, glad to hab yo', take off yor t'ings. Did yo' hab a gran' sermon dis mornin'?"

"Yes'm, very good, but everybody is dat 'cited 'bout de Millers dat no one scare knowed what de preacher said attall."

"Is dat so?"

"Yes'm, yo' know Silas Miller leaves fo' de No'th, Monday?"

"Yes'm, Aunt Mollie, I hyeahs dat, too!"

"Now, Sis Mariah, doan yo' t'ink John Miller is plum crazy to let dat lit'l upstart of a boy go gaddin' aroun' to de Lord knows whar by hissef?"

"Well, Aunt Mollie, I doan hardly know what to say 'bout Brother Miller."

"Ah sez dat he is crazier dan a musrat," said Aunt Mollie, holding her hands and shaking her head.

"Yo' know dem Millers allus had high-fluten notions. I wuz talkin' to Brother Miller mahse'f de udder day."

"What did he say, Sis Mariah?" Aunt Mollie asked, rolling her chair closer so as to catch every word.

"Well, he's tickled to death. Yo' should of heard him talk of his son. Says I to him, 'Ain't yo' kind'r skeered to 'low dat boy go so far away from yo'?' He jes' says, 'I can trust mah boy to do de right thing!'"

"Now, what do yo' t'ink ob dat fo' a civilized father?" said Aunt Mollie, rolling her beady eyes in disgust. An' he said also dat it would be an edicatin' fo' him."

"Ah doan know what dis world am comin' to, Sis Mariah. Ah wish yo' could heb seen Si dis marnin, a buttin' an' a scrapin' an' a bowin' wors'n any peacock dat yo' eber seen. Now, when we wuz young, our parents told us what to do an' we did it; but to-day, yo' jest born de chillens into de world an' wen dey is knee-high to a grasshopper, dey finish raisin' demself an stahts to bossin' dey ma an' pa."

"Yo' sho don sed it all now, Aunt Mollie," said Sis Maria, "but yo' can't 'spect any mo' from dem Miller chillens, 'cause Silas' mother wus a queer critter herse'f. She had all dese hyeah noti'ns 'bout edicatin' an sich t'ings. Dey say she kep piles ob books, an' read an' studied all de time. Now, a' tells yo' de truth. Ah ain't got no faith in dis hyeah sendin' yo' chillens some whar way up No'th to get an edicatin', 'cause dar wuz Sister Gibbs; she sint her boy to college in Noo Yak while she worked herse'f simple an' went ha'f naked an' haf starved. Says I to her one day, 'When is yo' boy goin to get gradiated from college?' She says, 'It's two mo' years he's got, yet, den mah boy will be a doctah; ah sartinly will be a proud mother!' Well, de nex' t'ing ah knows, her son done comes home. He had married some ole widder wif fo' yung'uns an' she ole 'nuf to be his ma!"

"Yo' don't say so, Aunt Mollie! Po' t'ing. I guess she was terrible hurt."

"Ah doan know how much hurt she war, but ah knows she drapped dead de nex' day. She aworkin' hersef to death to edicate her son to kech an ole widder an' fo' yung'ns wuz too much fo' her. No, I doan believe in sendin' dem away. Ah said to one ob de sisters to-day, 'Dars Miller asendin' his son away to some strange man dat he knows nothin' bout; he is lak'ly to be one ob dese student doctahs dat dey say am po'ful plentiful in de cities dis time ob de year. Ah'd feel maghty sorry fo' de boy ef one did kech him, but it would teach his pa some sense."

By this time the bell had rung for Sunday school. Aunt Mollie bade Sister Maria good-bye and left.

CHAPTER IV.

LEAVING HOME

As anxious as Silas had been to go, when the time came he felt downhearted and almost wished he had not planned to go. Then he made up his mind to let nothing stand in his way. Nett had gotten up early that morning and packed Silas' few clothes in a little basket; she put in a few biscuits that her step-mother had baked the day before. Wishing to give him something for remembrance, she put in her little gold locket that she had worn from babyhood, and a New Testament that had belonged to her mother.

The day before Silas had sent Nett over to Mr. Baxter to get his reference from him. Curiosity overtook her when he handed her the envelope unsealed. After walking a little way, she stopped and opened it. She read:

"To Whom It May Concern: Silas Miller has worked for me nearly two years.

I have always found him a good, honest boy, a willing worker, a little slow but his work always well done. He will grow to be a good trusty farm hand and servant."

"Humph," said Nett, as she searched in her pocket for a pencil and a piece of paper, which she quickly found. Sitting down by the roadside, she wrote: "And maybe it may concern you to know, too, that Silas Miller don't intend to be a 'trusty servant' always, but a real business man. He has started already, so please don't think he is good for nothing but a servant. Please be kind to him for his sister's sake.—Nett."

She re-read this note with great pride and placed it in the envelope and sealed it.

That morning, while packing his things, she placed the envelope in the Testament with her little gift.

The hour came, his father drove to the door in the family surrey. Silas kissed them all good-bye. Nett went to the station with them. On the way Nett told Silas she was going to take good care of the pigs and would write him each week and tell him all the news. She talked and talked, and at last she grew so silent that Silas asked her what she was thinking about.

"I was thinking that when you get start-

THE RESENTMENT

ed, would you help me to do something?"

"Certainly, Nett, what is it?"

"Oh, I sha'n't tell you now."

"All right, whatever it is I am sure it is right and I shall help you all I can."

At this answer, Nett hugged him and told him he was a dear brother.

As the train steamed out of Chestertown, Silas waved good-bye to his father and Nett. It was his first trip on a train and he enjoyed it immensely. It seemed as if he would never reach Philadelphia. He made friends with an elderly gentleman that sat near him. When the conductor called Philadelphia, Silas began to feel a little nervous, but the stranger assured him that he would stay with him until he found the party he was looking for.

"Are you sure the man will meet you and do you know him?"

"Yes, sir, he said he would meet me and would be standing at the gate."

"Very well, then, we'll wait until we reach the gate," said the stranger.

It was a wonderful sight to Silas to see the many trains in this large shed, and hundreds of persons hurrying to and fro on all sides. They walked slowly behind the great crowds that were leaving the trains.

Just as they reached the gate, a tall, swarthy-looking white man came forward. Lifting his hat, he asked: "Is this the young colored man that I am looking for? Silas Miller is the name, I believe. I am Mr. Dayton."

"Yes, sir, this is Silas Miller." Turning to the stranger, Silas thanked him for his kindness. In return the man gave Silas his name and address, inviting him to call to see him when visiting Philadelphia. To Silas the Broad Street Station was the most wonderful place he had ever seen.

Mr. Dayton left him in the waiting room while he went to attend to some business. That gave Silas a chance to see much of the station, with its beautiful waiting room, its lunch rooms, the calling of the different trains and the steady stream of human beings going and coming ceaselessly, was a great sight to this child who had only seen the little station and the three-coach trains of his home town.

Mr. Dayton returned in a short time. "Well, Silas, we shall start for home. I suppose you are tired and hungry, but the madam will have dinner ready for us and I am sure we can do justice to it when we get there."

THE RESENTMENT

Mr. Dayton lived on a large farm in Bucks County, about twenty miles from the city, and as they drove along the country roads Silas had a chance to get a good look at his future employer. He saw at once that he was kindhearted and pleasant. As they turned into a lane leading to a small farmhouse, not far from the main road, Mr. Dayton said: "Here we are, this is our home." At this he gave a long, loud whistle, and in answer to it, a pleasant looking woman came to the door. "Here's our boy, and that's my wife, Silas, Mrs. Dayton, a finer woman never lived."

Mrs. Dayton shook hands with Silas and told him she would show him to his room and then they would have dinner.

Was it possible that this was his room with its white bed and clean, white linen, a bureau, a little stand and two chairs, matting on the floor and dainty white curtains at the windows?—everything was immaculate. Silas stood in the middle of the room. "I wonder if this is really my room?" he thought. To be sure he called Mrs. Dayton and asked did she mean this was his room.

"Yes, Silas, is it all right?"

"Yes'm, it's fine, only I thought I had gotten into the wrong room."

"Hurry down, we shall have dinner at once, because I know you must be hungry."

Silas clasped his hands with joy; his first thought was, "I wish Nett could see this." He loved his mischievous little sister; she had been his chum and partner in everything since they were children.

That night Mr. Dayton read Silas' references from Mr. Baxter. When he read the other note, he was amused, but said nothing to Silas about it.

Mr. and Mrs. Dayton became very fond of Silas. They found what Mr. Baxter said was very true. He was an industrious boy and a slave to duty.

He ate with them and in the evening sat with them in the drawing room and read their papers and books. Mrs. Dayton did everything to make him feel at home. All of this, which he was so unused to in the South did not turn Silas. He showed his appreciation of their kindness, but was very quiet and seldom spoke unless he was spoken to.

When company came, he went to his room (which was a haven to him) without being told or hinted at. In everything he showed good home training or self-culture.

THE RESENTMENT

For this the Daytons admired him. He worked well, learning the business quickly and doing his work so well that after six months Mr. Dayton made him foreman.

One day after working hard in helping Mr. Dayton with his hogs, preparing them for sale, Mr. Dayton said to a friend: "I have never seen such a boy. I would never have gotten through to-day had he not taken such interest and given good suggestions here and there which helped me so much."

That night Mr. Dayton recalled the contents of the little note written on the slip of paper enclosed with Silas' reference. He asked his wife if she had kept it as he wanted it. Mrs. Dayton got it for him; he read it again and again. Turning to his wife, he said, "Whoever Nett is, she is right. Silas will never be contented to work as a mere laborer for others. His wits are as sharp as steel."

"Yes, I noticed the first day he was here that he was brilliant and intelligent."

When Silas came in from work that evening, Mr. Dayton asked him about his family at home, if he had any brothers or sisters.

"Yes, sir, I have two brothers and one sister."

"What is your sister's name?"

THE RESENTMENT

"Nett," Silas replied.

That night when Silas was fast asleep Mr. Dayton wrote a letter to Nett. " Dear little Nett," it read, "I got the note you sent me. I am glad to say that all that you said is true. Silas is a good boy and takes great interest in his work. We are very fond of him, yes, a boy so tactful as he will never be contented to labor for others. I admire his ability to strive to become a man of worth. We shall hate to lose such a boy, but he is not ours to keep long. I will add, we shall be kind to him for his own sake, and yours. Very truly yours, Mr. Dayton."

When little Nett got that letter, there wasn't a happier girl alive. After reading it she took down an old picture that hung in her bedroom, and placed the letter in the back of it. There it hung for many years with its secret.

CHAPTER V.

SEEING CITY LIFE

Silas was very happy but lonely. He met two boys who worked on adjoining farms. They both had been reared in the city, but their parents had come from the South years ago. When work was dull in the city they would come and work on the farm for a little while. They met Silas and became friendly at once. He was glad to have a little company, for at times he grew very homesick. Horace Turner's and Bob Dale's parents had worked hard to give them a good education, but after finishing grammar school, they refused to go further or to take up any good trade. Like a ship without a rudder, tossed and driven without a sure destination, so were Horace and Bob. They had chosen the road of sports, doing easy work and when they could not obtain this kind, they did a little hard work to keep pocket change. When they met Silas, they called him a "Green-horn," from down in the sticks. "We'll take him around and teach him to spend his change," said Bob.

"I don't know about that; he doesn't look so soft," slowly replied Horace.

After being acquainted for some time, they asked Silas to go into the city. Silas was anxious to go but consulted Mr. Dayton first. "Silas, I hardly know what to say. You never know who strangers are, but if you think you are strong enough by all means go." Silas did not understand just what he meant by "being strong enough," yet he did not ask and Mr. Dayton did not say.

A few weeks later, Silas went to stay over Sunday with the boys. He was introduced to their parents and their sisters. Both families lived together in one large house. Bob's sister played the piano and Horace's sister sang like a nightingale.

Silas had heard good voices, but not trained ones. He sat almost afraid to move out of the corner. Both girls saw how timid he was and took great delight to show their ability or rather "show off."

Later in the evening, the boys took him out to meet some of their friends and see their city. From the first Silas felt far beneath them. They were well dressed and seemed to know so much. As he looked down at his clothes, cheap and shabby, but

THE RESENTMENT

clean, he felt out of place. He thought of what Nett would say, "Snap in, old boy." With this thought he soon forgot himself.

Several of the boys laughed when they introduced Silas. "Just from down the sticks, ain't he?" whispered some of the boys. Silas heard this remark and answered, "yes, just from down the sticks, and met these two fine, young gentlemen working on farms near me, doing the same kind of work that I am, as for the same purpose I do not know. One thing I do know, if they have the same viewpoint as I, we shall be lifetime friends."

Bob and Horace would like to have choked Silas. They would not for worlds have had their friends know that they were working on the farm. Bob was very angry, but Horace was much amused and said nothing.

"Boys, this will never do, standing here, where shall we go for sport?" "Let's go down and stand on the corner of 'A' street and watch the girls," said one. "Let's go over to the pool room and pull a little change first," said another. "What will our friend, Mr. Miller, suggest?" asked another. "I don't know," said Silas, shaking his head," "this is my first visit to the city and I know nothing of the places of amusement here."

"You just follow us, and we will initiate you to real city life." On the way to the pool room they passed a crowd of boys shooting crap on the corner. Crap games, cards and drinking Silas was prepared against; he had seen these things in the country and his humble Christian mother and father had taught him the wrongs of such things. Silas Miller did not know how many other sins—deep, dark, black, blacker sins—existed in this world. On entering the pool room, they played a while and then asked Silas to join them.

"Is it gambling?" he asked.

"No, you blockhead, it is good sport and easy money."

"You all go ahead and play, I will look on this time until I get more acquainted with the game."

Seeing that they could not get him to spend his money here, they decided to take in a movie show, asking Silas to treat them by paying their fares, which he willingly did.

"We will make him spend his change yet if we keep at it long enough," they whispered.

Silas enjoyed the show very much. It was the first one of its kind he had ever seen. After leaving the theatre, Silas said, "Suppose we go home; you know I'm not used to staying up so late. I guess you'll think me rather 'sissy,' but I must get accustomed to the city before becoming one of you."

They had already begun to see that Silas had a depth of mind that one could not readily fathom. However well prepared, you could not guess just what he would say or do next. The slightest whisper reached his keen ears; he seemed to read one's thoughts and answered accordingly. Being a close observer he could detect the slightest wink or hint. This made the boys very careful. As bad and mischievous as they were, they did not care to have Silas catch them at their tricks. They had intended to stay out later and take in a cabaret, but when Silas suggested going home, they thought it best not to say anything if they ever expected him to go out with them again.

Sunday being a rest day, city folks, tired and weary from the week's toil, take advantage of this day to sleep a little late, getting up just in time to rush off to church services that begin about 11 o'clock, but Silas being used to rising with the sun, could

60 THE RESENTMENT

not sleep later than six o'clock; so he decided to dress and take a walk. It was a beautiful April morning and Easter Sunday. The sun was shining brightly and warm; the trees were putting forth their beautiful green leaves, along the street here and there little patches of green grass, showing that Nature was spreading her green mantle. The birds sang and chirped as if they were glad that the long winter was passed and spring had come, and they seemed to be pouring forth their thanks to God. Silas walked and walked. He saw great throngs of people going to and from large churches, while bells rang and chimes pealed out some of the hymns that he had heard so often. His heart was full and his eyes filled with tears, when he thought of the folks at home and of the little chapel where he had learned to recite his first Easter recitation.

On his return he told them of his walk. "I am a great lover of Nature, and seem to get wonderful inspiration in the early morning."

As they sat down to breakfast that morning, both families saw that Silas was far more cultured than their children, whom they idolized. His manner in eating and

THE RESENTMENT 61

speaking commanded great admiration and respect from them. Even Eva Dale who had in her mind to show off to the country lad, soon found herself of little importance. Silas Miller held the winning cards and he played them.

After breakfast they all prepared for church. It being Easter Sunday they were all dressed in their new spring suits. They asked Silas to go but hoped he would not accept their invitation as they did not care to take him, so poorly dressed, to their fine church among their fashionable set.

Instinct seemed to have forewarned him and he answered that he would rather stay and sit on the front steps and watch the people as they passed; then he added: "I have nothing nice to wear." They were very pleased and of course did not urge him to go. Mrs. Turner gave him a book and told him to read it if he became lonely. "We shall not be gone more than two hours," she said.

He had just started to read when Margaret Kempt, a young girl living two doors away, came out all dressed for church. She recognized him as being the boy who was visiting the Turner's home. She was so surprised to see him sitting there alone, she exclaimed, "Oh, aren't you going to church with the folks?"

"No, I'm going to sit and read until they come home."

"But goodness, this is Easter and you should go today, by all means."

Seeing that Margaret was a friendly little girl, he said, "I did not have anything to wear, so I decided not to go. I hear that your churches are so fine and the people so fashionably dressed here."

"Oh, don't stay away for that cause; come and go with me. Mother is not feeling so well and father is going to stay with her, so I am going alone. Besides, we belong to the Episcopal Church and we go there to worship and not for fashion."

Silas felt the warmth of this friendly invitation and decided to go.

As they entered the church it was a beautiful sight. The great pipe organ with its thundering music; the choir dressed in their peculiar-looking gowns—how they sang, "Christ is risen!"

The minister in his long robe read from St. John 3:16: "God so loved the world that He gave his only begotten Son that whosoever believeth on Him should not perish, but have everlasting life." The service was

THE RESENTMENT

quiet and simple, but very impressive; it seemed to touch the hearts of the entire congregation. Silas said he would always remember that wonderful sermon.

Returning from church, they met Horace and Bob; each walking with a beautiful girl. The boys were nearly shocked out of their wits with surprise when they saw Silas with Margaret Kempt.

Margaret Kempt was the only child of Mr. and Mrs. Kempt. Her father was the most prominent and prosperous colored lawyer of the city. They had reared their child not to be selfish or conceited. She was much loved by all who knew her, and at the early age of fifteen could be trusted to make good friends. Her parents would always say, "whenever you make acquaintances, Margaret, invite them to your home; we are older and experienced, and can help you to judge in selecting friends." In this way little Margaret and her parents grew to be great chums instead of becoming estranged as most children are with their parents at this age.

Silas told Margaret of his determination; why he had left the country and how he had intended to return as soon as he had made money enough to start in business on a larger scale. Margaret, in return, told him she was taking a business course with the view of becoming her father's secretary. "My father is doing good business, now, and I shall be glad when I am proficient enough to be in the office with him."

When they reached the house Margaret asked Silas to call that evening to meet her parents, as they were glad to meet young men who are trying to make good in the world."

When he went into the house the boys laughed and asked him if he was not reaching high up to be walking and talking so friendly with Miss Kempt.

"You know she's the daughter of one of wealthiest lawyers of the city."

"Yes, she told me her father was a lawyer; she also invited me in this evening to meet her parents before leaving for the farm."

"Is that so?" said Mrs. Turner, who had made many unsuccessful attempts to get her children on better social terms with Margaret Kempt.

"Aren't you afraid you'll get kicked out of the house?" said Eva Turner, with a sneer.

"No, Miss Turner, not unless I give him

THE RESENTMENT 65

good cause for such an offense."
Finding it useless to argue with Silas, she stopped at his last remark.
During the afternoon company came. Silas enjoyed the playing and singing, but sat quietly; he was not one to push himself upon others unasked. About five o'clock Margaret rang the bell and asked if Silas Miller could come in for a few minutes. "I want father and mother to meet him." Excusing himself, Silas went with Margaret and was introduced to her parents.
When Silas left the room Mrs. Turner said she did not know what Attorney Kempt was thinking of to let his daughter pick up any boy or girl that she chanced to find on the street and ask them into their home as friends: "Now she sees this boy and had the nerve to drag him off to church with her, and ask him in to spend the evening."
"And he hadn't any more sense than to go, looking like an Arab," said Eva.
"If you had said he had sense enough to go, I think you'd made better time," said Eva's father.
"Papa, who asked your opinion on the subject?"
"No one. I usually give my opinion free of asking," he said, laughing good natured-

ly. "I suppose the old lawyer knows what he is doing. If you and Horace possessed a little of the culture that young Miller has, I am sure you would be better liked."

"Oh, Will, you are always contrasting your children with someone else, and I hate that; they are as good as he. I suppose Margaret pitied him sitting there so forlorn and shabby-looking. He should have had gumption enough to have stayed on the farm until he got better clothes to come visiting decent people," said Mrs. Turner, suppressing something akin to rage.

"That's the trouble with you all now; you think that clothes is the whole thing; but let me tell you, it goes far from making the man or woman. Most of our people carry more on their backs than in their heads. Of course, I must admit that clothes help, but it is far from being the whole thing."

"Papa always has to give a long sermon on every little thing that is said."

"Yes, daughter, I hope some day you will understand what papa means."

"If you mean that I must pick up all kinds of persons for friends, I shall never understand you, papa."

"I suppose that's the way old Kempt made his money; by associating with such ignor-

THE RESENTMENT

ant people so that they would come to him with all their trouble," said Mrs. Turner.

"Mother, you should not say such things, Attorney Kempt is considered the shrewdest lawyer that we have, and it is said that he touches nothing that is chicane, and they all take their hats off to him. He is sociable because he was once a poor boy himself and worked his way up to his present standing, and Henry Kempt is not one to forget so soon," corrected Mr. Turner.

Mrs. Turner, finding no other subterfuge, said, "I hope they'll have a pleasant evening."

Never before had Silas met such learned people of his own race. They made him feel, not as a stranger but as a friend in their magnificent home. Margaret had told them of Silas' mission in the North. They both encouraged him very much and offered to assist him in any matter where their advise would be of service.

When Silas left, he thanked Mr. and Mrs. Turner for their hospitality, and also the boys for inviting him in to see the city. The most memorable object of that visit was Margaret Kempt. Who could not admire her sweet congenial manner and air, so different from the other girls whose sole object was to attract attention?

Monday night, Silas wrote a long letter to Nett, telling her of his visit to the city and everything that he thought would interest her. But Nett noticed that Margaret Kempt seemed to be the chief object of interest.

The boys kept friends with Silas and were more friendly than ever when they found that he was making good with the daughter of one of their neighbors. Finding that they could not persuade him to spend much money, they tried to coax him to join their set. They invited him to the city often; Silas going when it was his time off.

One who goes through life without falling, is weaker than he who falls; but is made stronger by the fall.

Silas had worked four months. He had spent but little money, but decided to buy a new suit of clothes when he came in town that evening. The boys, knowing that he had money with him, tempted him to play pool. They told him it was an easy way to make money to start in business sooner and that it was not gambling or the city would not permit it in public places.

This seemed possible to Silas. He had

THE RESENTMENT

brought ten dollars with him, so decided to play once. He could not understand, but soon found that he had lost five dollars, and when they let him stop, he had only three dollars left. It was a bitter lesson to this boy, but a good one.

When Margaret asked him was he going to church the next morning, he shook his head sadly and said, "No, Margaret, but I do want to speak to your father; I have something to ask him."

Margaret was delighted to call him. Attorney Kempt came into the drawing room to find Silas so haggard and forlorn-looking.

"Why, Silas, old fellow, what's the matter? You look ready to drop," he said, laughing as he reached Silas his hand.

Silas stood up and tried to smile, but he could not. So he simply said, "Mr. Kempt, I came to ask you, is playing pool gambling?"

"Yes, Silas, it is, in a way; although many claim that it is not."

"The boys asked me to play with them, last night; they said it was not gambling, but I lost seven dollars."

Mr. Kempt stood thinking for a moment, then he said slowly, "Silas, I am glad you lost, but sorry it was so much. No one could ever have convinced you that it is wrong as much as you are convinced now. Seven dollars could have done much to help you, but it has helped you to become strong against the many temptations of the city."

Silas hung his head. Walking over to him, Mr. Kempt placed his hand on his shoulder and said, "Do not be ashamed, Silas, you came to me for advice—one to whom you could tell the truth. I was once a boy, too, and I can sympathize with you.

"Dear boy, playing pool or any other such games are dangerous to the average youth, and particularly to the boy who must depend upon himself and hard work to obtain money for higher purposes. Because, after becoming an expert, and if circumstances ever cross his path, he will—if not masterful-minded (and nine cases out of ten he is not—be tempted to use this means to obtain money; and, being experienced, he will easily victimize the inexperienced player. Thus, both he and others will slowly but surely be drawn down to a gambler's hell.

"I want to impress upon you now, that there is no easy way to make money. No easy way to true success. This comes only to the man who is willing to work and work

THE RESENTMENT

hard. Let your dollars be honestly earned, and when your work is done, you can retire with a clear conscience to yourself and your fellowman.

"Miller, I have been at the bar for nearly twenty years. I have, through hard work, won honor and fame. There is not a living soul that can say through me he did not get justice. No man has dared to come to me guilty and expect me to plead or lie for him. I cannot be bought; but I will fight through a burning hell to right a wrong. For this, many hate me, and the same ones respect me. I could be far more richer today than I am, but I am rich in consciousness. I have few friends, but they are loyal and true ones.

"I could talk for hours, but it will take just such happening to convince you. However much I might say, will only serve as a map by which you may journey. You must do your own traveling. Wisdom comes with experience and age.

"I am glad you came to me. I admire the man in you."

"And so do I."

Attorney Kempt looked to see his little sunbeam standing in the doorway.

Silas felt proud that he had come to this man for advice. He also told Mr. and Mrs. Dayton that afternoon, when he went to the farm.

"That is what I meant when I said go to the city by all means, if you are strong enough," explained Mr. Dayton.

Later that afternoon, Bob Dale said to Margaret. "I see your pious Mr. Miller is a crackerjack pool player; lost quite a sum of money last night; should have known better than to have played with those city fellows."

"Yes, he came to father this morning and told him of his experience and asked him his advice. You are just the meanest boys alive. You know he had never seen a pool game in his life before." said Margaret, her face almost purple with rage.

"Oh," said Bob, sheepishly, "did he tell your father?"

He had intended to put Margaret against Silas, but was very much fooled and felt rather afraid that Silas had exposed them by telling Mr. Kempt. Margaret stood waiting to see what else he was going to say, but he turned and walked slowly away.

Silas had paid dearly for his wits, but it had taught him to wax strong against temptation by so-called friends. He did not

THE RESENTMENT

wholly shun the boys, but was careful where he went and what he did.

He had just begun to realize the full meaning of his father's words, when he said, "I am afraid the city life will make you forget us and the thoughts of becoming a business man."

He thought of how weak he had been, how easily he had fallen when he had thought himself so strong. "I wondered at my father's fear, but now I know," he said to himself.

CHAPTER VI.

NET DETERMINES HER COURSE

"I want every boy and girl to do his and her best today," said Mr. Price, the teacher. "I am expecting the Examiner about two or three o'clock today. I want you to be attentive, pay strict attention to what he says and try to answer as best you can. Please do not get nervous and answer anything. If you do not know, keep quiet and say nothing."

This day was always an exciting day to the rural district school children. The Examiner was a dreaded visitor to them. He usually frightened them all so badly that half of them could not tell whether the sun rose in the east or west, or how old they were or what grade they were in. It was very trying for the teacher, who wished to have his scholars at their best.

It was nearly three o'clock. They had given up hopes that he would come that day, when there came a loud knock upon the door. Mr. Keller entered. He was a large,

THE RESENTMENT

red faced, red headed white man, with a heavy voice. "Good afternoon, scholars," he said, bowing to the boys on the right and the girls on the left. "Good afternoon, sir," came the weak response.

After hearing several classes recite, he called the sixth grade, which consisted of five scholars, Nett Miller being at the head of the class. Each child seemed well prepared as they answered question after question. Mr. Keller was pleased and praised both the teacher and pupils. "The little girl at the head of the class is an unusually bright colored child."

"How old are you?" was asked.

"Fifteen years old, sir."

After asking several other questions, he started at the foot of the class and asked each child what he or she intended to do.

Some said they didn't know. Others just shook their heads, and still others laughed. He seemed almost despaired at not getting any intelligent answers and was about to dismiss the class, when he asked, "Well, what does my little girl at the head of the class intend to be?"

Nett said in a loud, distinct voice, "An old maid and a trained nurse, sir."

There was a loud roar of laughter, both

the teacher and the Examiner smiled, but Nett did not see anything funny about it.

Mr. Keller said, "Child, you have certainly chosen a noble field in which to work; you have the right idea—she who would seek her mission here, must make many sacrifices and could not do full justice to her work if a married woman. I am glad to know that at your age, you have some idea of what you should like to do."

Mr. Keller dismissed the class, talked awhile to the teacher, then left. There was a general snickering throughout the schoolroom. Nett Miller, one of the proudest girls in this county, wants to be an old maid," whispered the children among themselves. Mr. Price soon stopped the teasing and praised her for her good manner in speaking out so intelligently, and not giggling and laughing as did many of the pupils.

Nett wrote to Silas and told him how she had passed in her studies; she also added that she had been looking for a wife for him, but could not find a girl that seemed just right. She told him of all the little incidents that happened at school, but withheld her secret of wanting to go to the city to study to become a trained nurse.

School closed the tenth of May. Nett had

taken good care of the pigs, she worked late, and rose early in the morning. Her father, seeing how faithfully she worked, gave them entirely to her care.

About a week after school had closed, a farmer stopped one day to see if any of the Miller children were old enough to pick strawberries. Mrs. Miller thought that they were too busy at home to let them go, but Nett and little John begged so hard that at last she consented to let them go. "We have quite a number of school children, and that will make it pleasant for them," said the farmer. "I shall expect you all about seven o'clock in the morning. In the afternoon we pick from two until five."

Nett got her work done and retired early. She and little John could hardly wait until morning came. All the others had started picking when she and her brother arrived. "For goodness sake, look who's here!" they all exclaimed as they entered the patch. The foreman gave each a box and told them where to start.

"You must pick your vines clean, but be careful that the berries are not too ripe; you must not crush or mash them. Go slowly until you have learned to pick well. I am sure you will get along all right. What you do not know, do not be afraid to ask me."

It was a day Nett never forgot; the dew was so heavy in the morning that she swore that she was nearly drowned; in the afternoon the sun became so hot that she nearly roasted. But, in spite of these obstacles, she stuck to her post. It was indeed amusing to see Nett Miller appear upon the scene the next day with old gloves and a veil that she had begged her step-mother to give her.

"Poor little saint; girls, I really think that Nett Miller is the proudest and vainest girl alive," said Mary Stewart.

"I must admit that she is proud, but not at all vain. She possesses the kind of pride that doesn't hurt," said Mattie King, a girl older than the others.

In spite of the pride and all that was said about her, Nett proved to be one of the best workers.

She worked hard; it was the first money she had ever earned. Each night she would count her checks to see how fast her dollars were growing.

"We only get a cent a quart, and if I want to make ten dollars, I shall have to learn to pick faster than I do," she said to her mother.

THE RESENTMENT

She planned to buy a new white dress, a hat and new shoes, and then give the balance to help buy new things for her little brothers.

It was on the last day of the picking. Nett returned home in high spirits with nine dollars and eighty-seven cents. Giving the money to her mother, she rushed off to feed the pigs, only to find one dead. Poor child, she was dumbfounded; she had worked so hard to keep them fat and healthy. And they were growing so nicely. Now, one had to go and die. She cried until her little heart nearly burst. Her father and mother tried to console her; they told her that in every business, one loses as well as gain.

"You have nine left out of ten, and it could have nine dead and only one alive; you have much to be thankful for, Nett," said her father.

After this talk Nett was relieved, yet she was not contented.

Two days later, Nett counted out five dollars of her money; tying it in an old stocking, she went as fast as her feet would carry her to Mr. Baxter's.

"Well, well, Nett Miller, what brings you here so early this morning?"

"I came to buy a pig, sir."

"Holy smokes! are you going to raise pigs, too?"

"No, sir, Si left his in my care when he went away, and one of them had to die," said Nett, almost in tears.

"Well, don't look so hurt about it; we shall see what we can do."

Mr. Baxter left Nett standing in the barn yard while he went to look over his hogs. He returned a few minutes later driving a small young shoat before him.

"How about this one, Nett?"

"O, it is grand; it's a little larger than the one that died. How much is it, Mr. Baxter?"

"Why, I'll let you have it for two dollars."

Her heart leaped with joy; "I will still have money enough to buy my white dress and hat for Children's Day," she said, clapping her hands in childish glee.

She paid Mr. Baxter, and proudly drove "Jim" (as she named her new protege), home.

When her father returned from work that evening, Nett called him to see the pig she had bought. Mr. Miller was surprised.

"Where did you get it, Nett?"

"I bought it today, from Mr. Baxter."

"But, where did you get the money to

THE RESENTMENT 81

pay for it?" asked her father, more puzzled than he cared to show.

Seeing this, Nett said, "Why, papa, don't look scared to death; I cross my heart, I did not go out and rob any bank; I picked strawberries for three long weeks and made nearly ten dollars, so I took some of the money and bought the pig. I just couldn't rest, papa; I had to replace the one that died: I was afraid Si would think I had neglected them."

Mr. Miller laid his hand upon his daughter's head and said, "Nett, you are a darling. I am glad that you are so kind hearted; God will bless you for your good deeds, some day."

Had her father been able to witness the battle that occurred within Nett for two days; how she had struggled against the forces of selfishness and unselfishness, until she could not sleep; how these two spirits fought a mighty battle, one against the other, but unselfishness won. Nett gave up the white dress and the shoes to buy the pig. Had her father been able to witness that scene, he would have said, "Well done, my little girl."

This was the beginning; Providence had chosen this child for a purpose. The noble characters which He had instilled within her had lain concealed in her bosom to grow to maturity. And now, the first to steal forth from its hiding place was the virtue of unselfishness. Like unto the rose-bud that can no longer retain the flower, but bursting forth, and, unfurling its petals, drinks in the dew, the air, and the sunshine; and in return, gives forth its sweet fragrance. So would Nett Miller give to the world noble deeds that would seem almost supernatural. This was the first time she had been brought to test, and she had not been found wanting. She was so overjoyed at having enough money left to buy the hat and dress that she had forgotten the shoes.

It was the Friday before Children's Day She was showing her father her new hat and the dress her mother had made for her, when he asked, "Where are your shoes, dear? I thought you were going to buy new ones!"

"I did not get them, papa; I only made a little more than nine dollars. I gave mother three dollars to help get the other children ready, and after I got my hat and dress and paid for the pig, I did not have enough to buy new shoes. But mother bought a bottle of shoe polish, and I am going to polish the old ones and put new strings in them. They will look all right."

Her father said nothing, but told her mother that night, if it took the last cent he possessed, Nett should have a new pair of shoes.

Sunday came, all the children were excited and in a hurry to get dressed. Nett had helped her mother all the morning with the younger ones, and went to get dressed herself; she had put on her stockings and reached for her shoes which she had placed beside the bed after she had polished them, early that morning. She opened wide her large, brown eyes when she found a pair of new black slippers in the place of the old polished shoes. "Am I awake? I certainly must be dreaming; no, it is true, brand new slippers."

Her father had come quietly up the stairs to take a look at her; it was a beautiful sight to him to see his child bending over, admiring the slipper on one foot, while she held the other in her hand. "Ain't they pretty?" she was saying to herself.

"Do you like them, dear?" asked her father, walking into the room.

"O, papa, you nearly frightened me to death."

Rushing to him and putting her arms around his neck, she nearly smothered him with kisses.

"Papa, how did you know I wanted slippers?" she asked. "You don't know how happy you have made me."

Her father smiled and said, "If you make others happy, Nett, you too shall be happy."

Too young to know the full meaning of his words, she said, "I have never made anybody as happy as you have made me today, but I shall try, after this."

Years afterward, she put these words into effect.

CHAPTER VII.

STEP BY STEP

Two years have passed since Silas left. He had made one visit home. Nett and her father had sold some of the hogs and bought others. She had acquired a good business acumen.

While Silas worked in the North, she worked on the farm at home for him. He had shipped home several fine breeds of hogs that he had bought from Mr. Dayton.

Nett placed them in different lots, and, under no circumstances could she be persuaded to sell even one of them.

Silas had saved the amount of money he thought sufficient to start business on a larger scale with and was preparing to leave the North.

While foreman of Mr. Dayton's farm, he was loved by all the men employed there. No one ever thought of consulting Mr. Dayton concerning anything when Silas was near. It was always, "Where is Miller?" or "Ask Miller." In giving orders he always used good manners; he never forgot to say "please" or "thank you." He showed no egotism, nor ever made the slightest reference to the position he held over them.

He had taken advantage of the evening business school at Bristol, a little town nearby, and was well prepared to begin his life's work.

In these two years he had seen enough of the life in the city to be well prepared against the sin and vice that existed anywhere.

Mr. Dayton gave him a letter of recommendation that would help him to obtain any position in the world. Handing it to him, he said, "Silas, I can't say enough for you. With your interest and willingness to serve, with the pride you manifest in your work, and with your determination, success is yours. Come to see us when you can, and write us often."

He went to say "Good-bye" to the few—we cannot say friends—acquaintances that he had made. Even Horace and Bob regretted his leaving, while they did not associate with him extensively, they had learned to esteem him for the interest he maintained in himself and the respect he had for others.

He said "good-bye" to Mrs. Kempt and Margaret; he went over to Attorney Kempt and said, "Mr. Kempt, I have come to say good-bye, and thank you for the advice you gave me; it has helped me so much."

Attorney Kempt stood with his hands on Silas' shoulders; looking down into Silas' face, he said, "This is the *little* man; I shall be waiting to hear of the *big* man. It may take years, Silas, but don't disappoint me; I shall be surprised should I hear that you had given up because a little effort confronted you."

"I shall do my best, Mr. Kempt." "That is all one can do."

"We shall be glad to see you at any time; I hope you will always think of us as real friends," said Mr. Kempt.

As he left the room, Margaret said, "Don't forget to write."

Two days later Silas Miller left the North to take up his work again in the South. He had been encouraged so much that he felt sure he would make good.

At home once more, he went to work in earnest. We see him today on his father's place, a proud young man of nineteen years. One could hardly deem it possible that it was the same Silas Miller who left here just a

THE RESENTMENT

little more than two years ago.

Even Aunt Mollie Noble said, "I do declar' he looks a heap bettah den befo'! an' I t'ink de North has tuk out some of them airs, too."

While the other boys bought horses and carriages to drive around and enjoy the evening hours, Silas put every dollar that he made into his business.

All the farmers around had begun to notice that Silas Miller had the best hogs in the country. It was indeed wonderful to notice how rapidly he progressed. In calling upon Silas, the farmers would shake their heads and say after learning his prices, "Miller, you are selling too high." Then there would follow a long talk; Silas had learned to talk well. He often rehearsed the business talk that he had heard Mr. Dayton and his customers engage in. The farmers would listen attentively, then say, "Well, Miller, I s'pose you're right, after all." They usually ended by paying him his price.

Nett was always by his side; she loved the work, but she always seemed to be thinking of something afar off.

One day Silas told her that he had rented a larger farm for the next year. "Our business is getting so large we cannot stay here any longer. I shall also hire two more men."

"That is grand, Si, I know that you are happy."

"Yes," Nett, "I am; aren't you?"

"Well, y'e, yes, Si," she said, slowly. Silas noticed the unusual hesitation, as his sister, whom he loved so well, and asked, "What is it, Nett? You have worked so hard and faithfully for me; without your help, I could not have gotten on. You stayed here and worked while I was away, but Nett, you don't seem so happy. You know, if you don't tell me, I cannot help you."

Nett stood thinking for a while, then said, "Silas, I want to go to the city to study to become a trained nurse."

If Nett had told her brother that she wanted to go to Africa to catch tigers he could not have looked any more horror-stricken.

"Oh, Nell! You go to the city?" His heart nearly stopped beating.

"Yes, Si, I cannot stay here; something seems to call me, this is not my sphere."

Like a flash, the thoughts of what he had seen and heard in the city dawned upon him; he had heard men vie with each other in trying to win girls to their way of living.

He had seen girls dancing, thinly clad, in cabarets—young and beautiful girls. He had seen others staggering from hotels, half drunk, in the late house of the night, and most of these girls, he had been told, had migrated from the South. They had come of good, Christian families, but, not being properly prepared against the evils of the city, they soon fell an easy prey to these things, which at first seemed harmless.. "My God, if Nett would fall to such evils, it would drive me crazy. She is a woman, and, if she should lose her character and virtue, however innocent she may be, the world would never forgive her; she would carry the stain to her grave. But, how can I say 'No?' He looked again at his sister, and, for the first time, he saw that she was a woman, not the little Nett he had always thought of; childhood had flown, there she stood at the age of seventeen, in the full bloom of youth, and at the most critical period of her life.

Nett, seeing the shadows upon her brother's face, asked, "What is the matter, Si?"

He drew a long breath and said, "Nett, it would grieve me to see you go to the city alone and unprotected. You do not know how many temptations exist there; it takes a strong-minded person, and one with a deal of foresight, to resist them, and I am afraid the strongest often falls."

"But, Si, you went and returned all right."

"Yes, I went and returned but——."

His voice faltered; Nett saw that there was something that seemed unpleasant for him to recall. Then he told her the whole story of his temptation. After he had finished, Nett said, "But you are better and stronger than ever before."

"Yes, sister, but it seems that the scar will always remain; yet I cannot be selfish; we will talk the matter over with father and mother. If they are willing, I must be, too."

At supper that night, Silas told his parents of Nett's wish. At first they both were inclined to say no, but when they saw the pleading look in her eyes, they realized how good and faithful she had been, and consented to her wish—who could have said "no" to this girl?

About a week later Silas made a business trip to town. Upon his return he called Nett and told her that he had good news for her, but she must guess what it was.

"No, I cannot guess; please do not hold me in suspense."

"Mrs. Thompson stopped me today and asked me if I thought you would like to go to Philadelphia to live with her daughter who has recently married. I told her that you were thinking of going away in the near future. She told me to tell you that her daughter, Mrs. Schafer, would like you to do light housework for her; she also said she would give you good wages and take good care of you."

"Silas, that is fine; I shall never have words to thank you."

Turning to her parents, she asked them if it would be all right. Poor Mr. Miller nearly groaned at the thought of his only daughter leaving them, but he knew that she could not get sufficient education in the country to become a trained nurse. He told her if she would do as well as Si had done, he would be willing that she should go.

Mrs. Thompson called to see Mrs. Miller about Nett. She was charmed with the manner of the young colored girl, so cultured and refined. It was soon settled that she should go.

If Silas' going away had caused much comment, Nett caused more. When Aunt Mollie heard the news, she made many vigorous attacks upon her snuff box before

THE RESENTMENT

she said anything; then she said, "I s'pose John Miller thinks dis goin' away plan is all right. It may be all right for dee boy, but for de sak ob me, I caint see how he has de heart to sen' dat li'l gal away; but, I s'pose she'll git along all right, 'cayse she seems lak she's mo' fitted fo' an angel in Heab'n den any whars I knows ob. She done choosed a good work, 'cause she'll make a good Nu'se fo' de po' an' de 'flicted."

As Nett grew to womanhood she was loved by all. The little Sunday School class that she had taught for over four years loved her as few women are loved by children other than their own mothers. Hearing that she was about to leave them, they saved their pennies and bought her a little prayer book with these words inscribed upon the back: *By their fruits ye shall know them.*

On the first day of April, Nett left home to take her place amongst the thousands of women toilers of the city. That morning she felt sad when she saw her little brothers standing with tearful eyes, waiting to say "good-bye," but she played her part well. "Now please don't look as if I were about to start upon a funeral march; I am going to write you long letters every

94 THE RESENTMENT

week and tell you all I see and do," she said gayly as she came down the stairs. "And, of course, you know I will spend my vacation here, on this glorious old spot, as your guest."

She said so many other funny things that everybody was soon laughing. Silas felt the worst. "I am losing my right hand, my best friend, but one good turn deserves another. This rural life is too narrow for our ambitions, unselfish, broad-minded Nett."

He thought again and again to warn her against considering every acquaintance she chanced to meet, a confidential friend, but he thought it best to let her use her own judgment. With this decision, he kissed her good-bye.

The next morning Nett Miller awoke to find herself in a strange city, among strange people. But ere she had been here long, she had made a few warm friends. She was well liked by everybody. Mrs. Schafer taught her her way of working; she was very quick to learn, but found things so different from what she had been used to in her humble home in the South.

She wrote home at the end of each week as she had promised. Her letters were long and interesting, and so funny that all roared with laughter until the end was reached.

One day Mrs. Schafer invited some company to supper. After eating, they congratulated Mrs. Schafer on the well-prepared meal and asked where they got such a good girl. She told them that she had come from the South and had been with them only a short while. "She is an unusual girl, and seems to take more interest in her work than most girls who work out and whose main object is to just get through some how. She seems more like one of the family than a servant. I do hope she will stay with us for years." Mr. Schafer added, "Yes, but I am afraid that she is not made to be a house servant long; in several cases I have seen such girls who proved far more intelligent and rose to great heights than the persons by whom they were employed."

"I find that that is very true, especially amongst the colored people," said Mr. Catlin. "From experience, I find that the white man can seldom fathom the Negro; I know of one particular case that I often recall. A young colored boy worked for an intimate friend of mine. He worked there several years, then he left, telling them he was going to follow another vocation; he being a colored boy, they paid little or no attention

THE RESENTMENT

to this remark. After that, he would call unexpectedly some time during each year to see if they had any extra work they wanted done. They always found something for him to do, as they liked him and the children went wild about 'Tom.' To us he did not show any knowledge above that of a mere working boy, but he possessed good manners, quiet, clean habits. Often, we both referred to these good qualities in him and gave the cause to the fact that he had worked for our race of people since a child. |The real fact was—it takes the keenest and most scientific white man to discover the great, deep qualities of the black man.| My friend was one of the greatest surgeons of the State, but it never once occurred to him to talk of his great knowledge of medical science to that boy. Years passed and they had seen nor heard nothing of Tom. One day my friend was called to witness a very difficult operation; he has told me more than a dozen times that he was nearly dumbfounded to learn that the doctor who was to perform the operation was colored; and when he looked more closely and found it was Tom, his surprise was complete."

"Yes," said Mr. Schafer. "I have thought from the first that Nett is a girl for far great-

THE RESENTMENT 97

er service than ours."

Nett overheard part of the conversation as she flitted here and there doing her work. "Yes," she said to herself, "and here's another colored child somebody's going to hear from in years to come," clapping her hands playfully.

As anxious as Nett was to work, she often grew homesick and would sometimes cry, but she said nothing of this in her letters.

Mrs. Schafer found that they lived near a church owned by colored people. She told Nett this, and made it convenient for her to attend Sunday School there every Sunday afternoon. Nett found it very much different here than the little chapel in the country where she had attended Sunday School since a little girl. There everybody knew her and was glad to see her; here they hardly noticed her. She was assigned to a class, but they all being city-raised girls, were barely civil to her. She did not mind this much as she did not intend to let so small a thing spoil her career.

Mrs. Schafer saw that she was fond of reading and gave her free access to the library. This helped Nett and proved to be great company for her.

Unlike most ladies who employ help, Mrs.

Schafer did not think that a servant was a mer machine to grind out work day by day without a little recreation. She would find out if any of her friends had good colored girls, then she would make arrangements for Nett to go out with them, to see some of the city sights, such as Willow Grove, to photo-plays and other good places of amusement. When she could not find the right girls she took Nett herself. She took her to the large department stores and taught her how to buy good materials and not cheap, gaudy things. Mrs. Schafer also encouraged her to save a little money each month out of her wages. This she did not have to ever refer to, because it was Nett's one idea to save money to enter the training school for nurses.

Several ladies were having a tea with Mrs. Schafer one afternoon when one of the ladies, a Mrs. Gregg, asked her how did she manage to keep a girl so long.

"By treating her like a human being,' answered Mrs. Schafer.

"I don't find any worth treating as a human being," said Mrs. Wise. "If you treat them right, they don't appreciate it and by the time you have them trained into your way of working, they will walk off to some

THE RESENTMENT

other place for a few pennies more."

"I think it takes a fair-minded employer and a good, conscientious employee to get along good," said Mrs. Schafer.

"That's patting your own self on the back," snapped Mrs. Gregg.

"Well, maybe I am a little conceited," answered Mrs. Schafer, "but nevertheless, I always keep my girls, you see that, I suppose."

"Yes, some people will tolerate any kind of a girl, to keep from doing their work themselves," said Mrs. Gregg, conclusively.

"Hand it to me, Mrs. Gregg, I think that you will find my house as well kept as any," answered Mrs. Schafer, good-naturedly.

"See here, ladies, don't let us get on cross terms about hired girls; life is too short for such things, and you, Mrs. Schafer, wait until you have been hiring girls for thirty year, then you can talk," said Mrs. Baird, who was very quiet and had had little to say.

At this remark the ladies turned their conversation to other interesting things.

Nett met several girls who worked near her. She told them of her chosen course and how she planned to work for her education. To her surprise, they did not seem at

100 THE RESENTMENT

all interested, nor did they encourage her. They told her that she was crazy to work herself to death and deprive herself of clothes and pleasure just to go to school. One of the girls asked her if she ever intended to catch a city beau and if she did, she certainly would have to dress better. "No," said Nett, with a gleam of heated defiance in her eyes. "I hope you do not think that I came all the way up from the South to work to catch a city beau, and if I did, I am sure I would let him do the 'catching.'".

But her temper softened when she thought that they did not understand her. She talked long, trying to show them how education lifted them above the masses of the peoples and fitted them to deal proficiently with the difficult things of the world that confronted her race at a period when the best men and women obtainable are in great demand to help the less fortunate of the coming generation.

Poor Nett's words fell like seed on a desert's waste, they could neither grasp nor absorb them. Even while she talked, they would be winking and calling her the preacher in undertone voices. It made her weep to think that she could not make the others see or understand things as she did.

THE RESENTMENT

Nett Miller did not know that she lived far ahead of her time. Her thoughts and ideas were too progressive for their weak and undeveloped mind. Many have been like Nett Miller, striving and struggling to convince others to see their ideas of thinking and doing; such persons often die wrecked and heart-broken, but years afterward, while they slept the eternal sleep, the seed that they have sown took root and slowly pushed through the uncultivated soil. Such seeds would be readily recognized.

Dear readers, if you are striving to convince this slow-awakening race to some idea or purpose, do not tire, if at first they seem unable to grasp your meaning. Ere many years have passed, if not you, others will see the efforts of your work.

CHAPTER VIII.

"I SHALL NOT ALWAYS BE CALLED A NIGGER"

Several years passed since Silas Miller stood in the field on Mr. Baxter's farm with tears streaming down his face and in hot rebellion uttered the words that head this chapter. It seems that he is about to make good this statement. He purchased the large farm, the farm which he had told Nett of the day she expressed her desire to go to the city. Now, after six months, it was not large enough. The demand for hogs was far greater than he could fill. The feeding and care of them were great responsibilities. He employed several men, but one knows it is hard to get help who will take real interest in such work. This made Silas work hard during the day, and plan and think out the difficult problems at night. Several times he thought of trying to persuade Nett to come back and help him. He had already employed a girl from town to help in the office with the letters and the bills. But, not being so well experienced she could not keep pace with the heavy work. He knew that Nett could manage things better, yet he was afraid that if he did so, he would change her plans. She had helped him to get his start. Silas had become the chief object of interest in Kent County. Each day some farmer would say to another, "Have you bought any of Miller's hogs?" Or, in answer to where they could buy some good hogs, they would say, "Have you tried at Miller's? He is said to have the best hogs in this State." Others would say to some of their friends, "Don't you know that Miller is going ahead fast, give him a few years longer and he will be at the top of the ladder." And still others referred to him as "that smart black man," but no one ever called him "Nigger"—he had passed that stage.

Silas already saw the necessity of a good typist to attend to his work. He tried several times to obtain one, but it seemed a difficult task. None of the city girls cared to come to the country to live, and typists in the country were as scarce as "hen teeth." Silas thought often of Margaret Kempt. He had written to her occasionally, as he had promised, and she answered promptly each time. But he thought she did so just to make good her promise.

Margaret had completed her course at the business school and was working in her father's office. She had grown to be a beautiful young woman, quiet and reserved. Many called her vain, but when they knew her well, they loved her. Many young men called and tried to interest Margaret, but she treated them all alike. Leonard Morgan, the son of one of Mr. Kempt's most intimate friends, had called frequently. Both families had looked forward to this match, but Margaret could not be persuaded to entertain the slightest interest in him. Leonard Morgan was everything that one could wish a young man to be, having graduated from the School of Pharmacy at one of the leading colleges; he was also well accomplished in music. He belonged to several well-known clubs, and was one of the foremost young men in the younger social set. Most girls would have gladly accepted him, but Margaret was only sociably polite.

Both her father and mother wished to see their only daughter well-stationed in married life, and insisted that she should accept Mr. Morgan.

One day her father reminded her that she

should be more sociable and courteous to the young callers. "You know, Margaret, you are my all, and ———."

Margaret did not let her father finish; she went to where he was sitting, putting her arms around his neck, she said, "Dear Dad, you and mother are *my* all. I cannot think of leaving you yet, besides, I want to be free years and years to enjoy this glorious life. Furthermore, Papa, these young men disgust me; I cannot tolerate them. All they think of is women, and women and sport. I wish I had wings, I would fly away and find men who could find something sensible to talk about."

"Yes, Margaret, I know that we all love each other, but it would be so selfish if we would wish to keep you to ourselves. God gave you to us late in life; we are both getting old. This life is short, but death is certain. It would grieve me to leave you alone and unprotected. Margaret, darling, I would be happy to see you married to some good, young man; besides, mother and I would love to hold a little grandchild in our arms." Mr. Kempt's words were soft and pleading. It was a beautiful sight to see father and daughter sitting with their arms around each other. Her jet black hair was against his silvery gray hair.

Margaret thought a while, then said, "When I find a young man who really loves me for what I am, and *not* for what shall be mine some day; when I find a man that can honor good womanhood and appreciate me because I have tried to live to be a good woman, then, father, I shall marry; but," Margaret shook her head sadly, and said "But Dad, I am afraid I shall have a long wait."

Attorney Kempt looked aghast at his child, so young, so pure and innocent, but by no means ignorant of the ways of men.

"Dad, if I should marry, I shall ask God to give me sons, a half-dozen sons, then I would spare nothing to teach them the sacred duty toward women. To have good women we *must* have better men. Don't you think, Father, that men would be different if they were taught from childhood, by their parents, the sacredness of the virtue of women?"

The great ,learned attorney bowed his head and said, "Yes, daughter, you are right, I guess."

When Margaret went back to her desk, her father sat long, with his head resting in his hands, buried in deep thought. Here sat a man thinking and thinking upon a subject that should have required no thought for him. He was a man that few men could approach with any subject that he could not readily and openly converse on. The great problems that confront races and nations to-day were naught to him. Many had heard this learned man in the courts where he spoke concisely and with great ease. They had commended on his great ability of discussion, but to-day he faltered and stammered before the simple question of his daughter. His little Margaret, whom he had planned to make one of the leading belles of the city, and whom he had hoped would marry into some wealthy family of his associates, had chosen an entirely different course. He saw the great love of purity ebbing through her soul, and the effect was that she wanted sons, that she might teach them the sacredness of man's duty toward woman that the women of her race might be better.

How openly she had talked with hem, and in these years he had said nothing to help his girl to battle against the temptation of men. He had willingly ushered young men into his home without a thought of their care for his child; without thought of their intentions, whether good or bad. He wondered if his wife had told Margaret any of these things; they had both taught her etiquette of social life, how to choose company from the best of families, but the deep things which Margaret had spoken of to-day, seemed to him so immodest until he heard them from the lips of his own daughter. "There must be something wrong or Margaret would not have wished to bring sons into the world to make better men," thought her father.

This conversation made father and daughter inseparable companions. Mr. Kempt told Margaret many things that fathers should tell their daughters. He found that it was his duty as well as the mother's.

One day, after Margaret and her mother had had some heated words over Mr. Morgan, Mr. Kempt came in and found them both in tears. "Mother, I know both you and I would like to see Margaret marry Leonard. To us, he seems to be an ideal man, but we must not interfere. I am sure that she can be trusted to choose a good husband. Margaret and I have talked a great deal together, lately, and I find that she has noble ideas. We will let her instinctive powers lead her to the right man. We must not let this thing make a gulf between us. I strictly forbid that this matter should ever be mentioned to her again." Then Mr. Kempt kissed both women who were so dear to him, and the source of all his happiness.

A few weeks after this conversation Margaret received a letter from Silas. After reading it, she went to her father and asked him to guess who the letter was from. "I don't know, dear, you get so many letters I am afraid I'd have a fine time guessing."

"Well, if you have given it up, I shall have to tell you. It's from Silas Miller, and just look, Dad ———." Margaret held up a hand full of circulars and advertising matter. A long folding card contained a picture of the farm and buildings; here and there were large groups of hogs scattered over several lots and many fields of growing grain.

Mr. Kempt took the card and looked at it for some time. He read how Silas Miller the coming Hog King of the State, had worked his way from a single litter of six hogs, in a little back lot, to the ownership of a three-hundred-acre farm and thousands of the best hogs in the country. "Wonderful," exclaimed Mr. Kempt, "I knew from the first day that I saw him that he would make a good man." Mr. Kempt read Silas' letter

THE RESENTMENT

to Margaret. Silas invited Margaret and her parents to come to see him, and said, "I shall never forget how you made it easy for me to bear the loneliness of being away from home, and how your father's words helped me when I was heartbroken over the money which I lost in the pool room that night, due to my ignorance of the game. Margaret, you do not know how your words "when you go back on the farm" made me stick more firmly to the promise that I made father before leaving home. I am doing fine, but am putting every effort forward to do better, each year of my life. Nett, my dear sister, is in your city. She expects to enter a training school for nurses there, in the near future. You cannot imagine how much I miss her. At first, it seemed almost impossible to get along without her help. Her advice has always been so helpful, and she could do so many little things that I would never have thought of. I do hope some day that you two shall meet. It would make me so happy."

Silas wrote a long letter. After reading it, Mr. Kempt marveled at the splendid manhood. Only a country lad, not yet twenty-three years old, and to have braved such vicissitudes to become an independent man.

Handing the letter back to Margaret, he said, "A thoroughbred young man, dear."
"Yes, father, I think he's great."
That night Margaret lay awake thinking of Silas and Nett. She recalled all her acquaintances among young men, but not one measured up to Silas Miller. "My friends may laugh at me for liking a country boy, but who could help liking Silas! I certainly would be glad to meet Nett," so musing she fell asleep.
Time passed quickly by. Nett had just returned from her vacation. She worked six months longer, then Mrs. Schafer helped to gain admittance to ―――― Hospital. It was hard work, but not a girl in the class was more industrious or faithful to duty than Nett Miller. When the other girls murmured and complained about the unpleasant work of a probationer, she was always cheerful and willing.
She had chosen her course and accepted whatever duties assigned her without complaint. This won for her great commendation from the hospital staff, but made her less popular amongst the members of her class. They called her "green-horn" and accused her of seeking favoritism of the instructors and trying to artract the atten-

THE RESENTMENT

tion of the internes. They were jealous and would not associate with her, but she did not for once heed their uncultured remarks or petty taunts.

The patients with whom she came in contact all loved her. It was always, "Where is Miss Miller?" or "Can Miss Miller wait on me?" and it was always Nett who took the place of others when off duty. Often she would do the work of two, trying to help some girl along. When off duty she would read and write long, interesting letters home, and take long walks. She was always quiet and thoughtful most of the time, but, like other girls, she liked fun and friends; yet, both seemed to be denied her.

It was near Christmas; all the girls were looking forward to the holidays; each was expecting something from home. Nett knew she would get a check from Silas, but when she went to breakfast Christmas morning, she was surprised to find two packages, one was a box of candy and the other contained a beautiful fountain pen. Nett stood speechless, "Who could have sent them? And the pen is just what I needed."

"O, girls, look what I have, but I can't imagine who sent them," she explained.

THE RESENTMENT

"Oh, Nett Miller, you can't bluff us, you are always trying to play 'Meeky Moses;' you know some of your numerous admirers sent them," said Daisy Smith.

Nett did not reply to this remark, and Anna Gould added, "Nett makes me tired, she tries to be Miss Goody-good, and there isn't a doctor here that hasn't got his eyes open."

"Now, girls, don't tell tales out of school," said Lucy Beck.

"Oh, it doesn't matter, let them enjoy themselves," said Nett in an indignant manner, not understanding the sarcasm in Lucy Beck's remark.

Several days after Christmas one of the strictest rules of the hospital was broken by some of the nurses; no one seemed to know who did it, and the guilty one would not acknowledge the deed.

Anna Gould frankly declared that Nett Miller did it. She had always been envious of Nett and took this opportunity to give vent to her feelings by saying something to reflect upon her character, or demerit her in her class.

Poor Nett's heart nearly failed her when she thought of the disgrace of being demerited and the hard work she would have

THE RESENTMENT

to do as a punishment for an act she had not committed.

When the Superintendent asked her about it, she said, "I will tell you truthfully, I did not do it; but I can take the punishment and save some poor, unfortunate girl who is too narrow-minded to admit her own guilt. It is hard, but I can bear it for her sake."

All the girls hung their heads, they had suspected a heated resentment from Nett, but she took the unjust accusation so submissively that it struck home to the heart of every girl, yet none dare to own the deed.

Miss Wolf, Superintendent of the Hospital, not being too courteous with the girls, and who never let them forget her authority to rule, said, "Miss Miller, you shall do double duty beginning tonight, for one week; it must be understood that rules in this place cannot be broken, and, if so, that person or persons must bear the penalty."

Nett went on duty that night with heart aflame with anger. While she accepted the blame, she was wholly guiltless and could not help feeling the sting of shame. But, when she heard the groans of the sick and dying, all was forgotten. Her heart swelled with pity, "I should thank God that I am

able to do duty, instead of being angry," she thought to herself. She then went quietly among her patients humming within herself her favorite hymn:
"Does Jesus care when the way seems dark,
Too deep for mirth or pain."
She had hardly begun her work when she heard whispers amongst the patients, "Miss Miller is on duty." Everyone loved her; she was so patient, so kind, and the very touch of her soft, brown hands seemed to ease the severest pain.

Nett did not know that, as she moved to and fro, straightening a pillow here to make a patient more comfortable, or coaxing another to try to sleep, or to wipe a tear from the eyes of a poor, home-sick soul, that two eyes were watching her; nor did she know that this noble deed had lifted her to the heights of angels in the eyes of the one who watched. But she did know that Dr. Lionel came and asked her how she was getting along. "Oh, fine, I thank you," she replied. He said nothing more. Nett so loved her work that she soon forgot she was being punished for another's deed.

Dr. Lionel, one of the internes at the hospital, knew who had broken the rule, and

THE RESENTMENT

he had gone purposely that night, to see how Nett worked. He had watched for more than half an hour before he said anything. He had suspected to find her pouting and sulking; but, when he saw her at work, and heard her sweet, soft voice speaking so gently to the patients, he said to himself, "I have never seen such a woman; she is an angel of pity." He had seen and knew who had broken the rule and had also heard the plot to put the blame on Nett.

At the table, or wherever Nett met the other girls, they felt somewhat penitent to see that she was not even angry with them. The memory of her deed would never be erased from their hearts.

Several times Miss Dunn urged Anna Gould to let her tell the truth about it. "I think you are the silliest goose that ever was born, if you ever were born; sometimes I doubt if you were, you have so little sense. Now the thing is forgotten and you want to stir it up again; I don't see where Nett is any the worse off for setting up a few nights when it was not her turn. Maybe she will let her head down a little now, and not go around looking like some saint just dropped from the sky. It will give a good chance to be an angel, because we usually pay for everything in this world."

"Yes, Anna, I am afraid we do," replied Katie Dunn.

But Anna Gould did not fully realize the meaning of the words, "we pay."

CHAPTER IX.

OBSTACLES

We go on in life working, hoping, comtemplating success. But it is not the nature of man to contemplate failure. This we accept generally without premeditation, but as failures are often hidden blessings how much better it is to happen in early life, when we are young and can easily eradicate the pangs of disappointments. As it is in youth when we can withstand the scene of shadowed air castles or day dreams without losing hope. It is at this period of life we can with little encouragement work through.

Since his return to the farm, Silas had been rapidly sailing on peaceful waters, but like a thunder bolt out of clear skies, came a disease. An epidemic, that wrought havoc among the hogs of all the farmers in several States, the South being the most effected. The best veterinarians were summoned, and every known drug made for dumb animals was used, but to little or no avail. Poor Silas was compelled to watch some of his best breed entirely wiped out, and little hopes for the surviving ones.

Farmers visited farmers in hopes of gaining some helpful information, for it seemed that each within himself had given up all hopes. Even when facing a thing that seemed hopeless. Silas Miller displayed that same determination that had brought him thus far.

"Miller, we are done for." he would be told several times during the day, and when Mr. Poland, a well-to-do white farmer said, "Miller, it is all up with us," Silas shook his head and answered, "No, Mr. Poland, there must be something, if we can only find it."

"Well, Si, if there is anything, you go and find it, and I hope a shad may shoot me, if there is a farmer within a hundred miles that won't buy it from you, excusing the price," said Mr. Poland in an indignant manner.

"That is what I'm going to do," answered Silas with a little touch of that old confidential air that he usually possessed when being repulsed by another.

On his way home, Silas met Mr. Baxter. "Good morning, Si. How are things going over your way?"

"I cannot complain, Mr. Baxter. I have

THE RESENTMENT 121

lost a great many hogs, but to the present, I have managed to save the greater portion."

"Then, I must say, boy, the gods seem to have been with you. I have lost every single hog, that I owned."

"But remember, Mr. Baxter, I have about twenty times as many as you, so I may not be any more blessed, but I have more to give."

"That is true, too. I must say, Si, you the the most optimistic young man that I have ever known. You have an act of seeing rays of sunlight behind the darkest clouds."

"True to the old race, Mr. Baxter. I am now on my way to see if I cannot find something to help fight this terrible disease."

"If there is anything to be found, you will find it, Si Miller," said Mr. Baxter, laughing.

"Let us hope."

"If there is anything I can do to help, do not fail to let me know, Si."

Silas thanked Mr. Baxter, and started for home in a more hopeful spirit. On reaching home he found his father standing in the doorway looking very downcasted.

"Father, please don't look as if the world

THE RESENTMENT

has come to an end," he said in a cheerful manner.

"I am mighty glad you can take things so lightly," his father answered almost abruptly. "With all the work and money and time and everything you have in this business, and to see things going the way they are, appears to me you would be mighty nigh crazy, and for the life of me, I can't see that things are getting any better."

"Dad, it is the hand of fate," said Silas.

Mr. Miller fairly groaned. It seemed to him that Silas had lost all sense of reasoning.

Seeing that his father was completely discouraged with his optimisticness, Silas put his hands gently on his father's shoulder in his old familiar way and said, "Dear Dad, to become a good business man, you must expect failure with success, and one must also be a good loser. Yes, I do realize I have put much in this business, but in this life, we can't expect more than we are willing to give."

"Then, I don't suppose I have given much because it seems I don't get much."

"Now, Dad, you know you are wrong. You are a rich man, and I dare say there

THE RESENTMENT

are thousands that envy you this very moment."

Mr. Miller looked at Silas as if he thought he had been suddenly bereft of his senses, but before he had time to ask what on earth did he mean, Silas continued by saying, "Just think of Nett, Dad! How much in cash would you take for her?"

The clouds immediately disappeared from his father's face.

"Silas, child, in all the years of my life, I have never thought of such a thing. Well, there is not enough money in the United States Treasury or even in the entire world, to buy, not only Nett, but a single child I have."

"Then Dad, you possess priceless jewelry."

Mr. Miller stood thinking, while Silas went to his little room, where he had spent many hours trying formula after formula. His heart was heavy, but he dare not waver in hopes. He worked far into the night, hoping ere the dawn of another day, that something could be found, but the morning's mail brought an added burden.

Officials of several States had issued a rigid warning *To all farmers holding hogs affected or likely to be infected must be killed* within ten days after the issue of warning unless a permanent cure has been produced. All persons keeping such hogs on their premises would be subject to imprisonment or heavy fine or both.

In spite of Silas Miller's forced optimisticness, when he read this statement, he bowed his head and wept. It seemed as if this was more than he could bear. He wrote a long letter to Nett and one to Margaret. How anxiously he waited for Nett's answer which he knew would be full of hope and encouragement. In the return mail came Margaret's answer, full of sympathy, and several lines from Attorney Kempt which gave strength to hope, but Nett, why don't she write? He wondered at her delay, she who was always so punctilious. Oh! I suppose she is writing a book. Her letters are always so long.

Several days passed; then came Nett's reply. When Silas took the letter handed to him by the rural post delivery, it was so thin that he held it up to see if it contained anything beside the envelope. "Oh I suppose poor Nett is so tired trying to bear everybody else burdens and we can't blame her either," he soliloquized as he opened the letter. All it contained was a little verse

THE RESENTMENT

clipped from a book or magazine and pinned to half sheet of paper, which read:

"Thy fate is the common fate of all,
Into each life some rain must fall,
Some days are dark and dreary."
—Tennyson.

Beneath this Nett wrote:
Dear Silas:
Tennyson wrote this for you. Don't give up hope.
Lovingly,
NETT.

Silas was so disappointed that it was some time before he could really grasp the meaning of that verse. He read and reread it until at length he realized the strength of the words. "Yes, the great poet has in that one verse expressed more than Nett could have written in six long letters. But Nett is my very own, and one word from her is more to me than volumes from the greatest poets that the world has ever produced," Silas said as he placed the letter in a little drawer in his desk.

Days passed rapidly on with no signs of relief. It was on the eve of the fifth day

THE RESENTMENT

since the State had issued the order. Driven almost to despair, Silas went to his room immediately after supper. He wrung his hands in anguish, as he thought of the sacrifices he had made, and the struggles he had endured, and now it seemed that it were to end so.

Silas like most men and women as they prosper in life and rise to position and wealth, they are inclined to lean away from religion or its teaching. He had not become wholly skeptical, he was just too busy for such things, but God has a way of jogging our memories sometime. As he sat there thinking, slowly came the memories of his boyhood teachings. He recalled how a few years hence he had climbed the stairs to the dark and lonely bed room. How he had knelt beside the little pallet bed and asked that God whom his humble mother had taught him to ever serve and trust, to care for him and now when he should have trusted Him, he had nearly forgotten. Without further meditation, he knelt beside his bed and prayed for divine help to fight this epidemic. He lacked that great childish faith as in former days, but he felt relieved.

Aunt Mollie Noble had suffered much from rheumatism, and had been forced to stay

THE RESENTMENT 127

at home the greater part of the time, so had missed much of the news and gossip of the neighborhood. When Mrs. Lee, one of the neighbors, brought her the startling news that there was a terrible disease amongst the hogs, and that they were all dying, and what wasn't dying would be killed in the next few days, Aunt Mollie exclaimed, "What's dat, you say? My Lor, child, what's dat?"

"Yes'um, its true, and dere is Si Miller, dey say his'm all dying, and I s'pose his all gits killed too. Bless de Lor," said Aunt Mollie.

As Mrs. Lee did not see anything to bless the Lord for, she continued, "Well, you know, Aunt Mollie, 'taint no use for us colored folks to be reaching up so high and trying to get rich like the white folks, for we is shur to get fetched down."

If Mrs. Lee had expected a hearty response in her favor, she must have been both disappointed and astonished when Aunt Mollie answered barely audibly, "Um-hum." In fact Mrs. Lee looked up as if she thought Aunt Mollie had not quite understood her, because when it came to condemning prosperity, Aunt Mollie Noble seldom or never had to think for words. Instead she sat with folded arms staring into space. She had so little to say that Mrs. Lee asked, "if she was feeling well," to which she replied, "Just tolerable, Sister Lee. But I am thinking about poor Si. 'Tis likely he would be de most 'fected around here. It sho does seem ashamed for de chile, he has wurk so hard, but why don't they send for some of dem animal doctors from the city?"

"They has done everything Aunt Mollie, and dat is the reason they are going to kill the hogs to see if they can't stop it."

Aunt Mollie sat down in her old rocker and began rocking and thinking. She had so little to say that Mrs. Lee soon left. A few minutes later, Aunt Mollie climbed the rickety old stairs that led to the attic. Pushing the little door aside she said. "I wonder if I kin git through here. It has bin many a day since I was up here, and this doorway looks mighty small for my size." After a rather squeezing effort, she managed to get through it. "It's mighty dark and dusky, up har, and dat little window don't let in much light, but I know de old trunk a mile away," she said as she stepped cautiously over the creaking boards.

She soon found the prize piece of paper. "Dat's it," she exclaimed, wiping the dust away. "I knowed it was in there. I will run over to get Mary Liza's gal to put it on another piece of paper, as this is about to drop to pieces."

Aunt Mollie had always been known to be the greatest prayer in the church; besides, being one of its strongest supporters. Each rising generation had been taught these things about her, until it seemed that no one ever thought of her possessing another virtue. In fact, the young people had long since found it impossible to listen to a well-prepared sermon without being annoyed almost to distraction by her numerous ejaculations.

Often the young minister just from Morgan College, and eager to show to his congregation how well he had prepared himself to teach the Scripture, would be forced to stop in the middle of his sermon to let Aunt Mollie have a good shout. At other times he could succeed in keeping her quiet by repeatedly saying, "Now, Sister Noble, listen," and then at the end of each sentence, she would yell at the top of her voice, "A-A-men!"

If he could just keep her at this point, he would be satisfied, but the congregation would be interestedly listening to him intoning the Scripture, when Aunt Mollie would suddenly throw up her hands and send forth several loud shrieking screams, while the startled congregation would be wondering what had happened. She would shout: "Preach it! Preach it!" Then everybody knew Aunt Mollie was in the spirit, and every young girl within an arm's reach would feel shaky about her spring bonnet; and every young man would eye anxiously his prize panama held by some young girl, because when Aunt Mollie was in the spirit she was no respector of hats nor heads. Many a young lass had returned from church carrying the remains of her hat in her hand, while the lads usually left theirs to the fate of the sweeper.

To all who knew her, this was about the length of her religion, and the entire community would have been surprised could they have witnessed her movements now.

When she had gotten the recipe re-written, she made hasty preparation to make her secret call on Silas Miller the next morning. Silas had just finished breakfast, and had gone to his little office when he heard Aunt Mollie's voice, "Good morning, Brother Miller, how's all this morning?" he head her ask his father. "Goodness me, here comes

THE RESENTMENT

the old gossiper; I do hope she'll stay out there and talk to father and mother, as I am in no frame of mind to listen to a lot of nonsense this morning." He had barely uttered the words when she knocked at the office door. Silas moved slowly toward it with a mind to tell her he was so busy that he could not receive callers. But when he opened the door, Aunt Mollie popped in without an invitation.

Seating herself in the first chair she saw, she asked, "How is you to-day, Si?"

"Oh, fairly well, Aunt Mollie, how are you?"

"Well, just tolerable," she replied.

Instead of being annoyed, Silas found he felt rather kindly towards the old lady. He often said afterwards that something he had never seen before shone in her face.

"How is you making out, honey," she asked in a voice so full of sympathy and tenderness that he replied, "Oh, Aunt Mollie, we are done for, there is no help."

"Now, Si, don't say that, chile, has you prayed?"

"Yes, Aunt Mollie," answered Silas, bowing his head, yet he was conscious of a slight embarrassment or shame, at which Aunt

Mollie took no notice, for she replied, "Thank God."

Reaching her hand far down in the bosom of her waist she drew forth a little piece of crumpled paper. "Der Silas is a recipe that old Marse Causdon used to use for his hogs when dey got sick, and my Sammy used to use it for his'm too, when we were raising hogs."

" 'Tis so old that I could scarcely read it, so I went over and got Mary Liza's gal to write it off for me, and brung it here with me dis morning. It's been many a long day since I seen it used, but it's good. You jest read it and let me har how she is got it down, 'cause des har young things scribble so fast dey don't gib you time to ketch your breath before dey is asking 'what next'; and when dey get it all down, dey can't read it demselves and how dey spects any one else to know beats me."

How eagerly Silas Miller bent down and read that little note. After reading it himself he read it to Aunt Mollie.

"Dat's it, de very stuff. You go and get a big iron pot, and I'll help you get some of it mixed."

Aunt Mollie worked the entire afternoon. Having seen remedies of the best veterinarians failed, Silas seemed to have no doubt about Aunt Mollie's. When she had finished Silas insisted on taking her home in his car.

"No, chile," she said, shaking her head vigorously. "When I gets into one of dem chariots, I wants to go clean home to glory. Dese things sends you up, and den you comes down. No, I shall walk and den I know I shall get dere safe."

"Now Si, you jest feed some of dat stuff to each hog. Den you get down on your knees and git hold of dat wire dat leads from earth to glory and you ring til you gits an answer.

"Si Miller, don't you be like dese har folks dat call themselves de fore hundred. Dey is dat proud dat dey is skeptic. After God has gib dem their health and strength to earn de libbing by the sweat of der brow, den dey has de gall to stand up and say 'Der aint no God.' If dey own Him dey call Him by so many big names, dat you hab to stand and think who dey is talking about."

"Der was old Abe Lincoln. He never got so high up dat he could not git down on his knees. Don't you git too proud to pray, Silas," she said as she walkd slowing toward the gate.

THE RESENTMENT

As Aunt Mollie walked along the lonely country road, she prayed and pleaded with God as only a child can plead with his earthly father. "Now, dear Father, I don't ask for myself, but for dat humble chile, Si Miller. Dear Father, you heard me when I prayed in de cotton patches, when my po old back was aching and my feet were blistered. Dear Father, don't forsake me now."

How little did she or Silas suspect that that little slip of paper contained the answer to their prayers.

Not even Aunt Mollie's closest friend, Sister Maria Dudley, could have deemed it possible that Aunt Mollie had gne and worked an entire day without a word of gossip, but with encouraging words so full of faith.

Twelve hours passed, and Silas saw a change that was almost miraculous. He sent word and help to many of the farmers requesting them to pass the good news on to others. Thus, the news that Miller had produced a cure spread like wild-fire. When Mr. Baxter heard it, he came over to see for himself if it was true.

After Silas had shown the farmer the proof, he said, "I must admit that I was a doubting Thomas. Si, we have thought you a wonder for some time, but by golly I do

THE RESENTMENT

believe you are a wizard."

"But you are wrong for once, Mr. Baxter, everything I tried failed."

The astonished farmer looked his surprise. "I don't understand you, Si. Here are all of your hogs recovering and all of the farmers that have used the remedy report the same success, and you stand here and say all of your remedies failed."

"Could not some one else produce a cure?"

"Yes, but it seemed that no one did."

"But some one did, and not I."

"Gracious, goodness whom, Si Miller?"

"Aunt Mollie Noble."

"Do you mean Aunt shouting Mollie?"

"The same," replied Si, pleased to see the perplexed look on Mr. Baxter's face.

"When she heard of this disease, she brought me a recipe of an old remedy they used when she was a slave, and stayed all day helping me to get it made."

"Si, do you remember that quotation that Lincoln wrote about the good and bad in us? I guess there is a lot of truth in that saying," said Mr. Baxter, meekly.

A week later, Silas drove to Aunt Mollie's humble shanty. It was a bright, warm April day. The balmy spring air felt refreshing to Silas. The great nerve strain of the past

weeks showed plainly upon him. He seemed to have grown years older, but to-day his face bore that bright, happy look possessed only when the heart is at ease. He found her with work all done, and sitting on a low stool in the doorway with a large family Bible on her lap, with her specks nearly on the end of her nose. She was moving her finger slowly along, half spelling, half reading the passage, "I hear even the sparrow's cry."
"How true," she was saying when Silas called, "Good morning, Aunt Mollie."
"Now look here boy, you might night scarer me to death."
"Did you thing I was an angel, Aunt Mollie?"
"Now, Si Miller, you ought to be ashamed of yourself. An angel your color, and nary a wing hab you got."
"You see I am young, and maybe they haven't grown out yet, and as to color, are all angels white, Aunt Mollie?"
Aunt Mollie readjusted her specks, putting them back in the same place, then said, "I often wonder dat myself, Si. If I can jest get in the glory land, I ain't so particular about changing this old color."
"It's genuine isn't it, Aunt Mollie, don't fade or wrinkle."

THE RESENTMENT

"You said it, now chile," both laughed heartily.

"We is been so busy talking that I ain't tuk time to say come in, Si."

"No, I thank you, Aunt Mollie. I came over to bring you good news."

"What's dat, honey?"

"Your remedy has proved genuine."

"Oh, praise de Lord."

"And I came to thank you and——"

"Did you thank de Lord, chile?"

"Yes, Aunt Mollie." This time without any of that false pride that he was conscious of before."

"Den chile, don't you bother about a pore old worthless worm like me."

"But, Aunt Mollie, you must take something. If any one else had been able to have done as much, it would have cost a small fortune."

"Now, Si Miller, does you want to hurt my pore old feelings, dose you, Si?"

"Jest think I would take money for helping out in the time of distress! I knew dey don't 'sider me much, but thank de Lord I can do a little kindness."

"But, Aunt Mollie——"

"No, sir, Si, not a cent does this humble servant take."

Silas was about to give up, when he asked, "Maybe there is something that you have been wanting for these many years. See if there is anything that you would like me to give you; I must give you something."

After a few minutes, Aunt Mollie said, "Yes, Silas, there is something that I has been wanting."

"What is it, Aunt Mollie?"

"It is one of dem dar stones dat the kin folks put at de grave of their loved ones when dey die, but dey is so 'spensive, and I have always wanted one for Sammy. I has managed to put by a little against it, but am nowhere nigh it yet."

"Oh! Aunt Mollie, you mean a tombstone."

"Is dat what dey call dem? I have plumb forgot the name."

"Well, you go and have one made, just the kind you want, and then let them send me the bill."

"But, Si, they are powerfully high."

Then thinking that she would not have as nice a one as he wanted her to have, Silas changed his mind, and asked her what she wanted on it.

"I want Sammy's age, death and his discharge from the Civil War."

THE RESENTMENT 139

"All right, Aunt Mollie, you shall have it." Large drops of tears stood in her eyes as she tried to thank Silas for his noble gift. "Now, chile, I shall not forget you as long as I live, and I don't calculate dat is long, for I am getting old."

"Yes, Aunt Mollie, your is the evening of life."

"Dat's right, honey, and den comes de night, wid it de rest."

"Eternal rest, Aunt Mollie."

As Silas drove homeward that day, he realized that it is not ours to pass judgment upon our fellow man. While Aunt Mollie still bore the name of a gossiper, there was one who knew it was only a weakness, and in her heart she carried a debt of charitableness that could not be fathomed by human minds.

Some weeks later when the young minister shook hands with Aunt Mollie saying, "There is more in you than shouting and praying," she shook her head and said, "A-ah, Lord, chile," a favorite expression which she used when she did not want to say out right, "Not all old folks are fools."

She was indeed rewarded when a few months later she went to the cemetery and

140 THE RESENTMENT

saw the beautiful tomb-stone Silas had erected at her beloved husband's grave. In expressing her delight she exclaimed, "the Lord bless Silas Miller—and won't de folks be envious when dey sees dis beautiful stone. Why it's taller than any out here," she mused as she looked around as far as her dim eyes could behold. Then she unwrapped a small bundle that she had brought with her and displayed a beautiful silk American flag, which she proudly wrapped about the stone.

It was sometime before Silas could grasp the same working spirit as he hitherto had possessed. He said, "It was like climbing a mighty mountain, when about half way up, to find oneself suddenly plunged to the very bottom, to begin all over again."

Silas Miller's courage had nearly failed him, his faith was shaking, but he had withstood the test. It had made him less arrogant, more sympathetic, more patient with others that had failed, and had not the courage to go on, more considerate of the less fortunate. In fact, this calamity was a hidden blessing.

Some months later, we see him preparing for the sale that made for him the name that he bore forever afterwards, "The Hog King of the States."

CHAPTER X.
TWO GREAT EVENTS

It was a beautiful day on the twentieth of June, the sun was peeping behind the Eastern horizon. Already many vehicles were coming in from every direction over the different country roads. If one could ask where they were going, they would be told that they were going to the wonderful sale at Miller's. For weeks, hundreds of persons, especially farmers, had looked forward to this day. It had been extensively advertised in every paper and magazine throughout the country. Already, hundreds of letters had arrived. The work was heavy, Silas and his hired men were kept busy. "I do not know what I shall do," said Silas to a friend, "I must get a girl more capable to take full charge of the heavy mail orders." He had kept up a continuous correspondence with Margaret and wrote and asked her if her parents could arrange to let her come down for a week to help him superintend the work in the office during the week of the sale. "You see, I am just now accepting the offer of assistance you made me, some time ago. Your help to me at this time will be invaluable. My father and mother will do all they can to make it pleasant for you. If you cannot come, I shall suffer a great loss through mail orders."

When Margaret read this letter, and had gotten the consent of her parents to go, no one knew it, but it was the happiest moment of her life. Silas Miller was the prince of her heart. A few days later, Margaret Kempt sat in Silas Miller's office, and worked with lightning speed on the typewriter. Everyone marveled at the rapidity of speed she possessed. Letter after letter was read and answered. She placed everything in order, making it easier for the men to get the orders filled. She had done business for her father but nothing like this. She was pleased when Silas praised her at the end of a day. He told her that she had done more work in one day than they had been able to get out in a week. They stopped work at five o'clock each day, then went for a little recreation; Silas was teaching her to ride horseback, and there was nothing Margaret liked better than to ride along the country road and watch the beautiful Southern sunset.

THE RESENTMENT 145

All was in readiness; the farm was a picturesque place: all over the fields were pens and stalls with the names of the different breeds of hogs that were enclosed.

Never in all of his life was Silas so excited; he had spent hundreds of dollars in advertisements and improvements to make this a great day. Long before ten o'clock he had taken in more money and sold more hogs than he had during his entire years of business. By noon that day, more than five thousand persons had visited the farm. When they stopped at five o'clock, every hog had been sold, and every order filled. The farmers who lived in that vicinity said they had never seen such a sale; and every thing so well arranged. There was no auction; everything was sold in lots and pairs at set prices.

Mr. Baxter shook his head at some of the farmers and said, "Ain't Miller coming, though? Yes, I tell you, in another year or so, he will be a wealthy man."

During the entire day many comments were heard amongst the white farmers. Some wanted to know how he got his start; others marveled at the excellent business way in which he had arranged his sale, and still others doubted that he was doing business for himself.

Mr. Baxter was proud to say that Silas worked for him when a boy, always adding, "And a finer boy, I never saw."

A few days later, Silas was astonished to get a letter from Mr. Walker; it was a letter full of praise and encouragement. He told Silas of having seen the advertisement in his home paper, and he also said Mr. Baxter had told him of the great sale he had had. "I am as proud as you are, Silas," he said; and ended by saying, "Now, Silas, I am going to give you the advice I have given to hundreds of my young men—you have gotten a start; get married while you are young. Do not wait until you are old, or until you have accumulated more wealth; but now, while you are young and can become adapted to each other's ways; then bring into the world strong, healthy children. I have only one, but she is more precious to me than the millions of dollars I have made."

After reading this letter, Silas thought for a while. It was indeed true that success seemed his; each year he grew more prosperous; yet, there seemed to be something amiss. He had met many girls, but the great character of Love had lain—undisturbed.

That afternoon, as Margaret and Silas went for their daily ride, he told her of his plans to buy a larger place—it contained nearly twelve hundred acres. Margaret listened attentively; she was always interested in anything that Silas said or did. "I am going to let father and mother have the place where we are now," said Silas. "Shall we drive around to see the new place?" "O, yes," answered Margaret, clapping her hands in childish glee.

It was a beautiful tract of land, situated upon a hill that sloped down toward the main road. Silas pointed out the different improvements that could be made to beautify the place. Beyond the orchard, in back of the house, a beautiful stream meandered through one side of the farm to a small creek at the edge of a pine forest. Margaret stood looking.

"Isn't it beautiful?" she exclaimed.

"Do you really like it, Margaret?"

"Oh, I think it is just grand, and just think, Silas, you have made enough money to buy it."

"And pay cash for it, too, Margaret," continued Silas.

Her large, dark eyes shone with happiness as she said, "I am so glad you have made good, I am——we are all so proud of you, Silas."

"Are you, Margaret?" he said, looking at her with his deep, frank eyes. "If you are, will you share it with me, Margaret? You were a real friend to me when I was a lonely, shabby, country boy; you took me to church with you that Easter Sunday morning when no other living soul would dare to. That day you became one of the dearest friends that I had, and now, when I called upon you to come and help me, you came. Who could have filled your place? If you did so much to make me happy then, I know that your faithfulness need not be questioned, now. I did not know until you came last week that I really loved you, Margaret; it is sometime hard to differentiate between love and friendship. In my case, it is both. I know no other woman I would want for a wife and the mother of my children. I am not offering you wealth or position; you have both. But come and share what you have helped me to make."

Margaret had learned to love Silas, but she dared not hope this. We do not know just what Margaret answered, but, when they returned to the house, she was Silas Miller's promised wife.

THE RESENTMENT 149

At the end of the week, when Margaret left for home, Silas told her to tell her parents that he was coming to them again for advice.

Nett and her classmates were preparing for Commencement on the twenty-eighth of June. It had been three years of hard work. Soon, they were to say good-bye to the Hospital where they had learned, by theory and fact, the science of Nursing.

In these years, many of the girls learned that nursing was one of the greatest professions that any woman could follow.

To look down upon a sick person and be able to know what to give or to do to relieve suffering, was, to Nett, a wonderful knowledge.

Others who had chosen this course to please some parent or guardian or to keep from working in the kitchen had been firmly convinced that it was a stepping-stone from hard work to harder work. Yet, as Commencement day drew nearer, they all looked forward to it with much pride. Nett was as happy and gay as any, but a little quiet and more reserved. She had worked hard and had hoped to receive class honors, but she knew that any girl who had been demerited or punished could not have such distinction conferred upon her. She seemed to feel this keener as the time for graduation drew near. Several prominent speakers had been chosen for the evening. Miss Dunn was Valedictorian of the class. Nett was much surprised when Miss Wolf asked her to prepare a short talk on "The Duties of a Nurse." She explained to Nett that the girl assigned that part seemed too nervous to face the audience. Nett was delighted to substitute and went to work to prepare the essay.

Silas had sent her a check and a long letter telling her how proud they all were. He told her that he could not attend the Graduating exercise, but would be in the city on the first of the month. "I want to take you to see Margaret Kempt, my promised wife!" He also told her how Margaret had come and helped him during the week of the sale. "She is the second most unselfish girl that I have ever known; you are the first, Nett. I cannot wait until you are dead, I must give you the roses now. You are the dearest little sister that a brother could have!"

As she read this letter her heart burned with joy, to know that her brother had not forgotten the efforts she had made to help him.

THE RESENTMENT

At eight-thirty o'clock, on the evening of the twenty-eighth day of June, fourteen girls—dressed in white, representing the emblem of purity—marched on to the platform to the strains of the orchestra's music.

The overcrowded assembly room greeted them with a series of loud applause. One girl thought that she had not a relative or friend present; she did not know that in that audience a young girl looked anxiously into the face of every graduate. At last, she turned to an elderly lady and gentelman sitting beside her and said, "O, mother, and look, father, that is Nett; just like Silas, isn't she?"

"Yes, there can be no mistake, she bears a striking resemblance to Silas!" said her father.

"Isn't she a dear? What a fine, composed face; one can see the goodness shining through her eyes!" said Mrs. Kempt.

The girls were seated. Speaker after speaker paid worthy tribute to the young women who had prepared themselves to minister to suffering humanity. The house rang again and again with applause throughout the entire program.

Upon the platform with the other speakers a young man sat, buried deep in thoguht.

He seemed to pay little or no attention to what was being said by the other speakers. He looked now and then at the girls. His eyes seemed to rest long upon Nett; then he seemed to come to a decided conclusion. At last, the master of ceremonies introduced him to the audience as the last speaker of the evening, and as being one who had served in the same hospital. He had seen every girl at her best and knew the character and disposition of each.

Dr. Lionel walked slowly to the centre of the platform; his deep, clear, concise voice soon gave him the full attention of the entire audience. He talked from the subject, "Working Through!" He emphasized the value of a good nurse. Every few minutes the audience broke forth into thunderous applause; then he said, "I have a story to tell of a nurse in a certain hospital. One day one of the strictest rules of the hospital was broken by some of the nurses; no one would admit the deed but the blame was placed upon one—for what purpose it was not generally known. The accused girl frankly admitted that she did not commit the act charged against her, but said she could take the punishment and thereby save the girl who would not admit hre own guilt.

"That nurse had to do double duty for the whole week. During the first night, one of the doctors went purposely to see how she was accepting the unjust punishment. Instead of finding her sulking and pouting on duty, as he had suspected, he found her cheerfully working amongst the patients— surrounded by a halo that hardly belonged to an earthly being. She had forgotten that she was being punished for another's deed. The doctor knew who had done the deed and why the blame was put on this certain nurse." Dr. Lionel again referred to the work and then said, "The doctor will never forget that nurse and that noble act."

The audience sat spell-bound during the recital; one could have heard the slightest whisper; each individual seemed to be trying to grasp each word as they came from the lips of the speaker. Dr. Lionel came to a conclusion by saying, "She who can do this has already fitted herself for this great work, and—and"—his strong voice quivered —"I am proud to say that that girl stands here amongst these fourteen, to-night; by name—Miss Nett Mliler!" Then he fairly pushed Nett to the middle of the platform.

Did the audience hear aright? There was silence; then there rose such an applause that nearly sent the roof from the building. Many stood to get a glimpse of the little woman. Nett could barely restrain the tears from falling as she delivered her essay, which was short and simple, but very impressive. As she was leaving the assembly hall, Lucy Dunn came to her and said, "Nett Miller, can you ever forgive me? I did not mean to let you bear the blame and take the punishment for my wrong-doing; but, when we were discussing whom to tell, or what to say about the matter, one of the girls said, 'You should worry; say that little, pumpkinhead greenhorn from the country did it; they will not punish her half as hard as one of us who is not so pious as she. You know they're all daffy about her; but what they see in her, heaven only knows.' Thinking they were only joking, I said 'all right,' but did not think for once that the girl was going to say you did it when the Superintendent asked about it the following morning; and I was such a coward that I would not even own it after your emphatic denial. Each day I thought to confess, but as time passed, it grew hard to broach the subject; so I let it remain as it was; but, Nett, I have suffered more than you have. No punishment they could have given me would have brought so many tears and such heartaches as did your noble act; and not a harsh word to any of us did you say. I am so sorry that I have been so narrow-minded; I do not ask you to forget it, that you cannot do, but can you forgive me?"

Nett put her arms around her and said, "Dear Lucy, I can both forgive and forget; don't think of it, life is too short to worry over the past. Sometimes such things are good for us all; one heart has been tested; anuother purged. That little incident, I'm sure, will make you more careful in the future. Lucy, we are soon to leave this hospital; maybe, forever--where we have studied and worked together for three years. Our paths may lead through different avenues, but we may meet again; let us part true friends."

"But, Nett, everyone will hate me."

"No, Lucy, remember Dr. Lionel did not call any names; he did not even tell who it was. You can be sure he will not say any more than he has already said."

The two girls shook hands and parted.

Nett had been so busy talking and receiving congratulations that she had not stopped to look at the several presents that she had received: From Mr. and Mrs. Kempt, a leather medicine case; a bouquet of flowers from Margaret; and a medical thermometer from Dr. Lionel. Nett was overjoyed. "Just thinkn, these from Mr. and Mrs. Kempt and Margaret, friends whom I have never seen; and so thoughtful of Dr. Lionel to have remembered me with so useful a gift."

Nett Miller left the assembly that evening with part of her ambition obtained—a graduated nurse, with her diploma, to start a few days hence in the broad field of her calling amongst the sick and suffering.

Nett had sent several invitations to the folks at home; as none could attend the exercises, Silas mailed them to Margaret and her parents, asking them to go to the graduation of they possibly could. Margaret had talked her parents "deaf, dumb and blind" as they expressed it, until they consented to accompany her.

Silas came to the city on the first day of July. He was glad to see his sister; she was so happy, but a little tired. In showing him the beautiful present that Mr. and Mrs. Kemtp had given her, she said, "I could not imagine from whom they came until I saw the name; I was in ecstacy when I saw that

THE RESENTMENT

your friends had remembered me!"

"Yes, Nett, I have made few friends in life, but good ones."

They had luncheon together; then he took her to meet the Kempts. It was a joyous meeting; Margaret had heard of Nett, and Nett of Margaret, until they felt that they had known each other for years. There seemed to be no disappointment in the meeting. Nett felt herself at home in the palatial home of the Kempts. They invited her to stay a week with them.

The day had been hot and sultry; during the evening, Mr. Kempt suggested that the girls go for ice cream.

Silas took advantage of their absence to tell Mr. and Mrs. Kempt the purpose of his visit. "Mr. Kempt, a few years ago I came to you for advice; you gave it to me; I followed it and benefited by it. To-day I have come to you again for advice."

"Well, Silas, what is it? Whatever it is, I shall do my best to assist you in whatever way I can."

"I have come to ask your advice and consent in marrying your daughter."

Mr. Kempt was silent; he was not surprised, for he had seen for some time that there was something more binding than a mere friendship between Margaret and Silas. He turned to his wife and said, "Mother?"

"For our Margaret?" she queried.

"Yes, Mrs. Kempt, I know that she is your all and it will be hard for you to part with her, but it will be harder for me to live without her; I promise nothing, but let me prove to you what I shall be. I am not offering her money or position, but a life that I am not ashamed of."

His last statement went directly to the hearts of the elderly couple. Mr. Kempt said, "Silas, I could not say what you have said when I asked permission to marry my wife. The life you have lived makes you eligible to marry any good woman. Our men of to-day do not thing of preparing themselves to become good husbands and fathers; but live a life so full of vice and so corrupt until, at the earliest marriageable age they can only offer a girl a sickly, weak, diseased body. We shall hate to part with her, but are proud to know that the man whom she has chosen is a good man. We only hope that she will prove to be a true wife and a good mother."

Mrs. Kempt gave her consent. Like all mothers, she did not say much. To her,

Margaret still seemed only a baby.

When the girls returned, Mr. Kempt kissed his daughter and told her that they had given their consent for her to marry the best man alive. "I know you think so, don't you, dear?" he asked, patting her on the head.

"Margaret, do you wish to leave father and me?" asked her mother a little sadly.

"Yes, mother, I love you and father dearly, but there is something that makes me ly want to leave you for this man; I don't know what it is, but it is something."

"Yes, dear; we understand," said her father, "don't we, mother?"

Mr. Kempt was not like most parents who think it a disgrace to own that they ever were in love, or still loved each other.

"Nett, you must come and be our daugher; you know we shall be very lonely when Margaret leaves us."

"Dear Mrs. Kempt, I shall come as often as it is possible; I shall begin my work soon and will not have much time for visiting or pleasure, but I thank you so much for your kindness, said Nett.

That week was a pleasant one for Nett. Ere she will have spent another week of such happiness, Nett Miller will have paid the price: Angels pay to be angels.

Margaret's engagement was announced at an informal dinner given by her parents. News spread far and wide. In every home of the social set the coming marriage of Margaret Kempt to Silas Miller, the young Southern farmer, was much discussed. Few of Margaret's friends had met Silas and knew little or nothing about him.

Mrs. Crumpton, one of the leading matrons of the four-hundred set, said, "I cannot see where Attorney Kempt's senses are to marry his daughter off to such a person. Of course no one would dare broach the subject to him; he would explode like a keg of gunpowder."

"No," said Mrs. Townsend, "when Henry Kempt sets his mind on anything and thinks that thing is right, there is no turning him around. I suppose the man is some fortune hunter, marrying Margaret for her money and she is so heels-over-head in love with him that she can't see it."

"Well, I do hope she'll keep him in the country and not bring him up North and try to push him into our set."

"That's one thing I must say about the Kempts; they don't do any pushing; everybody I know is too glad to have them for

THE RESENTMENT 161

associates, and, if there is any pushing done, the other party generally does it," said Mrs. Townsend, conclusively.

When Aunt Mollie Noble heard of Silas' engagement she sat down and folded her arms and said, "Dar now; what did I tell you sis Mariah? Gone clean up to the city to marry somebody—'taint none ob de gals 'roun' heah good 'nuf fo' him. Done made a little money now, an' his head is dat swell dat he mus' marry some city 'oman; well, who eber she is, if she comes from de city, 'twont take her long to help him spend it."

"Yo' sure don said a mouf full, now Aunt Mollie; and besides, dey say it is dat girl dat he had come down heah to help him during the wek ob dat big sale dey hab hyeah."

Aunt Mollie stood up; kimbowing herself, said, "Yo' doan mean to tell me dat Silas Miller is goin' to marry dat little stripplin' of a peanut?"

"Dat's jes' what I hears, Aunt Mollie."

"Well, sah, I'se nevah heard of sich a foolish thing in all my life; why Sis Mariah, she's dat brazen, an' I seed her wid mah own eyes ridin' horseback 'roun' here 'straddle, jes' lak a man; an' when I speaks to brother Miller about it, he says, dat's de way dey rides in de city. Sez I, 'it may be city style, but it ain't no way fo' no decent 'oman to ride.' An' she's dat little dat she won't be able to lif' a pot from de stove. Who do yo s'pose do all de cookin' fo' de hands? Guess he'll be dunce 'nuf to try to do it hisself."

"No, dey say he's goin' to hire a cook."

"Hursh, Sis' Mariah, I done heard so much foolishness dat I'll had de heart trubble de res' ob dis week. Jes' t'ink ob his ma and pa working all dese years an' he astrutin' off to de city to marry some S'iety 'oman an' den hirin' a cook fo' her."

"I am a little 'fraid dat he will fin' dat she is not much fitted fo' dis life; de only t'ing, we'll wait an' see how she gets along," said Sis' Mariah.

"I s'pose he ca'culates on us po' ole workin' folks turnin' out an' helpin' her to cook an' keep house; but I fo' one, don't tend to move one step from dis hyear shanty, cayse ain't nobody goin' t' hire us any cooks when we gits too ole to work," assured Aunt Mollie.

"As I 'foresaid, Aunt Mollie, let us wait an' see how she gits along."

THE WEDDING

On the twenty-fourth day of October, two persons awoke to remember it was their wedding day. It was a typical autumn day; Jack Frost had made his appearance a few nights before, making the air keen and crisp; the leaves were falling and everywhere Nature seemed to be unrobing herself for the coming winter.

In a beautiful home in a northern city, a young girl lay restlessly counting the passing hours; she had slept but little during the night and, at the first peep of dawn, she awoke and went to the room of her parents —tapping lightly on the door, at the same time asking if they were awake. "No, dear. you awoke us, come in."

"Have you been up all night?"

"No, papa, but I didn't sleep much."

"I didn't either, a certain night about thirty years ago, but nothing disturbs me now," said Mr. Kempt laughingly.

"And mother, are you awake, too?" she asked.

"Yes, dear."

Neither the father nor the daughter knew that during the entire night the mother had secretly wiped the tears away, as the thought dawned upon her that, before another sunrise, her daughter would belong to another.

In the South, on the farm, a father walked nervously up and down the yard. He repeatedly asked his son, "Are you sure, Si, that Margaret will be contented to live here? You know that a week's visit in the country is far different from a life-time stay. I am afraid that she will soon tire of this dull, monotonous country life." Silas reassured his father not to worry; he told him that if Margaret had consented to come, she will have made up her mind to accept things as they were. "She is the kind that can readily adapt herself to anything—provided that thing is right."

A few hours later Silas left for the city on the early train. He recalled his first trip to Philadelphia—how differently! Then, a poor, penniless boy, with only hope and ambition before him; today, a man of considerable wealth, with some of those hopes realized and new ones formulating.

Whe he changed trains and boarded a north-bound express, several white persons recognized him and said to their friends who sat with them, "That's Miller." "Yes, I see it is; a fine-looking fellow, and they say he's

THE RESENTMENT 165

getting rich qpick." "Well, I don't know about the quickness, but if he keeps on at the rate he is going, there will not be a white man in the State richer than he."

"Who is Miller, papa?" asked a little boy sitting beside his father, who was one of the men of the group.. "He is the little colored boy you have often heard Mr. Baxter speak of and tell how he worked his way from a penniless boy to a prosperous business man."

While they talked, Silas was thinking of the future, and what it would mean to him. If it will only be as well as the past, I shall not complain," he soliloquized.

About six o'clock that evening a number of their intimate friends gathered in the parlor of Attorney and Mrs. Kempt to witness the marriage of their daughter.

Much comment could be heard while the guests waited anxiously for the hour. As the clock was striking six, the bridal party marched in the drawing room; and when Silas Miller entered, accompanied by the best man, who was a cousin of the bride, not another word was heard. Everyone gazed with astonished admiration at the tall, erect figure of the well-groomed and composed-looking young man. Many of the girls who sat there would willingly have taken Margaret's place, and they were not too selfish to tell her so.

Thus two girls changed places: Margaret Kempt, a city-bred girl, left behind her the fascinating scenes of a large city for the quiet life of the country; and Nett Miller gave up the fields, the flowers, the song birds, and the rural social life to work for suffering humanity in the hot, dusty, noisy city.

News was spread that Silas would return Saturday evening and would visit the church the following morning with his bride. Many invitations had been issued, asking all the neighboring friends to a housewarming party, Wednesday evening.

When Aunt Mollie got her invitation to the affair she took it to the home of a neighbor to see what it contained.

"A hous' warmin' pahty!" she exclaimed. "I'se nevah hyeahed of sich befo' in mah life, an' Ah am nigh on to de sixties. Ah tells yo', Ida, des' hyeah young peepl' don't know what to git at; a 'vitin' company to warm up de hous! Now, when we got married, we jes' put up a stove an' put some wood in thar. When de stove got hot, it hetted up de hous' an' de only envitation youse got

THE RESENTMENT

war to wahm up on de wood pile by heppin' to cut up some ob de wood. Yes'm, dats de truth, dis is funny notions dey is got."

"Ain't you goin' Aunt Mollie?" asked Miss Long.

"Yo' bet I doan miss it," she said.

Sunday morning, Aunt Mollie got up early. She almost forgot to feed the chickens and had to go back to get her snuff box and see if she had locked the door after she had started for church.

By hurrying so fast, she was almost breathless when she reached the church. Seeing Sister Maria Dudley she leaned over the pew and asked, "Has dey come yet?"

"Has who come, Aunt Mollie?"

"De bride an' groom. An' did yo' git an envitation to de pahty?"

"Yes, I did git some kind of letter, but I didn't jes' un'erstan' what it meant."

"An' nobody else. Ah guess its jest some ob dese hyeah high flutin' notions dat dese city folks am got, an' a waste of lots ob money; but, ah gess ah'll go jest de same to see what it is lak. Ain't yo' goin,' Sis Mariah?"

"Yes, I t'ink all is goin' dat got envited."

The minister had just finished reading the Scripture, and the choir was singing when Silas entered with his bride. There was a general "Um-m" throughout the congregation.

Aunt Mollie never knew what was said or done after she found that they had arrived. Touching Sis Maria lightly on the shoulder, she whispered, "She looks mighty puny to me, an' I declar' she ain't much bigger den a kildee. I 'spec' he'll wish mo' den once dat he had married some good, strong, country-fed gal."

"Now, don't over-ca'culate de t'ing, Aunt Mollie; I t'ink she'll be all right when she's hyeah a while," said Sis' Maria.

"Maybe so, but thars no telling."

After the service, Silas introduced Margaret to all, and in spite of all that she had said, Aunt Mollie said afterward, "A sweeter little o'man Ah hab neveh met in all ob mah life."

At the party, Margaret won many friends, and ere she had been in that community long she was beloved by all. This made Silas proud of the woman he had chosen for a wife.

Mr. Miller said, "I have never seen such a girl; a splendid housekeeper, and a good manager. I do not think that Silas could have found a better girl even if she had been

THE RESENTMENT 169

reared in the country."

While Silas prospered each year, he did not forget the humble folks with whom he was reared; both he and Margaret took active part in all the events for social uplift and beneficial affairs. The people soon found that Margaret was more proficient in dealing with the problems that concerned the welfare of the community than they, and willingly gave these matters into her hands. Margaret soon grew to love these quaint and humble folks and they in return respected and honored her.

Silas was elected president of a club for young men; and through his efforts many received help to start in business. He never forgot his boyhood days.

In this new life, his happiness was inexpressible. With Margaret, his first and only love, and his home. Nothing he enjoyed now as much as the quiet evenings with her by his side.

TEN YEARS LATER

Ten years has passed, Silas Miller is now said to be the wealthiest colored man in the State, and is reputed to be worth almost a million dollars. His name has reached every State in the Union and foreign papers refer to him as the Hog King of the States. During this time, four sons had been born to this union. It seemed that God had almost granted Margaret her wish. Never was there a more faithful wife nor a better mother. Both Silas and Margaret loved these sturdy little fellows, but, of course, they were left a great deal with their mother —Silas being busy most of the time.

One day when little Kempt was coaxing him to play ball, Silas said in a very impatient tone, "Don't worry father, I am busy. Go play with your brothers," pushing the little fellow almost roughly aside. Margaret had seen the incident from a window that overlooked the broad lawn; her heart almost sank within her when she heard the child say to his brother, "Papa's so mean, I almost hate him."

"This will never do; I must speak to Silas about that to-night," said Margaret to herself.

That night when the children were fast asleep, Margaret and Silas were sitting together in the library; she said, "Silas, dear little Kempt was very much hurt when you would not play ball with him this afternoon."

"But, Margaret, you don't know how much I have to do and think about; I have no time to be bothered playing ball. Why can't they play together? I give them everything that youngsters need to make them happy. I am planning to buy Kempt a pony and cart for his birthday; I am willing to give them anything that money can buy."

"And withhold from them the thing that they crave most," said Margaret more reprovingly than he had ever heard her speak.

"Margaret, you talk so foolish; what on earth do I keep from them?"

"A father's love."

Silas looked astonished. "Oh, Margaret, how can you say that?"

"It is hard, Silas, but it is true; I heard little Kempt say to-day that you were mean and he hated you. Silas, I would die if our children grew to dislike you—the only man in the world to me. The child wanted you to play ball with him; you are always too busy. You love them, I know, but if you do not devote a little time to amuse them, the children and you will grow up as strangers; they are too young to understand I did not awaken to this fact myself, until I heard Kempt's remark to-day."

Silas sat listening—ashen and pale—un-

THE RESENTMENT

shed tears stood in his eyes.

"Oh, Margaret!"

"Yes, God has given them to us; they are what we wished and hoped for. But if you thrust them aside now to make money and lose their love, what joy will you get out of it? If you want their love and respect when they are grown men, and you and I are old, give them a little of your time during their play hours; this is a child's idea of love. It will be worth more than the million that you have made, or the millions that you may make."

Silas went over to Margaret, putting his arms around her, he said, "Mother, you are righth; don't let me make such a blunder; what would I ever do without you? You have always been my guiding star." He fondled and kissed her. She smiled happily.

After that Silas devoted a few hours each day to his children. He was amazed to see how differently they regarded him; they always looked forward to the hours when "papa" would play with them. Silas began to feel a closer tie than ever before. He realized that they had almost been strangers. One day, after their usual romp, little Kempt came into the house for some cookies. "And some for papa, too, mother," he said, dancing around in a great hurry.

"Why are you in such a hurry? What have you been doing, you are so warm from running?"

"We have been playing 'Tiger' with papa and, O, mother, the fun! Papa is just great, isn't he, mother? Come on and watch us," With this invitation, he raced out of the kitchen as fast as his little legs could carry him.

It made the mother very happy to see the children and their father playing together and she said, "Thank God, the gulf was bridged before it was too late."

CHAPTER XI.

LET ME BUILD MY HOUSE BY THE SIDE OF THE ROAD AND BE A FRIEND TO MAN

During thes intervening years Nett worked in the hospital. After four years of faithful work she was promoted to the office of Superintendent. In this position she was loved and esteemed by all. She had seen so much suffering that she often wondered if the Heavenly Father was really merciful. She held the position of Superintendent for two years, then came time for her to go out into wider fields.

One day there was a meeting of the doctors at the hospital in reference to securing nurses for community and slum district work. A few days later, all of the nurses were summoned to meet in the assembly hall and the proposition was placed before them.

Calling the meeting to order the speaker addressed them, saying, "Dear friends, we are gathered here for a very important purpose; that purpose is to secure two efficient, trained nurses from this hospital to work amongst the poor, unfortunate class of our people in this city. You realize with us the extent of the influx of our people to this city yearly; they live here in congested districts under the most unsanitary conditions and not being used to this life, many have become ill and are dying for the want of good attention. We doctors do our best, but the chief want among them is god ursing. We all have at some time or other, migrated here from different parts; if we didn't our parents did. If we let these poor people go unnoticed and in want, whom shall they look to for succor? Not to the white people, by no means; they have their own poor to help, and we must help ours. We want nurses to volunteer to help. Of course, it must be understood that this club is securing these nurses and shall not be able to pay them the full fee. We can only promise twelve dollars per week, and whatever some of the people are able to pay. It must be a sacrifice on the part of the ones who volunteer."

The speaker, Dr. Waftner, talked a few minutes longer. He told of how he had given his services to many of them, free of charge; then he asked if there were two who

THE RESENTMENT 177

would volunteer to go.

There was silence, then Nurse Miller arose and volunteered her services by saying, "I will go." Miss Dunn also volunteered.

The entire staff objected to Nett resigning her position to work in the charity field.

"It is a broad field; they need me, and maybe I need them," she said in reply to many protests.

There was one who would have said much rather than see this young woman, of whom he had grown so fond, leave the position which she so worthily filled to go to work in the slum district. But when he heard her say "They need me," it filled his heart to know that she was so unselfish; and he knew it would make him seem almost inhuman in her sight if he openly objected.

After resigning her position, Nett rented a small room with a quiet, respectable family. Within these walls and at her work she spent a greater part of ten years. She worked unceasingly in and out amongst the poorest of the poor; up and down long flights of dirty, ill-smelling stairs, and into alleys and courts where it seemed almost impossible for humanity to exist.

She scrubbed floors, washed soiled bedding, cooked nourishing food, washed and dressed little, neglected children. How precious they all were to her! She never tired of her work. She taught these innocent mothers the art of cleanliness and how to protect their children from many minor diseases. Nett made herself one of them. She eliminated that stiff, professional ari— so prevalent amongst some doctors and nurses.

She worked hard from early morn until late at night. Hopeless as it seemed at first, they gradually grasped the true meaning of what she tried to teach them. Her efforts were not fruitless; she was indeed a happy woman when she saw them slowly awakening and the rays of the sun of Thriftness began to pierce the awful gloom.

They had learned to love her; many of the sick would lay and count the hours until she would return and they knew her very footsteps. She had made many sacrifices to make them comfortable and it was wonderful to see how these poor people would save a dollar here, or fifty cents there, and sometimes she would be surprised to be handed an envelope with five dollars in it from some husband or father, in appreciation of her work. Nett would not hurt their pride by refusing to accept it. She listened to various stories of misfortune and hardship; she soothed many an aching heart and pillowed many a dying head on her bosom.

While merry throngs of young people crowded the dance halls, theatres, parks and the saeshore in their respective seasons, and were being invited here and there to parties and luncheons, Nett Miller worked on—not that she was any less human than any of the other girls, but her work must be done.

Several young men had called, but after a few visits they came to the conclusion that she was too slow. She was dumbfounded to be frankly told by one young man that "you try to be different from the other girls; there was once a time when women preserved themselves for marriage, but that day is passed now," he said. Nett bowed her head and said, "I have my own ideas of life; let each one live his or her own way."

At first she had thought a great deal of this young man, but she knew that a man who would consider a good woman of so little value would not make a suitable companion for any woman. Tears came into her eyes as she watched him slowly descend the stairs. "How could a young man so well educated (he having graduated from one of the best colleges of the country) speak so?" Then she pitied him. "No one has taught him; he does not know any better, and he is not broad-minded enough to know the better woman," she said.

Nett was called one night to the bedside of a very sick girl. She had just fixed the patient comfortably and was about to leave the room when she was startled to hear the feeble voice of the patient call her by her first name; she turned quickly and went back to the bed.

"Nett, Nett, don't you know me?"

"No, I'm afraid not."

"Make a brighter light."

Nett did so and was very much astonished to look down upon the emaciated countenance of Anna Gould—her former classmate at ——— Hospital.

"Anna!" she exclaimed.

"Yes, it is Anna."

"What on earth are you doing here, and so sick?"

"I'm dying!"

"O, Anna!"

"Yes, Nett, I'm dying—that is the reason I sent for you to-night."

Here spasms of coughing seized her, after which she was almost too weak to talk. Nett begged her to rest and not talk.

"No, I cannot rest—there is no rest for me until after to-morrow." A shadow of distress clouded her thin face. "Close the door and sit down beside me and hear my story." "I left the hospital disgusted with nursing. I would never have finished the course had it not been for my mother who was so anxious to see me do something besides house work. I was considered a beautiful girl and thought of nothing but dress and good times. To dress well, I must have money and I had made up my mind not to work hard for it. With my acclaimed beauty I was quite an attraction among the men. I soon realized the extent of my influence and it mattered not to me whether they were married or single men, as long as they spent the money." Here she paused a while to get her breath. "I drifted from one man to another—not men of low class, but the best and most successful of our men. O, the life that I have lived! If some of those men would have said one word to induce me to do better I would not be here to-day. Look at this wasted form, the pain and agony I am enduring—all this for a few gaudy, perishable clothes—my beauty, my youth and womanhood all sacrificed and they are in their comfortable homes around the firesides with their wives and children; I am here alone, forgotten and dying."

She put her hands over her face as if to ward off a terrible scene. "And, Nett, the worst of all is the wrong I have done my mother. Thank God! She doesn't know. I have lied to her; told her that I was working at my profession and sent her money. Once she came here to see me; I was ashamed of her and told my acquaintances that she was my foster-mother. I had forgotten that she had washed and ironed, day and night, to keep me in training school and clothed me until I had finished, I soon hurried her back home—telling her that I had other appointments and did not want her to be alone. To-day I long for that home and that mother. If she know, she would be the only one to forgive me; but she cannot, she must not know—it would kill her.

"Take this message to other girls, Nett, and show them the fruits of disobedience and sin."

The tears streamed down Nett's face as she listened to this sad story. She looked at the once beautiful face, now marred by sin and distorted by suffering; placing her hand on the damp forehead, where there already lurked the hectic bloom of death, she said: "Anna, don't give up—while there is life there is hope."

"No, Nett, no, not for me."

"Through such avenues, Anna, God has wrought many wonderful things."

Nett racked her brain to think of something more to say to cheer the dying girl. She referred to many adverse conditions in the lives of different people who eventually benefited as a result of the adversity; such as slavery and hardship endured by the early Christians that Christianity might be established permanently.

She ended by saying, "Anna, you are sending a greater message to our girls to-day on your dying bed than I could have given in all the years of my life. God's works are so mysterious that we cannot fathom them. He, no doubt, has suffered you to come to this that thousands of other girls might avoid this path, and, if so, you shall not have died in vain."

"Do you really think so, Nett?"

"Yes, dear girl, I do."

A quiet calm settled upon the face. "I feel so much better, now, but I am very tired—tired of this world that was once so wonderful to me. Let me rest."

Nett arranged the pillows comfortably

around her and turned the light low. Anna slept the entire night, waking only when seized by a coughing spell.

The next morning as the sun's bright rays shone into the room Anna said: "Isn't it beautiful? But it is the last sun that shall ever rise for me."

Towards the latter part of the afternoon she called Nett and told her that she had an endowment for five hundred dollars insurance. "I want you to see that these humble, but good people get one hundred dollars for their kindness to me. What is left over the expenses goes to my mother."

Then she asked Nett to get a little jewelry box out of the top chiffonier drawer. Anna opened the box, took out a beautiful diamond ring and gave it to Nett. **She said,** "I know you don't want this, but grant my dying wish by accepting it."

Nett sighed as though pained at the thought of the approaching death. "Very well, dear, I shall keep it in memory of you, my classmate."

"And, Nett, when you hear the footsteps of the tens of thousands of day-toilers wending their way homeward, how often have I sat at the window and watched them, tired and worn, but they were going home—call

THE RESENTMENT

me; I am going home, too; I am so tired."

Ere the little nurse could call her patient, she had answered the call of Him who said: "Come unto Me, all ye that are weary and heavy laden and I will give you rest."

If Anna Gould was beautiful in life, she was surpassingly beautiful in death.

Nett looked down upon the still form whence had flown the mysterious forces that had kept it astir; tears glistened upon the long, dark lashes that rested lightly upon the pale cheeks; the lips were parted with a half smile, as if the sufferer were about to say to that unseen Visitor whose presence it is said is a terror to all, "You are welcome."

Nett wondered with throbbing heart if Anna Gould could be called from that slumber would she care to come back to this world of sorrow and sin. Oh! no, she had paid the price. "The wages of sin is death."

Anna Gould was an only child; her father had died when she was but five months old, which left her to be reared by a loving and over-indulgent mother who withheld nothing from her that a poor working mother could give her child. She was very much spoiled.

She was beautiful, fair, with long, black

curly hair; and as she grew year by year she was considered an unusually brilliant child.

As the years slowly advanced and Anna passed from childhood to womanhood her beauty became fatal to her. She grew vain and haughty. Fnding that most men were more readily fascinated by beauty than intelligence, she coerced herself into believing that her beauty was all that was necessary to help her obtain place and position. She entered the nurses' training school because her mother repeatedly insisted that she should do so. Had Mrs. Gould been able to have made a better introspection of her child's character, she would have kept her nearer and possibly saved her from much suffering and a premature grave.

After graduating, Anna said to her classmates: "Any one who wants to work at this profession may do so; I have no objections whatever. But I, for one, resign on the spot. It may be all right for some country 'Greenhorn' (referring to Nett), who would be glad to get a lift from the cotton patches or cornfields, but not for me." Several of the girls who heard the remark severely reprimanded her by saying that it was an outright insult to Nett.

"Now, girls, please don't quarrel over such

THE RESENTMENT

trifling remarks. As I said before, we are leaving soon, let us part as friends; who knows but we all might mete again?" said Nett.

Anna, turning scornfully away with a cold, haughty laugh, said, "I wonder who on earth will be so crazy to meet her again? I am sick of such a saint already."

"I don't think you should speak so, Anna; none of us know what we are coming to; we are all born, but not buried," said Lucy.

"What dunce doesn't know that, please tell me?" snapped Anna.

"You for one, it seems."

"Oh! when did you get to be so pious, Miss Dunn? I see you took care to let Nett be punished for your doings."

"Yes, Anna, you told Miss Wolf that Nett did it and I was such a coward and so afraid of you that I dared not say that you lied. Nevertheless, I have suffered more than she ever did, but I am glad she knows the truth now."

"Oh, then I suppose you squealed and let me in," said Anna, looking startled and frightened.

"No, I took all the blame myself."

"I am going or I shall be a fit subject for the insane asylum—listening to such quakerism. If you ever meet me please don't let on that you ever knew me. I wouldn't want my set to know that I ever dabbled around with such old nuns."

"All right, Anna, be sure you won't need some of us first," answered Lucy.

Anna kept good her word. She often met the girls of her class, but seldom recognized them. Through her beauty she had gained admittance to the best social circles and dressed and lived far above the means of a poor girl.

While the other girls worked, Anna lived her life. She lived, dressed and associated with the best of people.

At length she became ill. For some time she lived with the hope of getting better, but each week she grew worse. She went to doctor after doctor, but each gave her little hope of recovering entirely. "We can patch you up to last a while, but at the best, we can give you but little hope," they would say. She was also advised to go away to the country or to the mountains to regain some of her lost strength.

Poor Anna, with her fading beauty and failing health, she was soon forgotten. She rented a little back room from a humble, but good Christian family. She took most of

THE RESENTMENT

her jewels and pawned them, and was astonished to find how expensive it was. It had been given to her by some of her most ardent admirers. They brought enough monen to keep her for some time.

It was within the walls of that little room and in the home of those good people that this girl---after repeated daily meditations—realized the fruits of evil. It was hard for her to become submissive to her fate. Again and again she would say, "I am getting stronger," but instead she gradually grew weaker and weaker until at last she was too sick to leave her bed.

Here on her dying bed she passed before the awful judgment of God. "If I had only worked and lived an honest life, I would be willing to die young, but I cannot think of a single good deed that I have done," she said to Mrs. Hutt.

"But, do you know that God forgives everything—even the blacket sin?"

Anna could not be persuaded to accept this great promise of the Great Redeemer. "Do you believe that there is a hell worse than the one I am suffering? Oh! if my mother had warned me when I was just a babe of these things, I might have been better, she said to Mrs. Hutt, who reproved her by saying:

"Anna, do not blame someone else, for you were a girl with good home training and well learned. You certainly must have seen something of the fruits of vice and sin during your training in the hospital. But it was your vanity that you let lead you into such a chasm."

"Anna did not answer for some time, then she said in a tone more meek than anyone had heard her speak, "You are right, Mrs. Hutt, I guess it was my own folly and haughtiness that has brought me to this."

After that day it was sad to see the dying girl preparing to leave this world. For weeks she suffered untold agonies. It was just a few days before she died that she realized that the strain was too great on Mrs. Hutt. Anna called her and asked her to write a letter for her to a nurse. "Ask her to call and see a very sick patient at the above address; don't sign any name. She will come; I shall only need her for a short time."

Poor Anna! She could not make up her mind to have any of the other girls that she knew, neither could she pay a private nurse, and she knew that Nett was doing charity work. She thought of the many mean

THE RESENTMENT

things she said to hurt her, but "I know if anyone can forgive me it is Nett Miller," she said.

During the latter part of the afternoon Anna heard Mrs. Hutt singing Nett's favorite hymn—"Does Jesus Care?" How often had she laughed at Nett whenever she sang it, but to-day, that hymn seemed as a spring of cooling water to her sin-burned soul. How she listened to hear Nett's footsteps! "I know she will come."

It was getting late and the sick girl had despaired of her coming that day when she heard the bell ring. "Yes, the same soft, sweet voice." Anna recognized it at once, although it had been years since she had seen her. The door opened quietly; the little white-clad nurse walked in and turned up the light.

"The same Nett, only her hair is graying and she looks a little tired, but O, so happy!" Nett went over the sick girl inch by inch—examining her thoroughly. Being sensitive to the slightest touch Anna felt more at ease during this examination than any previous one. Nett was so gentle! She handled her like a babe.

But a fear crept over her when she saw that Nett did not recognize her. "Can it be possible that she still remembers what I said, or is it my condition? Although I know I said enough to hurt her, it will break my heart should Nett Miller fail me at this hour. I am dying; who would not forgive a dying woman!" Such were Anna's thoughts while Nett was examining her. After completing the examination and fixing her comfortably, Nett started to leave the room when Anna called her. It was then that she told her story.

Dear Reader: Do not forget that we always pay for the life we live. Do not let beauty bring you to Anna Gould's fate. Remember, beauty fascinates, but never holds.

What did Anna Gould give for a few perishable clothes and foolish pleasures? Her youth, her health, her virtue, her womanhood, a mother's love and confidence, loyal friends and a noble profession. And what did she receive in return? Sorrow and suffering and filled, a premature grave.

CHAPTER XIII.

THE REWARD

More than a year has passed since the death of Anna Gould; Nett had not ceased to work; she had seen the fruits of her labor. In all these years she had not taken more than a few day's vacation at a time; these days she usually spent on the farm with Silas and Margaret. Had it not been for this generous brother, Nett could have barely existed. He had never failed to send her a check each month; with this she was always comfortable. Both Silas and Margaret had tried to induce her to give up her work and come and live with them, but her answer was always "No, I cannot give them up yet."

Even when visiting here she did not get rest; her old friends were constantly calling or inviting her to their homes. Nothing they enjoyed better than recalling that afternoon in school when Nett made known her desire to become a trained nurse and an old maid. How they would laugh. "All of the members of that class are married but you, Nett," they would say.

"Yes, I have realized both wishes," she would reply.

"But, Nett, you are so changed," said Mattie Reynolds (who we knew in an earlier chapter as Mattie King). Those eyes that held so much defiance in them are now so soft in their depths one can read sympathy and pity."

"Yes, dear girl, when you have seen as much suffering as I, you can feel both."

"And your hair is getting gray, too."

"You do not realize that I am getting old, do you?"

"Yes, but we can only think of you as little Nett," they would laughingly say.

One day, after a hard day's work, Nett felt unusually tired; her head ached dreadfully; as she walked home she made up her mind to attend a theatre that evening. St. Elmo was being played at one of the theatres and she wanted to see the play as she had read the book so often. "It will be a little recreation for me, I am so tired and lonely." She purchased a small bouquet of flowers to wear with her new pale gray satin dress which she had bought some time before, but had not worn.

After dressing, she pinned the flowers in her corsage. She found that she was ready an hour before time to leave so she decided to read a while.

She was hardly seated when there was a ring at the door. She heard a voice ask: "Is Miss Miller, the nurse, in?"

"Yes, but I think she is going out," said Mrs. Hart, the lady of the house, "but I will call her."

When Nett came down she found an anxious, worried-looking man pacing the hall. "Oh, nurce, will you come? My baby, my only child is dying; do come for God's sake, don't say 'no'," he said, when he saw the disappointed look on her face.

It was the first time during her career that she had to decide, but it was only for a moment. "I will come," she said in a soft, sweet voice.

"Nett went. All night long she stood by the bedside of the tiny, pain-racked sufferer, battling against death. For hours it seemed that death would win.

"The doctor will be here early in the morning; he had just left when I came for you. He could give me no hope," said the father.

"Well, nurse, how is she?"

Nett was surprised to look and see Dr.

Lionel. "Very sick, doctor, but I feel there is hope."

Dr. Lionel left rigid instructions. "If there is any hope, it remains with the nursing." He did not fear, for he knew Nett Miller would leave nothing undone. Three days and nights, and the crisis was passed.

"Thank God, she will live!" said the nurse, as she saw the change. She had neither slept nor eaten; hardly five minutes had she left the bedside. As Dr. Lionel entered the bedroom that evening, Nett said, "She lives, thank God, she lives——" and fainted.

Knowing that the baby was out of danger, the doctor turned his entire attention to the nurse. She was soon revived. "I guess I am a little tired," she said.

"Nett—-Miss Miller, I am going to phone Mrs. Kempt; you are going there to rest and from there to the country—-not home by no means, but somewhere where you can rest without entertaining or being entertained. You have done your duty—double duty," he said.

Nett lay and listneed to his orders. She had given orders for years, but to-day orders were being given to her. She accepted his orders and said, "Yes, doctor, I feel too tired to go on."

THE RESENTMENT

That night she was made comfortable in Attorney and Mrs. Kempt's home. They told her that they wished she would stay with them all ways.

As Dr. Lionel was leaving he said, "Remember, Miss Miller, you are off duty until I give you orders to go back again." Then he added, "I saw that night when I entered the sick room that you were too tired to take the case, but I knew nothing could convince you of the fact but a complete breakdown or something like this." Nett marveled at herself for being so obedient.

Nett did not think it unusual that Dr. Lionel called every day, but she looked forward to the time that he would call with an interest that was deeper than professional. When she left for the country, Dr. Lionel asked her to write and inform him of how she was improving. "I shall come to see you as often as is possible."

One day he motored out in his new roadster and took Nett for a long drive through the country. "I am getting back to my old self again; I shall soon be able to go back to my people, don't you think, doctor?" Seeing that the doctor did not answer, she continued: "I feel better than I have for a long time, and Oh, I miss them so much." Dr. Lionel saw that if he did not speak now there would be no hope when once Nett got back to work, so he told her his long story; how he had waited for her to taste both the joys and sorrows of the course that she had so nobly chosen; how he had watched her give the love (that he had hoped some day would be his) to hundreds of sick, unfortunate and poverty-stricken people. "Ten long years have I worked and waited, the thought of you always foremost in my mind, has made me a good man. During my practice many homes have been open to me; men have trusted their wives and daughters into my care; I can truthfully say, until now, not once have I betrayed their trust. Not that I was not tempted (because men of my profession have enough of that before them), but these men paid me their hard-earned wages; I ministered to them, still I depended on them for my livelihood. I fought hard not to yield to things so low."

"Nett, I have loved as few men ever love; often I have tried to shut you out of my mind, but your shadow seemed ever before me. This great love has made me unselfish. I could not take you away from the work which needed you so much; you have given them ten years of your life—will you give me the rest?"

Nett's eyes filled with tears; through them shone unexpressible happiness, for love is a good woman's idea of a great reward; no fame, position or wealth can bring to her more happiness than to be truly loved and honored by a good man.

Years afterward, Nett said: "It was worth the trouble; the struggle, the hours of loneliness, the sacrifice and the love I gave to them because I got so much in return—a good husband."

And Dr. Lionel said: "I wish every young man could see through the eyes of virtue; I can never express in language its worth."

After their marriage, Dr. Lionel forbade Nett to even help him in his office, which she wanted so much to do. "No, dear, you must rest. You have worked long enough for a while at least." Nett did not try to argue with him because she knew he was right.

When they were married a little over a year a little daughter was born to them. The baby took much of Nett's time, but she divided her love—she was too sensible to let the baby take her entire attention away from the husband and father as most young mothers do. Dr. Lionel said: "When I found out there was to be a baby, I was glad, but I could almost see myself as lonely as I was before I was married. I have seen so many cases where the baby completely changed the home because the mother forgot everything except the baby. I had prepared myself for such a change, but, Nett, you have managed so well that we both have gotten full share of your love."

"Yes, Walter, I have often discussed such cases with my friends, and have repeatedly said it was a mistake that could be easily avoided if the mother was careful. I have said also that the wife and husband should always put each other before the children. This may seem hard, but it should be done. Children grow up and, however much we love them, they leave home. I tried when little Nett was born to avoid this error."

"You have not only tried, but you have done so, Nett," said her husband, affectionately.

When little Nett was four years old and was going to the kindergarten, Nett became very lonely. Dr. Lionel noticed this and when he questioned her, she said, "I suppose I have rested so much until I am tired of resting; the baby is going to school and you

THE RESENTMENT

are busy; I am most of the time alone."

Dr. Lionel made no reply, but while making his calls that day he thought seriously over what she had said and decided to let her help him one afternoon and evening each week.

On his return that evening he told Nett of his proposition. She was very much pleased and said, "You are the dearest man alive, Walter."

In a few weeks he noticed a decided change in her. The bloom returned to her face and there was a complete return of the old self. "I believe she would have died had I kept her from her work much longer," he thought.

It was soon known that Nett was helping in the office every Wednesday. On that day the waiting rooms would be overcrowded. So many persons called for her that the doctor decided to let her help him a little each day. How she worked! Nett was in her "Seventh Heaven."

Early one morning she got a check from Silas for several thousand dollars; it was accompanied by a little note, saying:

"Dear Nett: Enclosed is a check from Margaret and me. We want you to take

THE RESENTMENT

this, and with it do the thing that will bring you the most happiness. Spend all of this for that one thing. We shall forward this amount to you yearly for that cause, whatever it may be.
"Very truly yours,
"SILAS and MARGARET."

When she told her husband, he said, "It is yours; do whatever you wish with it."

No painter could paint, nor bards write, nor psalmodists sing of the supreme joy that swept through her heart as she stood with this gift in her hand. It had been her wish, her hope, her day dream—some day to erect a building where women could go to get free medical treatment from the best women doctors and nurses obtainable, and remain there until they became capable of caring for themselves. But she never thoughth that she would ever be able to do that thing herself. Dr. Lionel told her that she could not do a better thing. "I do not know of anything that would be more appreciated by the people or bring you more happiness," he said.

In answer to Silas' letter that evening she said: "I have tried every word in the English language to express my happiness and thankfulness, but I cannot find one. So I

THE RESENTMENT

shall let you see in the near future that which I most desire."

Some months later at a certain hospital workmen were busy building an annex to the main building. Many had already heard it was Miss Nett's—as she was generally called—gift to the hospital. The interior of the building was beautifully finished. Nett purposely had this building made more home-like than an ordinary hospital, so that the patients would feel more satisfied to stay. There was a beautiful rest room with a large, open fireplace and handsome bookcase containing many interesting books by Colored authors; a large dining room, a sun parlor and a small lecture room to grace the first floor.

Nett directed all the most important arrangements. The staff was composed of the best women doctors and nurses she could secure. To these she gave her orders: "There must be no hurrying here; each patient must receive full justice of your ability and knowledge.

"There must be patience exerted by all. You must not only be able to administer professionally, but also be able to give encouragement to the least hopeful.

"It is my urgent request that these orders be strictly followed."

Nett had advertised for a special nurse; she had just heard several applicants when she was surprised to find the last one was Miss Dunn. The two girls clasped hands; for a few moments there were no words. "And we meet again," said Katie. "Yes," answered Nett, smiling.

Nett called one of the doctors and said: "We need look no further because I have found the nurse who is capable of filling this position; we can give the general management entirely into her care." "Goodness! Nett, you don't know whether I came for a position or as a patient."

"I am taking it for granted. One look at you would readily convince us that you are not applying for medical treatment."

"Well, looks don't always tell, you know, Nett, and besides you don't know whether I would accept the position," said Katie Dunn.

"That is why I am accepting it for you," she replied.

"And do you think I can worthily fill the position? Suppose I might break some of the rules?"

"Now, Katie, I will not have any 'supposes'; I know more about the incident that you are referring to than you do. We will say nothing more about it. let 'the dead past bury its dead.,"

Katie took the position. She became a frequent visitor at the home of Dr. Lionel; they spent many happy hours together.

After the building was completed, Nett wrote asking Silas and Margaret to come and see what a beautiful diamond she had bought with her gift. They were both puzzled at Nett's letter. "Think of Nett buying diamonds and inviting us all the way to Philadelphia to see it! Why, jewelry was the last thing I would have thought of her buying," said Silas.

"Why Silas, that was perfectly all right; we told her to buy whatever she wanted most, did we not?"

"Yes, but it seems so odd for *her*, Margaret."

"That means that you don't quite understand women. We are all odd; some a little more so than others."

"But the thing I want to know is, are we going."

"Yes, if my sister has taken that money and bought diamonds, it is worth going to the end of the world to see," said Silas so seriously that Margaret nearly laughed herself into hysterics.

"I can't see anything so funny, Margaret (impatiently)."

"Dear, don't be angry, I couldn't help laughing, you seem so disappointed."

They left for the city a few days later, arriving there early in the morning. Nett and her husband talked of many different things, but neither said anything of the diamonds. This puzzled them more than ever.

It was late in the afternoon when Nett suggested that they all go driving in the car with Dr. Lionel when he went to make his calls. When Dr. Lionel stopped in front of the hospital, Margaret said, "How well I remember this place." "Would you like to go in?" asked Nett.

"Very much, indeed, Nett; and I am sure Silas will be glad to see once more the place where you obtained the knowledge of your profession and spent many years of hard work."

As they started up to the main entrance Margaret saw the new annex and exclaimed, "O, they have erected a new building—I didn't know that."

"Come, we'll go in and see it," said Nett.

When they entered the beautiful rest

room, Margaret stood with clasped hands, "isn't this wonderful?" she exclaimed. "I never saw anything so well arranged in my life." Both she and Silas admired the place.

"Have my parents seen it, Nett?"

"No, it has been completed only a week and we intend to invite the public to a formal opening later, and I hope to have your father as one of the speakers."

"How do you like it, brother?"

"I think it is great, Nett."

Then Nett said, "I am glad that you both like my 'diamond.'"

Silas and Margaret stood looking amazed at their sister.

"This is the diamond I wrote and asked you to come and see."

"Well, Margaret, this solves the puzzle."

"Silas could not understand why on earth you would buy a diamond with the money," Margaret explained.

"Yes, it did seem queer to me because I had secretly thought of something like this, we might have over-estimated what it was like."

Hundreds of women visited this part of the hospital weekly. It was said this was the hospital owned and lontrolled by Colcolored people where women were properly treated by doctors of their own race and sex.

Nett made three weekly visits to the hospital; two afternoons she set apart to lecture to boys and girls between twelve and sixteen years of age. She gave a series of lectures on Ethics and Care of Self; she considered this a most important part of a child's education which she found so badly neglected during her time as slum district and community nurse.

In addition to this, she issued pamphlets appealing to parents to eliminate all false modesty and teach their children the things that they should know ere they reach the age of puberty; thus preventing the ruination of so many young lives—that we may have a cleaner and stronger generation in the future.

So to Nett Miller-Lionel, may she

"Reap her joys in the sweet bye and bye,
By the seed she sows today."

CHAPTER XIII.

TWO GREAT MEN MEET

The Frenn, Silas Miller's beautiful home, surrounded by trees and shrubbery, stood in magnificent splendor upon a hill with its beautiful lawns sloping towards the main road. It was considered the most complete estate in that section of the country. One could hardly recognize it as being the same place that he purchased immediately after his first big sale, twenty-six years previous.

It was a beautiful day in the latter part of June; it had been very hot and sultry; the sun was slowly wending her way toward the western horizon, while a cooling breeze gently blew across the lawn. Silas walked up and down the broad piazza with his hands folded behind him, apparently in deep thought. Taking a closer look at him we find him the same shrewd, keen, conscientious man now as in earlier years. His once dark hair is graying. Everywhere one could see wealth and success. He looks and is happy. A portly, pleasant faced woman came out on the porch and called, "Daddy, dear, are you having a cake-walk out here all alone?"

"No, dear; I am thinking."

"Of what, please tell me?"

"Of you."

"Oh, Silas, for goodness sake don't you ever get tired of flattering me? Do respect my old age and gray hair," said Mrs. Miller, laughingly.

"But, dear, Margaret, do you know that it was just twenty-six years ago this month that three of the happiest events that ever occurred in my life took place? I had my first big sale, you became my promised wife, and Nett was graduated from the nurses' training school."

"At that time I thought you were the dearest girl alive."

"And do you think of me now?"

Walking over to her, he took her face between his hands and looking deep into her eyes he said, "at that time I *thought*, but now I know."

In all these years Silas never forgot to give her the praise that a wife so hungers for; she was his partner and companion. He had always thanked God for giving him such a good woman. With her he had pass-

THE RESENTMENT

ed the twenty-sixth milestone of married life; she had helped him to bridge many difficulties that mark the path of man striving to reach success ere life's evening tinges his brow with sunset glow.

Silas Miller stood and looked back over that path, and vividly recalled the source from which all his success had sprung. He said, "Margaret, I was thinking of what one writer said: 'Our chief want in life is someone to make us do what we can do.'"

"If Mr. Baxter had not continued to call me a 'nigger' I would have been working for him or someone else today. At that time that word seemed to me to be the worst word that could be uttered by human lips of a civilized individual.

"I have learned that when we help ourselves, others will help us. It has been a great misunderstanding among many persons of our race that the white man hates us; but I have found that the intelligent white man honors and respects the intelligent and prosperous black man.

"After I had got started and he saw that I meant to go on, who gave me more encouragement than Mr. Baxter? He not only purchased stock from me yearly, but sent many other farmers to me."

Although rich and prosperous, Silas was much beloved by all. The white people honored him because of his ability and worth; the colored people loved him because he was their very own. The boys of his schooldays —now men—gathered annually to renew the vow they made years ago. Then, there were twenty-eight; now there are only ten living.

Mr. and Mrs. Kempt had visited the farm often. After the first visit, Mrs. Kempt said to her husband, "Henry. I am glad you were firm in your decision that we should let Margaret choose her own husband. Nothing but your firmness would have made me give over at that time; but I am so glad that you took matters into your own hands, or our child might have been very unhappy. Leonard Morgan has already been twice divorced, and is now said to be infatuated with some young actress."

"That is the reason why I urged that she be let alone. I had helped to untie so many unhappy marriages that I did not want to sit and listen to someone untie my daughter's."

They had had their wish; they had seen their daughter's children. While she was not a society leader she was a true wife, a

THE RESENTMENT

good mother and a happy woman. What more could parents wish?

Now they slept the sleep from which none ever awakes.

Aunt Mollie Noble who had grown old and feeble had repeatedly said of Margaret, "She does beat anything ah ever seen. I doan say dat Silas did bad after all." Margaret often visited Aunt Mollie. In spite of all Aunt Mollie had said, they became warm friends. When she was very sick, and dying, Margaret went every day to see her and took her nourishing food. She marveled at the great child-like faith the dying woman had in God; when in great pain, she would say, "De Lord doan put any more on his chill'n den dey's able to bear." And just before she died she whispered, "I'se goin' home, Mis' Margaret."

Dr. Lionel and Nett visited the farm as often as was convenient; they could never stay long as his large and extensive practice demanded their time in the city.

Silas' two younger sons had completed the Agriucultural course at Tuskegee and were working with their father.

The two older ones had attended school in the North; one was graduated from law school and the other was State Instructor in canning fruits and vegetables in the State of Texas.

Silas and Margaret were proud of their children. He had never ceased to be chums with them since that day Margaret called his attention to his unintentional neglect of them.

He had just finished saying to Margaret, "I wish I could show hundreds of young men of my race the way to success."

"Yes, dear, but you cannot do it by yourself; it will take the co-operation of the people of the race. We can do our best; but time and the evolution of circumstances will bring about that which we so earnestly desire. As it is, we see a nation rising slowly up out of the dust—with most most of its future before it."

"Yes, Margaret, and we should be proud to be members of that race; and I shall—."

A beautiful car turned into the lane and came slowly toward the house. Silas took his hat and went down to see who his new visitors were. One gentleman had gotten out and had turned to assist an elderly, white-haired man out.

"Hello, there, Miller."

"Why, it's Mr. Baxter," said Silas. "It has been several years since I saw you."

"I am indeed glad to see you," said Mr. Baxter, shaking hands. "Do you know who this is?"

Silas looked and then exclaimed, "Why, it's Mr. Walker."

Both men clasped hands as only men do when they are truly glad to meet.

"And you know me!"

"Know you! Could I forget the man who gave me the first money and the first encouragement to start in life? This is the fruit of your encouragement and my labor," he said, with a sweep of his hand.

Walking to the porch he called Margaret, and in introducing her, said, "Mr. Walker, this is my jewel!"

Both men laughed heartily. Their visit was short; Mr. Walker was getting old and could not stay out late.

Preparing to leave he shook hands, sayin, "You've done well, Miller; I shall not come East again; I am getting too old to travel. My days are nearly done. Good-bye, and may God bless you with a long life to enjoy the fruits of your labors."

As they drove down the beautiful drive, both men lifted their hats and said good-bye.

In the vanishing twilight, Silas and Margaret walked slowly back to the porch.

Silas Miller had made good his vows: "And—we'll take off our hats to each other."

THE END.

ABOUT THE EDITORS

Henry Louis Gates, Jr., is the W. E. B. Du Bois Professor of the Humanities, Chair of the Afro-American Studies Department, and Director of the W. E. B. Du Bois Institute for Afro-American Research at Harvard University. One of the leading scholars of African-American literature and culture, he is the author of *Figures in Black: Words, Signs, and the Racial Self* (1987), *The Signifying Monkey: A Theory of Afro-American Literary Criticism* (1988), *Loose Canons: Notes on the Culture Wars* (1992), and the memoir *Colored People* (1994).

Jennifer Burton is in the Ph.D. program in English Language and Literature at Harvard University. She is the volume editor of *The Prize Plays and Other One-Acts* in this series. She was a contributor to *Great Lives from History: American Women*, and, with her mother and sister, coauthored two one-act plays, *Rita's Haircut* and *Litany of the Clothes*. Her creative non-fiction has appeared in *There and Back* and *Buffalo*, the Sunday magazine of the *Buffalo News*.

P. Gabrielle Foreman is Assistant Professor of English at Occidental College. Her writings on African-American and nineteenth-century literature have appeared in *Representations*, *Feminist Studies*, *Callaloo*, and *Black American Literature Forum*.

FEB - 6 1997